HALF-PAST DAWN

ALSO BY RICHARD DOETSCH

The 13th Hour

The Thieves of Heaven

The Thieves of Faith

The Thieves of Darkness

A THRILLER

RICHARD DOETSCH

HALF-PAST DAWN

ATRIA BOOKS

NEW YORK LONDON TORONTO SYDNEY NEW DELHI

ATRIA B O O K S
A Division of Simon & Schuster, Inc.
1230 Avenue of the Americas
New York, NY 10020

First Atria Books hardcover edition September 2011

ATRIA B O O K S and colophon are trademarks of Simon & Schuster, Inc.

For information about special discounts for bulk purchases,
please contact Simon & Schuster Special Sales at 1-866-506-1949
or business@simonandschuster.com.

The Simon & Schuster Speakers Bureau can bring authors to your live event.
For more information or to book an event, contact the Simon & Schuster Speakers Bureau at 1-866-248-3049 or visit our website at www.simonspeakers.com.

Manufactured in the United States of America

10   9   8   7   6   5   4   3   2   1

ISBN 978-1-4391-8397-7
ISBN 978-1-4391-8399-1 (ebook)

For Virginia,
My best friend,
I love you with all of my heart.

Each man is the architect of his own fate.

—APPIUS CLAUDIUS

I am not an adventurer by choice but by fate.

—VINCENT VAN GOGH

It is what a man thinks of himself that really determines his fate.

—HENRY DAVID THOREAU

HALF-PAST DAWN

CHAPTER 1

HALF-PAST DAWN, THE WORLD slowly came to life. The sun crept along the freshly cut grass, over the scattered toys on the back lawn, and through the rear windows of the modest colonial house, the country kitchen filling with morning light as it danced over cream tiles and a wide-plank oak floor.

A tall man walked into the kitchen, his black hair mussed and astray, his lean, muscular body wrapped in a blue robe. His face was strong and intelligent, but carried a certain toughness, while his dark brown eyes had the appearance of seeing far more years than the thirty-nine he had lived.

A Bernese Mountain dog ran to his side, and he crouched down, running his hands through the large dog's black, brown, and white coat, rubbing his belly and behind his ears. "Hey, Fruck," he whispered. He always loved giving his pets obscure names that never failed to become conversation starters.

He reached into the fridge, grabbed a Coke, popped it open, and drank half of it as if it were desperately needed air for his lungs. He wasn't a coffee guy, never had been, preferring his caffeine jolt cold and sweet. He looked around the kitchen, at the overflowing garbage he had promised his wife he would take out more than a day ago, at the ever-growing stack of bills by the phone, and finally, at the lack of bagels, cream cheese, and newspaper on the counter.

Heading through the hallway of the small house, he opened the front door to find the newspaper on the slate step. He picked it up, tucked it under his arm, and took a long, deep breath of the summer morning air. There was a crispness to it, fresh and clean and full of hope. Fruck charged by him, through the door, and out onto the lawn, jumping around in hopes of an early-morning romp. But that would have to wait.

Jack went back to the kitchen, tossed the newspaper onto the counter, and opened the garage door. He shook his head in bemused understanding as he saw his wife's freshly washed blue Audi parked there. He walked over to it with a smile on his face, opened the door, looked at the gas gauge, and laughed. Empty. Which explained why *his* white Chevy Tahoe was gone. It had been a forever pet peeve; she would drive on fumes before pulling into a gas station. The following day, without a word, Mia would snatch his car, leaving him to roll the dice on making it to the gas station and come up with an explanation for why he was late for work again.

Mia had always been a morning person, up at 6:00, down to the deli by 6:15 for coffee and bagels, back home, lunches made, the girls packed off to the bus by 7:00 and gone. Mia had probably been up at 5:30, accomplished a day's worth of work, and was already on her way to the city.

Jack Keeler hadn't seen 5:30 except from the other side of sleep, when he would crawl into bed and pray for the sun to skip its rise for the day. He always seemed to hit a second wind at 9:00 p.m., his mind kicking into overdrive as thoughts about work and life suddenly became clear. But at 6:30 every morning, his body would wake, whether it had taken in eight hours of sleep or two. Of course, the pain factor would determine if it was a one- or two-Coca-Cola morning.

He grabbed a second can from the fridge and headed upstairs, peering into Hope and Sara's room—the pink beds made, toys tucked away, the room cleaner than it had been in weeks. The five-and six-year-old Irish twins were inseparable and loved nothing more than climbing all over Jack at night when he arrived home from work. It had been a ritual since they could crawl and was topped only by their love of the ocean.

Jack cut through his bedroom and into the bathroom. As he brushed his teeth, thoughts of the day began to filter in: what awaited him on his desk, what needed to be dealt with. Leaning over the sink, he finally looked into the mirror . . . and was confused by what he saw.

Above his right eye was a scabbed-over wound, a wound he had no recollection of getting. He ran his finger over it, the sharp, stinging pain shocking him. He leaned closer to the mirror to examine it and noticed the other scrapes along his cheek and neck—not as dramatic but surely something he would have remembered getting.

As he began to probe his memory, something on his left wrist caught his attention. A dark marking on his skin peered out from beneath the sleeve of his terry-cloth bathrobe. Fearing another wound, he quickly slid the sleeve up, only to reveal the last thing he expected.

The tattoo was detailed, intricate, created by an artist's hands. The design covered his entire forearm, running from wrist to elbow. The ink was of a single dark color, just short of black. The tattoo appeared to be an elaborate woven design of vines and rope, but upon further examination, lettering of a language he had never seen came into a focus like an optical illusion revealed to the mind's eye.

As he studied the detail, his mind searched back, and the absence of memory scared him. He had no recollection of needles on his skin, of being drunk, of being a fool. He did have a tattoo of a dancing skeleton on his right hip, a drunken mistake made when he was eighteen. He and two friends had them done at three in the morning on the Jersey shore, the alcohol-induced foolishness of youth. To this day, only Mia and four ex-girlfriends were aware of its existence; not even his parents knew. But the small skeleton on his hip was forever undercover; the markings that covered his arm couldn't be concealed, couldn't be hidden for long.

Jack turned on the hot water, running his arm through the scalding stream, the underlying skin growing crimson, making the artwork pop. He rubbed his forearm with a bar of soap, grabbed the washcloth, and scrubbed his skin raw. But it was to no avail. The markings were deep . . . and permanent. Mia was going to be furious.

But the surprise of the tattoo and the facial wounds was quickly forgotten as he removed his robe.

The shock of what he saw sent panic running through him, and he nearly collapsed to the tile floor. The wound was like nothing he had ever seen—black, haphazard stitches holding a dime-sized wound together, dark blue bruises radiating out from its center.

He tilted it toward the mirror and felt nausea rise in him. Something had pierced his shoulder just below the lower left collarbone, and he had no memory of it. There was no question; the improvised checkerboard stitches were not done by a physician. He ran his finger close to it and nearly doubled over in pain, as if he had just felt the bullet make contact.

Without thought, he reached into the cabinet and grabbed the bottle of peroxide, poured it over the wound, and then applied a wide mesh bandage over it. He raced to his closet and quickly dressed in a pair of jeans and a long-sleeved button-down shirt. As he slipped on a pair of shoes, he saw a pair of dress pants, muddy and wet in a ball in the corner. Picking them up only proved to cloud his mind further as they were torn and ruined. He couldn't remember wearing them, but when he reached into the pockets, he found them filled with his personal effects, proving that, despite his lack of memory, he had worn them recently.

Jack pulled out his wallet from the wet pocket and checked its contents: nothing missing. He found twenty dollars, some change, and the small blue jewelry box that Mia had given him the week before. Opening it, he found it to contain not the cross she had bought him but her pearl choker, the one he had given to her on her birthday three months earlier. Without further thought, he tucked it all in his pocket and raced downstairs.

He picked up the phone and quickly dialed Mia's cell. Usually known for a calm demeanor and a clear head in a crisis, Jack was in a full-blown panic, his mind on the verge of a nervous breakdown. He had no recollection of receiving the wounds on his body, no memory of what had occurred the night before or even yesterday, now that he thought on it. His mind was slipping through his fingers, and there was only one person he could turn to.

Mia's cell phone rang once, twice, three times before going to voice mail, and just as Jack began to leave a message, his eyes were drawn to the kitchen counter . . . to the newspaper that lay there.

He zeroed in on the large center photo, the artificially lit night-time photo of a bridge, the guard rail missing, black tire marks on the roadway disappearing over the edge.

And above it all, the headline screamed across the page:

New York City District Attorney Jack Keeler Dead

CHAPTER 2

FRANK ARCHER WAS THREE months into his retirement and already missing his former life. At 6:35 on a Friday morning, he should have been baiting a hook, hitting golf balls, or at his desk, anywhere but in his backyard planting begonias in his wife's garden. His world had become chores, a routine not of his choosing but of his wife's, and his thirty-year dream of retirement, of fishing and golf, was a fool's dream. It was as if his life was over at fifty-five.

He wasn't about to complain to Lisa. He loved her as much as the day they were married—most days, anyway. Frank always discounted the times she threw him out for drinking, for the biblical fights when she ran off to her mother's, the weeks of silent treatment and no sex when he forgot her birthday. But all things being equal, she was his life partner and the one he had retired from a satisfying career to be with.

Finished planting the last flower, he stood up and examined his work of the past hour. He stood no taller than five and a half feet, but his wide shoulders and still powerful arms gave the perception of a taller man, a younger man by at least ten years. He continued to work out almost daily, as he had his whole life, running, lifting weights, whatever it took to forestall Father Time. He wasn't about to become a cliché retiree.

The neighborhood was quiet at this peaceful hour, with life slowly returning to the world for another day. He looked at his watch and was surprised that he had yet to see Lisa. She was usually out there, giving direction, asking him in her sweet passive-aggressive way to rearrange everything he had just planted. While he did all the work, the garden was her design, something she took all the credit for when friends praised its beauty. It never bothered him, though, being the type to defer recognition. He required only nine holes in the afternoon in exchange for his sweat-inducing work.

With dirt-covered hands, he used his forearm to push back his salt-and-pepper hair and then walked in through the back door of the small Cape-style house, only to find Lisa sitting at the dining-room table, her eyes red with tears. A sour feeling formed in his stomach as fear began to fill his mind. He sensed, no, he knew, someone was dead. He didn't need his wife to say a thing to know it was someone close.

He finally saw the newspaper on the table before her and closed his eyes in shock, the headline confirming his fears.

Then the cell phone in his back pocket began to vibrate, causing him to jump, startling him from his grief. Since he had left his job, no one called at this hour, and there was no one he wanted to speak to as he came to terms with the news of his friend's death. He pulled the phone from his pocket to turn it off . . .

And his heart nearly stopped as he looked at the caller ID.

JACK PUT DOWN his cell phone and stared at the newspaper—its headline proclaiming his demise—and he could barely focus as the gravity of the situation enveloped him. His hands were shaking; he was unsure if it was from somehow being shot and not remembering it or reading his own front-page obituary. With trembling hands, he finally picked up the paper and began to read.

Three times over, he read it, his agony growing with each sentence. The description of his death, of the wounds to his body, the strange markings on his arm, was but an afterthought as the words sank in. It was as if someone had ripped away the floor he was standing on. He had never imagined it, even with her line of work . . . the thought of such a tragedy had not entered his mind until now. Somehow, his worst nightmare had come to pass.

His wife, Mia, was dead.

EVERYONE KNEW MIA Keeler when she entered a room, even if they didn't know her. Her dark brown hair was long and thick and flecked with natural auburn highlights. She had a dancer's body, not that of a waifish ballerina but that of a Latin dancer, strong and lean, with perfect feminine curves. Her large, dark brown eyes were always alive and filled with expression, a trait she used equally well in her job and at home staring down her children when they did wrong. She possessed a classic beauty, a face lightly tanned, which had yet to know a wrinkle despite the worries her daughters had engendered.

Jack Keeler and Mia Norris had met at Fordham Law. It was their second year. Jack was a man in transition, a police detective hoping for a redo in life, seeking out a second career only four years after his first one began and ended with the tragic death of his partner. Mia, however, had always had a distinct, singular focus: the FBI. Like her stepfather before her, she felt the pull. She had a passion for law enforcement, a mind for puzzles, crisis, and problem solving, a Supergirl instinct for saving the helpless and fighting for truth, justice, and the good old American way.

Their first date consisted of gelato from an Italian street vendor and wandering around the Upper West Side of Manhattan, finally ending up in Central Park on the Bow Bridge, legs dangling over the lake, lost in conversation for hours. The following day, it was hot dogs along the Hudson and the next, a Friday, an actual formal sit-down date at Shun Lee Palace on 55th Street.

They laughed at how neither was really a serious student until senior year of high school, both preferring the joys of sports and socializing. They shared a passion for the Rolling Stones, Aretha, and Buddy Guy and would have flown anywhere in the world for a Led Zeppelin reunion.

As the weeks went on, they played baseball on Tuesday nights and spent weekends climbing the Shawangunk Mountains in New Paltz, New York, with ropes on their backs and pitons clipped to their waists. Jack taught her how to ride his motorcycle and win in mock trials, and they went head-to-head in skeet and trap shooting, neither one giving quarter.

After a month, they found themselves in Jack's small apartment on Bleecker Street deep in conversation while the strains of Clapton's "Layla" played in the background. Mia told Jack of her tough-as-nails mask. Opening up her soul, she told him of her fears of life and failure, of the expectations her parents had always placed on her to be nothing but the best. She had rebelled against them as a teen but by twelfth grade had made everything in her life about pleasing them, about meeting their ideals, about avoiding that all-too-common disappointed stare.

And as Clapton's heartfelt guitar cried the song's final notes, Mia told him of her life up to when she was a young teen, things she hadn't spoken of in years, a pain buried deep down of an event no child should ever endure: the death of her father in her arms at the age of fourteen.

She allowed the memories to rise as Jack's gentle words, his presence and warmth, conveyed an understanding she had never known. And as she spoke in soft whispers, it was cathartic, akin to confessing one's sins. Mia told him of the pain, the horror that had forever changed her life and set her on a path that had been anything but linear yet had become at times an obsession.

Although she fought with everything she had to contain her emotions, the tears pooled on the lower lids of her eyes. He gently reached out, a simple brush of her arm, his touch conveying his heart, his sympathy. Their eyes locked, time slowing until a silent understanding flowed between them. He took her in his arms, allowing her pain to come up finally in quiet gasps.

And as her grief was purged, as her trembling subsided, a truth emerged. Her head rose from his shoulder, their faces inches apart, feeling each other's breath on their skin, a near kiss that built in sexual tension. The moment hung there, their breathing falling into a synchronized rhythm, until the unspoken barrier finally dissolved away.

It was like nothing Jack had ever experienced in his life. Mia's lips were full and warm, filled with passion. They inhaled each other's soul until they were one. Tearing each other's clothes off, they fell to the couch in a tangle of arms and legs, seeking and giving pleasure. It was animalistic yet heartfelt, sensual and honest, a moment of perfection that neither had dreamed of. Thoughts and worries drifted away. They were safe in each other's embrace, complete in the moment. The music continued to play, growing ever distant as they fell into their own world, where the only sounds were their passionate sighs of urging and joy, their quickened breaths and pounding hearts.

And in the after-moments of silence, their beating hearts slowing, the sheen of sweat cooling their heat, they understood.

Without a single word necessary, they knew.

So often, as love takes hold, it sharpens the focus, the selflessness, imbuing confidence in one's abilities, providing the self-assurance to be able to achieve anything. It fills the heart with hope and possibilities, opening the eyes to the joys of life that can become obscured by the trials and tragedies in life's journey.

And so, what was to be a fifteen-minute frozen snack to discuss tort reform and judicial process turned into a sixteen-year relationship, with two kids, mountains of bills and stress, but a deep satisfaction and reward from a life filled with love.

Jack looked back down at the article one final time:

> *District Attorney Jack Keeler and his wife, Mia, were killed just after midnight, their car plunging off the Rider's Bridge. Their bodies have yet to be recovered from the Byram River, the recovery effort proving to be futile in the raging, storm-swelled waters.*
>
> *Unconfirmed reports of bullet casings at the scene have bolstered rumors of foul play and that the accident is being treated as murder.*

HE PUSHED HIS grief aside and allowed his logical mind to begin to take over. He was the one who could always see the forest for the trees, who could sift through the evidence and glean the truth where others saw nothing but disjointed facts.

The sensational nature of newspapers, any headline to sell a copy, always angered Jack. How could the newspaper declare him dead when a coroner had not, when his body had yet to be recovered (which, point in fact, wasn't about to happen)?

And if he was standing there, then maybe . . .

Mia was tougher than any woman he had ever known. If there was even a shred of possibility . . .

As he stood there in the kitchen, a glimmer of hope began growing in his mind, but it grew only so much as it hit an obstacle. It was as if the memory of the night before was hidden behind a wall that he couldn't get around, couldn't climb, couldn't penetrate. His frustration grew to be overwhelming as he realized that he had lost some part of his mind.

CHAPTER 3

RANK ARCHER STOOD IN the Keelers' kitchen, his hand on Jack's shoulder, his eyes equally confused and relieved, looking as if he were staring at a ghost.

The two had sat in silence for more than three minutes, both coming to terms with the situation. Jack had explained everything he knew. He showed his injuries, the wound in his shoulder, the cuts on his face and neck; he showed his mud-encrusted, wet pants. Finally, he unbuttoned the cuff of his shirt and slowly rolled it up to reveal the dark tattoo that wrapped his forearm.

Frank looked at it a moment, his eyes darting between the macabre piece of artwork and Jack's troubled eyes. Jack slowly rolled down his sleeve, waiting for his friend to speak.

"How can you not remember last night?" Frank finally asked. "You were dreading it for weeks. You were so pissed about giving up your tickets for the Yankees game—which was rained out, by the way—having to celebrate the life of the man who had yet to offer you a simple sign of respect. Don't you remember making him his present? Ten nights you spent working on that thing, creating it from scratch, all those pieces. You're a better man than I. I wouldn't even have bought him a card."

"I've got nothing," Jack said. "Not an image, a thought. It's like someone threw a white can of paint on my mind. Yesterday just isn't there."

"Think. What time did you and Mia leave the party? Did you leave together? You didn't just drive off that bridge, did you? And the gunshot wound?" Frank pointed at Jack's shoulder. "It didn't just appear. Is someone after you? Which is a distinct possibility. Most criminals hold the man who throws them in jail responsible for the troubles in their lives. You put your fair share away."

No matter how hard Jack thought on it, his mind was blank.

"Think back," Frank said. "What is the last memory you had before this morning? You remember me, not that I'm the forgettable type."

Jack's mind was on overload, as if it had short-circuited. He couldn't hold a coherent thought as he tried to reflect back to the last memory before that morning. It was like lifting an impossible weight, his brain straining with the effort.

Last Friday, a week ago, appeared within a fog in his mind. In his office. Images started to come into focus. Reviewing pending cases with his assistant, Joy. But none of the cases was of any significance. He had arrived at work later than usual. Skipped lunch, early dinner with Mia and the girls . . . and then it completely fogged over.

"Ok," Jack finally said as he looked up. "Last Friday."

"Good." Frank smiled. "It's a start."

But his mind was already back on Mia and the hollow feeling of being alone in the world, of grief, how he would tell his daughters that their mother was dead. He couldn't bear to look in their eyes. He wouldn't know how to answer "Daddy, I don't understand. Why isn't she coming back?"

"Hey," Frank snapped. "I see your face. Your mind is spinning tales of supposition. Stay focused. Think. Something's got to spark your memory. A song, a piece of clothing."

Jack ran his hands down his face. Everything made him think of Mia. The kitchen table they sat at, which she'd bought from a friend and was so proud of after he had sanded it down and polished it in his shop. The kitchen she designed, the wallpaper, the framed pictures of her and the kids on the windowsill. Everything in his life made him think of Mia. She was part of the fabric of his being.

He walked through the house, hoping that something would just pop out and fill in the holes in his memory. Past the living room, glancing at the piano, which sparked a vision of his girls whining about Thursday lessons with Mrs. Henry. Past the dining room, which only pulled up memories of Mia's home-cooked Thanksgiving dinner for twenty-eight. The front hall: nothing. Feeling a fool, he headed back to the kitchen, and as he passed the powder room, it hit him. Her perfume, Chanel, hung in the air, its faint scent still lingering from . . . the night before. It was what she always wore, part of her essence since college, the smell of Mia. It was what filled his mind as he drifted off to sleep, what he smelled on her pillow, on her clothes, on her neck when he held her.

He froze where he stood, motionless by the powder-room door, trying to coax the memory of the night before from the dark hollow of his brain, but it kept slipping away, drifting off just out of reach.

Frank poked his head out of the kitchen, seeing Jack standing there, lost in thought, and remained silent.

And then Jack saw her in his mind's eye, standing there in all of her beauty, looking at the mirror as she brushed her long dark hair one last time, yelling at him to get dressed, that they were going to be late . . . again.

It was as if a wellspring opened, flooding with images, thoughts, and sounds. Like from a separate life, distinct and apart from his own. It all came in, all of the joy and sounds of the party, of the never-ending rain, of the catered food. A movie unwinding before him.

He nearly collapsed, grabbing the wall for stability, sliding down against it, coming to rest on the floor as he started to shake. His emotions were building up inside him, and last night's moments of joy and anticipation shattered as rage and anger and fury filled him. He felt the pounding of the rain on his face, his body soaked and bloodied. And he finally boiled over as if awakened from one life to be thrust into another, where the shadows were darker, where pain was everywhere and life hung in the balance.

He finally looked up at Frank, tears welling up . . . for his memory of the night before had returned.

He knew what had happened.

CHAPTER 4

M IA WORE A BLACK dress, long, elegant, her lithe legs gliding along the floor as she walked arm-in-arm with Jack across the marble lobby of her parents' house. The stately home was just short of a mansion, a brick dwelling with large rooms and high ceilings that dated back to the 1920s. Servants scampered around, carrying trays, adjusting floral arrangements, preparing for a party.

Jack readjusted a birthday gift under his left arm. Wrapped haphazardly in fishing-themed paper, the eighteen-inch-square box was awkward and difficult to carry.

They opened double doors and entered a small, cozy gentleman's den. An oversized desk sat before the bay window, nothing on it but a brass elephant paperweight and a humidor. A life's worth of books filled the shelves, and family pictures were scattered around, of Mia with her mother and stepfather below a white lighthouse, at the beach, skiing, of friends, family, and life, of Mia standing with a strong military man in dress uniform.

"I know it's a day early, but happy birthday," Mia said.

On the red button-tuck leather couch sat a white-haired gentlemen, his broad shoulders projecting strength despite the evident years on his face. Dressed in a pale green blazer and dark slacks, he had an exacting style that matched his demeanor. He finally looked up with cold, assessing eyes at Jack and Mia.

"Your mother will use any excuse for a party," the man said. His voice was deep, with no sense of celebration.

Jack handed the gentleman the colorfully wrapped package. The man's dark eyes narrowed as he took in the crinkled paper of the unevenly wrapped gift.

"The girls spent a lot of time picking out that paper," Mia said as she pointed out the bigmouth bass and the fishing rod. "Open it," she urged him.

He sat back on his leather couch, placing the package on the coffee table in front of him. He pushed aside his newspapers and muted the TV.

He was born on July 1, and his mother named him Samuel, as her due date had been the Fourth of July and she had grown attached to it. But Sam Norris hated that name and hadn't gone by it since grade school.

Leaning forward, Sam wrapped his large hand around the present and tore off the wrapping, revealing a polished wooden box, its cherry wood waxed to a high sheen. He lifted the lid of the furniture-quality case to find an assortment of small individual packages adorned in the crooked bows of a child's hand: a fly-fishing reel, flies, string, lures.

"The girls are still waiting for you to live up to that promise of taking them on one of your fishing jaunts."

Mia's stepfather smiled as he held up the box, looking at its detail, at its perfect joints and recessed hinges.

"Jack made the box," Mia said.

"A box?" Sam looked at Jack, a playful taunting in his voice.

"Well," Jack began, trying not to sound defensive, "actually, it's a—"

"Dad," Mia cut in, "he spent a lot of time on that."

"Thanks." Sam smiled as he looked at Jack, stood, and headed for the door.

And as he passed Jack, he leaned into his ear, out of Mia's range, and whispered, "I hear the campaign is kind of rough."

"Well," Jack said, "if it doesn't work out, I can always make boxes for a living."

Sam looked back at the box, tilting his head in doubt. "I don't know much about carpentry, but if you need help with the campaign, you let me know."

Jack smiled. "Happy birthday, Sam."

Norris opened up the door to reveal a massive party in full swing, the crowd noise pouring into the den as he walked out.

Jack watched Norris disappear into the crowd of well-wishers, who slapped his back, patted his shoulder, and shook his hand, greeting him as if he were king.

"He never should have retired," Mia said. "What did he say? Was he taunting you about the campaign numbers?"

"Mia." Jack laughed. "He was just expressing his appreciation."

The couple turned and stepped through the doorway, into the joyous mood of the party.

"I don't believe you. It's not funny," Mia said as she grabbed two glasses of champagne from a passing waiter and passed one to her husband. "For once, I wish he would just say thank you without having to add a comment."

"Mia, when you're the former director of the FBI, it's hard to let go. Sometimes you still need to throw your weight around."

"Not at the people you're supposed to care about. Not at family."

Jack leaned over, looking his wife in the eyes. "He's a dad. He takes pleasure in ribbing the man who took away his little girl, his only child."

"After sixteen years, it's time for him to get over it."

"You think I'll be any different with our girls?" Jack smiled.

"Yeah, I do." Mia paused with a smile. "You'll be worse."

"Damn straight." Jack put on a false grimace.

"How's your headache?" Mia asked. "I'm sure tonight is really helping."

"No big thing; two Tylenol and two Cokes, and it's almost gone."

"Yeah? Well, I think I'm catching it—"

"Hey, Mia," a gruff voice whispered.

Mia turned to see a bespectacled, older man.

"Mr. Turner," Mia said. "You are the last person I expected to see here tonight."

"And I'll be the first one to leave," Turner said. "Already saw your father. I just wanted see you, say hello, and remind you that you really belong on the world stage. The FBI is so limiting."

Mia smiled. "When it's time to make a change, you know you will be my first call."

Turner nodded gruffly and headed for the front door.

In point of fact, Stuart Turner was a man known for tactical genius not only within the world intelligence community but inside the Beltway of Washington. He had been CIA director for the past three years, deputy director for six years before that, and had spent his earlier career in various State Department posts throughout the world. Known as a man who could cut through the bullshit and get things done, he possessed an abrasive manner that struck fear into those who didn't know him. But after knowing him for eighteen years, Mia couldn't help but smile at his social peculiarities.

"Jack." A man approached, his brown hair perfectly parted, his suit perfectly pressed. He warmly grasped Jack's shoulder as he shook his hand.

"Peter," Jack said.

"Hi, Mia," Peter said as he leaned over, giving her a kiss.

"Hey, Peter. Is Katherine here?"

"No, I'm solo. She and the kids are out in the Hamptons. Figured I had to show up to kiss the ring of the man."

"He's retired, Peter. No need for anyone to kiss his ring or his ass anymore," Mia said with a knowing smile.

"But you know that's my specialty, kissing ass and currying favor."

"Spoken like a true politician."

Peter Womack was, in fact, a federal prosecutor. At the age of thirty-six, he was the youngest U.S. attorney for the Southern District of New York, overseeing the federal government's most important and visible office. He and Jack had worked together on occasion, while their wives had become friendly at one too many political functions.

"Special Agent Keeler?" a deep voice called out.

Mia spun around to see the current director of the FBI, her boss's boss, Lance Warren, standing in the hallway behind her. A career government man, having previously served in the military, the CIA, the NSA, and the State Department, Warren was the rare breed favored by both political parties not only for his finesse in coordinating between foreign and domestic intelligence agencies but also for his tenacity and get-it-done yesterday approach. A handsome man, he stood tall in a blue blazer with his hand thrust out toward Mia. Mia took it as he shook it in congratulatory fashion.

"So many jobs well done, Mia." Warren said.

"Thank you, sir."

"Mia . . ." Warren said admonishingly.

"Lance." Mia relented. "You know my dad raised me formally in addressing my elders."

They had known each other since Mia was in high school and Warren and her father worked together in Washington. He had helped to shepherd her career far more than her father had.

"Jack." Warren turned. "How have you been?"

"Terrific, Lance. And you?"

"Great. How's the district attorney's office? You ever thinking of leaving there?"

"Every day." Jack smiled. "We'll let you guys catch up. I'm going to find some food."

As Jack and Peter both turned to a passing waiter, grabbing bacon-wrapped scallops, Warren's face grew serious. "I understand there may be an evidence file that is missing."

"Missing?" Mia smiled.

"I got a call from Gene Tierney about a murder earlier this week at a hotel."

"Yes, the Waldorf."

"He mentioned a number of people are interested in reviewing the case, seeing the evidence."

"Of my case?" Mia was never one to hide her emotions, even from her superiors.

"Mia." Warren threw up his hands in surrender. "It's your case, I just got the call. I'm not pulling rank, especially for someone like Tierney."

"Thank you."

"In confidence, you haven't lost the evidence file, have you?"

"Just misplaced." Mia shook her head and smiled. "We're working with New York City on this. Evidence administrators filed it under the wrong name. No one likes to admit how often it happens."

"Ah," Warren said with relief as he raised his glass in a toast. "Here's to hating the bureaucracy that employs us."

JUST AFTER MIDNIGHT, Mia kissed her mother and father good-bye and slipped out of the party that was finally winding down. She and Jack ran out the front door into the pouring rain and climbed into his white Tahoe, slamming the doors and exhaling, taking a moment to enjoy the silence,

"Live to fight another day," Jack said with relief as he took off his wet sportcoat and laid it on the console between them. "I ran out of small talk two hours ago."

Mia reached into the back and grabbed a blue button-down sweater, pulling it on and buttoning it up, shaking out the cold rain from her hair.

Settling back in the passenger seat, Mia took Jack's hand and gently squeezed it, a warm, loving smile washed over her face. "Thank you. I know how much you hate those things."

Jack leaned across the seat and kissed her softly on the cheek. "I'd survive far worse than your father for you."

"You're just saying that in hopes of getting lucky."

"Is it working?" he said with a laugh. He started up the car and drove out into the rain-soaked night.

"No," she replied, but her serious look quickly dissolved into a smile. "Well . . . the kids are sleeping at your mom's. Suppose it would be an awful waste of freedom to let the evening pass us by."

"It would be a shame; you know what they say about opportunity lost?"

"Guess that means your headache's gone," Mia said as she ran her hand through his hair.

"Headache? What headache?" Jack smiled.

As they drove up Route 22, Mia spied a lump in the breast pocket of Jack's sportcoat on the center console. She reached in his pocket and withdrew a blue jewelry box.

She turned her head, raising an eyebrow, and opened the small box to find a gold cross attached to a simple gold chain tucked into the black velvet slit.

"You haven't even taken it out of the box yet," Mia said.

"I know." Jack laughed a guilty laugh. "I will."

"I got that for you weeks ago. You need a little bit of faith, Jack. I can't even remember the last time you were in church."

"You know me, as long as you believe in me and I believe in you, that's all the faith I need. Besides, when have you known me to wear any jewelry? I don't even wear a watch."

"When you wear this"—Mia held up the box like a spokesmodel, withdrawing the gold cross—"you can think of me."

She leaned across the center island of the car and put the cross around Jack's neck.

"I don't need a piece of jewelry to remind me of you. How about you wear it?"

"Because I got it for you."

They came to a stoplight in the middle of nowhere, the red light shining on Jack's sudden smile. "In that case," he said as he took the box out of her hands and lifted the velvet interior to reveal a second necklace.

Mia leaned forward, looking at it. "It's beautiful."

The chain was platinum and suspended an intricate pattern of varying blue stones: topaz, blue onyx, and small sapphires. Shards of blue light danced and leaped through the polished stones' crystal centers, seeming to bring the necklace to life.

"What's the occasion?"

Jack removed the necklace from the box. "Indulge me."

Jack leaned forward. Mia reluctantly obliged, tilting her head down as he clasped the necklace around her neck. He gently removed the single pearl choker he had given her for their wedding anniversary and tucked it into the jewelry box, then slipped it back into his pocket.

He tilted his head, assessing the piece as shards of light refracted off its precious stones. Jack unbuttoned the top two buttons of Mia's sweater and loosened the top of her dress to expose a bit more cleavage, allowing the blue stones to contrast against her skin. He ran his finger around her soft white neck, trailing it down her chest. "It looks great on you."

"I don't think you're looking at the necklace." Mia smiled as the light turned green. She pointed at the light and cleared her throat for effect.

Jack gave her a smirk, turned his attention back to the road, and continued up the highway.

"You know you were already on your way to getting lucky tonight?" Mia said. "You should have saved this for a day when I'm angry with you."

"There are so many of those, how could I possibly choose?" Jack smiled.

Mia reached over and stroked her hand down Jack's face. "Thank you."

They headed up Route 22 toward Byram Hills, both in silent thought as the rain pounded the windshield, its pitter-patter competing with the thumping of the rhythmic wipers. As they approached Rider's Bridge, they could see the raging river fifty feet below, a churning cauldron that rose well above the banks, pulling anything and everything into its rapids-like flow.

As the SUV hit the bridge pavement, the rear wheels lost their traction, and the Tahoe went into a sudden fishtail. Jack held tight to the wheel as the vehicle skirted left to right and back again, pulling hard to bring it under control. Mia's right hand shot up and gripped the passenger strap above the door. Their collective breath caught in their throats as the car spun headfirst toward the guardrail.

But Jack finally gained control. Slowing down to catch his breath, he had turned toward Mia with a that-was-close smile when the flashing red lights lit up his rearview mirror and the back of the car.

"Tell me you didn't have more than two glasses," Mia said as she caught her breath.

"God, that was close," Jack said as he pulled over to the side of the two-lane overpass that spanned the rushing Byram River. "I'm perfectly fine, though I think I shaved five years off my life with that little maneuver."

The flashing roof light slowly passed them. It was atop a black Chevy Suburban, and it came to a stop just in front of them.

Jack rolled down his window, the pouring rain instantly soaking his arm and the interior door of his car, stoking his mood. "This is bullshit."

"Shhh, let's keep it in check," Mia said as she smiled and rubbed his leg. "Take the ticket like a man, and we'll be home in ten minutes. Then you can continue playing with my new necklace."

They both sat silently, staring straight ahead, the thump of the windshield wipers rhythmically droning as a man in a dark suit approached. Jack glanced at the blue necklace and Mia's cleavage, motioning with his eyes.

Mia, feeling exposed, buttoned up her sweater.

Suddenly, to Jack's shock, there was a gun in his face, the black steel barrel coming to rest inches from his left eye.

"Hands on the wheel," the man in the black suit said quietly. His blond hair was plastered with rain to his head. He looked at Mia, "And you, hands on the dash."

Mia slowly put her hands on the dashboard above the glove compartment and turned to her right to see a second man in black, skinny, with a sharp long nose, his gun aimed at her head.

As if on cue, both doors were ripped open, and Jack and Mia were violently pulled from the car into the pouring rain. The skinny man thrust Mia against the car.

"What the hell is going on?"

"Quiet," the skinny man snapped, his red hair already soaked in the storm.

"You have no idea who you're messing with," Mia said through gritted teeth as the rain ran down her face. "You may want to open my purse and check my badge, because, I swear to God—"

The man brought the gun to rest inches from her eye, silencing her. He was painfully thin, his neck and jaw almost skeletal. With the rain running down his face, over his unblinking eyes, he looked like something out of a nightmare.

The blond man spun Jack around, kicking his legs out as he assumed the position of a perp. The man frisked him from stem to stern, pulling the blue box from Jack's pocket. He opened it and spied the pearl choker. Without interest, he closed the box and threw it into the car. He grabbed Jack by the neck, punched him hard in the kidneys, and threw him to the rain-soaked pavement.

The skinny assailant spun Mia around, running his hands up and down her torso, her legs, frisking her through her soaked sweater and black gown, while a third man, linebacker-sized, in a black suit, popped the trunk of their Tahoe.

The team of three operated with military efficiency, as if every move was planned, as if they had a singular goal to accomplish on a hair-trigger timeline.

"Where is the case?" the skinny man demanded.

Mia just stared at him.

"Case seven-one-three-eight?" The thin man leaned in, his breath assaulting her senses.

Mia looked at Jack and began to mouth something—

"Got it," the third man cried out as he hoisted a long black metal box from the rear of the Tahoe.

As the skinny man looked through the teeming rain at his partner, Mia drove her knee into the man's crotch, following it up with a hard elbow to the nose. But while her FBI training was thoroughly ingrained in her mind, it didn't prevent the powerful blow the man countered with and unleashed into her jaw, driving her 125-pound body into the car as he rammed his pistol into her forehead.

At the same time, Jack, who lay on the bridge, spun his leg left, sweeping out his assailant's legs, sending him crashing to the ground, his head hitting the pavement, his gun skittering away. Jack dove on top of the man, drawing back his fist and unloading it into the man's throat, stunning him. He continued to pound his knuckles into the man's face but was suddenly grabbed around the neck and yanked backward. The third man was much larger, pushing 275. His fist crushed into the side of Jack's head nearly knocking him out. For extra measure, the man didn't stop, hitting Jack twice more, opening up a large gash on his brow and his cheek.

And then a gun exploded, the crack of the percussion echoing in the rainy distance. Jack collapsed, a bullet lodged just below his shoulder. He looked up to see the bloodied, raging face of the blond man he'd beaten, leering down on him in anger before he was tugged away by the linebacker.

The skinny man dragged Mia toward the black Suburban as she kicked and screamed, fighting with all of her will to break free and get to her wounded husband.

Jack struggled to focus in spite of the pain that coursed through his body, his heart aching as he could barely move, unable to stop the men who were taking Mia.

"Let her go!" Jack shouted through a bloodied mouth. "Take me, take me, please . . ." As his words faded, he was hoisted up and tossed into the passenger seat of his car.

The large man climbed into the driver's seat, threw the car into neutral, and hit the gas, revving the engine to redline. With a last bit of strength, Jack tried to get out of the vehicle, but the man drove a punch into his bullet wound, sending crippling shards of pain through his body.

The man kept his foot on the gas pedal, the engine howled with pent-up energy, and he threw the Tahoe into drive.

The wheels screamed as they spun on the wet bridge, struggling to gain traction, smoking until they finally caught and launched the SUV into the rail of the bridge. The linebacker dove through the open driver's-side door, hit the roadway, and rolled clear.

Inside the vehicle, Jack looked with half-mast eyes to see Mia break free from her captors and chase after the Tahoe. He then caught a sudden glimpse of the small blue box that lay on the seat next to him and, without a thought, picked it up, holding it tight, as if it was the last piece of Mia he would ever touch, and slid it into his pocket.

The car crashed through the rail, sailing out over the river like a bird taking flight, but gravity soon took hold, and the Tahoe began its arc toward the rushing waters, knifing into the raging river, an explosion of water hurled nearly bridge-high. The car bobbed, quickly caught in the flow, tossed around as it slowly sank. As it neared the river bend, its taillights finally disappeared, their red glow hovering below the surface before fading to nothingness.

• • •

DESPITE THE DRIVING rain and the churning waters, there was a silence over the valley, the white noise of the downpour obscuring and absorbing all other sounds, creating a quiet over the Byram River, as if in reverence. The downpour continued to rage, roughing up the waterway, the storm surge carrying the water high up on the banks.

And then, out of the black water, climbing up into the dark night, he clawed his way onto the shore. His shirt was torn, hanging from his body, and blood poured from his shoulder.

He crawled through the mud and finally collapsed, gasping for air, rolling onto his back. His mind was blank, as dark and empty as the night around him; it struggled for purchase. Jack reached up, pressing his fist into the bullet wound on his shoulder, and his mind finally cleared, his thoughts returned, pouring in with panicked awareness as he realized . . .

Mia was gone.

CHAPTER 5

STANDING IN THE KITCHEN, as the realization that Mia must have been kidnapped washed over him, an even worse thought stabbed at his heart.

"Where are my girls?" Jack spat out, his voice desperate. He raced past Frank, up the stairs again, into their bedroom, looking around. Everything was in place; he checked the drawers, the closets, as if he would find some clue. He had no idea what he was looking for as he searched under their beds. He stopped and looked at the innocence around him, their toys, their books, the stuffed animals on their beds.

With all of his focus on the night before, on Mia, Jack had forgotten about his daughters, always thinking them safe, out of harm's way. His mind filled with panic, the feeling a parent gets when a child is hurt or in pain, when a child gets momentarily lost in the supermarket, but this was far worse.

Frank arrived upstairs. Standing in the doorway, he looked at Jack, with no answer but a face filled with equal panic.

The sound of a closing door broke the moment. Jack looked out the front window to see a dark blue car at the curb, and a man walking up to the front door.

"Where did you park?" Jack quickly asked.

"In the back," Frank said as he peered out the window. The two raced down the stairs and into the kitchen, looking out the side window at the dark-haired man.

"Reporter?" Jack asked as the man arrived at the front door.

"No way. Looks like law. Just not sure which side he might be on."

The knock at the door was loud.

Jack and Frank didn't make a move. Waiting.

The knock was louder this time, pounding. And the doorbell rang.

There was no more knocking; the moment seemed to draw out. And then the door opened.

With unspoken understanding, Jack and Frank stepped from the window and quietly slipped into the powder room. Through a crack in the door, they could see the man enter the house. He stood in the hallway, listening, eyes shifting around . . . and he disappeared. Frank slowly drew his gun.

Jack could hear the man walking around, into the kitchen, opening the garage door. They saw him again, back in the hallway. He stepped into the den. Jack could hear him tearing open the drawers of his desk, opening the armoire and the file cabinet, papers rustling, things falling off the desk and the shelf. Then the room fell silent.

And the man burst out of the den, heading upstairs.

Jack and Frank stepped from the powder room and silently walked through the kitchen. Out of sight, they crouched on either side of the stairs. Waiting.

The intruder came down the stairs, carrying something in each hand.

Without waiting, Jack tackled the man hard into the wall, driving his fist into the man's gut. The man dropped what he was carrying and drew back his fist, but Frank's fist caught him first, square in the jaw, knocking him to the ground. Frank shoved his gun into the man's face, ending any further struggle.

Jack glared at the intruder, but his eyes were quickly drawn to what he was carrying. The file was thick, notations in varying pen and pencil covered the outside, and the header was labeled *Keeler*.

Jack snatched it up.

"What is that?" Frank asked.

"Nothing." Jack headed into the den and put the file away.

"Interesting file," the intruder said. "Keeping secrets from people?"

"What's in the file?" Frank asked again.

"Nothing," Jack said. "Just personal stuff."

But the file was quickly forgotten as Jack saw the other two things the man was carrying.

"Why the hell would you take these?" Jack yelled at the thief.

They lay there in all of their innocence on the floor. And Jack's blood began to boil. He had bought them almost a year earlier, they were "just because" gifts, simple yet filled with meaning. Hope and Sara loved the two stuffed bears. One blue, one brown, they always brought smiles to their faces.

Jack grabbed the man, hoisting him up. He slammed his head into the wall. "Why?"

"They're for your girls," the intruder said. "To make them happy. To comfort them, give them something to play with."

"Who the hell are you?"

The intruder stared at him.

"Where are my girls?" Jack pulled the man in close, doing everything he could to restrain himself from killing him.

"Why, did you lose them?" The man smiled, taunting him. "Misplace them?"

"Where are they?" Jack pulled him closer, face-to-face. "Did you take them? Who took them?"

Frank stepped toward him, his gun aimed at the man. He placed his hand on Jack's arm, the action calming him, getting him to back off.

Jack frisked the man, searching under his suit jacket. He found a gun in a shoulder holster, took it, ejected the clip, tossed it aside. He checked his pockets, finding nothing but a cell phone.

He flipped it open, checked the call log, found nothing. He passed it to Frank.

"It's new," Frank said. "A onetime phone so it can't be traced."

Jack snatched the phone back out of Frank's hand and violently threw it against the wall, smashing it to pieces. "Who do you work for? Where are my wife and children?"

The man looked at Jack, his dark eyes curious, questioning. "The whole world thinks you're dead."

"Answer my question."

"How did you survive?" the man asked. "When he finds out you're alive—"

"Who?" Jack screamed in his face.

"—your wife won't even make it until dawn."

"What do you mean?" Jack's voice was unable to hide his fear.

"He's leaving the country at dawn tomorrow. Why bother keeping her alive when he could have you?"

And Jack suddenly realized that no one could know he was alive, no one could know he didn't lie at the bottom of the river, or Mia would surely die.

"Who is he?" Jack screamed as he grabbed the man, his rage trembling in his arms.

But the man fell silent and looked away in defiance.

Frank looked at Jack. "We need to turn him over to the cops—"

"We can't," Jack snapped as he let the man go. "What if he's right? We can't let this guy out in the open, or it will leak to the press that I'm alive. What if whoever has Mia finds out that the papers are wrong? Then what's stopping him from killing her, even killing my children?"

He turned back on the man with new anger, grabbing him by the lapel of his jacket. "They're children, how could you?"

"Jack . . ." Frank said, trying to calm his friend.

"What the hell are we going to do with him?" Jack turned on the man again and raged into his face. "Where are they?"

Frank thought a moment. "We drop him at a friend's house."

"What? Who?"

"Someone I trust even more than you. He'll keep an eye on him until we can figure out how best to use him. And if need be, he's the type of person who's had practice at extracting information. If this guy knows where Mia and the kids are, he'll find out."

WITH THE MAN'S hands bound together with duct tape, they tossed him into the rear seat of Frank's Jeep. Before Frank closed the door, Jack flicked the switch of the child lock. He followed suit on the other door and climbed into the passenger seat, and Frank drove off.

The back roads of Byram Hills were vacant in the early-morning hours of the day before Fourth of July weekend, people having headed off either to work or on vacation.

"You truly have no idea what's going on, do you?" the man asked, his eyes focused out the window.

Jack looked back over the seat. "Why don't you tell me what's going on?"

The man remained silent.

"Don't bother," Frank said to Jack. "We'll get our answers."

Two minutes on, they stopped at a red light on a vacant, tree-lined street. As they silently waited for the light to change, time seeming to drag out forever.

Without warning, the man rolled onto his back in the rear seat and kicked out the window; he dove from the vehicle, hit the ground hard, and was up and running. Jack and Frank leaped from the car and raced after him.

The man sprinted down the road, his feet pounding the pavement, his arms awkwardly swinging from his bound wrists. A noise grew as they ran on, soft, growing louder until they were running across the overpass of a major highway. He was fast, running for his life, but Jack was running for his wife, his children, and couldn't let his only connection to them get away. His legs drove him faster and he was suddenly upon the man. He tackled him to the hot black-top, road-rashing their skin. Frank caught up and violently lifted the man, throwing him against the guardrail of the overpass.

"Do that again, and I'll throw your ass off this bridge." Frank drew his gun for emphasis, grabbed the man by his right arm, and held on tight. The man finally relaxed, closing his eyes in defeat.

Jack got to his feet, catching his breath. "You sure your friend is going to be able to hold this guy?"

"Yeah. Ben's not just a good friend, he's a military friend, tough. He doesn't suffer fools like this."

Without warning, the man opened his eyes, tore away from Frank, and leaped over the guardrail, falling feet-first to the rush-hour traffic below.

Jack realized that escape wasn't his intention. He knew exactly what he was doing and where he was going, he timed it perfectly.

The fifteen-ton tractor-trailer never even locked up its brakes. The driver didn't see the man falling into the path of his seventy-mile-an-hour truck until it was too late.

CHAPTER 6

RIDER'S BRIDGE WAS AWASH in emergency vehicles, while scores of people had gathered, lining the bridge rail, watching the search unfold. News trucks lay in wait at the bridge entrance, their cameras fixed on the arrival of an enormous crane. Two ropes were tied to and disappeared off the bridge edge, stretching down into the roiling waters below. A team of scuba divers held tight to the ropes, fighting the rushing current before slipping beneath the surface to continue their search.

A limousine arrived on the bridge, and all eyes turned. News cameras swarmed it. And what little noise was in the air fell away. All waited and watched. After three minutes, Sam Norris exited the rear of the car, accompanied by FBI director Lance Warren. The two tall men had always exuded power and leadership, but today they exuded only sorrow and pain.

They stared at the small numbered evidence markers along the roadway, the black skid marks that led to the missing guardrail. Without a word, they walked to the bridge edge, as everyone gave

Mia's father and Director Warren a wide, respectful birth. As Norris watched the activity below, he clenched his jaw, holding back his emotions. He knew what he would see. He knew it had been best to leave Pat at home; she was already inconsolable with grief.

Warren laid his hand on Norris's shoulder. He had called him with the news, sparing his friend from learning about it from a newspaper or a cheery reporter on TV.

A man arrived at Warren's side. Warren walked away with him so that Norris wouldn't overhear.

"They found the vehicle."

"But no bodies?" Warren asked.

"No, sir." The man was young, efficient, and direct. "The dive team says with the heavy current, the search grid is large, it could take twelve or more hours."

"What do we know on the bullet?"

"We don't know yet. Everyone is working on possible scenarios."

"How do we know they were in the car?"

"At least one airbag is deployed, the driver's side. They don't blow unless someone is in the seat."

"Anyone think this was a hit? Because it's looking that way, and if that's the case . . . These were real good people, Sheldon."

"I know, sir," Sheldon said, nodding.

"If they were in the car, what are the chances they survived?"

Sheldon looked at Warren and shook his head.

Warren looked over at Norris, whose eyes were fixed on the dive team in the river. "Double our efforts."

"Yes, sir."

"And Sheldon, Mia and I discussed an evidence case that had gone missing, a bureaucratic screw-up. Let's be sure it was the bureaucracy and not something worse. Find out what cases she was working on. Hook up with Keeler's office, find out what was going on with him. Call Deputy Director Tierney. I want him to handle this personally. If this was murder, I want the bastards found."

Warren walked back over to Norris and looked out at the raging river. In unspoken understanding, the two men turned as if leaving a funeral. All eyes followed them. The press remained silent, microphones held down at their sides in respect. Warren held the door for his friend and got in behind him, and they drove away.

CHAPTER 7

IF THAT GUY PREFERRED jumping off a bridge into a tractor-trailer, if that was the only alternative in his mind . . ." Frank said, but he never finished stating what Jack was already aware of.

"I know," Jack said, more to himself than to Frank. They were back at his house, trying to regroup. With the death of the man on the bridge, they were thankful no one had seen them.

As much as the man's suicide scared Jack, his fear for his children was far worse. He had lost the only link to them, the only link to Mia.

Standing in the foyer, he looked at the cell phone he had smashed in anger, wondering if he had destroyed a crucial piece of evidence that would have led him to her. He leaned down and picked up the blue bear. He remembered giving it to Hope last October. He had been working late on a racketeering case for weeks, spending most of his weekends in the office. He had missed them terribly but knew they missed him even more. When the trial finally ended in victory, he had stopped at the toy store and grabbed the blue and brown bears. After arriving home after ten to find Mia sound asleep, he crept into the girls' room and sat in a desk chair watching over them. He had missed them as if he hadn't seen them in months. Knowing that the next day would only bring more routine—school, work, dinner, bedtime—he had leaned over Hope and kissed her cheek, then quickly turned and kissed Sara.

The two girls had awoken, sleep dripping from their eyes until they saw their dad. They had leaped into his arms, holding tight so he couldn't escape.

"Daddy," Sara had said, "it's the middle of the night."

And Jack had held out the bears. They had snatched them up, hugging them close, but soon returned to hugging their father.

"Thank you," Hope had said.

"I just want you to know I love you."

"Is that what the bear's for?"

Jack had nodded.

With a warm smile, he had picked them up, carried them downstairs, pulled out a box of Oreos, and poured three glasses of milk. They had headed into the den, cuddled up under a blanket, and watched *Willy Wonka* until four in the morning, when they all finally fell asleep. Needless to say, Mia hadn't been happy when she found them at 6:15 but soon forgave them, allowing them to sleep, everybody taking the day off and spending it together.

And now, as Jack stared at the bear, the wellspring of his subconcious reopened, flooding his mind with images, thoughts, and sounds. But it was last night, early this morning . . . all of the pain, all of his emotions from twelve hours ago, building up. His life shattered, the rage and anger and fury filling him as Mia was torn away into the night; the wound in his shoulder once again sharp with pain; he was keenly aware of the cut above his eye. He felt the pounding of the rain on his face, his body soaked through and bloodied.

Then he finally burst through it, all of the pain gone, his mind clear, as if he had to travel through hell to venture into the recesses of his mind.

• • •

FIVE DAYS AGO. Sunday's drive out to his parents' house was suddenly as clear as if it was five minutes ago. They had dropped the girls off for the week. He and Mia needed alone time, time to talk, to reconnect, time for Jack to explain some things that were happening in his life and career.

Jack could still hear Mia's voice as she calmed the girls, standing in his parents' driveway, wiping the tears from Hope's and Sara's eyes as they cried about leaving behind their pillows, their stuffed animals, and how much they would miss them.

"Honey." crouching down, she took each of them into her embrace, "both of you, give me your hands."

The two girls held out their right hands, which Mia gently grasped. She warmly kissed their palms and then closed their small fingers around the kiss so it wouldn't escape.

"Do you know what that is?"

The girls shook their heads in unison.

"That's a kissing hand. Whenever you miss me, need me, or are scared, you place it against your cheek." Mia placed her palm against her cheek in demonstration; both the girls followed her lead. "Do you feel it?"

The girls smiled and nodded.

"I do," Hope said.

"You both hold on to those." She pulled them close and whispered in their ears, "They last forever."

With the girls now smiling and their eyes focused on the beach, Jack and Mia handed them and their bags to his mom and were back on the road. They loved their children more than life but realized that they had sacrificed so much of themselves to the point of forgetting about each other.

All of their money went into their house, their government salaries not affording them the luxury of vacations. And so they embraced those moments of slowing down, turning their lives around, modifying their day to make it a vacation of the mind.

Their conversation on the way home had nothing to do with play dates, juice boxes, or Fineas and Ferb. It was about each other, catching up on things missed as a result of work and children.

After walking through the door of their home, they reveled in the silence. It was like the peace of walking into a hotel after a long journey, dropping the bags onto the floor, and collapsing on the bed. They read the paper, walked around in their underwear without care, talked for hours, and fell silent for long spells, taking pleasure from simply being in each other's company. There were things Jack wanted to talk about, things about life and the future, but in the recaptured feeling when one first falls in love, Jack decided that things could wait, that some secrets could hold for a few more days.

Mia made garlic mashed potatoes and green beans while Jack seared the steak. They made love on the sofa like teenagers whose parents were out for the evening, watched movies, and lost themselves in the moment. At eight o'clock, they piled a sea of pillows and comforters on the floor of the sunroom and fell sound asleep in each other's arms.

Besides the night before, it was the last full memory of the week he could form. He looked again at the blue bear, leaned down and picked up the brown one. He knew where he would take them.

FRANK DROVE THEM up the Merritt Parkway, heading north, the glare of the early-morning sun filling his Jeep.

Jack dialed his cell phone. His mom had always been an early riser, so he felt no guilt about calling so early. He needed to hear that the girls were OK, needed to know they were safe. The phone rang.

He had given his mom a cell phone, taught her how to use it, insisted that she always carry it in case of emergency, but he knew she had tucked it into the back of a drawer where the battery died and had forgotten all about it.

The phone rang again. And again. Four times now. No answer. He cursed her for not having an answering machine, for not keeping up with the times.

On the sixth ring, Jack began to panic, and Frank hit the accelerator.

CHAPTER 8

JACK BURST THROUGH THE side door of his childhood home, raced through the small New England foyer, and charged up the stairs. He tore open the door at the end of the hall and peered into the dark room.

The curtains were drawn; daylight had yet to arrive in his old bedroom. His eyes struggled to focus as he stepped in, careful not to trip on the scattered toys. And as his eyes finally adjusted, he sighed in relief. Hope and Sara lay sound asleep in his old queen-sized bed, their small bodies lost amid the sheets and pillows. He smiled to see Hope's right palm resting on her cheek, her kissing hand protecting her as her mother had promised.

Jack headed back downstairs to search for his mother. Assuming that she was walking her dog, he stepped outside and took a breath of fresh sea air.

The white clapboard house sat on a two-acre parcel of land surrounded on three sides by a forty-acre preserve; on the fourth side, behind sea-grass-covered dunes, was the Atlantic Ocean. The roar of the early-morning waves rolling over the sandy hills instilled a temporary peace in Jack, one that he always felt at his childhood home.

With momentary relief, he stood on the dunes, staring out at the ocean, absorbing the serenity, hoping that it would help him focus and fill the holes that dotted his memory, where he knew that the answer to finding Mia lay.

His gaze was drawn to Trudeau Island, the spit of land two miles off the Connecticut shore, the private enclave where Marguerite Trudeau used to throw her lavish parties back in the '30s for the New York high-society crowd. Jack and his friends spent too many summer nights to count riding Doug Reiberg's boat out, beaching it on the southern shore, and throwing makeshift keg parties on the beach with bonfires, music, and girls.

The southern section of the island had become a potter's field, donated by the Trudeaus in the 1940s to the city of New York for the unclaimed bodies of John and Jane Does, for orphaned children who died alone, for prisoners whose sentences of banishment from society would be extended into eternity. It was said that the hundred-acre southern section had been filled up by the '50s and so they began doubling up the graves, burying the dead upon the dead. By the '60s, the city had turned to cremation, and by the '80s, the potter's field was nothing more than a graveyard overgrown with trees, shrubbery, and weeds, erasing the memory of the forgotten.

It made for great stories around the beach bonfires, tales that grew more outlandish as the beer consumption increased, stories that would send the girls into the arms of their boyfriends. And while Jack never believed in ghosts, it always disturbed him that so many died alone, forgotten, with no one to speak of their lives.

The cries of the distant gulls startled him out of his thoughts, and he turned to see his mother emerge from the paths of the nature preserve. Theo, her golden Lab, fought to break free of his leash, howling with excitement at the sight of Jack. As her ninety-eight-pound body fought to hold him back, Jack's mom nearly collapsed when she saw her son. Jack raced to her, and she clasped him as she did when he was child and stayed out past dark.

"The news said . . ." She gasped, her small body trembling.

"I know."

"I tried to call . . ." Heidi Keeler said as she brushed her gray hair from her face. "Where's Mia?"

Jack looked into his mother's fragile blue eyes, seeing the fear in his answer. "I don't know."

MORNING SUN POURED through the large picture window of the great room as Heidi Keeler busied herself cooking the way she always did when she was stressed. Eggs and bacon sizzled on the stove, English muffins toasted under the broiler, and the smell of fresh coffee filled the air.

With the blue and brown bears tucked under his arm, Jack raced around the great room, determined and without pause, reaching behind the media console to disconnect the TV and unplug the radio.

"You didn't need to bring those bears. We have so many toys here—"

"No television, no radio today, Mom. Keep the girls out at the beach and away from phones."

"OK," his mom said. "Is your friend going to come into the house, or should I bring his breakfast out to the car?"

"He's on the phone. We can't stay long."

"Then I'll pack something up for him," Heidi said as she pulled out the tin foil.

"Where's your computer?"

"In the study on the—"

But Jack was already out of the room and in the adjacent study. It was paneled in a bleached oak; driftwood and shells were scattered on the shelves between the books on yachting, golf, fishing, and finance. He found his mother's computer on the desk, lit with a screensaver of Hope and Sara, and turned to the all-in-one printer-scanner on the side table. He quickly rolled up his sleeve, lifted the scanner cover, and laid his tattooed left arm on the glass. After closing the lid, he hit scan and watched as the bright light poured through the machine. Within a few seconds, the scan of his arm filled the computer screen, looking like some Maori appendage that one might see in a *Smithsonian* magazine article.

"What did you do to yourself?"

Jack turned to see his mom alternately staring at the computer and his arm. "Long story."

"What's going on, Jack?"

He took a seat at the computer and opened his mother's e-mail. He attached a copy of the tattoo image to a document and hit send. "I have no idea and not much time. You don't know any language experts, do you?"

His mother shook her head as she leaned in and studied the tattoo on his arm. "That thing is horrific."

"Thanks."

"Columbia."

"What?" Jack's BlackBerry beeped. He pulled it out and saw the incoming e-mail he had just sent himself.

"They have a huge language and sociology department." Heidi looked closer at the tattoo. "And I'm pretty sure linguistics and anthropology. Jeez, Jack, that thing is ugly."

"Remember what I said about the girls." Jack kissed her cheek and ran from the room.

He headed back up the stairs and stepped into his old bedroom to see the girls still fast asleep. He stared at them, taking comfort in the knowledge that they were safe, that they had no idea what was going on; their young minds were still unblemished with the dangers and realities of life. He silently walked to the bed and tucked the two bears under the covers between them.

As he turned to leave, he nearly jumped out of his skin, for sitting there was the one man he didn't expect to see. If Jack's relationship with his father-in-law was bad, the one with his own father was far worse. They hadn't spoken in months, and the conversations they did have over the years were few and far between. They would start out cordial, with false smiles and handshakes, talking of the weather and the girls and maybe the Yankees, but after thirty seconds of niceties, David Keeler would only speak of himself, his world, his fishing and golf, how hard he worked. And the conversation would soon devolve into criticism and words of disappointment. His father was critical of his career choice, wasting his education on politics, living the life of an elected official; he never saw his son's life as one of sacrifice, of protecting the people, of fighting crime. He would tell him he was wearing a white shirt in a blue-collar world.

He made Jack feel like a child, inadequate and small, with a diminished mind not worthy of a life.

But as Jack stared at his father, sitting calmly in his old wooden desk chair, his father looked back with eyes Jack hadn't seen in years. They were filled with concern, with worry, so contrary to his usual expression of disappointment.

Jack stared at him for a long moment and walked out of the room without a word.

CHAPTER 9

J ACK KEELER COULD HARDLY remem-
ber a time when he and his father didn't disagree,
didn't fight, didn't go for long spells without speaking.

Jack had grown up in a family of privilege, though not multi-
millionaires. His father's successful career in finance left Jack wanting
for nothing. He lived inside a bubble, his friends and family from similar backgrounds with similar morals and viewpoints. As far as Jack was
concerned, life as it was in his town was the way the world was.

Jack had been the goalie on his high school hockey team and
rode his talent to play Division III at Williams College in Massachu-
setts. While his father had pushed him to play Division I—the stepping stone to the pros—Jack was under no illusion of ever having the
skill set to play in the NHL. He was happy having a good time and
enjoying the sport for what it was. It had allowed him to attend a
school that his grades couldn't get him into, and it kept him the center of attention on campus for the first two seasons.

Jack was all of twenty when his world was turned upside down.
His father was a senior VP of a small investment firm and had been

pushing his son toward the power world of finance, badgering him about his grades, his appearance, his reputation. When he ventured into the city, his father ensured that he met with all of the movers and shakers, laying the groundwork for the future. In the summer of his freshman year, he interned at the investment bank Millar and Peabody in Manhattan, and his sophomore year saw him spend eight weeks at Wyeth Investments. But the experience did not have the effect his father had hoped for.

Earl Nathanson was their neighbor, a successful investment banker, a thrice-divorced father of five who regularly had forgone seeing his children's baseball games and swim meets for work and the track. Earl's house next to the Keelers' was the finest on the block. He always claimed that it would have been three times its size if he didn't have to pay his three ex-wives and so much child support.

Jack's father truly hated the man. He found him despicable not only in his personal life but also in business, having made his money off of questionable trades and the backs of others. They both worked at Wyeth Investments but in different offices. Earl was considered a star in the company, and many said he was the man to learn from, but Jack's father told him that he was the type to avoid, the type never to aspire to be.

But three weeks after that lecture, Earl and his father did a significant deal together, one that made them both a considerable amount of money. And in the small celebration in the firm's conference room, with champagne flowing, Jack watched as his father shook the hand of the man he despised, all the while smiling and laughing, choosing money over principles.

He looked around the room, seeing men with phony smiles that masked hidden jealousy and agendas, employees driven by greed, all secretly hoping that the next champagne toast would be to them. Jack wondered how many of them would put aside their convictions and dreams to chase the dollar.

Jack silently railed against his father, his moral compromise for financial success, his lack of genuine honesty in his job. He swore that he was not going to let his dreams die, compromise himself for anything. Unbeknownst to his father, Jack formed his own plans.

It was in the summer, just before the start of his junior year, that he finally declared his major: criminal justice, a major that his father frowned upon.

Jack Keeler took the New York City police entrance exam in his senior year of college and headed to the Police Academy—much to the disappointment of his father—the day after graduation, his degree and pedigree making him a unique commodity in the New York City Police department.

It turned out that Jack was gifted with a gun, finishing head of his class at the range. He represented the N.Y. Police Academy at several competitions, always taking home the top prize. He never had a love for guns but found them to be like an extension of his body. His skill with a pistol in the obstacle-laden practical shooting courses was only bested by his ability with a rifle. His instructors recommended him for SWAT and made the military aware of his talent, but Jack would have none of it. He wanted to be engaged in fighting crime, solving crime; he wanted to use his mind far more than a firearm.

With the honors bestowed upon him, Jack was given accelerated entry into homicide, the division where he thought he could do the most good, applying his deductive reasoning to capturing those who committed the most heinous acts.

With an affection for puzzles since his teens, he was a natural as a detective. His aptitude helped him get assigned to a six-month apprenticeship under Detective Frank Archer. The department believed that the veteran would impart his wisdom and skills to someone with youthful energy, drive, and passion for police work.

Frank at first thought Keeler was some rich kid playing cops and robbers, a showboater who would be the front-page poster child of the "new" kind of cop. The fact of the matter was that Jack was not rich in the sense of privilege, having been raised in the upper-middle-class world afforded by his father's income. Jack had all but rejected his father's monetary assistance and connections upon graduating from college. He was neither arrogant nor vain, and his passion turned out to be entirely genuine.

Although Frank was fifteen years Jack's senior, they became fast friends, working together on multiple cases over the six-month period. Jack absorbed his new friend's knowledge, while Frank found Jack's drive and commitment refreshing in a world where work ethics were as ephemeral as a cool summer breeze.

Frank's world was the antithesis of the life Jack had started out in. He was street-tough and spoke his mind without thought; his bulldog body and attitude were the outward manifestation of his heart. Frank had spent ten years in homicide and had yet to become jaded. Bronx-born and -raised, at the age of eighteen, he joined the Army in search of adventure but ended up spending the majority of his ten years of service as a sergeant stateside, barring a single tour in Germany.

His wife, Lisa, never complained as they crisscrossed the country from base to base for six-month stints, but she exacted a promise from Frank that once he was out of the Army, he would figure out a way to buy her a small house with a garden, where they could settle down and have kids.

Frank fit right in at the NYPD, which was happy to embrace a military man. He worked his way through narcotics, robbery, and special units, finally settling into homicide. Lisa had feared for his life far more than she ever had when he was in the army.

She had hoped to overcome that by focusing on family and children. But despite all the years of trying, despite all of the doctors' promises and bills, a child was not in their future. They dealt with their heartbreak as they did with so many of the problems they had faced in life: distraction. Lisa became a teacher, indirectly sating her maternal instinct by helping to form the lives of other people's children, taking pleasure in her third-grade class and the students' magical, inquisitive minds.

Frank found an even greater focus at work, rising to the top of his game, with multiple accommodations and countless convictions. He and Lisa purchased a small Cape Cod–style house in Byram Hills and had finally found a peaceful balance to life.

CHAPTER 10

JACK ROLLED UP HIS sleeve and stared at the intricate tattoo on his left forearm. It was truly like nothing he had ever seen before, not in print, not on canvas, and certainly not on skin. He looked at it closely, examining the dark ink, the tightly woven pattern, the odd lettering from a language he couldn't fathom. He wracked his brain but could find no recollection of getting it. It certainly wasn't something he would have chosen. The one on his hip was one thing, a drunken mistake. This was different, and while his memory of the last two days seemed to have slipped away, he knew that this mosaic on his flesh was somehow connected to Mia's disappearance.

"Like my body art?" Jack asked, trying keep a little humor in the car before Mia's situation overwhelmed them. He rolled down his sleeve.

"You know"—Frank suppressed a smile as he ate the bacon sandwich Jack's mom had made for him—"that's going to come up in this year's campaign."

"Front-page material," Jack said.

"Mia's not going to be happy." Frank spoke as if confident that finding her was already a given.

"Hell," Jack said, "she probably knows about it. Who's to say we haven't already fought about it?"

"Did it occur to you that maybe it was her idea? She may have had you branded, trying to make sure her prize cattle didn't get lost."

Jack reached around to his side and pulled out his Sig Sauer. He had fetched it from the oversized gun safe in his workshop before they left. He rarely touched it except to clean it, having left his particular talent with the weapon in his past.

"I haven't seen you holding that in forever," Frank said. "You remember how to use it?"

"Yeah," Jack said quietly. "Don't worry about me."

"Why don't you let me handle things involving weapons?" Frank smiled. "I have an aversion to being shot."

Jack ignored the joke. "We'll cross that bridge when we get there."

"You've got to learn to put that guilt away." Frank admonished his friend as if he were his son. "Everyone else has except you."

Jack didn't respond. The car fell silent as Frank turned his eyes on the highway ahead.

Jack Keeler was dead—the world thought it, the papers screamed it, and it was the lead story on every local news channel. In the matter of an hour, Jack's mind had gone from confusion to fear to relief and back to confusion. While the faint odor of Mia's perfume had sparked his memory of the night before, and the two bears had helped fill in his memory from the beginning of the week, nothing else came forth. He tried everything: he looked at pictures, looked at her clothes in her closet, read her various Post-it note reminders around the house in hopes of dredging up those lost days, but he found no key to unleash his recent past.

"You know, if someone sees you alive," Frank said, "it's going to create a lot of questions."

"Whoever has her thinks I'm dead. It's an advantage for the moment."

"Do you think this is connected to a case out of your office?"

"I'm sure the list of people who want me dead isn't small, but then, why ask Mia about the box?"

"And you didn't see the box before?"

He heard their demand; it still rang in his ears, box 7138. No matter how he tried, he could remember nothing about a box. When he saw it pulled from the rear of the Tahoe, he was more than sur-prised. Mia must have hidden it there underneath the tons of crap—soccer balls and tennis rackets, water bottles and blankets, shoppin bags and toys—that they had accumulated over the summer. An what it contained he had no idea.

"No. At least, I don't think—" Jack paused. Something gnawe at the periphery of his mind, just out of reach of clear thought, lil a two-day-old dream that was discarded as insignificant . . . althou he couldn't grasp it.

"Listen," Frank said, "you said you remember last night, you member the attack, going over the bridge, climbing out of the wa But how did you get home?"

Jack remained silent.

"Someone else was there," Frank said slowly.

Jack didn't respond.

"Stitched you up. Do you remember and are just not saying?

"No," Jack said.

"Jack?"

"Don't you think if I could remember, I would?"

"Someone helped you, kept you alive. Maybe if we could fi out how you got home—"

"How did I get home?" Jack asked rhetorically. "How the he I survive the fall off the bridge? Being shot? I'm not Rasputin. sewed me up, got me back to my house? Who wrote this crap o arm?" Jack pulled up his sleeve, revealing the dense black syn the unfamiliar language. "What the hell is going on?"

• • •

IT WAS ON a hot August day when Jack completed his tenure with Frank. And while Jack regretted parting ways, he was looking forward to shedding his apprentice label and getting more actively involved in homicide. There were six guys in the Manhattan Detective Bureau's Homicide Division, a breed apart from the other divisions. They were tenacious, hardened by what they had seen, and thankful for new blood with Jack's arrival. It was more akin to a club, with their own way of doing business, ensuring arrests, making sure the cases they built were seamlessly turned over to the DA's office for successful prosecution. No cop wanted a murderer back on the street as a result of his incompetence.

A tight group, they all had nicknames for one another: Double D for Dicky Donaldson; Shank, short for Hank the Shank, whose real name was Hank Ramón and who had a tee shot that went forever to the right; Sean Sullivan arrived at homicide with the name Red for obvious follicle reasons; Two used to be called Two Ton Tonelli but had lost so much weight that they shortened his name; for Apollo, there was debate about whether the name came from the Greek god, the solving of some murder near the Apollo Theater up in Harlem, or Rocky Balboa's toughest opponent and friend, Apollo Creed; and there was Deuce, not to be confused with Two, who loved playing poker, both literally and figuratively.

That evening, Jack was asked by Shank to follow up on a lead on a gang murder. When he got into the car, he found Apollo in the driver's seat, his thick, meaty hands wrapped around the wheel as he drove out of the garage.

"So, Jack, unless you came into homicide with a nickname like I did, we get to name you."

"So, the name Apollo has nothing to do with a murder at the Apollo Theater?

"You don't see the slight resemblance to Apollo Creed?"

Jack smiled.

"Irony of ironies, I was on a case near the Apollo Theater, but truth be told, my uncle was kind of a mythology buff and gave me the moniker when I was eleven."

"Why?"

"You want to hear the big story?

Jack nodded.

"There isn't one." Apollo laughed. "It's what my uncle called my father when they were kids."

Jack rolled his eyes.

"Laugh it up, Shooter."

"Shooter? You're kidding, right?"

"Well, we thought about Lily for Lily White, you being so pure, but that would be too cruel. Then Golden for Golden Boy, seeing you were the pride of the force who got fast-tracked onto our team. But Shooter won out, because we all had to admit it, you're a hell of a shot."

They drove over to Alphabet City, and Jack hopped out of the car while Apollo parked. Although Apollo had told Jack to wait, Jack was overanxious and figured nothing could go wrong in speaking with the grandmother of the victim. Apollo would only be two minutes behind him.

Jack met the grandmother in her apartment on the sixth floor of the 1920s walk-up and asked her a few routine questions about the grandson she had raised only to see him lose his life at the age of sixteen during a drug deal gone bad. Jack promised her that they would do everything to find his killer.

As Jack emerged from the tenement, he saw Apollo racing down the street, pursuing two thugs. Jack took up the chase, following the three as they sprinted across the city streets. They cut down through the subway, leaping turnstiles, across platforms, hopping up the far stairs, emerging onto the street and crashing into a vacant loft building. Apollo and the thugs seemed to have vanished as Jack entered just steps behind them.

The building was dark. Rats scurried in the shadows, and the stench of urine filled Jack's nostrils. Several homeless people lay on cardboard in their makeshift homes, casting their eyes downward, paying no attention to the pursuit in their midst.

Jack crept along, working his way up the stairs, four stories up, following the elusive sounds of racing footfalls.

There was a sudden shouting of "Police! Stop where you are! Drop your weapon!"

And then a gunshot. And another. And another.

Jack honed in on the cacophony of violence and burst through a door to see the two thugs with their guns aimed at Apollo, who was pinned behind a column in the wide-open space. A hail of bullets erupted, shredding the column, skipping along the floor around Apollo.

The world seemed to slow down. It was as if Jack could see every bullet explode from the barrels of the guns, as if life had fallen to half-time while his senses and reflexes doubled.

And for the briefest of seconds, Jack froze.

On the range, with paper targets popping up left and right, Jack was supreme, decisions made on instinct, his reaction time barely measurable. But this was real life, with real consequences; this wasn't for a medal, a trophy, or first place. This was for survival, both his and Apollo's.

Jack quickly recovered. His hand suddenly rocketed to his hip, quickly drawing his Sig Sauer. He raised his weapon and, without hesitation, fired two shots. The two assailants were thrust back as if a rope had wrapped around their bodies and yanked at them, a single bullet erupting out of the backs of their heads. They were both dead before they hit the floor.

Jack ran over to the two bodies and leaned down, confirming that they no longer posed a threat. He looked at the small bullet wounds in their foreheads, almost identical in placement, just like in target practice. And while the backs of their heads had been blown out, their faces were serene and unmarred but for the single bullet hole. And it hit Jack that the two young faces before him were not men, as he had assumed—they were teens, hardened children of the street, and he had killed them both. It was the first time he had killed, and he was overwhelmed by what he had done, a sudden nausea taking over his body.

He heard movement, a subtle moan. He raced to Apollo's side, where he lay sprawled on the bare concrete floor, a bullet wound to the chest.

"Took you long enough," Apollo said with a smile.

And the world seemed to fall into double-time, moving at hyperspeed now. The bullet had missed the bulletproof vest; like threading a needle, it had found the small gap beneath Apollo's armpit. Jack tore Apollo's shirt open, ripped the vest off, and quickly examined the wound. Blood pumped out of the hole on the left side of Apollo's chest in a rhythmic pulse, his life flowing out of him with every beat of his heart.

Knowing that he was in a war zone, Jack hoisted Apollo off the floor and threw him over his shoulder. He raced down the stairs, his partner on his back, and out the door.

After laying him down on the sidewalk, Jack grabbed the med kit from the back of his car, trying desperately to plug the wound while he waited for the ambulance to respond to the "officer down" call.

But despite his efforts, despite everything he could do, Apollo died. They were partners for all of one hour.

In the wake of the incident, a tragedy that hit the front page of every newspaper, Jack nearly succumbed to his grief. The guilt he carried over the deaths of his partner and the two teens was overwhelming. If he hadn't hesitated, if he had listened to Apollo about waiting for him, if he had held his emotions in check and instead followed procedure, Apollo would still be alive.

And although Jack was cleared of any wrongdoing, he knew that the death was his fault. The irony of his nickname in the wake of his failure was like a heavy chain around his body.

At such a young age, Jack found himself at a crossroads in life. He resolved to push ahead. He swore that he would never pick up a gun again in the line of duty, he would never take a life, he would find other ways of carrying out law enforcement.

He enrolled in Fordham Law, attending at night, dreaming of a way out of the life he had chosen. He remained on the police force, taking a desk job until he could finish law school, all with the under-standing and respect of his superiors and the men in homicide.

When Jack graduated, he was a natural for the DA's office. He was an attorney from the street who could bridge the gap between cops and lawyers. His conviction rate was high, and his reputation grew.

After ten years, he became the natural choice to succeed the retiring district attorney. Handsome, successful, with a beauti-ful wife in the FBI and two baby girls, he was packaged and sold by the powers-that-be and won his first election by a ten-percent margin. His first year in office saw a rise in investigations and con-victions, but his new reality set in after that. As a cop, things were black-and-white; either a crime was committed or it wasn't. But the DA didn't just handle crimes of the street. There was the more nuanced realm of white-collar crime, subjective areas where politi-cal favors were sought, where things beyond facts and reality came to bear.

In his second year, his office became involved in the unsuccess-ful pursuit of the real estate industry, while the third dealt with Wall Street—something that further distanced him from his father. In his fourth year, the final year of his term, the powers-that-be were look-ing for his successor, since they had no tolerance for backing a man who would seek to end their livelihoods. If Jack wanted to remain in office, he would have to play the game.

Jack loved his job. He loved carrying out justice, amassing con-victions. And as much as he didn't want to admit it, he had enjoyed the limelight, the prestige of the office.

What he had first thought of with disdain eventually lured him in. He had gone out glad-handing, soliciting money, wearing false smiles, and making promises that he knew couldn't be fulfilled. But it was all in sacrifice to his career, to the job, to getting reelected; the end justifyied the means.

And with his compromised values, Jack realized that he had become his father.

CHAPTER 11

CRISTOS AWOKE WITH THE sun, its warm summer rays spilling across the white sheets, urging him out of bed. For forty-five minutes, he put his body through the fluid motions of an ancient routine taught to him in his youth; it at once worked out the body, the mind, and the soul. The routine was not a martial arts kata or yoga, although its ancient rites found a foothold in both. The sweeping motions of his legs and arms, the delicate balance achieved on a single hand or foot, the inverted crunches and situps, the spiritual emptying of his mind, all combining to awaken his muscles, heart, and spirit, preparing them for the arduous day ahead.

Through years of discipline, pushing himself to the physical limit, Nowaji Cristos had built his body into an instrument of perfection—one of power, capable of not only immense strength but also subtle dexterity and coordination that afforded him the tools to perform his expertise.

Completing his routine, he arose from the floor and looked around the elegantly appointed room, his home for the last five days. The room was masculine, with heavy, dark wood furnishings: an armoire, a nightstand, and a matching dresser filled with recently purchased clothes. He stared at the luxury king-sized bed, his thoughts filling with memories. He had slept on all manner of surfaces, from the beds at the George V hotel in Paris to the jungle floors of Borneo. No matter where he closed his eyes, he could find a restful sleep, free of worry and anxiety, his body thriving on six hours of rest, the circadian rhythm of his mind like a precise clock. For forty-one years, through turmoil, death, and agony, he had never been troubled at night, but this week proved different. His dreams, usually few and far between, had become frequent nightmares, as if all of the dead had returned to exact their vengeance upon him.

With the look of a man fifteen years his junior, no one would have guessed his age. In spite of his large size and long black hair, he could lose himself in any environment, in any crowd, no matter where he was on earth. While he prided himself on his refined appearance and despite the notoriety he had gained the world over, his face was not known except to a handful of people. No photo or video existed of him—he was spoken of as myth, with descriptions ranging widely, from having been born on five different continents to possessing the appearance of varying ethnicities. Like a chameleon, he could adapt to any environment. The mix of clothing within the armoire would shape his appearance as everything from a day laborer to a homeless man of the street to an investment banker.

In the blue-tiled bathroom, he meticulously laid out his shaving kit—an old-fashioned single-blade razor, a soft camel-hair shaving brush, a heavy bar of Rhist soap—placing them on the washcloth on the counter. He filled the sink with scalding water, dipped the brush and the bar of soap in, and rubbed them together, building up a frothing lather. With the attention of an artist, he shaved his skin smooth, his dark eyes staring in the mirror as he examined his skin, ensuring that he hadn't missed a spot. His face was strong, hardlined, its tone just above a mild tan. Some may have called it the color of weak tea, a color found in many races of men: dark-skinned Caucasian, Mediterranean, Asian, South American.

He turned on the shower, allowing the steam to build, to fill the air with mist, fogging the mirror so he could avoid seeing his reflection as he removed his T-shirt.

While his face was pure, his body was marred. Jagged flesh, raised and ghostly white, had restrung itself along his left side, and his back was littered with crisscross striations, worn like a badge of honor for surviving torture during capture. Scars along the right side of his torso leaked down his body like melted wax, pouring down from the base of his neck, repulsing him at every glance while terrifying anyone who cast their eyes on it. The burns robbed his tan flesh of color, the grafted skin, grotesquely taut over his large muscles, stretching in odd folding shapes when his body flexed or grew taut. The pain of the countless surgeries had lasted for months, an agony forever etched in his mind.

Yet somehow, despite all of the brutality he had endured, his face had remained without blemish. It never exposed what lay beneath the designer suits he had grown fond of wearing, his damaged body concealed like the violence in his heart.

DRESSED IN A black Armani suit, starched white shirt, and pale blue silk tie, Cristos inspected himself in the mirror. He picked up two EpiPens off the counter and slipped them into his breast pocket. He exited the bedroom and entered the small office-like sitting room. His jet-black hair was pulled tight in a ponytail, his fingers were perfectly manicured, and a gold watch wrapped his left wrist. With the appearance of a refined Wall Street executive, he took a seat at a large partners' desk. He glanced at the long black box that sat on the table in the corner, at the number 7138 along the side, but quickly directed his attention to the array of monitors before him. He read the first; the bank accounts in Sri Lanka, Switzerland, and Prague reflected balances in excess of fifty million dollars each. Each account was under the ownership of an elaborate string of shell companies, each legitimate in its own right, with a diversity of holdings in real estate, textiles, and manufacturing.

The second and third monitors reflected his latest intel, dossiers, and photos pertaining to his various employees and contracts.

Cristos's computer system was secure, with an encryption system that would be the envy of any government. But there were certain secrets for which he reserved other methods.

Unlike much of society, governments, and institutions, he did not trust his most important information to a silicon chip. He was taught at an early age that if one was to keep secrets, there was no greater location, no place more impenetrable, than his own mind. Computers could be hacked, vaults could be cracked open, associates could be coerced with everything from bribery to chemicals. But as sharp as his mind was, as good as his memory was, there were some things that needed to be recorded. In his simple homeland, a forgotten world that shunned technology in favor of a more spiritual existence, methods existed whose simplicity had been forgotten by modern society.

Cristos rose from his desk and stepped to the table where the rectangular box lay. He removed a small billfold from the breast pocket of his suit jacket, opened it, and withdrew two thin strips of metal, one L-shaped, the other with a multiwaved tip. He kneeled before the box and slipped the two sticklike objects into the lock on the near end, and with a surgeon's careful hand, he picked the lock. After placing his tools back in their pouch and slipping it back into his pocket, he stood up, lifted the lid, and peered inside.

He stared for a moment and finally reached into the case, withdrawing a single envelope. He tore it open and removed a handwritten note. He read it through twice, before putting it back in the envelope and into his pocket.

He picked up his cell phone—satellite technology, multiple relays, and encryption software made it virtually untraceable for up to three minutes, which was twice as long as any conversation he ever needed to have—and quickly dialed.

"Hello," a voice answered.

"Good morning," Cristos said in a deep Eurasian accent.

"Well?" the person on the other end of the phone asked. "Do you have the case?"

"I do." Cristos turned his head and stared at the long black box. "But it seems your intelligence—a word so inappropriate—was wrong."

"What do you mean?"

"The case was empty."

"Empty?"

"I never had much faith in you, anyway."

"You listen to me, I could end your life with—"

Cristos tuned out the angry voice. It always made him laugh when his employers would threaten him with death when it was that precise expertise he was hired for. The egos of the rich and powerful blinded them to reality, which always made them so surprised when they found the tables turned, when they didn't get their way, when death turned its eye on them.

"Good-bye." With the man still screaming on the other end, Cristos folded up his cell phone.

He walked to the door and opened it, nodding his head.

Three men entered.

"Where's Tobin?"

"Dead," the blond man said. "Jumped off a bridge, hit a by a tractor-trailer."

"I take it, then, we have no files on Keeler, no toys from the girls' room?"

The blond man shook his head no.

Cristos nodded, thinking before continuing. "The intel we received on the box in the rear of the Keelers' car was faulty. It could be a decoy or just plain wrong."

The three stood there

"Which one of you shot Jack Keeler?"

"I did," the blond man said quietly.

"Your name?"

"Gallagher."

Cristos nodded, his dark eyes staring off into space, although truth be told, they were looking inward. "You knew what was to be in the case, correct?"

Gallagher gave a subtle nod, like a child in school.

Cristos lifted the lid of the box, displaying its inside to Gallagher. "So you killed him without verifying its contents."

And with a sudden whip of his arm, Cristos's hand snapped out, wrapping around Gallagher's neck, pulling him close, staring into his eyes as he slowly began to squeeze. Gallagher's face grew crimson, the veins at his temples growing with each pulse, throbbing with agony.

Gallagher grabbed Cristos's hands around his throat, trying in vain to pull them away. He desperately swung his fists, flailing his arms like a child in his first fight, attacking his assailant with clenched hands, but Cristos's powerful left arm extended, his grip continuing to tighten as he blocked every blow with his right arm. And with a swipe of his leg, Cristos knocked Gallagher's feet from beneath him, leaving him dangling.

Gallagher's face was impossibly red, his eyes bulging in stress and fear, for he knew there was no escape.

The other two stared in shock as the life was literally squeezed out of their associate, but neither made a move, as a single step would be like raising a hand to die next.

Gallagher's body began to twitch and vibrate as if each muscle was doing its part to escape. Robbed of his last breath, as if at the bottom of the sea, his eyes began to lose focus, his body stiffened . . . and he was finally released, crumpling to the ground gasping, his hands rubbing his throat.

"I wanted you to taste death, something you rendered so quickly to Jack Keeler before accomplishing your task." Cristos looked at the three men before him. "I want you to know fear. I want you to know that no one was allowed to kill him except me."

Cristos methodically closed the box. It was a moment. The only sound was Gallagher's labored breathing as he climbed to his feet.

"You have six hours to find me that box."

And the three left.

Cristos reached into his pocket and withdrew the envelope. He stared at it a moment, knowing the words written within. He didn't know how its author possessed the forethought to write it; only a select few knew he was in the country. While the expression on his face was placid, calm, it was entirely contrary to his emotions.

For the letter in the box he had stolen was addressed to him.

CHAPTER 12

FRANK HUSTLED DOWN THE long embankment that led to the river's edge. The churning waters were still near flood stage after the previous night's rains, inhibiting the recovery effort that was already well under way. He had parked his Jeep a quarter-mile up the road behind a string of emergency vehicles, flashing his old police badge to gain access to the site. Frank looked up at the crowd that stood on Rider's Bridge in silent, rapt attention. They were not the usual rubberneckers, the morbid curious hoping to see a body. They were a mix of law enforcement, friends of Jack and Mia from the FBI, the DA's office, and both local and city police. Even from his fifty-yard distance, he could see the grief in their faces, in their body language.

And as Frank continued to look, he felt an uneasy shame, a horrible feeling of deception for allowing so many to think the couple dead. He knew the pain he had felt at hearing of his friends' deaths and knew it was a communal feeling shared by all of their colleagues. Although he wanted to shout out about Jack's survival, he knew it would only further endanger Mia, wherever she might be.

Frank turned his attention to the enormous crane that sat mid-span, its cable line disappearing into the churning river below, where a small pocket of bubbles turned into a froth. An enormous man, six-four, at least 220 pounds, emerged from the water, climbing up the bank. He removed the regulator from his mouth and pushed his dive mask up onto his head.

The two men nodded to each other.

"I hate this," the man said in a deep voice, pushing his wet blond hair from his face.

"I know. Anytime a rescue turns into a recovery, it's heartbreaking to all." Frank avoided the man's eyes, hoping his deception would not be evident in his face. "Look," Frank said slowly, pausing as he formed his words. "I need a favor, and I need your discretion."

Frank had known Matt Daly for twenty years. He was local, part of the fabric of the community. He had retired from the Byram Hills police force at the ripe old age of thirty-nine and owned a local bar called GG's North. He still responded as part of the dive team whenever the need arose.

"Discretion . . ." Matt nodded. "There's a word with implications."

"The people in this river are family."

"I think it's safe to say they're everyone's family." Daly looked up at the horde of people on the bridge.

"I know, everyone feels that way, but to me and my wife, they really are family. Do you know how long it will be before you recover the bodies?" Frank asked, knowing that the recovery effort would never yield a soul.

Daly inhaled. "I've got six guys working the river. The current's rough, the bottom's rocky. They could be anywhere between here and a half-mile downriver in the spillway. There's no way to know."

"If you had to make a guess . . ."

Daly knew something was up but didn't ask. "It could take an hour, it could be twenty-four. There's no way of knowing. It's one of those things I wish I could get over with but dread the final goal. Do you want to tell me where you're going with this?"

"I need you to call me when you find their bodies. Jack's parents found out by seeing the morning paper. I don't want them seeing it as another breaking news story. They deserve a modicum of respect."

Daly nodded. "You still have the same cell number?"

"You think maybe you could keep me updated on your progress?"

"Of course," Daly said as he looked at Frank. "We both know there's far more to this than a car accident and what you're telling me."

Frank inhaled, his face speaking the truth that his words couldn't say.

"Good luck, then," Daly said in all sincerity.

Daly turned to see his team of divers climbing out of the water. He slowly counted heads twice before looking up at a man in a hard hat who stood by the crane. Daly gave him a thumbs-up, and within seconds the low rumble of its engine grew. The winch engaged and slowly began to spool up. All eyes were glued to the heavy wire, watching in anticipation, fearful of what they would see but unable to avert their eyes. And then the water started to churn, and in near slow motion, the trunk section of the white Tahoe emerged from the water, rising like a rebirth. As more of the vehicle emerged, the extreme damage began to sink in. The right side of the SUV was crushed in as if someone had taken a giant sledge hammer to the door panels. The driver's side was demolished. The car continued to rise out of the water until the last bit of its front end was revealed and it began its fifty-foot climb into the sky. Frank could almost hear the gasps as the front accordioned section was seen; the windshield was missing, as was the driver's-side door. Water cascaded out of the doors, out of the crumbled front end, like a waterfall, as the car ascended toward the bridge.

As Frank headed back up the embankment, he knew they would never find a body; he knew they would be working through the day and well into the night before they concluded what he already knew. Jack's and Mia's bodies weren't in the water.

• • •

JACK SAT IN the passenger seat of Frank's Jeep. With the car sitting far back from the activity and with Frank's license plate still possessing the police tag IDs, no one paid the vehicle any mind. Jack had tucked his black hair under a dark blue Yankees cap. He chose to avoid sunglasses, the preferred "disguise" for those who wanted to remain anonymous, but as he knew, the effect was the antithesis; it called attention to the individual, made him appear either suspicious or famous or, at the very least, someone who deserved a second glance.

Jack's confusion was even greater since he'd left his parents' home. He wasn't sure what disturbed him more, seeing his tearful mother or his father sitting watch over his daughters. He had remained silent for fifteen minutes after rushing from the house. Jack almost mentioned seeing his father, as Frank knew their relationship, the harsh words his father always threw his way, the distance between them. But he thought better of it. He'd deal with his father later.

Despite the fact that his kids were at his parents' house, despite the fact that his father was watching over them, he had Frank call his friend Ben. The ex-military man who didn't suffer fools had taken up position at the beginning of the single access road that led to his parents' house. His car parked on the side, he would remain there until Frank gave him the all clear, ensuring that no one got near Jack's girls.

A surreal feeling filled Jack as he watched the distant crowd standing in collective grief for his and Mia's purported deaths. He had never imagined his own wake or funeral, who would attend, what people would say with his passing. He was never one of those who fantasized about being eulogized, having his friends or some priest stand at the pulpit extolling his virtues, his accomplishments and example in life. He always wondered why people never expressed their true feelings for one another while they were alive, instead of waiting to say the kindest things when they were no longer able to hear it, when they had left this earth for their final reward.

Truth be told, Jack's faith had wavered; he no longer clung to the notion of an afterlife. His life and career, all of the death and cruelty he had seen, made him question the existence of God. On the other hand, while she was not outwardly spiritual, Mia's unspoken convictions had been strong since she was a child. She knew of Jack's diminished beliefs, which is why she bought him the crucifix that had hung around his neck for the last twelve hours in the hopes that it would bring him protection, instill him with faith, ensure God's beneficence upon him. As he thumbed the talisman around his neck, he refused to attribute to it the fact that he had survived being shot and nearly drowned, but if it had somehow played a role, then he hoped the blue necklace he had given her was equally, if not more, imbued with spiritual protection.

In this moment, Jack swore he would believe in anything if it would save Mia. He'd believe in the power of the cross, he'd believe in God, in the afterlife, in Elvis . . . whatever would ensure her survival.

The thrumping engine of the crane pulled Jack's attention back to the recovery effort. He watched his white Tahoe rise over the bridge guardrail, the crane slowly swinging about, the SUV dangling, swaying back and forth as the construction vehicle guided the wrecked truck over the flatbed that lay in wait. He could hear the metal twisting, screaming in protest, as it was lowered onto the tow truck. The crumpled front end was a reminder of how lucky he truly was. He didn't just survive the bullet wound, he survived a vertical car crash, he survived drowning, being trapped within an SUV coffin. While he had recaptured most of the memories of the night before, he had no recollection of what had happened after hitting the surface of the water. His mind was truly blank.

He watched as the crowd followed the Tahoe's journey, watched as it was secured to the truck. There were no murmurs, no gasps, the only sound being the grinding of the crane's gears and the gentle sobs of the people who had individually and collectively concluded that Jack and Mia Keeler were dead.

And as he continued to watch, he could see their individual faces. Joe Gasparri, the newest member of the DA's office; Margo Libreros, his tough-as-nails lead prosecutor; Stanley Boil, the rumpled veteran who refused to retire. There were cops, local officials, and people in mourning he didn't even know.

But the sight that struck him the hardest, the one person he felt ashamed for deceiving, stood there alone, off to the side, silently weeping, tears running down her face. She made no effort to wipe them away, allowing them to pour down as if they would somehow wash away her agony.

Joy had been his assistant for twelve years and had come upstairs with him to his current position as DA. She was everything that made him successful; she kept him timely, organized; she knew his faults and weaknesses and always countered them, never allowing the outside world to know of her boss's shortcomings. She was like the sister who always kept him in line, kept his ego in check if it ever got out of control after winning some big case or being featured in the newspaper.

And as he looked at her, at her forever-young face, at the black purse he had given her for her birthday slung over her shoulder, his head began to pound, his heart suddenly racing as his emotions built up inside him. Last night's rage and anger and fury filled him once again.

His mind began to open. He felt the memories coalesce. Joy's pain, her suffering and tears, and, in an odd way, the purse on her shoulder sparked it all. It was as if his brain was suddenly on overload. Thoughts, feelings, images, and memories from two days earlier poured forth as if it had been minutes ago, as if it was always there, in the forefront of his mind.

Jack remembered.

CHAPTER 13

IT WAS WEDNESDAY, 11:00 in the morning. Jack was staring at Joy, her eyes blue and clear, unmarred by tears and sorrow. Her wry smile flashed the usual I-told-you-so as she handed him a file.

"I told you to take the Richmond case file with you last night."

"I went straight to the conference room this morning."

"Mia leave you on empty again?" Joy laughed.

"You could have brought the file upstairs to the conference room."

"You could leave ten minutes earlier in the morning."

Jack handed her back the file. "A lot of good it's going to do me now."

Without missing a beat she took the file and handed him the newspaper and a new file. He raised his eyebrow in question.

"You need to read up on the polling numbers," Joy said. "And the *Times* didn't paint a very flattering picture of your first term in office."

Jack opened the file and glanced at his morning campaign brief. Although it was only June, the political prognosticators and the soothsaying polls had already projected his defeat in November. His opponent had raised more than double what his coffers held, most from the power brokers who had funded him four years ago. While many thought elections were up to the voters, they were really won with dollars and a theme.

While Jack had achieved much in three and a half years, there was no compelling theme to hang his hat on. Everyone needed buzz, every politician needed a defining moment that could be boiled down to a catch phrase that thirty million dollars could disseminate into the hearts and minds of the thirty-two percent of the public that pulled the lever on election day.

With his thoughts on more significant matters, Jack snapped the file closed and headed into his office.

The high-ceilinged space was the largest on the floor, as was fitting for the man who oversaw the prosecution of the New York City's crimes. The wood-grain walls matched the forty-year-old chipped and scarred desk that sat before the large picture window. New York Harbor's panorama was brightly lit under the summer sun, the vast waterway dotted with freighters and barges heading in and out of the local ports. A handful of sailboats piloted by those lucky enough to have the day off cruised the waterway, their sails filled with summer breeze.

Jack removed his jacket and draped it over his chair, loosened his muted blue-striped tie, and stared out at the view, regrouping after his early-morning trial conference, knowing he had a long day ahead. He finally looked at the *New York Times* and skimmed the article about his successes and failures in his first term, along with the odds against reelection. And as he turned, he nearly jumped out of his skin.

Sitting on the couch was the last person he ever expected. She had only been to his office once in all the years, and that was when she needed his signature on the legal papers to refinance their mortgage.

"I didn't mean to startle you," Mia said. She was sitting on the old, cracked leather couch, dressed in a long black pencil skirt and white shirt, far more fashionable than any FBI agent he had ever known. On the couch next to her was a long black metal box.

"Friggin' Joy," Jack said with a half-laugh. "She could have mentioned you were in here."

Mia smiled. "I told her I wanted to scare you."

"Well, you succeeded." He laughed.

He walked over, leaned down, and kissed her gently; it was a rare day when they saw each other in the morning, their divergent schedules pulling them in different directions. He hoped their lives would once again fall into sync but knew that was years off with both of their careers in high gear. "By the way, thanks for leaving me on empty."

"Sorry . . ." Mia smiled that get-out-of-jail-free smile, the one that always released her from Jack's anger. She had him so wrapped up in her heart that she could remove his limbs and he'd still forgive her with a thank you and a returned smile.

"Not a very nice article," Mia said as she pointed at the newspaper in Jack's hand.

"Don't believe everything you read in the papers," he said as he tossed the paper into the garbage. But then his eyes filled with sudden concern at her unaccustomed presence. "Are you all right?"

Mia nodded as she stood from the couch. "Yeah."

But Jack could see that she wasn't, his eyes falling on the case on his couch.

Mia walked to the window, looking out at the harbor. "You know, we never did properly christen this office."

Jack looked at her with raised eyebrows, glancing out through the open door at Joy, who was busily typing, hoping she didn't hear Mia's suggestive comment. He quickly closed the door.

"Hmm. You like that idea." Mia turned around and sat on the windowsill, her long legs exposed even more, a glint of mirth in her eyes. "I didn't expect that."

"Mia," Jack said with a smile, "as much as I would like to mark the occasion four years after the fact, as much as I would like to see the rest of those legs, I know you didn't come here for that."

"I need a big favor."

"You don't need to preface it."

"I need you to put this evidence case in the Tombs." Mia pointed to the box on the couch.

"The FBI evidence room isn't good enough?"

Mia didn't answer.

Jack looked at her, his concern growing. "Do you want to tell me what's going on?"

Mia shook her head.

Jack walked to the couch and picked up the case. It was a standard one-foot-by-three-foot evidence case, akin to a bank lock box. It was hinged along the short side, a single cylinder lock on the near end. The top was stamped *FBI 7138*.

"Do you want to tell me about it?"

"It's best you don't know."

The moment hung in the air, a host of unasked questions floating around the room. They both had secrets, things in their jobs that they didn't share: cases, investigations, rumors. It was the nature of their jobs. Jack and Mia had always been open and honest, even speaking those truths that are sometimes hard to hear. It was the foundation of their love. But in their careers, while often sharing war stories, tales of success and failure, advising each other as spouses so often do, there were aspects that they couldn't talk about.

"Mia, I've never questioned you, never told you what to do with your job." Jack stared at her. "But if you can't trust your own people . . ."

"I don't tell you how to do your job, Jack." There was a hint of stress in Mia's voice. "Can't you just help me without a lecture?"

Jack took a long breath and relaxed. "I'll have Joy bring it down—"

Mia shook her head. "I don't want anyone else to know."

"OK." Jack nodded. "I'll bring it down myself after lunch."

Mia continued to stare at him, the same look she gave him when he said he'd take the garbage out, the look that said it couldn't be done on Jack time, it had to be Mia time. It had to be done now, preferably five minutes ago.

Jack walked out of his office and thirty seconds later returned with a case nearly identical to Mia's but without the FBI sticker. "You're going to need to swap the contents of your box into one of mine."

Mia nodded. "Now?"

"You can do it on the ride over. We'll take the Tahoe."

Jack grabbed his suit jacket from the back of his chair, put it on, and straightened his tie. He picked up both metal boxes and walked out of his office, Mia two steps behind.

"Joy," Jack said to his assistant, "Mia and I are going to run and get a quick bite to eat."

"Well, that's a first," Joy said. "You guys have worked ten blocks apart for all these years, and in all that time, it was like you worked in different states."

Joy stared at the two large boxes under Jack's arm, then looked into her boss's eyes. They both knew that lunch was not really on the agenda.

THE MANHATTAN DETENTION Complex was located at 125 White Street and had a level of security that rivaled the New York Federal Reserve, where one of the world's largest gold stores resided only a half-mile away. But the contents of the Tombs were far from precious metal. The primary function was as a jail for holding criminals with pending cases in the adjacent courts, although it also functioned as a maximum-security prison for several of the country's most notorious criminals, from terrorists to serial killers. It was rarely spoken of, as both liberal and conservative voices would seek to have the facility shuttered for humanitarian or not-in-my-backyard reasons. The facility was actually two adjacent structures that rose eighteen stories into the Lower Manhattan skyline and extended down eight additional floors into the island's granite substrate. Configured with multiple checkpoints, electronic security, video, and nearly impenetrable walls, the Tombs was considered one of the most secure locations in the country. Without incident, it was a place of no hope for the incarcerated, as no one escaped the Tombs, ever. It was a place fittingly called a mausoleum for the living.

Of little note, unless one was familiar with the workings of the judicial system, was the function of sublevel five. With its central location to the courts, it had become the natural repository for the district attorney's evidence room. Five stories belowground, it was like a modern dungeon, secreted in the earth, carved out of Manhattan Island's bedrock.

Jack and Mia walked through the cavernous granite and marble lobby, a single black evidence case under Jack's arm.

Desk guard Larry Knoll's eyes lit up upon seeing him. "Mr. Keeler."

"Hey, Larry," Jack said warmly. He tapped the black evidence case. "I've got to see Charlie. Is he down there?"

"Is he ever not down there?"

"Good point. How is your wife?"

"Great, thank you. Daria's getting fat with our first."

"Congratulations." Jack laughed. "Never heard it put that way. There is nothing better than kids. Keep me posted."

"Thank you, sir."

Larry hit a button, and Jack and Mia walked through the security gate and headed to the elevator, the doors open awaiting their arrival.

"Fat with her first?" Mia repeated with a laugh. "Do you know every cop in the city personally?"

Jack smiled. "Hardly. If I could, I would, though."

Mia rubbed Jack's back. "Once a cop, always a cop."

Jack and Mia rode the car down and arrived in a small vestibule. There was a couch and two small chairs, their soft design in sharp contrast to the iron door and adjacent Plexiglas window on the far wall, its three-inch bullet-proof design distorting Charlie Brooks's round face like a carnival mirror. The small window revealed the head and shoulder of the sixty-year-old man who had been the facility's gatekeeper for twenty-two years.

"Whoa," Charlie said with a smile, his voice tinny and hollow through the small speaker. He glanced down with an arched brow at his lap. "If I knew the big cheese was coming down, I would have worn pants."

Jack smiled as he pulled Mia toward the glass into Charlie's view. "Charlie, I'd like you to meet my wife, Mia."

"I beg your pardon." All sense of mirth fell out of the old guard's face as he looked at her with contrite eyes. He quickly stood up in a chivalrous greeting while making a point to show his clothed legs. "I always wear pants to work."

The door lock fell back with a thud as a loud buzzer echoed through the halls.

Jack pulled open the heavy metal door and ushered Mia into a small hall, the door crashing closed behind him sealing them in the confined space. The small room was adorned with a metal desk; in the corner was an ancient cathode-ray TV atop a VHS player, its cable line draped along the ceiling, disappearing into a conduit. And while the room and its accoutrements were of a prior century's vintage, the computer setup on the desk appeared to come from the future, off of some starship: three flat-screen monitors, images of an elaborate file system on one, a security monitoring configuration on another, and the third displaying a picture of Jack with his fingerprints and statistics below. It all sat before Charlie, who was far larger than Mia expected. At six-two, the older man, in his crisp NYPD blues, looked as if he didn't need the protection of all the security or the 9mm pistol on his belt to fend off any intruder.

Jack laid the metal box on the table against the wall.

"How can I help you, Mr. Keeler?" Charlie's voice had taken on a forced formality.

"It's a lock box, highly sensitive case."

Charlie looked between the two of them as he began to type it into his computer. The evidence-tracking program came up.

"You need to do me a favor," Jack said as he laid his hand on Charlie's shoulder. "Don't log it into the system."

Charlie slowly turned and looked at Jack, his tone saying far more than the question he uttered. "How are we going to track it?"

Jack stared back, his eyes speaking volumes.

"Suppose something happens to you or me," Charlie said slowly. "How's anyone going to know where to look?"

"We'll just have to make sure nothing happens to you or me."

Charlie paused a moment, his mind working. "This isn't some elaborate way to hide Christmas presents or anything, is it?"

Mia smiled. "If the three of us tuck it away, there shouldn't be any problem."

Charlie shifted uncomfortably in his chair. "You know I can't let her beyond the gate—"

"She's FBI," Jack said.

Mia reached into her purse and flashed her credentials.

"You know that carries no weight." He nodded to Mia. "No offense."

Jack looked at Charlie, the moment dragging on.

Charlie flipped off his computer, reached into his desk, and withdrew a large white sticker with a long bar code on it. He slapped it on the metal case. "I guess being married to you carries some weight."

Charlie buzzed the door behind them, and the three headed through.

The evidence room was enormous, nearly the size of the building's footprint. The raw space of concrete floors and walls was filled with thousands of shelves, twelve feet high, their layout creating dozens upon dozens of rows and aisles that formed passages and walkways that ran on for hundreds of feet. The space was lit by harsh, bright fluorescent lights, although the shelves conspired to cast heavy shadows that ran off in every direction.

Boxes of all sizes filled the shelves, their contents varying from dime bags of marijuana to photographs of domestic-violence cases; expensive jewels from the latest store robbery to the two knives taken from the suspect in the slaying of an off-duty cop. Trials were won and lost on the evidence held within this facility.

Jack, Mia, and Charlie walked down the central aisle from which forty rows branched off toward the secondary aisles. One could truly get lost in the labyrinthine space, feeling like Theseus without a thread.

"You forget the scope of the justice system," Mia said. "And you handle all this yourself?"

"One man per shift," Charlie said. "It's really slow most of the time. I'm kind of like the librarian, checking things in and out."

"Do you ever get lonely?"

"Nah, kind of peaceful. Besides, there's usually a decent flow of people throughout the day to tell me what's going on in the world."

"What do you do if you get hungry?"

"I bring a bag lunch or dinner, but . . ."

Charlie smiled and tilted his head for them to follow him as he turned down row S. He reached up and pulled down a large cardboard box labeled *Evidence 9530273*. He lifted the lid to reveal a bag of Oreos, a six of beer, two bottles of water, some chips, magazines, and VHS tapes of *The Quiet Man, The Poseidon Adventure, True Grit,* and *Chitty Chitty Bang Bang.*

"I'm prepared for any scenario," he said in a mock-serious tone.

Jack and Mia laughed, appreciating the humor intended to break Mia's serious mood.

Charlie put the box away and led them back out to the center aisle. He finally turned and pointed to a vacant section of shelf on row Y. They all looked up.

"Stick it up there in the white-collar-crime section away from all the drugs, jewels, and guns. No one will have any interest in it over here." Charlie turned and headed back toward his office.

Jack turned to Mia and looked into her eyes. "You're not going to tell me what's in the case, are you?"

Mia slowly shook her head.

Jack looked at her as he slid the box onto the deep shelf seven feet up. "You're sure about this?"

Mia looked up into his eyes. She couldn't hide her worry. There was an intensity in her face, a focus like Jack had rarely seen. Mia was excellent at hiding her emotions, her thoughts, never betraying her inner feelings to the outside world. But Jack wasn't the outside world. He could read her as if she were an open book.

"I've never been more sure about anything," Mia softly said.

And finally, Jack realized that what he saw in his wife's eyes wasn't worry or concern about her latest case. It was a far more base emotion.

It was fear.

CHAPTER 14

MIA'S EYES OPENED WITH a start, her heart already pounding in her ears as she awoke from a nightmare into something far worse. She looked around the barren, windowless room, and except for the bed she lay on and the tray of food on the floor, there was nothing to offer any indication of where she was. The heavy brass knobs were polished to a high sheen, while the key mechanism for a dead bolt looked average and recently installed. There was a single lamp in the corner, its forty-watt bulb casting heavy shadows in the small, confined space. The room was not more than ten foot square, and she couldn't imagine its function beyond a jail cell.

She rose from the bed, her shoulder sore, her head throbbing, and reached for the brass doorknob, although she knew what she would find as she turned and tugged on the thick, heavy door. She laid her ear against the white oak and gently shook the door, listening to its hollow reverberation on the other side. There was no reaction, no approaching footsteps, just the soft echo of the knob turning to and fro and, in the distance, the faint sounds of the city.

Mia turned and looked at the tray of food on the floor. There was a sealed bottle of water. A loaf of bread, cheese, fruit, and a wedge of sausage, like a welcoming tray from some fine hotel. And although she felt hungry—starving, actually—the hollow pit in her stomach, the mix of fear and anger, was too overwhelming to allow her even to think of eating.

Mia had always been able to master her emotions, contain her fear, her pain, her disappointment. Her stepfather had instilled in her that the display of emotions was for the weak, the unintelligent, a sign of our animal heritage. The display of emotions—be it by man or woman—would only serve to fog the mind and impede one from clear thought.

Whether is was the disappointment she felt at being cut from the swim team in eleventh grade after dedicating so many years to the sport or being thrown from her horse at the age of fifteen, her father admonished her tears, scolded her for not burying the pain deep down, never to be spoken of again. She had learned it so well that she was thought of by many as cold and distant. But her face to the world was so contrary to the swirl of emotions she felt within, emotions she didn't display until she met Jack and he cracked the hard shell she had developed over the years. But those lessons her stepfather forced upon her, while not suitable for a child, had come in handy in her line of work. She was unreadable when she chose to be, masking her feelings with an expertise only seen through by her husband.

But as she thought of Jack, it all came pouring forth in her mind: the rainy bridge, the white Tahoe, the gunshot, her husband's eyes as he looked pleadingly at her as the car tumbled over into the churning river below.

Despite all of her mastery of her emotions, despite the desperate need to find a means of escape, Mia wrapped herself in her grief.

For the second time, the most important man in Mia's life had been murdered, violently taken from her as she was forced to bear witness.

And as all strength left her, she collapsed to the floor, her body wracked with sobs.

CHAPTER 15

THE CALL CAME AT 6:30 that morning. Cursing under her breath at whoever had the nerve to rattle her so early on a Friday, Joy Todd rolled over and grabbed the phone to hear her sister utter her name in a fateful tone. Joy sat up and swept her long blond hair out of her face as if it would help her to focus. She climbed out of bed, stretching the kinks out of her back when her sister began to sob.

"Sheila . . ." Joy said. "What's wrong?"

Sheila read the headline from the morning paper.

Joy's anger was immediately vanquished by grief, and she collapsed to the floor, unable to move.

She finally struggled to stand, wiping the tears from her blue eyes, and she knew where she had to go. It was an odd instinct, something that affected everyone when dealing with the tragic death of a loved one. It happened in plane crashes, motorcycle accidents, and shootings. Some kind of mystical tug on the heart and mind drew the grieving to the place of the incident, where they could try to touch the souls of their loved ones as if they lingered waiting to say good-bye. Makeshift memorials were constructed of flowers, candles, handwritten notes, some in pen, some in pencil, many in crayon bidding farewell, expressing their love and anguish to the ones they never got a chance to say good-bye to.

Joy emerged from her apartment on the Upper West Side of Manhattan. Two subways, one train, and a cab ride later, she found herself in Byram Hills, standing with the crowd on the bridge. She was not surprised at how many had followed the same instinct to gather and mourn Jack and Mia. They were the type who always listened, who helped others through their troubles and tragedies, yet never spoke of their own difficulties. It contributed to the fondness people held for them, to the genuine love their friends expressed over the years.

Joy knew Jack as well as, if not better than, anyone. In all the years they had worked together, she had seen him at his best and worst, yet he never buckled, never broke, no matter how hard the pressure. When her parents died and she didn't have money for the funeral, it was Jack who stepped in and paid. And while the gesture would warm anyone's heart, Joy knew that it was paid for from what little savings Jack and Mia had. She was there for the births of their daughters, helped them move into their house; she was the only one from their office who attended their holiday parties.

As she watched the Tahoe being lowered onto the bridge, tears rolling down her face, she barely felt the vibration of her phone in her jeans pocket. She pulled it out and flipped it open without seeing who called—she couldn't care less—and absentmindedly laid it on her ear.

And her heart nearly exploded for the second time that morning as she heard his voice. There was no doubt, no thought of some kind of trick; she knew who it was before the first uttered word was completed.

"Joy," Jack said, "please don't let anyone see you react to this call."

"Oh, my God," she said in a sobbing whisper.

"I need your help."

• • •

JOY SAT IN the backseat of Frank's Jeep, hugging Jack, holding on to him as if he was about to slip away from this earth again.

"What the hell?" She was genuinely pissed. "It's eleven a.m. and you couldn't have picked up the phone any earlier?"

"Sorry," Jack said with an apologetic smile as Frank shot him a glance.

"I'm serious." Joy leaned back and glared at him. "I thought you were dead. Do you have any idea how that feels?"

"I said I'm sorry."

"You're lucky I don't kill you now. Don't ever do that again." Joy's emotions flew all over the place, finally settling down into relief as she took a deep breath and leaned back in the seat. "How's Mia?"

Jack's look quickened her breath. He told her what had happened, about going over the bridge, his wounds and the tattoo, Mia's disappearance and his confidence in her still being alive, and the evidence case. After riding the emotional roller coaster again, Joy calmed herself and regained the focus she was known for.

"Do you understand that I need you?" Jack asked.

"You've always needed me," she said with a smirk, falling into their yin-and-yang work mode. "Which you can show your appreciation for by getting me a nice big present for my birthday next week."

"Don't I always?"

Joy smiled, then got serious. "Let me see that tat?"

"The what?" Frank asked from the driver's seat.

Jack rolled his eyes and rolled up his sleeve.

Joy smiled as she examined the tattoo.

"What's so funny?" Jack asked.

"That's not a tattoo, it's henna," Joy said as she ran her hand over the dark ink. "You're lucky. It's like the mehndi art that Asian woman get on their hands before they get married." Joy couldn't suppress a laugh.

"Joy . . ." Jack urged her on.

"In a few weeks, you'll never even know it was there."

"Great. Long sleeves in summer."

"It's better than long sleeves the rest of your life."

She took hold of his arm, looking at him for approval. Without a thought, he nodded and she began turning his arm, examining it closely.

"This is intricate writing; it's beautiful in a scary kind of way. A few of my goth friends would love this. Looks like some kind of a mix of Asian and Sanskrit."

"Well, how do we get it translated fast?"

"Not going to be easy on the Friday of the long Fourth of July weekend."

"Check with the universities, Columbia, NYU, Yale. I really don't care what you have to do, Joy." Jack's voice grew stern as he handed her his BlackBerry with the scan of his arm.

Joy shrugged it off. She understood the fear running through Jack, the fear he felt for his wife. She had always tended to combat stress with humor, some of it dark; it helped keep her mind from slipping into a black hole of pain that she knew would be hard to extract herself from.

She began working the phones, calling in favors, reaching out to academia, to the professionals they so often called on to render expert testimony. She had always been resourceful, street-smart; it was what allowed her to thrive in school, in work. She was tenacious beyond compare and could pull a rabbit out of a hat if the occasion called for it.

And right now, the occasion called for it more than ever.

"Did you ever give her that necklace?" Joy asked without looking up from the BlackBerry.

"Yeah," Jack said. "Last night, actually."

Joy nodded. "That's a good thing, then. Timing's everything."

"What do you mean?" Frank asked.

"Jack gave a speech at a UN Peace Council dinner a couple of weeks ago. It went over very well, mainly because I helped him write it. As a token of appreciation, they sent him a beautiful necklace. Their new representative, Manirak Coulhuse—"

"Marijha Toulouse," he corrected her.

"Right. His council was quite enamored with Jack."

"It was just a speech, and it's just a necklace," Jack said, his tone ending the conversation.

The blue necklace had arrived Monday in an elegant box with a personal letter.

Jack was at once hesitant; he had a deep-rooted fear of compromise. *Beware of strangers bearing gifts* rang in his ears the moment he became an assistant DA.

Jack had shared the handwritten note with Joy, having her confirm that the simple gift was truly an altruistic gesture with no implications that could compromise him politically, ethically, or morally. They had discussed returning it, but Joy had pointed out that it was an honorable gesture, and if Jack refused to accept it, it would be seen as an insult and an affront. So they created a paper trail, a detailed file documenting the gift, Jack's speech, Joy's research, and the Peace Council. And just before dropping the note in the file, Jack had read it once more:

Dear Mr. Keeler,

On behalf of our committee, I would like to thank you for speaking at our dinner, and while I did not have occasion to attend, I heard you were an inspiration to all.

This necklace is a token of our esteem; it represents peace and love, healing and long life. Though you may not subscribe to its religious implications or symbolism, you should know that it is given with the wishes of what it represents and we would consider it an honor if you would accept it.

It is something that is worn by the men of my Asian culture, but understanding your customs, perhaps you would not find it fitting with your mode of dress, though it may be more suited to your wife, her tastes and style. You would honor us by giving it to her, affording her our blessing for being the wife of Jack Keeler.

JACK SENT A note back, thanking Toulouse and the council for their generous gift, and had scheduled to meet with him next week as a gesture of appreciation.

Jack had looked at the blue stone necklace thinking of the copper bracelets that arthritics wear, believing in their unproven healing properties; he thought of the Star of David, of the Buddhist yin and yang, and of the holy cross. He reached up and fingered the cross around his own neck, thinking about how he had survived bullets, car crashes, and near drowning . . . And hoped that maybe the blue necklace Mia wore around her neck would somehow impart the intent of Marijha Toulouse: peace, love, and, most important, long life.

CHAPTER 16

MIA SAT ON THE edge of the bed, feeling hopeless, the sounds of the city droning in through the locked door.

There was a heavy click of the dead bolt, and the door opened, the sounds of the city growing louder as a tall man stepped into the room. He held a silver tray with a steaming etched kettle of water and blue china cups, along with a plate of pastries.

The man's skin was smooth like porcelain, the tone dark. His long black hair, pulled tight in a ponytail, hung just past his shoulders, which filled out a black pinstriped suit. He placed the tray on the table as someone pulled the door closed and the latch was reset, sealing them in.

The man pulled out a chair, sat, and crossed his legs as if in ceremony.

"Good morning," he said in a subtle Eurasian accent. "I'm sorry about your confined accommodations."

Without waiting for a response, he turned over the two china cups, picked up two small metal sieves packed tightly with tea leaves, and placed them in the cups. Grasping the kettle in his large hand, he poured the steaming water over the leaves, making a rich, hot tea.

There was a refinement to the man, in the way he talked, in the way he moved. He was precise, with each word spoken in perfect diction; the simple movement of his hand was slow and deliberate as he prepared the tea. With similar precision, he reached into his pocket, withdrew an envelope, and placed it on the table next to the tray.

Throughout the ritual, Mia remained silent, studying his every action. Beneath the tailored Savile Row black suit, there was no doubting his size, his broad shoulders, his powerful hands.

Mia sat there in shock as she recognized him. As impossible as it was, Nowaji Cristos was standing there now. And while she knew of the atrocities he had committed, what he was capable of, these were not what scared her the most.

"You should have no worries for your safety," Cristos said. "I have very strict instructions not to kill you."

Cristos smiled at Mia. A pregnant pause hung in the air.

"But I should make you aware, I've never been one who listens to orders or instructions. I follow my own path; if I don't get what I want by dawn tomorrow, I will kill you all."

With his manicured hand, Cristos pushed the elegant white envelope toward Mia, and without further word, without explanation of what was going on, without asking a single pointed question, the man stood and walked to the door. He gave it two sharp knocks, the door opened, and he disappeared. The door closed behind him, leaving Mia, once again, by herself.

Mia finally inhaled, deep and plentiful, to quell the fear that ran through her, to purge the adrenaline that coursed through her veins, making her tremble uncharacteristically. The impossibility of her encounter, of the man who held her captive, sent her mind into a world of confusion. She had thought, as so many others had, that he had died almost a year ago.

Mia sat there a moment, staring at the elegant tray that stood in sharp contrast to the rest of the room, her eyes drawn to the envelope, the gravity of its contents weighing on her mind, knowing that it portended something far from the proper breakfast that was just delivered to her. Despite his refinement, despite his gentle voice and manner, Mia knew what Cristos was truly capable of. Mia knew of the horrors this man had done in the past.

She finally picked up the envelope, glaring at the door as if the man on the other side could feel her stare as she lifted the flap. She peered inside, and the false composure of her face finally cracked, all color draining away as her eyes welled with tears.

She withdrew the picture; holding it up, she stared at it. It was taken from a distance, through a telephoto lens, the white sand bright in the early -morning sun. The date stamp in the lower corner read, *June 30.* Today.

There was no mistaking the older woman who sat in a beach chair watching over the children, but Mia paid her no mind. Her eyes were glued to the children playing in the surf. Her heart felt on fire with rage as she stared at the unmistakable faces of her daughters, Hope and Sara.

JACK SAT IN a small office, the desk and shelves stacked precariously high with papers and books all in total disarray. Although the mayhem did have some semblance of order known only to its owner, there was no doubt a single gust of wind would wipe it all away.

Much to her anger, Jack told Joy to stay with the car out on Broadway while he and Frank headed into Kent Hall to the Asian studies department of Columbia University. The old stone building on the far southeast end of campus was the quintessential image of college, with its ivy-covered granite walls and high steel-casement windows.

"Gentlemen." The voice was distinct, gravelly, its rough tone fermented by liquor and cigarettes. The elderly man wore a bow tie and suspenders, every bit the professorial image Jack expected, except that the man's years were far beyond what Jack thought possible.

"Not sure which one of you is Joy, but you look nothing like your voice," the man said, a hint of mirth in his tone.

"I'm Joy," Frank said in all seriousness as he pointed toward Jack. "This is DA Jack Keeler."

The man looked at Jack, a hint of surprise on his face. "Hello, Jack." He greeted Jack familiarly, as if his advanced years granted him the privilege. He held out his arthritic hand, the fingers locked in a curve.

Jack took his hand and gently shook it, afraid the man would break before him. "Killian Adoy."

The professor shuffled into the room, his stooped body struggling with the effort. While countless years had twisted his form and wrinkled his face with deep folds, his eyes were like those of a vibrant young man who savored life. He removed his hat, revealing a bald pate, wisps of gray hair scattered around like sparse weeds on a field of dust.

He laid the hat on the table and took a seat before Jack.

"Like Mark Twain, the report of your death seems exaggerated, Jack."

Jack smiled. Killian reminded him of his grandfather, someone who not only had a unique perspective on life and its folly but also took an interest in him for simply being him.

"I got the e-mail scan, but beyond identifying the language, I can't make a translation without seeing the text firsthand. I wasn't sure, was it on parchment or from a book?"

Without a word, Jack held out his arm and rolled up his sleeve, feeling like a child in the nurse's office.

Killian's brow arched with curiosity. "Let's take a look."

He took hold of Jack's arm and ran his gnarled, aged fingers along the surface, his eyes keenly focused on the intricate markings.

"This is the language of Cotis," Killian said with an academic air as he continued to study Jack's arm. "Some call it the language of the priests because it is so infrequently used except by scholars and clergy. Much like the language that emanated from Latium and ancient Rome spreading to become the language of Christianity, of scholars, and of science, it has faded away from everyday use. And like Latin, it's no longer spoken. The Cotis people are a small Asian society whose isolation and small population had caused their numbers to dwindle, their culture to be forgotten, swallowed up by the jungle where they lived. They are still in existence, though.

"Cotis has survived the centuries, thriving in its isolation, developing off of the framework of harmony with nature, with the earth, with the afterlife. Its central city was similar to but a on a much smaller scale than Angkor, the Hindu temple city that was mysteriously swallowed by the jungles of Cambodia with no clue to the fate of its people or culture."

"We're in kind of a rush here—"

Killian cut Frank off, "If you want to hear the translation, then you need to understand the culture."

Frank exhaled in frustration but otherwise remained silent.

"Cotis's stone temples soared high, parting the foliage to emerge above the treetops as if rising to heaven. They were constructed by skilled craftsmen millennia ago, eight central towers looking like tiered lotus buds, their footings connected in long, meandering passageways, a visual history in bas-relief depicted on the walls: an ancient king arriving atop a majestic elephant, priests plucking stars from the skies, burying horrific beasts in the fires of the sun, wild animals living among the people.

"An elaborate funerary lay on the perimeter; its entrance faced west toward the land of the dead, while its exit faced toward the east, the land of birth. The central palace was the home of the high priest and his family. But unlike the isolation of royalty practiced by the kingdoms of the world and usurped by presidents and dictators, the doors of the palace were forever open. The high priest, his sons, his daughters, and his wife lived with the people and viewed all as equals. The high station of ruler was an expression for the individual's attainment of enlightenment, of wisdom, as opposed to sovereignty and holding a superior position.

"The high priests were said to be able to communicate with the dead and converse with God; the membrane between the two worlds was easily pierced by the selfless disciple, which resulted in a lack of fear of death in the Cotis people, as they believed their time on earth was just a phase of their eternal life.

"There were always twelve monks on the Tietien, what some might call a council; they were the highest and most respected of the priestly order. But unlike so many religious orders, the Cotis priests could marry, as love was thought to be one of their god's greatest gifts and should not be denied to one who has dedicated his life to spirituality. The council was not gender-specific and included both priests and priestesses.

"As in so many temples in the distant Far East, the priests studied a method of combat, a form of self-defense, a martial art that emphasized turning opponents' strengths and aggressions into their greatest weakness. But these priests were also taught the deadliest methods of attack, a skill set that put the power of death in their bare hands. For while the priests were the symbol of peace, they were also the protectors of their heritage, their people, and would kill any intruder who sought to hurt even the smallest inhabitant of their village. They were a kind of military force that could silently kill intruders before they had a chance to strike, before they even noticed they were about to die.

"Although they abhorred man-made metal tools of death, they studied the weapons and incorporated them into their defenses, knowing that someday they might have to fight fire with fire. They were skilled not only in hand-to-hand combat but also in swordsmanship, archery, and, of late, guns.

"And while they were a prepared force of twelve, they never saw an attack except on three occasions. The first was in 1869, when a British contractor, an arrogant man of greed who thought the 'savage tribe' to be nothing more than inferior simpletons, entered their territory with the intent to mine the village. Looking to harvest precious stones that littered the rich volcanic soil, he and his team set out to round up and displace the 'tribe,' relocating the compliant and handling the resisters accordingly. They did not understand the Cotis or the abilities of their holy men and women. The British contractor and the bodies of his men were never found.

"The second attack on their culture came from a man of the cloth, a priest from another sect who sought to convert them all to his god, the *true* god. After being invited in amongst the Cotis people, sharing their meals and hospitality, he was told that the Cotis faith was strong. The Cotis, being a peace-loving society, voiced that there was more than enough room in the heavens and the hereafter for their gods to coexist. And with that, the foreign priest, unaccustomed to being rebuked, abruptly left. He returned days later with guns in hand to teach them of his greater god's vengeance. His mission never heard from him again.

"The third intruder was twenty years ago, actually another group of twelve. They were military elite, a mercenary group from various European and African nations who had come to commandeer the village for a secret base of operation, a place to conduct their trade far from the eye of society. The soldiers, dressed in black, were trapped in the labyrinthine confines of the temple and urged to leave empty-handed or face the consequences of their actions. Foolishly thinking themselves superior as a result of their training, intelligence, and weaponry, the soldiers refused and continued with their demands. When they didn't return, their loved ones were told they had been swallowed by the Asian jungle.

"To the outside world, the Cotis were thought to be a people out of myth, out of legend, filled with magic and an unusual harmony with the land, a culture whose example of peace was far more influential than the hollow words of politicians. Lately, though, there have been fractures in their society, the outside world infecting them with modern ideals—"

"Thanks for the history," Frank said, cutting him off. "But what does the tattoo on Jack's arm say? We don't have time to waste here."

Killian finally looked up toward Jack, pausing as he gathered his thoughts. "It talks about fate and destiny as if it was part of nature, part of the winds. Some kind of prayer for the dead, some kind of myth, ancient, that I don't understand."

"That's it?" Jack asked.

"No." Killian paused again, his steely academic façade cracking just a bit with foreboding. "The main topic of this mehndi-like tattoo is . . . It says you shall die at dawn, on the first day of the seventh month, killed by an enraged man who has lost everything he loves."

"What kind of bullshit is that?" Frank spat out, angry. "You're going to die tomorrow?"

"Relax," Jack said.

"Relax, my ass. What about today? Didn't you die earlier this morning? Where's the mention of that? How about the weather? Any mention of the weather on his arm there, Doc?"

Killian's eyes locked with Jack's. "I take it the report of your death in the paper this morning has everything to do with this?" Killian paused, academia slipping away to be replaced with genuine concern. "Someone has given you a warning . . . and as you have already experienced, someone is trying to kill you, Jack."

Jack rubbed his shoulder, wincing as his hand touched the wound. He turned to Frank.

"Well," Frank said, looking at the tattoo, "that was a waste of time."

"If they were after me, why not just kill me, ensure that I was dead on the riverbank? And why would someone take the time to scribble a warning on my arm? Why not just wake me up and tell me?"

Killian looked between the two friends, pointing at Jack's arm. "I can assure you, with the intricacies, the time it took to write this, the author was sending a very deliberate message."

Killian finally released Jack's arm.

"And you don't remember who did this to you?" Killian continued. "The complexity, the detail, This was not done in haste. He wrote this for a reason. I don't know if it's a warning, a reminder, or something to frighten you away . . ."

The room fell silent as Jack absorbed the man's words.

"Tell me you're not buying this shit," Frank finally said.

"I don't know what I believe right now," Jack said. "But after what happened this morning, after what I've seen today . . ."

"You can't be serious."

"Look, I don't believe it, but say . . . just say it's true, and I don't find Mia in time . . ." Jack let the supposition hang in the air.

"We're going to find her," Frank said. "And we're going to find her well before dawn tomorrow."

Jack rolled down his sleeve, covering up the words as if to make their prophetic declaration disappear from sight and mind and also to remove any chance of it coming to pass. But as much as he was skeptical, as much as logic told him there was no such thing as fate, fear welled inside him. It wasn't for himself—he had no fear of death—it was for Mia. If he was to die tomorrow at dawn, he had less than eighteen hours to save her.

CHAPTER 17

A S JACK STARED AT his arm, pondering the fateful words, he couldn't help shaking his head at the irony. So often in life, we hear predictions about tomorrow's weather, next week's championship game, or who will win the Oscar, and more often than not, those predictions, while not coming to pass, do have a shadow of truth. Through either random chance, analytical review, pure statistical odds, or just plain dumb luck, the modern-day soothsayers sometimes hit the mark, not always on target but with a semblance of accuracy.

In ancient Greece, it was the oracle of Delphi, the Middle Ages had Nostradamus, the early twentieth century had Rasputin, and for the last hundred or so years, there were astrologists, tarot card readers, and palmists, who preyed on the weak who were in search of hope and some way to make sense of their lives.

And with the tattoo, the mehndi piece of artwork on his arm, there was a semblance of truth to the prediction. The truth was just as dire; it was just that the timing and the cause of death were wrong.

Jack had had a nagging pain in his hip, something he ascribed to when he got hit by a pitch in a baseball game back in May between the DA's and the mayor's offices. While uncomfortable, it was nothing more than an inconvenience that would occasionally send a sharp pain through his body. He was actually proud of the injury, thinking it was like a war wound, as Deputy Mayor Brian McDonald's pitches were known to reach ninety miles an hour. While the curve ball cut its arc quicker than Jack had anticipated, knocking him to the ground, he was able to walk to first despite the pain and the oohs and ahs of the sympathetic crowd.

But ten days ago, when he finally mentioned it to his doctor and friend Ryan McCourt, he had him come in for an X-ray just to be sure there was no permanent damage.

When Ryan got the X-ray back, with Jack sitting in the embarrassing half-gown on the table, he examined it on the light wall for all of two seconds before ripping it down. As he turned to Jack, a grave shadow fell over his face.

Within ten minutes, Jack was being run through an MRI machine for a full-body scan. Blood was drawn, urine requested. He was poked and prodded as a team of doctors came forth discussing the results.

Ryan sat him down and suggested that he call and ask Mia to come meet them. But Jack would have none of that. He suspected where this was going the moment he saw his friend's face looking at the first X-ray.

Jack told him just to give him the news. He could deal with the treatment and would much prefer to have some time to formulate how he would break it to Mia and the girls that Daddy was sick but not to worry, that they had medicine and he would soon be on the mend.

But as Ryan sat down across from him, laying his hand on Jack's shoulder, he couldn't hold back his emotions.

Ryan told him that it was cancer and that it had long since spread, taking hold in his liver, his pancreas, and, worst of all, his brain. The disease had yet to manifest itself outwardly, but the most troubling tumor was pressing on an area of his cerebral cortex and could possibly affect his memory, cause him to hallucinate and become delusional, or interfere with a host of other higher brain functions.

Feeling as if he had been hit by a train, Jack walked out of Ryan's office.

THAT WAS TEN days ago. Since then, he had reformulated time and again how he would tell Mia, how he would find the words of assurance and hope that everything would be all right, even though he knew it wouldn't. He had arranged for the girls to go to his mom's for a week and had every intention of telling Mia of his prognosis when they arrived home. But when he took her in his arms, as she whispered in his ear about how much she had missed his touch, how much she needed him, his heart broke. The news could wait. They needed this time together. He made subtle hints about her staying focused in the moment, about turning off the phone and the BlackBerrys, finding uninterrupted comfort in the here and now, for he knew there would be no next year, next summer, next Christmas.

He had put up a façade not only to Mia but also to his friends, those at work, his campaign, even his mother. He had seen the devastation on her face when she thought he had died that morning and knew she couldn't handle news like that again.

Jack had no idea how to tell the world that he was dying. He was so good at dealing with other people's pain and suffering, being the voice of wisdom and reason. He had always been the shoulder to cry on, but now he did not want to reverse that role.

The doctors said they could begin chemo and radiation, but it would only forestall death, not prevent it or cure him. And it would, without question, destroy the quality of life he currently held on to. Jack wasn't about to become a burden, to have his wife look after him every day as he withered, slowly losing his mental faculties.

Ryan advised him that he should stop work and that the growth of the small tumor in his brain might be slowed with some radical treatment so he could at least have some more of what little life he had remaining.

Wrapped up in conviction rates, trial victories, and landmark settlements, Jack had forgotten to live, to embrace the simple pleasures around him, thinking himself immortal. What scared him deep down was that he had never imagined himself dying so young, dying in such a way. Modern medicine, with all of its treatments, prolonging life no matter the quality, eking out the last breath from a mindless, useless husk before allowing the soul to be surrendered to the hereafter, didn't seem modern at all. Jack couldn't help wondering if that was progress or regression in the evolving history of man.

In so many cultures, there were *good* deaths. Death on the battlefield, the greatest honor in the Viking world, to be carried off to Valhalla by the Valkyries with a sword thrust through your chest; a samurai dying in the heat of battle, giving his life in defending the empire of his deity the emperor; the soldier giving his life to save his comrades.

But Ryan's MRI and diagnosis made it clear: that wouldn't be the case for Jack. There would be no sword in hand, no supreme sacrifice in the name of God, no glorious death on the battlefield. And so, as he pondered the words of the fateful tattoo on his arm, Jack wondered what death had in store for him. Would it be a good death or simply an uneventful, powerless demise that he had no way of preventing?

And, he thought, if there was any truth to the markings, he was running out of time.

With Mia gone, with her life in danger, finding her and saving her were paramount. Getting her back was not just about how much he loved her but how much the girls would need her once he was gone. Whether he was to die tomorrow or six months from now, everything was about saving the only parent his children would have.

Jack would do whatever it took to get Mia back, he would face whoever had attacked them on that bridge, and if he died in saving her, if he gave his life so she would live. It would all be worth it, it would be a good death.

CHAPTER 18

MIA

MIA NORRIS WAS THOUGHT to have grown up in a life of privilege, the girl with everything, but nothing could be further from the truth. While Mia was the stepdaughter of the successful businessman and former director of the FBI Sam Norris, she was born Mia Sullivan, daughter of Joe and Patricia Sullivan.

Joe was a lieutenant in the Navy—a SEAL in his twenties, a strategic analyst in his thirties—and as a result, according to her father, the world was their home. While the world may have been their home, where she laid her head at night was in constant flux—eighteen beds, thirteen different countries, in fourteen years.

In all of the eighteen homes she lived in by the age of fourteen, she was never bitter. When her father would arrive home and announce a new exciting assignment in some foreign land, she would feel a tinge of sorrow at being suddenly uprooted when she was just getting her feet wet, but at least they were together. So many children in the military wouldn't see their fathers—and in some cases mothers—for six months or more at a time, and many of them kissed their parents for the last time when they left, not realizing that they would lose them on the battlefield. Mia was fortunate that her father had already spent ten years in serious combat around the world before she was three. His body proved it, dotted with scars from all types of minor wounds—except for the long not-so-minor squiggly one on his neck—with which Mia played connect the dots. Since becoming an analyst, he only endured paper cuts and jet lag, leaving the threat of dying for his country in the past.

Since Mia was a young child, she dreamed of flying, staring up at the soaring birds, riding the updrafts, the air current carrying them higher and higher, only to nose-dive back to earth. It was a child's fantasy, one she shared with her dad on more than one occasion. They would lie in a field or on the beach, staring at the clouds and the birds flittering about. He would feed her fantasy, telling her to close her eyes and imagine the feel of turning to and fro in flight.

Her mother, Pat, would always admonish him for encouraging her, but her dad would laugh her off and turn to Mia and say what he always said when faced with adversity: "Remember, Mia, nothing is impossible."

She loved her father. She loved that they shared a passion for junk food, candy, and chips; movies and early rock 'n' roll; sports and puzzles. Joe Sullivan was handsome, broad, and tall, unlike most kids' round-about-the-middle dads. He was sympathetic, knowing how difficult it must be for his daughter to sacrifice her childhood for his career. And so he compensated. His free time was not spent playing golf or cards, racing off to some hobby; his time was spent with Mia, teaching her to sail and shoot, showing her the cultures they dropped into for six months at a time. He taught her the value of being happy in your work, of the pain of sacrifice in pursuing your dreams, that the value of life was not in riches but in the richness of one's existence, in loving someone, in putting others before oneself. Simple lessons that had been forgotten by so much of the world.

It was on a Friday that Mia turned exactly fourteen and a half. Her father believed in celebrating not only birthdays but half-birthdays, too, always saying one shouldn't rejoice in someone only once a year. They had been back in the States all of three days, settling into a small two-bedroom house just outside of Naval Air Station Oceana in Virginia Beach, Virginia. It was a late-spring morning; school didn't start for an hour. Her mother was busy unpacking and getting breakfast ready when her dad snuck into her room and kidnapped her for a day of fun.

With the windows rolled down, the radio blaring, and two bags of chips, candy, and waters on the seat between them, they escaped.

Arriving at NAS Oceana, they drove around a road crew repairing pavement near the front entrance and stopped at the security gate. Joe introduced the three guards to Mia and, with a wink and a smile, continued on to a large hangar. Without a word, her father led her inside. The cavernous space was filled with F-35 Lightning II's, F/A-18 Hornets and Super Hornets, the greatest fighter jets the world had known, capable of speeds in excess of mach 1.8. Mia looked at her father with curious eyes as they walked toward a locker. He reached inside and pulled something out.

"Put this on," Joe said as he handed Mia a flight suit.

"What are we doing?" Mia begged with a smile

"Just go into the ladies' locker room and put that on." Joe pointed to the door before turning into the men's locker room.

Mia stared at the tan jumpsuit before looking at the two-seater jets and her heart began to race with excitement.

THREE MINUTES LATER, Mia exited the locker room, but her father was nowhere to be found. She left the hangar, looking at the nearly vacant runway, seeing nothing but a 757 jet, its engines whining in anticipation of takeoff. She saw no fighter jets prepped and ready, no planes of a smaller stature that her father would be taking her up in.

Then, from the doorway of the 757, she finally saw her dad in his jumpsuit, his short dark hair blowing in the morning breeze, waving to her. She waved back, a smile on her face that expertly hid her disappointment. Being the daughter of a naval officer, she had been in the cockpits of large jets such as this one on too many occasions to count. She had gotten her hopes up for something exciting and new. But she would never let him know.

Mia climbed the stairs and entered what she realized was not a typical 757. The room she stood in was like a scientific lab; instruments and computers abounded. Four young officers stood when she entered the plane and nodded hello. Her father quickly introduced them as naval scientists who were studying the effects of spatial awareness in low-gravity environments.

Her dad pointed her to a door that led into the cabin of the jet, and they entered what looked like an insane asylum. There were no windows, and the walls and ceiling were padded. Against the walls were harnesses, spaced evenly apart. Along each wall, the ceiling, and the floor were ladder rungs affixed to the body of the plane, running the length of the large tubular room.

"Let's strap in," Joe said, smiling at his daughter.

"What are we doing, Daddy?" Mia asked, her curiosity growing.

Joe just smiled as he sat on the floor against the padded wall and strapped himself in. Mia followed suit.

"What kind of plane is this?"

A red light on the far wall lit up, its glow painting the white wall padding bright crimson. The whine of the jet grew, and she could feel the four large engines vibrating as the jet lurched forward, quickly picking up speed. And although there were no windows, she could imagine the Virginia countryside whipping by. After thirty seconds, the roar of the engines peaking, she felt the jet jump into the air, the engines screaming as they climbed high into the sky.

"Mia," her father finally said, "in life we are faced with adversity, with tough choices, difficult decisions, but what you must remember is that there is always a solution. Nothing is impossible. Your mother doesn't believe this, and that's OK. But I do, and I know you do, too. I can't imagine what your heart must go through every time we pull you away from friends, how difficult it must be always to feel like a stranger, but that will soon end. I'm going to retire and move into the private sector. We're finally going to have a normal life."

Mia looked up at her dad and smiled. "To me, it's always been a normal life. I wouldn't trade a single moment."

The red light on the far wall winked out, replaced by a yellow one, and with it, the whine of the jet's engine disappeared.

Joe unstrapped himself, stood up, and nodded for Mia to do the same. He took her hand, and they walked to the rear wall.

"Remember, Mia," Joe said as he stared into her eyes with such love, "nothing is impossible."

The light on the far wall turned green, Mia felt her stomach grow light, and all at once she was floating, drifting hand-in-hand with her father. The weight of the world was literally gone.

"Put your feet against the wall," her father said, which they both did effortlessly.

He held tight to her hand, and they pushed off.

Mia couldn't help it—she could feel the tears forming in her eyes. Her dream had come true. She was flying.

They were soaring through the air, light as feathers, like birds on invisible wings.

Her heart was more alive than it had ever been. She was doing the impossible. Her mother said it could never be done, but her dad was right.

Holding hands, they sailed through the air down the length of the jet. Arriving at the far wall, her father released her, and they both planted their feet against the wall, quickly pushing off.

She was flying solo; as she had always imagined, she put her arms out, spinning around. She flipped over effortlessly, somersaulting over and over again without getting dizzy.

For two minutes, they defied gravity.

The light on the wall turned yellow, and Joe and Mia grabbed the ladder on the floor and pulled their way back to the wall. She could feel her weight returning as the engine's cry returned.

Her father explained that they were in a modified 757, which some affectionately called the Vomit Comet for those who experienced adverse reactions to weightlessness. The plane flew up and down in long parabolic arcs, the effect of which created a zero-gravity environment within the confines of the plane. The 757 was used to study weightlessness, train astronauts, and conduct experiments; today it was used for teaching Mia how to fly.

Eleven more times the light turned green. Eleven more times Mia flew. It was, without question, the greatest experience of her life, not just because she flew but also because her father made her realize her potential; he made her realize that nothing was impossible.

FIFTEEN MINUTES AFTER they landed, the bomb went off.

MIA AND HER father quickly changed out of their flight suits, grabbed their things, and hopped into the car. As they drove through the gate, they said goodnight to the three guards and headed toward home.

Fifty yards past the gate, Joe stopped the car. He looked at the full bag of uneaten food.

"Let me," Mia said. And without waiting for an answer, she grabbed the bag filled with candy, chips, and waters and took off for the guard shack.

The soldiers took the bag, smiling in appreciation, waving to the lieutenant.

And without warning, an explosion tore the front of Joe's car apart. A large fireball rolled into in the sky, black smoke curling upward, spreading out in a large cloud.

Joe stumbled from the car in shock, his eyes scanning for Mia. And once he saw her running toward him, once he saw that she was all right, he collapsed.

The three gatehouse guards were ten yards behind Mia, their guns drawn, yelling at her to stop, fearful of another bomb. But nothing could stop her from getting to her dad.

Joe Sullivan lay in the middle of the road, his car in flames behind him. Blood stained his burned clothing as his chest heaved and he gasped for air. Mia came charging to his side, kneeling beside him, lifting him into her lap, cradling his broken body to her chest. He was always bigger than life to her, but now . . .

"Dad? Look at me."

Joe struggled to breathe, his body convulsing in short bursts, his eyes struggling to stay open.

"Please!" Mia cried out. "Oh, God, please don't . . ."

The three guards looked at Joe, instantly assessing his condition. They formed a perimeter around the lieutenant and his daughter, guns aimed out, searching for the perpetrators, protecting Mia and her father in what they knew would be their final moments together.

Sirens blared in the distance as the soldiers spoke into their radios, but Mia heard none of it. All of her senses were focused on her father.

"Dad!" Mia pleaded as the tears poured down her face. "Please—"

His wheezing breaths grew shallow as every muscle in his body went limp.

Without a word, he looked up into Mia's eyes, a world of emotions passing between them, and he died.

JOE SULLIVAN HAD fought in three wars, had been in countless battles and firefights, had spent his naval career in some of the most hostile locations on earth, only to be felled by a car bomb in his own country.

What was first thought to be an act of international terrorism turned out to have been committed by a small domestic group known as Peace for All whose members preached passivity while demanding the withdrawal of U.S. forces from all countries and the abolition of the U.S. military. After a one-week manhunt, the three American perpetrators were captured by the FBI, tried, and executed.

Mia's world was shattered. Her father was everything to her. She felt adrift without his words of wisdom, his guidance in life, the sound of his voice as he arrived home at night after work. She couldn't wipe the image of his dying in her arms from her nightmares. And while her mother comforted her, Patricia Sullivan was equally devastated, often lost in her own grief, unable to function.

Within six months, her mother moved on, falling for the FBI agent who had captured the killers of her husband. No one spoke of the Freudian influence on her heart.

Sam Norris took them in, adopting and embracing Mia as his own. Against her wishes, Mia's mother made her change her name from Sullivan to Norris, explaining that she couldn't go through the pain of explaining how her daughter had a different name, that it would force her to relive the agony all too often, never realizing the betrayal it caused for Mia.

They moved to Washington, where her stepfather was made deputy director of the FBI. A year later, he began serving three years as director. He retired and moved to New York to start a security consulting business, a firm where he could capitalize on his vast government connections.

As Sam Norris's business expanded, their creature comforts grew. Mia's mother embraced their large home, her fancy car, their life of privilege, but to Mia, none of that could replace her father. The money made her uncomfortable. It seemed to be a patina over the lack of love and affection in their new family.

And so she became focused on herself. Although Sam Norris hadn't filled the vacancy left by her father's death, he did offer a window into the FBI, entrée into fighting people like the ones who killed her father. As she rose through the ranks, investigating and arresting criminals and terrorists, it was as if she was taking down her father's killers again and again and again.

Jack would have liked her dad. They were alike in so many re-spects: wise, selfless, extremely athletic yet always modest and always believing nothing was ever out of reach.

Mia looked around the small room, locked away in who-knows-where, thinking of the impossibility of escape, and she relived that day of flying with her father and embraced his words, knowing them to be true.

Nothing is impossible.

CHAPTER 19

AFTER FINDING OUT ABOUT the ominous warning on Jack's arm, Frank, Jack, and Joy agreed that there was one thing that held the answers they needed. Whatever was in the evidence case had frightened Mia as if it were death come to claim her soul. Jack beat himself up for respecting her wishes and for not forcing her to tell him what she was involved in, the gift of hindsight condemning him. The three agreed that the answer to finding Mia was not in the tattoo on Jack's arm; it was in the case.

IT WAS JUST after 12:30 when Frank walked through the lobby of the Tombs. There was no need to flash his badge, as he was greeted by his first name at every checkpoint he went through.

"Your disappearance from the force was just a rumor, hey?" the skinny guard with washed-out skin said as he stood up from the central reception desk.

"Good to see you," Frank said as he offered his hand, shaking Larry's warmly.

"I knew you wouldn't be gone for long. You're here about sublevel five?"

Frank was shocked that the young guard would know where he was going. "As a matter of fact . . ."

"I hate when the feds go sniffing around in our business."

Frank didn't respond, although his mind was already spinning.

"Surprised they didn't call you in earlier." Larry flicked the button under his desk, releasing the security lock to his gate and allowing Frank to enter the central lobby.

Frank walked through and headed for the bank of elevators against the far wall, then turned back to Larry.

"Thanks, Larry."

"I'm glad you're back," Larry said with a nod before returning to his post.

As Frank hit the elevator button, he knew that things were about to go far off track. If the feds were in sublevel five, the situation that couldn't get worse was already well past that point.

AS THE ELEVATOR doors opened on sublevel five, Frank saw yellow police tape stretched the length of the small lobby. Several black rolling cases of various sizes sat in the corner as if someone was moving in. Two men in dark suits said nothing as they stepped into the cab, not waiting for Frank to disembark, and hit the button for the ground floor.

Frank walked out, shaking his head. He ducked under the tape and stepped to the glass window, pulling out and placing his ID flush with the glass, rapping on the window with his knuckles.

Charlie spun around in his desk chair, his usually cheery face awash in grief.

"Frank," Charlie said with relief.

"Hey, Charlie." Frank nodded.

"This is god-awful." Charlie's usually perfect tie was askew, his hair mussed, making him look like someone at the end of a forty-eight hour shift. But Charlie had just arrived. "Their poor kids, both parents, how do you tell a kid their mother and father aren't coming back?"

Frank nodded, wishing he could wipe away the pain with the simple truth, but that was out of the question for the moment.

Charlie glanced at Frank's ID and buzzed the door. Frank pulled open the steel security door as the release buzzer screamed in his ear and headed straight into Charlie's small office.

"Police tape?" Frank said. "What the hell?"

"Feds are here, looking for an evidence case they say belongs to them."

"And that would be down here because . . ."

"They say Jack Keeler hid it down here for his wife."

"Did he?" Frank wasn't sure how much Charlie was involved.

"They're not going to find anything," Charlie said in unspoken understanding. "They come down here thinking they're smarter, that we're just a bunch of cops out of a Keystone movie."

"The feds are always so charming."

"Yes, we are."

Frank turned to see a tall man, thin and wiry, standing ramrod-straight in the doorway, his head seeming a little large for his body, what little hair he possessed buzz-cut short. The exhaustion in his eyes left no doubt that the man hadn't slept in days; the dark circles and humorless expression were not what anyone was accustomed to seeing in Gene Tierney. The FBI's assistant director in charge of the New York field office was known for his sense of humor, a dark, dry wit honed over a twenty-five-year career, which Frank had come across on several occasions. Frank would never consider Tierney to be a friend, but he respected him, which was something he could only say about one other FBI agent, and nobody knew where she was right now.

"Since when are you back on the force?" Tierney quickly said.

"What the hell's going on?" Frank asked.

Tierney stood there, troubled, mulling over Frank's question. "We're looking for an evidence box that Mia Keeler had, and it seems to have disappeared."

"And why would it be here?"

"Mia's smart. We believe she asked her husband to hide it down here."

"So you think Mia was hiding evidence and Jack was committing political suicide?"

"No, I didn't say that. But as with everything, there's more to the story that none of us knows."

"Do you know what's in the case?"

"Evidence from a murder investigation."

"And you think Jack and Mia are somehow involved?"

"Nobody is accusing them of wrongdoing. I've known Mia since she was a senior in high school, and her father forever. If she did something like this, she did it for a reason."

"So all this to figure out that reason, you just come in and take over?"

Tierney took a moment, running his hands through his bristly hair. "We got the mayor, the governor, and we have a warrant, which I haven't needed to wave around, because everyone is trying to work together on this. We're not saying Jack or Mia did anything wrong, but something got them killed. And we need that evidence case."

"So what's taking so long? You've got a whole team down here, and you can't find it?"

"Nothing is in the system," Charlie cut in.

"He's smart. He didn't log it in, which means either someone was helping him"—Tierney paused as he looked from Charlie to Frank—"Or he tucked it into some other case file."

"The DA's office has thousands of active cases. Are you telling me you're going to go through every evidence file?"

"Welcome to my hell," Tierney said as he took a step into the evidence room. Frank followed him into the enormous storage space. Frank had been in there too many times to count.

"Do you mind if I take a walk around?"

"Yes, I do," Tierney said, a tired tone of suspicion in his voice. "Until you tell me why someone who was so anxious to retire and get away from all of this is back."

Frank stared at him a moment. "You and I both know it was no accident; otherwise, *you* wouldn't be down here."

"It's no coincidence that we're both here right now. I know what I'm looking for. Why don't you tell me what you're looking for?"

Frank's mind was scrambling. He was never one for lies, always spitting out the truth before his mind could hold it in check.

"I heard you guys were here, something that's never happened before. Like you said, no coincidence."

"We've spent the entire morning looking at every ongoing case that Keeler was working on."

"And nothing is missing."

"Nothing's missing."

"You really give a shit if I look around?"

"Actually, I do, unless you've got something to offer, something that might point us in a direction?"

Frank nodded, looking down the corridor at the rows upon rows of enormous shelves of evidence. A group of white-shirt analysts sat at four makeshift tables, computers and boxes before them. They checked each and every case, pulling out files, guns, bags of drugs, whatever the box might hold, logging the information on their clipboards and computers. Two young agents wandered around, each one no more than thirty, eyes alive, their pistols visible on their belts.

Frank turned his eyes back down the central aisle, all the way to the end, all the way down to row Y, where he knew the case was hidden away. Second shelf from the top, seven feet up, Jack had said, a white bar code sticker on the top.

"No offense, Frank," Tierney said.

"It's OK, I understand." He did understand, but he was seething nevertheless. Mia's evidence case just slipped further away. "What the heck happens to any cop looking to log evidence in?"

"We have no problem with anything coming in," Tierney said. "We're not going to interrupt the process of law, but this place is under lockdown. Nothing goes out until Monday, and that's after being thoroughly inspected.

"Your suspicions only further confirm ours. Someone is after this case, and I think we've seen how far they're willing to go to get it. So, I'm keeping a team here until we get to the bottom of this. You guys may have great security, but a few extra guns never hurt. If that box is down here, it's not leaving with anyone but me."

JACK SAT IN Frank's Jeep. Joy had nodded off beside him, the ordeal of his death and resurrection exhausting her. Jack stared at the rear entrance to the Tombs, feeling impotent, completely and utterly helpless, trapped within a car while Frank did what he should be doing: retrieving Mia's evidence case. Yet all the while, Jack suspected that the real answer to everything—how he got back to his house, who helped him, who wrote the tattoo on his arm—lay somewhere in his own mind.

As he looked out at the city of New York, at its skyscrapers, its bustling sidewalks, the traffic-filled streets, he knew the search was not out there. The search was within, and all of his efforts should go to cracking open his memory. It was like some cruel puzzle, images, flittering impressions of the night before remaining just out of focus, like waking from a dream that he could no longer remember. While the tattoo was a mystery and the box that they had hidden away held some answers, Jack knew that if he could just recover his memory from after the crash, he would have his solution to find her.

He wondered if his memory loss was from the cancer, the small tumor in his brain manifesting itself in blackouts. Of all places to hit, of all times to attack—Jack thought the twist of fate was beyond cruel. A man known for his mind, for his memory of everything back to his earliest youth, was now rendered a mnemonic cripple. His greatest asset and skill was in solving problems, seeing solutions where others only saw frustration. And now, in his most desperate hour, he was like a novitiate without a guide, no map, no clue to what direction he should take.

It had been nearly fifteen minutes since Frank had ventured inside the Tombs. There was no word, no call on his cell phone, and the silence only confirmed the worst. Mia's evidence case was deposited two days ago in the one place they both thought secure. She had been insistent on hiding it away from the world, on keeping it out of reach of the people around her, all the while being terrified of its contents—which she never explained. But now that he thought on it, maybe she had. Maybe she had told him everything, what was going on, what scared her, what was in the box, and he just didn't remember. Jack wanted to scream.

Trying to calm his mind, he once again looked around the bustling streets of downtown Manhattan, and his focus was drawn to a blue Crown Victoria, the standard cop-issue, law-enforcement vehicle, that had come to a stop across the street. There were several of them parked in the reserved NYPD spaces, among the cop cars and prisoner-transport vans, but this one in particular drew his attention for a single reason. The man inside was staring at Frank's car.

Jack felt it in his gut, deep in his belly. He remained low in the passenger seat, comfortable in his anonymity behind the smoked windows, watching as the man's eyes alternated between the Jeep and the side door to the Tombs.

A heavy rumble shook the street, the subway that wound its way beneath the city reminding him that much of life was hidden beneath the surface. The man stepped out of his car. He stood just under six feet, his muscled arms stretching the sleeves of his short-sleeved shirt. His blond hair fluttered on the summer breeze, and all at once, Jack realized whom he was looking at.

Joy stirred beside him, opened her eyes, and looked at him staring intently out the window. She followed his gaze to the man across the street.

"Who's that?" Joy said, her voice hesitant, as if not really wanting the answer.

Jack didn't break his stare, the moment dragging on to almost the point of forgetting the question. His voice was low and steady as he answered her, although his tone was filled with vengeance. "That's the man who killed me."

FRANK STEPPED INTO the elevator with far more questions than answers. Whatever Mia had stumbled upon was worse than he had imagined. The effort mobilized to recover the case was being overseen by Tierney personally, and the assistant director only took on-site charge of an investigation when the matter had far-reaching implications.

The elevator ride back up into the world seemed to take forever, which suited Frank fine. His mind was churning with scenarios, thoughts, and ideas. He had no intention of leaving the Tombs without the case, no matter how many feds were down there.

As the doors to the lobby opened, Frank pulled out his cell phone, quickly dialing as he continued out into the rear hallway to get cell service.

IN THE CAR, Jack sat glaring at the man who shot him at point-blank range, who helped send him hurtling off Rider's Bridge. Rage clouded Jack's mind; thoughts of unquenchable revenge were all he could think of. He wanted to leap from the car and kill the man with his bare hands. But his thoughts were interrupted by the ring of his cell phone. He saw Frank's number and quickly answered it.

"Got it?"

"No," Frank said, pain in his voice.

"What?"

"It's a nightmare down there. Seems the whole world is looking for your box. The feds took the place over."

"Dammit." Jack slowly exhaled, trying to balance his nerves and focus as his only link to Mia slipped away. "We need that case—"

Jack stopped talking as the rumble of the street momentarily distracted him, but this time it wasn't the subway. He glanced in the rearview mirror to see a sanitation truck make its way down the road, two workers clinging to the white garbage truck's side, leaping off, grabbing and dumping waste cans that had been left for pickup. There was a line of cars behind the slow-moving vehicle, windows down, drivers cursing, laying on horns, which, as anyone who lived in a city knew, only made the truck move slower.

Jack turned his attention back to the man across the street.

"Jack?" Frank's tone was filled with concern.

"Jack," Joy echoed Frank. She could see the look on her boss's face and knew it all too well.

But Jack was lost in thought, staring at the blond man who now leaned on the Crown Victoria until he finally tilted the phone toward his mouth. "I've got to go—"

"Go?" Frank's voice grew loud with anger. "Go where?"

"There's someone I need to talk to—"

"Don't you dare get out of that car—"

Jack slammed the phone shut, stuck it back into his pocket, and watched the sanitation truck crawl up the street toward him. It finally came to a stop in the middle of the road, clogging traffic while obscuring his view of the Crown Victoria and the man who stood beside it.

"Jack," Joy said, "don't even think about it—"

Suddenly, on instinct and against reason, Jack leaped out of the car. Using the large white sanitation truck as cover, he stayed low and circled back around the Crown Victoria.

Just as Jack rounded the back of the truck, coming out behind the blue car, the blond man noticed his approach. The man's eyes grew wide with shock. He reached for his cell phone, quickly dialing, but before he could lift the phone to his ear, Jack was upon him, knocking the phone away, thrusting him against the car.

"Where's my wife?" Jack said through gritted teeth, his body like a coiled spring ready to release.

"I watched you die . . ." the man said in disbelief. He reached for his gun, but Jack snatched it from him, tucking it into the small of his back.

"Where is she?" Jack wrapped his hands around the man's throat. "I'll snap your neck."

While the element of surprise gave Jack the advantage, it was only temporary. The man quickly recovered his wits and, with lightning motion, swept his arms up, freeing himself from the stranglehold. His hand clenched into a fist and in a continuous arc struck Jack in the side of the jaw, stunning and knocking him backward.

The man took off, racing up the street. Without breaking stride, he grabbed his phone from where it lay in the gutter and kept running, dialing on the fly. Jack quickly recovered, regained his footing, and took off in pursuit. He couldn't afford the world knowing he was alive, not yet. He ran for everything he was worth, knowing that if the call went through, Mia's already meager life expectancy could drop down to minutes. He pressed on, pushing his legs to the limit.

The man cut across Center Street, up Chambers, and hung a right onto Broadway. He was fast, but Jack was faster, quickly gaining on him. They bobbed and weaved through oncoming traffic, as cars locked up their brakes and tires screeched, trying to avoid the two crazed men who ran through the streets of New York. The blond man leaped a fraction of a second before the front end of a yellow cab plowed into him, his butt sliding across the hood of the car, then practically landing in stride on the street as he fled. Jack didn't miss a beat as he leaped onto the hood of the cab, jumping to the roof of the next vehicle and back to the sidewalk, landing inches from his prey.

Jack reached out, a hair's breadth from grabbing him, when the man cut left and raced down a flight of subway entrance stairs, taking five at a time, stumbling but quickly gaining his footing. The man jumped the turnstile and charged along a darkened platform.

Jack never lost distance, hurdling the turnstile, never breaking stride. A moment of panic filled him as he watched the man charge the closing doors of a departing subway car but was quickly relieved as the doors sealed up and the car left the station.

Alone on the vacant platform of the subway, the man jumped onto the tracks and never stopped, the sound of his racing feet echoing through the shadowy, cavernous tunnel as he disappeared into the darkness.

Without hesitation, Jack also jumped to the tracks, the stench of urine and filth filling his lungs as he sprinted and gasped for breath, struggling to keep up with the man ahead of him. The footing grew precarious, the gravel fill intermittent and scattered and the gauged rail ties uneven with his stride.

They were both swallowed by the dark, the only light coming from the green and red subway lights affixed to the walls, their unnatural glow casting staccato shadows.

Jack's heart pounded in his ears. He had been sprinting for three minutes full-out, farther and faster than he had ever pushed himself.

But the rhythmic thrum was soon obscured. The heavy roar of an approaching train grew by the second, shaking the ground on which they ran and making it even more treacherous.

And then it was there, up ahead, rounding the corner to bear down on them, the wail of the train's horn shredding their ears as its harsh light blinded them. The subway brakes locked up, sparks flew, and the seized metal wheels let out a screaming cry. There would be no stopping the train in time.

But the blond man never stopped. His silhouette, ten feet ahead, seemed to accelerate as if playing chicken with the thirty-ton train.

And then, suddenly, he cut left through an opening in the wall as if he knew it was there all along. The train bore down on Jack, only feet away, milliseconds from crushing him.

He dove through a hole in the wall just as the train roared past, a mix of shrill brakes and rumbling motors. He could feel the heat of the lead car as it barely missed clipping his back.

Jack found himself in an adjacent tunnel, this one without the benefit of the red and green directional lights. The blackness felt like a veil over his senses. He lost his bearings as he turned around, listening for any sign of the man who had shot him. He caught a glimpse of light ahead, coming from above, and approached what he realized was a sidewalk grate.

By the time he felt the man's presence behind him, it was already too late.

The garrote had already wrapped around his neck.

FRANK STOOD ON the platform as the express train roared through the station without stopping. He had caught sight of Jack racing up Center Street and took chase, his body forgetting his age until he was forced to stop and wait for the train to pass. He doubled over, hands on his knees, swallowing air in large gulps. He was in good shape, but he was no match for Jack, who was fifteen years his junior. As the train continued by, Frank took the brief interlude to clear his mind of his anger. He couldn't have been more specific when telling Jack not to leave the car under any circumstance. After enduring the sight of the evidence room filled with feds and not getting his hands on the evidence case, he was floored to emerge from the building and find Jack out of the car, tossing some stranger against a Crown Victoria.

Before he could shout, the blond man had taken off with Jack in full pursuit. As Frank took up the chase, running with everything his half-century body had, he hoped to God no one recognized his friend; otherwise, what little advantage they had was gone.

As he stared into the dark tunnel where Jack had vanished, he feared the worst. The Lower Manhattan underground was a maze of subway tunnels, viaducts, and abandoned passages dating back almost 150 years, a world where one could get lost forever.

"WHERE IS IT?" the man screamed in Jack's ear.

As the garrote dug into Jack's neck, he could feel the warm moisture of blood trailing down his back. He struggled, his arms flailing, his head throbbing while his brain screamed out for oxygen. The man had taken him by surprise, positioning himself in the shadows beneath the sidewalk grate, lying in wait.

And then, with the thin wire wrapped tightly around his neck, the man kicked Jack to the ground of the abandoned tunnel, crushing his face into the dirt, where puddles of stench-filled water dotted the ground.

Jack's rage and anger were no longer directed at the man but were turned on himself for being so easily captured, where he was now about to die, where all hope for saving Mia would die along with him.

"Where is the case?" the man growled in his ear.

The question shocked Jack, and the tables turned as the man slammed his face into a puddle while tightening the garrote. But then the man lifted him out of the water and, to his surprise, loosened the garrote. As Jack gulped for air, drawing in a big breath, his face was shoved into the puddle, where he gasped nothing but water into his lungs. Reflexively choking, the man retightened the garrote, drowning Jack with a mouthful of water.

Jack's lungs burned as his mind began to turn black, darkness flowing in from the periphery of his vision. He could taste death as if he already knew its flavor.

But then a singular thought filled his mind: it was Mia in all of her beauty, in all of her grace and perfection. If Jack was to die, then she would have no hope, no chance of living, for her captors wouldn't be letting her go.

Despite all of his valiant thoughts, he lacked the strength to escape his captor. He would die in the darkest recesses of Manhattan, never to be found or heard of again, as if he had already died in the Byram River.

Again, his face was jammed into the puddle, the severe lack of oxygen kicking his body's automatic response to breathe when the garrote was released. The water flowed deeper into his lungs this time, burning like nothing he had ever felt before. But this time, under the pressure of imminent death, he didn't see the proverbial light or his family before his eyes; his life didn't replay like all of the myths.

What Jack saw in a burst of memory was the night before, as if the curtain was momentarily pulled back, allowing him a brief glimpse of something forbidden. Not vivid, more like a recaptured dream. The river raged beneath him as he lay on the shore. The world was filled with shadows beneath the driving rain. All around him were shattered trees and rocks. And the pain came charging back at him as if it had just happened, as if his body had a memory of its own that it couldn't suppress. The pain below his shoulder was like hot steel, his head throbbed, and the teeming rain poured down on his face as he struggled to breathe. He caught glimpses of debris on the soaked shore around him,

And he saw a man emerge from the woods, his face cloaked in the night. He looked around at the raging river, up at the bridge, skyward as the rain began to stop, while shafts of moonlight pierced the parting of the clouds. Jack could hear his own voice crying out.

"You have to help me . . ."

The man looked at Jack but said nothing.

"I think I'm dying, but my wife . . . I have to save my wife . . ."

Jack's recollections were suddenly shattered as the garrote grew tighter around his neck, and a knee jammed into the small of his back, pulling him out of his memories to dangle him at the edge of death.

His captor held his cell phone in his other hand, thumb dialing. The signal that struggled through the grate was weak, intermittent, the call static-filled. "Hey, it's Gallagher . . . Gallagher!" he repeated. "Listen to me. You're not going to believe this . . ."

FRANK TRUDGED HIS way through the tunnel. He hated the dark; he was terrified of it. With the unworldly sounds that permeated the lower depths of the city, his mind filled with images of rats and dead bodies, of the unknown lurking in the shadows. He kept his ears attuned for any sound of Jack, for any indication of an oncoming train, not knowing where Jack could have possibly turned within the confined space of the tunnel.

With the help of the red and green glow of the subway lights, he could see the disturbed gravel, and the intermittent footprints along the rail ties confirmed that he was heading in the right direction.

"Listen to me. You're not going to believe this."

Frank heard the voice up ahead, his ear pinpointing the distance. He drew his gun and caught sight of a small service opening in the wall.

"He's alive."

Frank felt like a moth drawn to the flame as he crept through the opening on silent feet. He stepped through the dark, catching sight of Jack and an assailant in the checkerboard light wash that poured in from above.

"Jack Keeler . . ."

Frank raised his gun as he saw Jack facedown in a puddle, a wire dog-tied around his neck, his assailant atop him with a flexed right arm wrapping the wire, his cell phone held in the other hand, pressed to his ear.

"Tell him Jack Keeler is alive."

Frank pulled the trigger, the report of his Sig Sauer sounding like a cannon in the confined space as the orange glow of the barrel flame momentarily lit the space.

The man fell to the ground, the sounds of death leaking from his mouth, from the exposed side of his head.

Jack rolled over in the puddle, gasping, rubbing his own neck as if it would impart air quicker. He heaved, his lungs expelling water with gut-wrenching coughs that echoed in the abandoned tunnel. He lay on his back, his eyes closed, his mind without focus, as his body struggled to recover from near death. Blood seeped from the razorlike wound that wrapped his neck, the surrounding skin swelling up.

Frank tucked his pistol back into his holster and leaned over the body of the dead man, rifling through his pockets, pulling out keys, a clip of bullets, his wallet. He picked up the cell phone, briefly looking at it, and tucked it into his pocket. He rolled the man over and removed his gun from his holster. He examined it, shaking his head before laying it on the ground.

Frank turned and knelt beside Jack, helping him to sit up. He pulled a handkerchief from his pocket and blotted the blood on Jack's neck, holding it to help stanch the flow of blood. "Jesus, are you OK?"

Jack nodded in reflex without thought of his condition. He finally looked up at Frank, looked into his friend's eyes, his voice hoarse, his throat raw. "I remember."

Frank stared at him. "What?"

"There was someone else there with me last night."

"Can you remember what they look like, a name, maybe?"

"No." Jack shook his head. "But whoever it is . . . he scares me."

"Yeah, well, we've got an even bigger problem. You sure this is the guy who drove you off the bridge, who kidnapped Mia?"

Jack nodded.

Frank held up the man's billfold, letting it drop open to reveal a badge and an ID that made Jack's blood run cold.

Steven Gallagher was FBI.

CHAPTER 20

CRISTOS ENTERED THE ROOM and laid a new silver tray of food and tea on the table before Mia, picked up the tray of tea and the now-empty plate, and handed it to a man at the door, who quickly departed. They were once again sealed in.

"How dare you!" Mia raged as she shook the picture of her children. "My children have nothing to do with this."

"I see we found our voice." Cristos's tone was calm and proper, like a nanny speaking to a child. "Your children are fine. I have not touched them, nor will I. Provided you help me."

"You killed my husband," Mia finally said, her eyes filled with anger. She was not going to give this man the satisfaction of crying, letting him see her pain, seeing her weak. "They're going to find me. The whole world of law enforcement is going to come down on your head."

"Actually," Cristos said in feigned sympathy, "the only place they are looking for you is at the bottom of a river." He picked up a newspaper from the silver tray and placed it before Mia, the headline screaming out the deaths of her and her husband.

Mia sat there in shock. What was stopping them from killing her now?

"I have a very simple question," Cristos said. "Where is the evidence case?"

Mia stared at Cristos.

"I know that you removed it from the FBI and hid it in the evidence room of the Tombs."

"How would someone like you know that?" Mia said, channeling her pain into anger.

Cristos stood and walked around the small room. He rubbed his fingers together as he stared off in thought before finally looking back at Mia. "I want you to look at me," he began as he took a seat next to Mia. "Where in the evidence room of the Tombs is the case?"

Mia stared at him, defiant and silent.

"Where is the case?" Cristos's voice was barely above a whisper as his dark eyes began to bore into her.

Mia continued staring, her silence taunting him.

He leaned forward into her face; she could smell the odor of cigarettes and wine on his breath. Their eyes were inches apart as he mouthed the words, "Where is the case?"

Mia stared back, but instead of answering, she did the one thing that she did when confronting an adversary, be it her father, her husband, or a suspect.

She simply gave a false, vindictive smile.

Cristos exploded, all refinement melting away, the veins and tendons in his neck distended and throbbing. *"Where is the case?"*

Mia had gotten to him. Without a single word, she had unearthed the madman beneath the silk and wool façade.

Suddenly, his hand shot out, grabbing her around the throat, while his other hand grabbed her by her hair. His trembling rage radiated down his arms, through his hands, and into her.

He slowly began to squeeze just enough to send a message that he could snap her neck with his bare hand. Her face began to redden, and although she tried not to react, fear rose into her eyes.

"Tell me where the case is, or this is what I will do to your children."

There was a knock on the door. The lock was released, and it opened. A dark-haired man no more than thirty, dressed in a suit, popped his head in. "You need to come here, right now. You're not going to believe this."

CHAPTER 21

A s JACK EXITED THE subway tunnel onto the street, the bright sun temporarily blinding him, he became aware of something he hadn't realized earlier. His senses had grown acute. His vision seemed more focused, colors more vibrant, he was cognizant of all of the sounds around him, not just the white noise of the city but also the subtle characteristics that made it city noise: car horns, a bus's pneumatic hoses exhausting air as its doors opened, the chatter of pedestrians as they walked the street, hailed cabs, and sang off-key tunes with their iPod ear buds in. He could smell the Hudson just a few blocks away, the smell of exhaust, of street-cart souvlaki and warming pretzels. He could see the expressions in people's faces, their happiness and pain, their lust and greed, as if their intentions were written on their skin. It was as if his body had just come out of a major tune-up that accentuated his very being.

Jack knew at once what was happening. While the accident had jarred his head, affecting his memory, these symptoms were unrelated to that. They were exactly what Dr. McCourt had said might occur and that when they did, he needed to get to the hospital right away.

But that was the last place he planned on going.

As they walked out through the subway tunnel, Frank demanded that Jack stay away from the Tombs to avoid risking anyone else seeing him. He took the north-side exit and headed off to grab the car, saying he would be back within ten minutes to pick him up.

On top of that, Frank had said it was time to get some real help. While it appeared that Mia's kidnapping might be some inside job involving rogue members of the FBI, that didn't mean that he and Frank didn't have their own people they could trust. Jack wasn't sure, though; beyond Frank and Joy, he trusted no one and wasn't about to put Mia's life in any further danger.

As Jack continued down the street, he flipped up his collar, tucked his head, stooped his shoulders forward, and disappeared inside the Friday crowd. He was glad he was in the city, where the true New Yorkers kept to themselves and paid little attention to their city brethren. Jack loved the urban jungle cliché. To an outsider, it was mysterious, alluring, and frightening, with unfamiliar creatures lying in wait to pounce on unsuspecting prey that strayed from the light. But to those familiar with its confines, it was wondrous and friendly, filled with magic and life.

Maintaining heightened caution, with his senses on overdrive, he soon realized that someone else was already watching him. Jack moved across the street, using the plate-glass windows of a Barnes & Noble to catch sight of the man's reflection. He saw the large man fall into lockstep a block back.

Without a thought, Jack quickly ducked into a deli and took a seat in the back. There was no one there except two men behind the counter. He turned to watch the door. The wound in his shoulder suddenly felt as if it was on fire. The pain had been on and off throughout the morning but seemed to grow as the day went on.

"Hello, Jack."

He was shocked to see the man who had been nearly a block behind him standing there; he was heavy-set, with a receding hairline. Jack didn't know whether to run or strike, as he was trying to comprehend how the man was so quickly upon him.

"I'm not a threat, Jack. Please relax. I just need to talk to you."

The man put his right hand up in supplication as he took a seat across from Jack.

"That wasn't a smart thing, chasing that guy down." The man's voice was sympathetic as he admonished Jack like a longtime friend.

Jack continued to assess the man before him as friend or foe, thinking that either way, he might be able to help him move one step closer to Mia. "Who are you?"

"A friend of Mia's."

"Prove it."

The man smiled. "Not an easy thing. I'm James Griffin, FBI forensics."

"ID?"

Griffin shook his head. "Not on me."

"Convenient."

"Yeah, well, when I heard what happened, I rushed out to find you, spent the better part of the day looking. Been to your house, your office. I've been watching the Tombs for the last hour, figuring either you'd show up or the people who are after the case would make an appearance."

Jack had heard of the man. Mia had spoken of Jimmy Griffin on occasion as one of those brilliant minds who should have been working in a think-tank or a pharmaceutical company, making ten times his FBI salary. She admired him for his passion and for not selling out like so many others.

"I know how scared she was of what was in that evidence case." Griffin rubbed his left hand. "I know she said there was only one person she could trust with it."

"I don't know what you're talking about," Jack lied. He wasn't about to confirm anything.

"I was with her on Tuesday."

"Yeah," Jack said. "Where was that?"

"Room 1408 at the Waldorf. A murder investigation."

Jack remained silent.

"The contents of the evidence box, the things that Mia so desperately wanted hidden away, are the belongings of a Cotis priest."

Jack's heart nearly stopped. He looked around the deli, no one there except the two men behind the counter, who paid Jack no mind. He glanced at his left forearm, realizing that everything was even more connected than he had imagined.

"Do you know what's in the box?"

Jimmy nodded. "You get that box, they won't dare hurt Mia."

"Who's they?"

Jimmy shook his head. "Not sure of the players, but Mia and I knew there were some of our fellow FBI guys in the mix. Don't really know who or how many. But I can tell you this, get that box, and they will, without question, trade it for her."

"What's in the case?"

"I don't know everything, but there's a ceremonial jewel-encrusted dagger, some prayer beads, two prayer books with some interesting notes etched in them, and some images."

"What kind of images?"

Griffin paused, again rubbing his left hand. "The scary kind, the kind that makes your blood run cold and makes you wish you could forget ever seeing."

THREE DAYS EARLIER, on Tuesday afternoon, Jimmy Griffin had opened the rear door of the hotel suite and quickly ushered Mia in, closing and locking the door behind them.

The executive suites at the Waldorf were decorated to resemble a home, designed to impart a warmth and comfort not associated with travel. The sofas were plush and deep, the leather wingback chairs comfortable enough to sleep in. The separate bedrooms were more like those in a ski lodge, with large four-poster beds, piled high with thick earth-tone pillows and comforters.

Mia had received the call a half-hour earlier and had rushed up-town, telling no one where she was going, adhering exactly to Jimmy's instructions. His words in that deep, resonant voice were brief and exact. "Room 1408. Waldorf. I've got a murder. I need to see you now. Tell no one."

Mia glanced toward the second bedroom. The curtains were drawn, the darkness covering all details.

Jimmy abruptly shut the door. "You've got to see this first."

He led Mia into an elegant bathroom, white marble, a Jacuzzi and sit-down shower. But the grandeur was tainted, awash in gore. Once-white towels littered the floor, stained dark brown with dried blood. Haphazard hand- and fingerprints streaked the counters and shower walls. A pile of blood-soaked bandages lay on a soiled pair of pants and shirt in the corner.

A pocket knife and a single misshapen bullet were on the counter. Although it was deformed, an intricate pattern could still be discerned on the flattened, bloodstained casing.

Jimmy handed Mia a pair of rubber gloves. She picked up the bullet, rolling it around in the palm of her hand. The warped lettering was elaborate and detailed, not what one would expect to see on an instrument of death. The language was foreign, and even if she understood it, she doubted the twisted metal would reveal its true meaning. But as she continued to examine the bullet, what surprised her was not the etched verbiage or the fact that she was holding an object that had robbed a man of his life. It was a barely discernible pinhole in the tip and the minute black stain that ringed the tiny opening.

She looked up at Jimmy

"Yeah." Jimmy nodded as he stepped from the bathroom. "Exactly what I thought."

Mia put the bullet back on the counter and followed him out into the hallway.

"You know I'm not one for drama, Jimmy."

"You have to bear with me on this." Jimmy pursed his pale lips. There was an unnatural quiver to his voice, a stroke of nerves in the usually composed man. Mia had known Jimmy Griffin when he was still considered skinny; most people couldn't believe the portly man could ever have passed for that classification. Over the last ten years, he was always her go-to guy when she ran into a wall. Jimmy had a knack for forensics and seeing the truth beneath the mystery. She had watched as the job literally aged him from a handsome, dark-haired man of twenty-eight to a balding, overweight, and prematurely gray man of thirty-seven. It was as if every crime solved and every arrest made took a year off his life, and she feared that what he was about to show her would shed at least a decade.

"Do we have an ID on the victim?"

Jimmy nodded.

"Wealthy?" Mia asked.

"No, he's a diplomat."

Mia's concern grew.

"So you know, the windows are bulletproof, and he had no visitors."

Jimmy opened the door and flicked the wall switch. As the light washed over the room, Mia saw a man of indiscernible age. He was laid on the four-poster bed in serene repose, his face relaxed and at peace. He wore white priestly robes that wrapped his body from shoulder to ankle, and while she was unsure, they seemed more Buddhist or Hindu than Christian. He lay atop the thick, downy covers, his hands folded on his belly, his feet bare.

As she circled the bed, she looked closely at his pristine skin, a hint of Asian descent in his cheekbones and eyes. His hair was closely cropped, its dark bristle yet to know the color gray. As she walked around, she looked at the soles of his feet, noting the thick calluses of someone who had frequently forgone shoes. Leaning in, she examined his fingers and recently groomed cuticles, which showed no hint of blood or grime. His entire body was almost antiseptically clean.

Mia had seen death on too many occasions to count; it always disturbed her, marring her mood not only for the moment but also for days to come. The victims were never people who had died naturally—they were always those whose last breath had been stolen away by another. But for some reason, this death was worse. She viewed the murder of a holy man as an affront to God. As evil and wicked as mankind could be, she thought there were some boundaries that should never be crossed.

"It was as if he prepared his own body for death, knowing it was inevitable," Mia said softly as she continued to look at his body, at all sides of his head, his neck, his chest. "Where's the fatal wound?"

Jimmy walked over and grasped the white gown in his gloved hands, slowly lifting it, parting its layers to discreetly reveal the man's torso.

What Mia saw was not what she expected.

On the left side of his stomach was the torn flesh from where the bullet had been extracted.

"It's his fingerprints on the knife and the bullet," Jimmy said.

"He took it out himself?"

Mia examined the crosswise incision, where the skin had been peeled back by the victim. Mia imagined the pain was excruciating as he dug into his own stomach to pull out the bullet.

As much as the thought of operating on oneself distressed her, what she saw around the wound shocked her even more.

Circling the point of the wound, a black, threadlike ooze radiated outward beneath the skin as if it had invaded the veins, replacing blood with darkness. The inky tentacles reached out through the body, spreading death from the point where the dermis had been breached. It drifted upward over the stomach and the sternum, over the ribs and lungs, circling the region of the heart as if it was drawn there. The tone of the flesh had been obliterated by the black-stained webs that rendered the surrounding unblemished skin a pasty white.

"This man had no chance," Jimmy said. "His self-operation was nothing but a vain attempt at survival. His fate was sealed the moment the bullet pierced his flesh. I believe it was a neurotoxin from an Asian sea snake used for its slow-acting, agonizing effect; the pain must have been excruciating.

"According to the front desk, he arrived at seven o'clock. He never called down for dinner, for anything."

"What is a priest doing staying in a room like this?" Mia asked.

"No idea . . . yet."

"OK, so this is on odd murder, I see that, but you still haven't told me why you called me here," Mia said.

"You need to take this case."

"Why?"

Jimmy pointed to the long desk against the wall, the elegant dark wood covered with a host of personal effects.

Mia knew the *how* and the *what* as it concerned this man's death, but it was the *who* and the *why* that drove her for the moment. She walked over to the desk, picked up and opened a dark red passport. The image was an exact match for the dead man in the bed, issued by the Cotis government. His occupation was listed as priest/diplomat. The pages were heavily stamped over the last month: Shanghai, Sydney, Tokyo, South Africa, Italy, India, London, and Sri Lanka.

She thumbed through the effects from his pockets, which Jimmy had laid on the desk blotter. Four hundred dollars in cash, two credit cards, a gold pocket watch, and the keycard for the room. There was an open-ended plane ticket to Mumbai, a taxi receipt, and a stick of gum. From his suit-jacket pocket, there was a small quill pen and two bottles of ink, one a deep brown, the other as black as the poison that ran through his body.

On a separate table, as if placed in reverence, was a set of wooden prayer beads on a simple necklace, organic, as if they had grown in nature themselves. Beside them was a gold jewel-encrusted dagger, looking more like a piece of artwork than something of deadly purpose. There were two identical red books, each the size of a paperback novel.

Mia picked up and examined one of them; the cover was red leather, weathered from years of use. Opening the pages, she found an unfamiliar language but noted its similarity to the etching on the bullet. Thumbing through the dog-eared pages, she imagined it to be a prayer book, the text laid out in a rhythmic cadence. Each and every page was water-stained as if the book had been dipped in the ocean. She suspected the book was of sentimental value to the owner, as it appeared worn and well used. She picked up the second and found it identical in every sense, including the water-stained pages.

She finally turned and looked at Jimmy. "This isn't why I'm here," she said, as if she could read his mind.

"No, it's not," Jimmy said, avoiding her unspoken question. "Anything you see in his personal effects that gives you pause?"

She reexamined the prayer books, picking each one up in turn, flipping through the pages, fanning them as if a secret might fly out. She finally nodded. "Two things." She held up the second book, opening it to the back. "A page is torn out of the back. Judging by its condition"—she ran her finger along the frayed edge of what remained of the paper near the spine of the book—"it was recent."

"And the second thing?"

"The pages are water-stained, yet the leather cover is not."

Jimmy smiled as he nodded his head. He disappeared and returned with a wet washcloth. He took the book from her hand, laid it down, opened it to the middle, and rubbed the page. At once the foreign language of the prayer vanished, revealing a handwritten text beneath.

"I think it's a diary," Jimmy said softly.

"What's it say?"

"I don't know, but it's a hell of a place to keep secrets."

Jimmy picked up the quill from the table. He opened the black ink bottle, dipped the quill in, and wrote on a piece of paper. They both watched as the lettering dried and disappeared.

Mia took the cloth, and with a single wipe of the page, the word reappeared.

"It's like a kid's magic trick."

"Yeah, we've gotten so complex with our encryptions and pass-words that we've forgotten the best place to hide is usually in plain sight."

"Makes you wonder what was on the torn-out page."

They both paused a moment, digesting the room.

"There's a whole team on their way," Jimmy finally said. "I need you to take this stuff before they get here. Keep it to yourself. The things hidden on the pages of those two books, I believe, are far more explosive than anyone realizes. I've reached out for a translator. I'm flying him in, but he won't be here until the weekend. I need you to hide this away till then. I'll get this case classified."

"You're sounding paranoid," Mia said.

"Have you ever known me to be paranoid?"

Mia shook her head; Jimmy was anything but. He was probably the most logical, methodical man she had ever worked with.

"I need to show you something," Jimmy said.

He took the washcloth from her and picked up the second book. Turning to the last page, he quickly wiped it to reveal a list of names, written in English, all in sharp contrast to the surrounding foreign characters. The list was short, five names. Fear ran through Mia as she realized that she knew them.

"I want you to take all of this now." Jimmy picked up a two-foot-by-ten-inch evidence case and swept all of the priest's personal effects into it. "You hide it away, far from any FBI, until we can figure out what to do."

Mia nodded in agreement. If she had her way, she'd bury the box for all eternity.

"How's Jack doing?" Jimmy asked, the question seeming odd in the middle of a murder scene.

"He's good, thanks."

"When did you see him last?"

"What?" Mia asked, confusion filling her voice. "Late last night. He got home late. I left before he was even awake."

"Did you talk to him today?"

"What's going on, Jimmy? You're scaring me."

"Just answer me. When did you speak to him last?"

"Dammit, Jimmy. Ten minutes ago."

"And he's OK?"

Mia glared at him, pissed.

"Is he working any crazy cases lately?"

Mia glared at Jimmy.

"Listen, Mia, I found something. It's real disturbing. And as much as I'd like to spare you the shock, you need to see it."

"Drop the preface, and show me. I hate when people do that. Everyone has to build the drama."

Jimmy pulled out two eight-by-eleven sheets of paper, each with an intricate, lifelike drawing on it, and handed them to her.

As shocked as Mia was by the body on the bed and the names in the book, these images shook her to her core, lifelike in every respect. Her knees nearly buckled as she realized who they were of and what they represented. Without a further glance, she stuffed them into the black metal case and slammed the lid closed.

AS JACK SAT in the deli listening intently to Jimmy's every word, he leaned forward. "What were the images of?"

"I can't say," Jimmy said.

"Why?"

"Because I promised your wife I would tell no one of their existence, especially you."

"Bullshit!" Jack's arm shot out and grabbed Jimmy by the shirt. "You tell me, and you tell me now, what were they of, and why did they scare her so much?"

"Jack, they are too difficult to explain. When you get the box, you will see them for yourself, and then you will understand why I can't speak of them and why they frightened Mia."

Jack glared at Jimmy, finally releasing him. He glanced over at the two men behind the counter and saw them staring back. "Tell me the names in the book."

Jimmy shook his head. "I promised Mia for a reason. I know she is your wife, but whether you know the names will not affect your getting that metal case. Jack," Jimmy said as he stood up, "you have to get the box. I know the Tombs is under lockdown, but the people who tried to kill you are going to try to get there first. I don't know how many are coming, but if they get that case, Mia is dead."

Jimmy turned to leave but suddenly turned back.

"One other thing," he said. "The body of the priest . . . it was stolen from the morgue last night."

As baffled as Jack was by Jimmy's last comment, he brushed it off. He couldn't imagine who would steal a body. Instead, his mind focused on Mia. He couldn't fathom how he would get the case, how he would possibly penetrate the depths of the Tombs. And if he couldn't . . .

Jack buried his head in his hands, drawing them down his face as if the action would somehow wash away his nightmare.

He finally looked up . . . Jimmy was gone.

CHAPTER 22

FRIDAY, 3:30 P.M.

FRANK PARKED SEVERAL STREETS away from Jack's house, on Sniffen Road, only three hundred yards through the woods to Jack's backyard. He had dropped Joy off at her office to see if she could uncover anything in Jack's files that could lead them to Mia and picked his friend up on the corner of Broadway and John Street. Jack made no mention of his conversation with Jimmy Griffin, as Frank was already all over him for being spotted and racing off into the subway tunnels of Manhattan to get nearly killed. And besides, there was something about Jimmy that Jack couldn't put his finger on. While he gave him some insight into Mia's fear of the case and clues to what it held, he offered no further information that would really help him find her.

Against Frank's opinion, they headed back to Byram Hills, circling Jack's house to make sure there was no one there before parking on the other side of the neighborhood. Jack had a suspicion, which he wouldn't voice until he could get his hands on a file in his study. As pissed as Frank was, it was the only direction they could take at the moment, and everything aside, he trusted Jack's instinct.

They ran at a fast clip along the old logging paths that had become the haven of hikers and kids on minibikes. There were no houses along the path, and with the summertime tree canopy, the chance of being seen was minimal. They came to Jack's backyard and remained in the heavy shadow of the woods as they looked around, listening, seeing if there was any other presence beyond their own.

They both feared the FBI or worse descending on the house at any moment, if they weren't already inside.

They looked at each other and in unspoken agreement sprinted across the backyard to the rear door of Jack's workshop. They drew their pistols, quietly counted to three, and slipped through the doorway.

Jack's shop had been turned upside down. What was once an impeccably organized workshop now looked like the twisted wreckage of a junkyard—tools everywhere, cabinets turned upside down. Handmade chairs were now splintered wood scattered across the floor; the tall doors of a dark cherry armoire hung wide open, revealing an empty interior.

The small workshop off his garage was Jack's haven, his sanctuary. When the days became too much and the house full of females left him feeling outnumbered, he'd fire up the power tools and build himself a bookshelf, a stool, a puzzle box, whatever it took to clear his mind. Some people found peace through yoga or golf; he found it through Craftsman and Dewalt power tools, knotty pieces of pine, and brass hammers.

The three-inch-thick steel door on the five-foot-tall gun case was ajar, its lock drilled out. Jack pulled back the heavy door and glanced inside. The guns still lay there in their racks, the ammunition drawers sat wide open, yet nothing was missing.

Frank laid his finger on his lips and held his gun high. He and Frank bisected the door into the house. Jack gripped his pistol as he wrapped his other hand about the knob and slowly turned it pulling open the door.

Peering into the kitchen, he could see every cabinet open, food and debris scattered across the floor. Before Jack could make a move, Frank rolled into the kitchen, gun at the ready. He spun around, backing himself through the room. Jack came in close behind, his gun held high, his finger on the trigger.

Jack's eyes were drawn to the picture on the floor, the one of Mia and the girls at the beach, honest smiles on their faces. He remembered that summer day last year as if it had just happened. He could still feel the warmth of the sun on his skin, the smell of the ocean as its breeze tousled the girls' hair. He remembered it all so well.

"Hey," Frank whispered.

Jack snapped back to the moment to see Frank pointing his gun at the pantry door. He motioned Jack to take up a low position as he angled himself to the right of the doorjamb and, without warning, ripped open the door.

Fruck charged out. Frank leaped back, shocked, as the 150-pound dog nearly bowled him over before running straight to Jack.

"Jesus, you didn't tell me you got a dog," Frank said as he lowered his gun.

Jack opened the back door, hustled the dog outside, and closed the door behind him. "Sorry about that."

Jack and Frank worked their way through the house, sweeping through the rooms: master bedroom, living room, study, basement. They were all ransacked.

"Whoever it was is long gone," Jack said.

"What were they looking for?"

"The case. I'm sure they were pissed when they found out they snagged an empty one from the back of our car. Or maybe something of Mia's that might point them in the right direction."

Jack walked into the study and found that both his and Mia's computers were missing, no doubt taken by the intruders, but he wasn't too worried about that. The drawers were upended, the shelves swept clean of their pictures, books and mementos strewn on the floor. Jack leaned down and picked up the file labeled *Keeler* that the intruder had tried to steal several hours ago before hurling himself in front of a tractor-trailer. It was a medical file, with X-rays, MRIs, and information packets on death. He picked up the center drawer, inserted it back into the desk, and tucked the file away, keeping it from Frank's sight.

"Is that the file from this morning?" Frank asked.

"Yeah, it's just my boring health records and physical. Whoever came here second didn't seem to want it."

"Then what were they looking for?"

Jack turned to a tall cherry-wood armoire, its twin doors wide open, its contents of books, papers, and trinkets on the floor, leaving nothing inside. The joints were smooth and pure; the dark cherry finish was his favorite and had taken almost a month to bring to its current gloss. Jack closed the left door, latching it up while leaving the right door wide open. He stuck his hands inside, and, placing them along the back seam in just the right spot, he gave a slight push. The lock sank, and the floor panel of the case popped up, revealing a hidden compartment. Like a magic box where the magician's assistant disappears only to come back moments later, it was a trick box, a puzzle case, the kind of thing he was fond of building. Mia always mocked him. "Why build a box when you can build a *magic box?* Why build a chair when you can build a *trick chair?*"

He lifted the lid to reveal a host of files. He thumbed through them and finally found what he was looking for. The file was thick with his personal notes and research that he had gathered on a case eighteen months ago. The file was, in fact, a duplicate file, the original remaining in his city office, but he wasn't about to go near there. The files were not of a secret nature requiring lock and key, but he preferred to tuck away anything that might frighten the eyes of curious children who loved to rummage through Dad's things when he wasn't looking.

Jack looked at the small sliver of tattoo protruding from his left sleeve, written in an obscure language, from a culture not many had heard of. In all honesty, when Professor Adoy had looked at his arm and mentioned the foreign tongue earlier that day, it wasn't the first time Jack had heard of the Cotis people. He had, in fact, prosecuted and won a conviction against one of them for triple homicide and had watched as that man was executed last fall.

In the file, there was a book on the Cotis people and the history of their small Asian country. He had read it through, trying to gain insight into the man he was prosecuting, but found the book to be filled with legends, mysteries, and myths, none of which helped him in his prosecution. There was the one-page dossier on the accused, whom they never could uncover background on and, most important, the detailed evidence that damned him to death by chemical injection.

Jack closed the file, the hidden door, and the armoire. He tucked the file under his arm and walked back into the kitchen.

"You got it?'

"Yeah."

"You going to tell me what you got?"

"I think Mia's kidnapping may be connected to a case I handled a while back."

"Yeah, how do you know?"

Jack put the thick file on the counter, pulled out and opened the book on the Cotis people, specifically to a page of their language. He rolled up his sleeve and laid his arm next to it. While the lettering was on a different scale and in different coloring, there was no question: it was similar.

"And you didn't mention this before because—"

"I wanted to be sure."

"Bullshit." Frank was pissed. "You better start sharing everything that you know if you want my help. That's what partners do, remember?"

Jack nodded. "Of course, I remember."

"I'm going to get the car."

"All right, let's go—"

"No. I'll pick you up in five minutes. I need to clear my head now, thank you very much."

As Jack watched Frank angrily walk out the side door, he closed the Cotis file. He looked again at his arm, the brown intricate writing continuous around his skin from elbow to wrist.

He thought himself insane for not remembering where it came from, how something so intricate could be applied, yet he had no memory of it. And as he continued to stare, he wondered whether Professor Adoy's translation was accurate. Maybe there was more to what was written than either of them realized.

Jack loved Greek mythology but was obsessed with puzzles and mysteries. It was what inspired him in his job, trying to unwrap the unknown, piecing together evidence into a coherent story, into the truth. Now he was the mystery.

He had been intrigued by puzzles since he was a child and started creating his own around the age of seventeen. It started out with word problems, progressed to numeric puzzles and then on to mechanical puzzles, those impossible metal knots. He would build wooden cubes of twenty pieces that fit together like a glove, his work progressing into hidden compartments in the furniture he crafted, puzzle boxes for his children to solve, where once they found the secret drawer, a gift would be waiting inside.

As Jack stared at his arm, he realized that he was within one of his own puzzles, trying to find his way out. While he remembered images of the man on the riverbank the night before, nothing else was forthcoming. He still had no idea how he was stitched up, how he got home.

And his senses . . . he felt as if he was in a hyperreality. Everything he looked at seemed brighter, richer; all of the sounds, no matter how far away, were clearer, the birds outside, Fruck panting as he ran around the yard. But with every hour, Jack felt as if his mind was failing him more and more.

He heard a noise at the side door. He quickly rolled down his sleeve and grabbed his gun off the counter.

As he spun around, he was faced with the last person he thought he would see.

"Jesus, you scared the shit out of me," Jack said.

His father stood there in the doorway. A moment passed as father and son looked at each other.

Jack and his father had never really gotten along, sometimes going almost a year without speaking. And it was something everyone was well aware of. Their friends and family had grown used to their constant fighting and intermittent estrangements and had tried to mediate between the two on too many occasions, finally leaving them to their own arguments, devices, and silence.

But this moment was different, his father's eyes holding a hint of uncharacteristic warmth.

"I think I'm losing my mind," Jack said.

David Keeler stared at him, the moment hanging there like a death knell, before he finally shook his head. "No, you're not."

Jack's father walked into the kitchen and stood across the counter from him.

As much as his father denied it, Jack could feel his mind unhinging. "I've always had the best memory. I can remember back to the womb, for Christ's sake." Jack paused, pulling up his sleeve. "Look at this. I can't remember getting it; I can't remember what happened after the accident. What is happening to me?"

David reached across the table and gently took his son's arm, turning it over, studying the tattoo before shaking his head. "I don't know. But I can tell you there is so much in this world that doesn't make sense and probably never will."

The two looked at each other. His father still held his arm. Jack could feel the warmth from him, something he hadn't felt since he was a child.

"So, any word on Mia?" David asked as he finally released Jack's arm.

"No." Jack looked at the file on the counter. "And I can't help thinking this is my fault."

"That's bullshit, and you know it. Stop feeling guilty and sorry for yourself."

"Sorry for myself?" Jack snapped.

"Yeah, the more time you sit wallowing in self-pity, the less time you have to save your wife." David paused. "How are you feeling?"

"What do you mean?"

"I'm your father; I see it in your eyes."

"I'm worried for my wife."

"How sick are you?" David asked, in a tone of concern that Jack didn't remember ever hearing in his father's voice. "Your mother noticed it this morning, but she's always been one to avoid difficult conversations."

"Unlike you, who can't allow a thought not to pass your lips?"

"You know I don't dance around tough topics."

"The more time we sit around talking about that, the less time I'll have to save Mia."

David stared at his son.

"With this hole in my memory . . . I think I'm losing my grip on reality—"

"Reality is all a matter of perspective, Jack. There's the reality of history books, which both you and I know is always fine-tuned. There is the individual reality that we each experience when observing an incident. Think of how often you get a reliable witness on the stand who tells an entirely different story from your star witness, even though both individuals were standing in the same room and both are sure of what they've seen."

Jack absorbed his father's words, looking closer at the man he hadn't seen in six months. "Why did you come back?"

"It was shouted to the world this morning that you and Mia were dead. Turns out she's missing, you're sick—though you don't want to admit it—and we both know that if someone killed you once and failed, they'll be trying again. You need me," his father said simply.

"Why?"

"Who else tells you when you're screwing up, tells you when you're wrong? I'm here to set your head straight, tell you that you can do this, and watch over your girls."

"Yeah, and if you came back to watch over them, why are you here talking to me?"

"Your mother is capable, and the man at the end of our driveway, the guy Frank sent, has an eye on them. And with respect to why I'm here—because you're my son, and as I've heard it, some fathers and sons talk."

"Look." Jack felt his guilt building. "I said some things . . ."

"Yeah, you sure did," David said. Jack waited for him to admit some culpability, but that wasn't forthcoming. "We're not going to waste time on those issues. Let's stay focused on getting Mia. I can't imagine what you're feeling, the fear, the worry and anxiety, but remember, this is where you thrive. No one thinks clearer under stress than you. When you were a kid, you were so good under pressure; it's what made you such a strong goalie. With games riding on your shoulders, no one was better at protecting the net, no matter how many shots were fired at you. You carried that talent into every aspect of your life.

"And this is hard to admit: you never listened to me about sports, school, your career. And you know what? You were right. You were right every time. You always listened to your heart, to that voice inside you. Listen to it now. Embrace the pressure as you've always done. It makes you think clearer, it allows you to see solutions where others don't." David paused. "You'll find Mia. Trust in yourself. I do."

Jack looked as his father, his words filling him with confidence.

"Jack," his father said, "let's keep this conversation between us. We wouldn't want people to get the wrong idea, especially your mother."

David patted Jack's shoulder, and it might as well have been a hug.

Jack smiled and nodded. "Thanks."

"I'll be watching over the girls," David said as he headed out the door. "You go find your wife."

Jack's cell phone rang, startling him. He didn't dare answer it unless it was Frank or Joy. He glanced at the caller ID, and his heart leaped. He couldn't answer Mia's call fast enough.

"Hello, Jack," the voice said.

"Who is this?"

"I see we've both risen from the dead."

Jack knew the voice instantly, the deep, haunting tone, the polished accent.

"You sent me to die, Jack. Not sure how *you* survived, but I guess you're wondering the same about me. You can stop wondering where Mia is. I've got her. She is so beautiful. Her hair dark like the night, her eyes filled with emotion, all kinds of emotion. And her smell, do you remember her smell?"

"You lay one hand on her—"

"Who says I haven't already? And there's not a thing you can do about it."

"I don't know how you're alive—"

"I guess it's fate that we're both alive, because I sure wouldn't call it coincidence. Cute trick keeping an empty evidence case in the car. Was that your idea or your wife's?"

"What are you talking about?"

"I got your note, Jack."

"What note?" Jack said in total confusion.

"I know you like puzzles and playing games, but I can assure you, this is no game."

Jack was silent, perplexed at the man's words. He hadn't written any note, let alone had any clue this man could possibly be alive.

"You know what I want, Jack, and you're going to get it for me."

"Not a chance."

"Oh, there's every chance. You and I, Jack, are going to get it together. A little match-up, a partnership between the executed and the executioner. Mr. DA is about to break every law in his little law book."

Jack looked down at the file on his kitchen counter. He knew exactly who was on the other end of the line. He had studied him, tried him, convicted him and, on April 15 of last year, watched as Nowaji Cristos, the man on the phone, was executed.

CHAPTER 23

"Hello," Frank said into his cell phone as he got into the car.

"Frank, Matt Daly."

"Hey."

"No bodies yet; we've got a torn shirt, probably Jack's," Matt said.

Frank had completely forgotten about Matt Daly's team dragging the river.

"Listen," Frank said, "you've got to do me a favor. Try to keep things from the press as long as you can. And keep it local. Byram Hills cops only. Think you can do that?"

"I'll do my best. We're working toward the spillway, probably eight hours before we reach it. Though there's a good chance their bodies could be hung up in the rocks."

"Thanks."

"And Frank, there's a bullet hole in the shirt, right above the heart. This was no accident."

"I know."

"I thought you'd say that. You're digging into this, aren't you?"

Frank's silence answered the question.

"I'll keep things under wraps as long as I can," Matt said. "You need any more help, you call me."

"Thanks again." Frank hung up the phone, slammed the door, and started the Jeep.

JACK LEAPED INTO the Audi. He looked at the gas gauge, near empty, and shook his head before he drove out of the driveway as fast as he could, the garage door auto-closing behind him. He headed east down Banksville Road, in the opposite direction that Frank would be coming from. Frank went out the door pissed and would arrive back any minute even more pissed when he found out that Jack had slipped away again. But Jack wasn't going to risk Mia's life by involving Frank or anyone else in what he was about to do.

Jack was on his way to meet a dead man. He had wondered what in his life had set him on this path. Was there a singular moment that made this day inevitable? Was it karma, fate, payback for a bad decision in his youth?

His mind jumped back to that night so many years ago when Apollo died, when he killed those two teens. He thought about the promise to himself never to kill again. He thought of how hard he had dedicated himself to fighting crime without a gun, doing whatever it took to get a conviction.

While he was so disturbed by the deaths in that loft building, the lives he took, the life he couldn't save, swearing off his gun, he realized that he didn't need the gun to kill. He had done it with the power of the justice system. And while he felt it was justified and within the constraints of the laws of the state, he had still taken the life of a man.

Now that man, Nowaji Cristos, had somehow returned and was exacting his revenge.

CHAPTER 24

ON FEBRUARY 8 TWO years ago, Nowaji Cristos lay prone above UN Plaza, his left eye nuzzled into the gun sight of the Israeli-made Galil sniper rifle. Dressed in a blue maintenance worker's jumper, his long black hair pulled tightly into a ponytail, he stared down, watching the motorcade's approach. Cristos knew that the escort by New York City cops on motorcycles was only for show, a gesture to make the Pashir general and ruler feel important, to boost the already oversized ego of a diminutive military man who rose to power through a coup d'état two years earlier.

The general was of little significance to the world order. His small jungle country had not moved much beyond colonial times, but he had grown to be a nuisance to certain countries' national interests, with his border skirmishes with Cotis, India, and Bangladesh, military posturing, and the nationalization of private companies—nationalization being his word for personal take-over. And so certain affected parties turned to Cristos, a man with a one-hundred-percent success rate, whose face was not known to the world and whose chosen name meant "the risen ghost."

Those who hired Cristos never imagined that he knew General Gjwain. He knew him as the ruthless, Napoleonic sadist who had killed his own family so as to inherit the family farm; he knew him as the man with not one iota of courage, military training, or experience who decorated his chest with medals of valor and bravery. Cristos knew Gjwain as the insignificant man who lived across the border not fifty miles from Cristos's place of birth, a man who was disappearing those who disagreed with him or stood in his way.

Cristos was a man without conscience, but he thought if he ever had one, it would not be burdened by his coming actions. In fact, he considered it a magnanimous gesture to the people who shared his heritage to remove the depraved ruler. He had accepted the job at his usual rate, but it wasn't about the money. It never was for Cristos. It was about the challenge, testing his skills, pushing his limits. In the end, if it did not raise his game, he would never accept, walking away in search of a new quest.

As the small general exited the black limo, his silver and gold medals glinting in the bright winter sun, Cristos lined up his gun sight, the cross hairs bisecting the diminutive man's buzz-cut head. He adjusted for the three-mph cross wind and the dry winter air. He wrapped his fingers around the trigger as he had so many times before, fully exhaled, long and slow, purging his body and mind, tuning his focus. He took a half-breath, held it. And finally pulled the trigger.

Cristos rolled over into a crouch behind the parapet wall and out of sight of the world. He quickly broke down the rifle as he moved, and he had it stowed by the time he arrived at the bulkhead door.

He stripped off the blue jumper to reveal a charcoal-gray pin-striped suit, custom-tailored over a powerful body. He looked every part the nouveau-riche Wall Street banker, with his blue iridescent tie, polished cap-toe shoes, and perfect ponytail, as he walked down the stairs to the thirty-third floor and entered apartment 33A.

The apartment belonged to Naveed and Jasmine Bonsley, a society couple who had emigrated from India forty years earlier and had amassed a fortune from thirteen pharmaceutical patents they held. Their four-million-dollar apartment had nine rooms with a view of the East River and a southerly view of Lower Manhattan.

The Bonsleys were in bed in the other room and had been all morning. They had been out the night before, arriving home after midnight to find Cristos sitting in a club chair and staring out the window.

Confused and impaired by too much champagne, Naveed questioned the man as his wife reached for the phone, but her fingers never made their way to the dial. With primal speed, Cristos burst out of the chair, his hand snapping out, grabbing her thin neck and lifting her six inches off the floor. Naveed stood there in panic as Jasmine's frail legs uselessly kicked the air, her hands wrapping around her assailant's as she struggled to breathe.

Cristos carried the fifty-five-year-old woman through the living room, past the dining room, to the master bedroom, flinging her about like a rag doll. He finally gripped her shoulder with his other hand and in a single move snapped her neck. He flung her to the bed, where her limbs splayed out as her dead eyes stared off.

Naveed ran to her side, clutching her, screaming her name as tears flooded his face. He turned to see Cristos above him and didn't flinch, didn't move—he just wanted it to end, to be reunited with his dead wife.

With the morning sun pouring in, Cristos looked out the living-room window to the south toward the entrance to the UN, where police had swarmed the area and cordoned off First Avenue. He knew the drill: they would fan out in hopes of finding the killer but knew he was probably long gone, lost in the city of eight million plus, never suspecting that he was five hundred yards away, looking down on them with the confidence of accomplishment and continued freedom.

Cristos stepped into the elevator, hitting the button for the ground floor. As the polished brass doors closed, he stared at his reflection, adjusting the small knot of his tie. His face was pure, unblemished, a façade to the world in so many ways.

His private charter was scheduled to leave the Westchester airport upon his arrival, and with the half-hour drive, he estimated wheels up for 11:15. The six-hour transatlantic flight would put him back home before midnight local time. He was exacting in all areas of life, planning, timing, playing out every scenario in his mind before engaging in any task, be it the purchase of a new Bugatti, making personal investments, or committing murder. While he had used the rifle that day—leaving it on the bed between the Bonsleys' cold bodies to taunt and confuse the authorities—he had engaged in all manners of dispensing death: poisons, accidents, knives slipped between the ribs of unsuspecting marks. There were assassinations of subterfuge and grandeur: politicians dying of heart attacks in the throes of illicit passion; crime figures sitting in Parisian cafés torn asunder by horrific explosions of world-headline proportions; prime ministers' wives trapped in their cars as they tumbled down mountainsides.

And all the while, there was never a single piece of evidence tying back to Cristos. Credit was never taken, responsibility never assigned. His disparate methods never allowed the connecting of any dots. Too often, in so many jobs, pride was the greatest enemy. When credit was taken, egos were inflated, dulling the mind, softening drive.

The feeling of invincibility flowed in with such delusions of grandeur, and while they might not prove life-threatening to an ad exec, it was deadly to someone like Cristos.

When he arrived last night, slipping past the sleeping concierge, he stepped into the elevator, confident that his image wouldn't be picked up by the security camera. The small device in his pocket emitted a magnetic pulse that interfered with the circuitry of the camera. It was of Israeli design, the Mosad having developed it to help them hide under a cloak of invisibility. Now, as he rode toward the lobby, he dug his hand into his pocket, running it over the small matchbook-sized device.

But all of the planning and preparation in the world cannot eliminate pure chance. Sometimes the wheels of fate turn in different ways. And in such a manner, the bearings on the counterweight cable of the elevator wore out with a belabored squeal, fusing themselves under the grinding pressure, bringing the cab that Cristos was riding in to a halt.

At the same time, a tall, matronly woman named Charlotte Newman arrived at the concierge desk, flowers in hand and a small elegant gift box under her arm. She was there to surprise her friend Jasmine Bonsley for her birthday and to whisk her off to a surprise-filled day of massages, facials, and lunch.

The cab was out of service for all of two minutes when the maintenance staff entered the shaftway one floor above the crippled elevator to make sure that none of their elderly tenants was in the car. With no video feed, no one was going to take the chance of some senior having a claustrophobic panic attack because of faulty security equipment.

But when they pried open the sixteenth-floor door and peered down the shaft onto the car ten feet below, they saw the impeccably dressed man climbing up through the emergency hatch, a man none of them recognized, a man who was now trapped with nowhere to go in the thirty-five-story shaftway.

With the sudden radio call about the horror found inside apartment 33A by Charlotte Newman happening in conjunction with the mayhem out in front of the UN, you didn't need a detective to put the pieces together.

The headlines screamed of the arrest of Nowaji Cristos, the murderer of the head of state of Pashir and the executioner of a wealthy couple in their bed. The New York City police were praised by all for apprehending the criminal so quickly. But as he was arrested, no one had any real idea who they had in custody or the atrocities he had committed the world over.

And so the man who had remained invisible to mankind, who killed without witness, who walked the world like a ghost, was brought down by the failure of a handful of twenty-cent ball bearings and an overeager best friend.

TWELVE HOURS LATER, under cover of darkness, a four-boat flotilla headed out to Trudeau Island. The boats were driven without running lights, their captains aided by infra-red goggles as they peered through the cold night.

Jack rode out with Peter Womack, the U.S. attorney for the Southern District. He knew him well; following parallel ascending career paths, they had worked together on several cases, even sharing dinner, with their wives, on occasion. While many complained about friction between the state and federal levels, none of that existed between Peter and Jack.

The evidence against the assassin was overwhelming. They had the rifle, the bodies, Cristos in the building at the time of incident, and while there were no prints, the circumstantial evidence was undeniable. The interim Pashir government, although secretly happy about the death of the despot, pressed for an expedient trial and execution, blaming the New York City police for the failure to protect their leader. The city of New York cried out for justice for the Bonsleys, and the public demanded a trial on the world stage to show that you don't mess with New York.

The debate facing them was whether to charge Cristos on the local, federal, or military level. As an enemy combatant, he would not be afforded the rights of an American citizen, but this alternative, while satisfying the Pashir government, would not provide needed justice to the city of New York. If there were separate trials—the general's murder in federal and the couple's by the state—the matter could drag on for years with independent resulting appeals, but if the matters were handled concurrently, swift justice could be served, satisfying all concerned.

The four boats pulled up to a long, deep water dock on the eastern side of the island. The varied topography of the small spit of land was mostly undulating hills of old-growth trees and scattered bedrock. The North Shore was truly a misnomer, as there was no shore, just a sixty-foot sheer dropoff onto a rocky, riptide sea. A once-grand lighthouse stood on a precipice, holding court with its outstretched hand of guiding light to the now-diminished fishing fleets returning home. The western and southern sides of the island were large, sandy beaches that would be the envy of any Hamptons resident and would fetch in the tens of millions for a fraction of their white sand and magnificent views, if not for the large stretch of graveyard just beyond the scrub and tree line, a potter's field of forgotten dead.

Jack and Peter watched as the twelve-man lead team of police, FBI, and Justice Department personnel disembarked and disappeared into the shadows of the windswept island to prep and secure the vacant facility.

From the second boat, four guards in black military fatigues, pistols strapped to their waists and rifles on their backs, climbed down onto the dock. The four turned as Cristos emerged from the boat's cabin with shackled wrists and leg irons around his ankles. The four guards flanked him as he shuffled down the gangway, and they, too, disappeared, swallowed by the cold night.

Jack and Peter, dressed in heavy winter coats, finally leaped from the boat as the two Justice Department guards tied it up.

A large man in a black pinstriped suit greeted Jack with an outstretched hand. "Special Agent Carter Dorran, FBI."

Carter stood just over six feet, a commanding presence in both stature and voice, with a deep tone that his fellow agents mocked behind his back. Despite the weather, he wore no coat and seemed unaffected by the elements.

"Jack Keeler," Jack said as he shook his hand.

Dorran helped his agents secure the unmarked powerboat and turned to Jack. "Please excuse the formality, but we need your ID and to check your person."

Jack smiled, his breath coming out in great clouds. He fully understood the procedure. He pulled out his wallet, flipped it open, and displayed the two-year-old picture. At Dorran's nod, Jack extended his arms out, allowing him to run his hands up and down his body in the usual manner. Jack looked at Peter, who was enduring the same treatment, smiling at the irony; neither had ever been on this side of a pat-down.

Under the glow of a full moon, Jack looked up at the mansion in the distance. The enormous Georgian-style house, made of fieldstone quarried from the island's bedrock, was more than twenty-five thousand square feet and was entirely self-sufficient, with a power plant, a water desalination station, and a communication center all installed in the late '70s when the mansion had seen extensive use as a classified government facility. Being off the radar, the island and the once-magnificent home were the perfect location to be forgotten. During the first half of the '80s, it had been used for everything from a safe house to a refuge for Russian defectors at the end of the Cold War. In recent years, its location and function had fallen off even the radar of the government.

Dorran led Jack and Peter up the gangway and ushered them into a waiting golf cart. He drove up the long cobblestone pathway, the sides of which were overgrown with knee-high grass and weeds that poked up through a dusting of snow. Several felled trees, evidence of hurricane season, had yet to be removed, their haphazard patterns adding to the ominous appearance of the mostly wooded island. The enormous Georgian mansion was overrun with ivy that wove and flittered along its stone, giving it a Gothic feel.

A belching choke filled the night, as a generator muscled to life in the distance. And almost immediately, lights around the estate began to go from a dull orange, intensifying like the rising sun, into a full glow. The shadows around the mansion were chased away as walkway lights and decorative sconces flanking the entranceway lit the stone home into a semblance of its former glory.

Arriving in the circular courtyard, Jack and Peter hopped out of the cart and walked past two large stone lions that flanked the slate step and led to an enormous mahogany entrance door.

The choice of venue was Jack's, which Peter, the FBI, and the Justice Department quickly agreed to in order to avoid the prying eyes of the press, or worse. It was the perfect location to hold Nowaji Cristos, the perfect place to conduct his interrogation.

Jack followed Dorran and Peter through the large doors and couldn't help pausing in wonder, looking around the place that only existed in his dreams, a place that had sat two miles from his childhood home. It had lived in his imagination, in tales from a bygone era, when high society arrived in magnificent yachts for weekend parties that dragged on all summer. He couldn't help picturing flappers and Gatsby types dancing until dawn, sipping champagne, the jazz band never tiring.

He had only seen the island from the perspective of sandy beaches and the overgrown graves in the potter's field on the far side. He had never thought that the grandeur might exceed his imagination. The marble foyer was cavernous, his footsteps echoing off the decorative floors and dark-paneled walls. Dual staircases mirrored each other, their polished banisters and maroon carpeted stairs leading up to fourteen bedrooms.

As they walked, Jack peered into the library, an Old World room wrapped in floor-to-ceiling shelves filled with books and ghostly mementos of those long gone. The fireplace was enormous, speaking of an age before furnaces and heat. The oversized mantel and the shelves and furniture were caked with dust.

They walked past a billiard room and a parlor, through a chef's kitchen that hadn't known the smell of food in years, and came to a stop in the rear service hall.

"Bit of a surreal setting," Peter said.

"Yeah, especially when the ghosts from the potter's field come out and you realize you're isolated on this island."

"Did you get a look at this guy yet?" Jack asked. "Any sense of what we're dealing with?"

"There is something in his eyes. A coldness. I don't know if he's practiced the look or it comes natural." Dorran shook his head. "Cute name, Nowaji Cristos, loosely translated as 'risen ghost.'"

"Nice," Jack said. "Safe to say that's not the name his mama gave him. Is this guy stable, or are we thinking he's going to play the insane card?"

"The docs will check him out, but I don't think he's insane at all. A sociopath, yeah, but his mind knows what he is doing. There is no disconnect."

"Do we have a file on him yet?" Jack asked.

"Beyond a name, we've got nothing else," Dorran said. "No intelligence, background, nothing. CIA, Interpol, all came up blank so far."

"No one has spoken to him, correct?"

"He was taken into federal custody, under my orders," Peter said. "Not a word was said."

"Think he was working alone?"

"Yes and no. He's a hired gun. Someone was paying his way, though he seems too fastidious, too confident, to rely on any accomplice. Weapon, clothes, watch, all expensive but untraceable."

"Any thought on who hired him?"

"CIA sent an operations officer; he's here somewhere. He's the expert on the political machinations of Pashir."

"He's not going to try to jockey for position, is he?"

"No, within our borders, it's just you, me, and Dorran's FBI," Peter said. "Consider him a source for all the things you can't find on Google."

"Seriously," a thin, prematurely balding twenty-five-year-old said as he came out of a side room. "I'm reduced to human search engine?"

"Cyril Latham," Dorran said as he pointed at Jack and Peter. "Womack and Keeler."

Latham handed them each a file. They quickly scanned them as they continued to walk. Peter finally looked up and said, "So, this guy he killed, this general, he's a despot?"

Latham nodded. "The list of people who wanted him dead is long. We're running ballistics against both ours and Interpol's database. We're cross-referencing everything Carter has given us against the world stage. This guy was bad news. The only person who would truly mourn him is his mother, but he killed her years ago."

"Nice," Peter said.

"As terrible as the general was," Latham said, "the United States has an international obligation to try this man."

"And the Pashir government isn't looking for extradition?"

"They barely have laws," Latham said, "let alone a judicial system. They want him tried and hung on our soil so as not to create a martyr or make a mistake."

"And the CIA's position on him?" Peter asked.

"Unless we can somehow tie him to some other activity, Director Turner will not stand in your way. He's currently an unknown to us."

"I suggest the three of us do the initial interrogation," Peter said to Jack and Dorran. "Let's see where this goes."

"I'll lead," Carter said. "Feel free to interject, ask questions, whenever you want."

Jack was actually a very skilled interrogator; he was good at getting people to speak, whether it be on the stand, in an interrogation room, or at a party, but he was happy to defer and step in when needed.

A man approached from the opposite end of the hall.

"This is Alex Casey," Dorran said, introducing Jack to the red-haired FBI agent.

"Mr. Casey will escort us and remain during the interrogation."

Jack looked the man over. He was dressed in dark loose-fitting clothes, not the usual dark suit and tie or blue windbreaker of the FBI. Like the other guards, he had a Sig Sauer 9mm pistol at his side, while an HK submachine gun was strapped over his shoulder. Casey possessed the lean, strong body of a swimmer, his eyes focused and alert. There was no question about the man's abilities.

Casey slipped his key into the lock, opened the door, and ushered Dorran, Peter, and Jack into a dark room. The only source of light leaked through enormous red velvet curtains that had been drawn across a picture window.

Casey flipped a switch, flooding the room with a harsh, bright light courtesy of a temporary flood in the corner of what was now seen to be a parlor. The walls were covered in chintz wallpaper, the floor in wall-to-wall burgundy carpet. A guard stood silently in the corner, his rifle clutched tightly against his chest.

All furniture had been stripped away except for a metal table in the center of the room and several hard wood chairs. Casey drew back the curtains, revealing an eerily lit backyard, the leaf-filled pool, a tennis court with a torn net. The picture window was obscured by a chain-link fence that reached from floor to ceiling; its galvanized metal links stood in sharp contrast to the room's décor.

In the center of the room sat Cristos in a large wooden high-backed chair, his wrists cuffed to the thick oak arms, his ankles chained to the heavy legs. He was dressed in the dark charcoal-gray suit he was captured in; the knot of his blue tie was perfect. His hair was pulled back in a ponytail. The day's growth on his face only served to enhance his ominous appearance, which agitated even the guards. It was as if they had caged Satan and were awaiting his retribution.

But it was his eyes that disturbed Jack the most. They were dark, malevolent, and fixed on Jack, like a predator lying in wait to strike down its innocent prey. He studied Jack for several seconds before turning his assessing eyes on Peter and Dorran.

Casey walked backward, practically disappearing into the corner. He spun his rifle forward, gripping it tightly to his chest, thumbing off the safety as if to send a message.

The three sat down before Cristos, Dorran in the middle, Peter to his left, Jack to his right.

"I am Special Agent Carter Dorran. You are in the custody of the United States government and the state of New York and are being charged with murder. This is Peter Womack from the U.S. Justice Department." Carter pointed at Peter and then at Jack. "And Jack Keeler, the DA from New York City. Would you like an attorney?"

"Not yet," Cristos said softly.

"Understand that our legal system provides—"

"You should be aware that I understand your judicial process as well as, if not better than, you." Cristos spoke as if he wasn't bound, as if he wasn't being interrogated, as if he was before a legal committee in a large corporation.

"Do you wish to offer a confession," Dorran said, "or should we proceed?"

Cristos nodded.

"Can you explain what you were doing in that building's elevator shaft?"

"No," Cristos answered.

"Were you in the Bonsleys' apartment?"

As Dorran continued his questioning, Jack opened the file and examined the images of the dead general, a single bullet hole above his left eye; of the Bonsleys' laid out against each other, their heads tilted at odd, impossible angles. Jack fought the sour feeling in his stomach, trying to hide the emotion from his face.

While most would succumb to the horror and reality of death, of brutal murder, their minds overcome with grief and revulsion, Jack was different. Anger had arisen in him at the violation of the most basic tenet of human existence.

As he continued listening to the line of questioning, in a slow reveal of emotion, Cristos smiled as he glimpsed Jack's reaction.

"You killed a head of state," Peter said. "Was this on behalf of a foreign government?"

Cristos took a deep breath and turned his full attention to Jack. "Mr. Keeler is the most skilled man in the room, yet he is silent."

Peter paused a moment before continuing. "Are you working on behalf—"

"I'm only going to have a conversation with one of you," Cristos said, still staring at Jack.

"You don't dictate how this interrogation goes," Dorran said.

Cristos glanced at Jack's wedding ring. "Married?"

Jack didn't respond.

"Children?" Cristos paused. "Children are amazing. They make us see the world from a whole new perspective. They teach us patience, tolerance, and sacrifice."

Jack stared at Cristos, assessing him, letting him continue.

"It's interesting how every child starts off innocent," Cristos continued, "but each follows a different path. Some become men like you; some become men like the general; some become like me." Cristos paused. "Do you think it's fate, someone pulling strings, or do we choose our own path?"

Jack had conducted too many interrogations to count. There were moments to listen, moments to speak, moments to challenge, and moments to play mind games. He knew the personality types: the passive-aggressive who attacked with charm; the ultraviolent whose rage was obvious and explosive; the compliant and cooperative who answered every question without hesitation, weaving stories on the spot that they believed as much as they hoped the interrogator would. And then there were the types like Cristos.

"What you did today was monstrous," Jack finally said.

Cristos leaned forward, becoming more attentive.

"In the last twenty-four hours," Jack continued, "you took three lives."

"And how many did I save in the process?"

"Save?" Jack asked with a raised brow.

"How many people would have died at the order of the general just in the next month?"

"So your defense is that you killed three to save more?" Dorran said, trying to reenter and resume control of the conversation. "Well, that's not how it works."

Cristos ignored Dorran and spoke directly to Jack. "When a soldier, a military man, kills another man, when a fighter jet drops a bomb destroying a village, it's for honor and country. But when an individual kills, it is called murder. Why is that?"

"Don't equate war with this," Jack said.

"We're all at war in some way or another. Some people use their words to fight, to tear the opposition apart emotionally. Others"—Cristos tilted his head at Jack and Peter—"use their legal system of laws, to take down and destroy their opponents' freedom and security. And others forgo destroying the character, choosing just to eliminate the individual altogether."

"Did the Bonsleys deserve to die?"

"Do the people in a poor village where an errant bomb was dropped deserve to die? Dispatching death in a war, when a country deems it necessary to success, is understood by humanity, but when it deals in eliminating a single man, when the public doesn't understand its purpose, it's horrific, shocking, evil."

"Did you kill those three people today?" Jack asked.

Cristos smiled. "You're going to have to do at least a little work here, Jack. Let me ask you a question. Are you the type who is more interested in justice, truth, or an eye for an eye?"

Jack said nothing.

"Could you look me in the eye and kill me so others might live? Put your lawyerly self aside. Could you be the hangman? Hold the pistol to my head and pull the trigger to save lives?" Cristos paused, waiting for Jack to answer. "I didn't think so. It's always so much easier from behind the curtain, pulling other people's strings to do your bidding. Well . . . I just think you should know, if you asked me the same question, I'd have no problem laying that pistol right up against your temple and pulling the trigger."

"Too bad you'll never get that chance. You no longer have control of any strings."

"You think you're in control here." Cristos smiled. "But are you?"

Jack stared at him.

"Do you know whom to trust? You don't think I've been captured before? You don't think I have ever escaped?" Cristos smiled again. "Always remember, control is tenuous at best."

"I'll remember that," Jack said with a placating tone as he looked at Cristos's chains.

The two men studied each other, the moment drawing out.

"OK," Dorran said. "I think—"

"I was in love once." Cristos ignored Dorran, cutting him off.

"And she loved you in return?" Jack asked.

"She died before I ever knew the truth."

"Is that supposed to make me sympathetic?"

"No, just a reminder." Cristos looked at Jack's wedding ring. "We never know how long we have with the ones we love."

Anger flowed into Jack's face, wiping his calm away as he realized that he had let Cristos lead the conversation. "We're done," Jack said as he stood up. Dorran and Peter followed his lead.

"Are we going to finish our conversation?" Cristos said.

"You are being charged with the murder of three individuals," Jack said as he looked into Cristos's dark eyes. "We have every intention to try, convict, and see you executed for the deeds you have done. Your smugness, your overconfidence, will only help me make this happen quicker."

Jack turned and headed for the door.

"I'd hold tight to your wife and kids," Cristos said. "God knows what might happen if a monster like me ever got hold of them."

JACK, PETER, AND Dorran silently walked through the grand mansion, past the library and the parlor; this time, the rooms didn't even register.

"What do you think?" Peter asked.

"This guy is far more than I or anyone thinks," Jack said.

"Meaning?"

"Hired gun, very cool, and very experienced. He has a résumé we probably couldn't even fathom." Jack looked at Dorran "Think we can tie him to anything else?"

"No. Not yet, at least," Dorran said. "The fact that we caught him is pure luck."

"Then let's get him formally charged and on trial," Peter said.

"State or fed?" Dorran asked.

"State will be quicker," Peter said to Jack. "If we get him convicted, the fed can wave off. Do you think your office can get a conviction?"

"Yeah, and I'll make sure he hangs."

SIX MONTHS LATER, Jack was sitting in the viewing theater at Cronos Correctional Facility in upstate New York. Although the state had reinstituted the death penalty two years before, not a single execution had been carried out.

But this matter was different. Convicted after a three-week trail, Cristos waived his right to appeal, demanding that his sentence of death by injection be carried out immediately. Although the liberal left had cried out to spare his life, he spat in their faces and railed against anyone who stood in the way of his execution. Cristos did have a final request: he wished to speak to Jack Keeler alone.

Against the advice of all, against the advice of Peter, Carter Dorran, Mia, Frank and everyone else he trusted, Jack walked out of the viewing room and was escorted down to death row, which was in a dark, windowless basement.

There had been no one to come forth for Cristos, no family, no friends; in fact, not a single person in the world stood up and said they even knew the man. He requested no priest, rabbi, monk. In fact, like everything about him, no one knew if he even had a religion.

As vile a man as Jack thought him to be, as dangerous as this man without a soul was, everyone deserved a last request, a final statement before dying.

Jack entered the basement cell to find Cristos sitting on the bed, his legs and arms chained. He was dressed in a deep blue suit, no tie or belt, and wore a pair of black Gucci loafers, looking as if he was about to go out for a fancy dinner. While the condemned were usually put to death in their prison uniform, Cristos had asked and was granted the right to die in his favorite suit.

He made no move as Jack sat in the chair across from him, their eyes settling on each other. The silent moment held; each could hear the other's breathing, the committer and the committed.

"How's the weather today?" Cristos asked in his low, accented voice.

Jack was surprised at the question. "Sunny, clear, a warm fall day."

Cristos nodded. "Did it occur to you what is happening here today?"

Jack said nothing, letting the condemned man say his last words.

"Jack, you accused me of murder, of ending lives, yet you are doing the same."

"This is your sentence for the lives you have taken."

"I asked you before, could you pull the trigger, Jack?"

Jack remained silent.

"I understand many years ago, your partner died and that you killed two people, children, I believe."

Jack felt his heart fall in his chest.

"Were you condemned for that? Did anyone hold you accountable for their deaths?"

"It wasn't like that," Jack hated that he was explaining himself to this man.

"Was it more like collateral damage in doing your job?"

"The Bonsleys weren't collateral damage."

"Oh, yes, they were. In order to stop a very wicked man. Even you have to admit after learning about that general that he deserved to die, that his death saved countless others. I bet you would have loved to put him on trial in your courts after all of the murders he committed."

"Is this how you wanted to spend your last moments? Imparting some kind of guilt?"

Cristos smiled, although his dark eyes stayed emotionless. "You should hold tightly to your family."

"Is that a threat? Is somebody after my family?"

"No, Jack. I have spoken to no one. But sometimes we lose sight of what is precious to us."

"Do you have family?"

Cristos paused. "I did."

Jack didn't respond. He had not thought of Cristos as anything but a murderer; his actions spoke nothing to the contrary. Jack wasn't sure if he was being played or seeing a glimpse of the man's soul.

"Is this what you wanted to see me about?

Cristos shook his head.

"What do you have to say, then?" Jack finally asked.

"Nothing is as it seems." Cristos looked Jack directly in the eye and whispered, "Remember this, death is not always final, not always permanent; death is never the end."

WITH CRISTOS'S WORDS ringing in his ears, Jack watched through the plate-glass window as the man he had convicted of murder was strapped down to a black leather gurney. The room was small, covered with lime-green tiles and taken up by several medical monitors. Cristos's Zenga suit jacket had been removed; the white sleeves on either arm were rolled up, exposing his thick forearms. Cristos lay on the gurney, staring straight up, his eyes focused elsewhere. There was no emotion on his face, no fear or anxiety in his body language. He appeared calm, as if awaiting a simple medical procedure.

Beside Jack in the viewing room, seated in the rows of chairs, were Peter Womack, Carter Dorran, the two grown children of the Bonsleys, members of a Pashir delegation who had flown in from Asia, and various members of the federal and state law-enforcement community. Not a word was spoken; a prayer-like silence had fallen over the room as if awaiting the start of some religious ceremony.

Within the execution chamber, two medical technicians entered and stood on either side of the gurney. Each swabbed Cristos's arms, inserted a needle in a vein in each arm, and a saline drip commenced, ensuring a proper flow into Cristos's system.

The lead technician, an overly tall and gaunt man, leaned over and unbuttoned, Cristos's shirt, exposing his chest. And as the tech's eyes fell on the condemned's torso, so did every other eye in the room, and an almost collective gasp cried out. No one expected to see what Cristos had hidden under his fine suits, masked from the world. His burned and scarred skin was inhuman, like melted flesh from a horror film.

The technician quickly set back to work, affixing the heart monitor to Cristos's mangled flesh, and checked the readout to ensure that it was working, surprised at the slow heartbeat of a man who was about to die.

At the subtle nod of his head, the two techs confirmed they were ready. They pressed a button on the wall and signaled the executioner.

In an adjacent room, unseen by all, sat a third technician before a console. The IV lines in Cristos's arms ran into this room, terminating at a middle-aged man in a lab coat who sat at a coldly white, antiseptic desk. Before him were three syringes, each conspicuously labeled.

With a methodical nature, he picked up the first syringe, flicked his finger against the needle, and slipped it into the port in the IV line. The administered drug was sodium thiopental, a barbiturate and anesthetic agent.

Out in the execution room, Cristos's eyes fell shut as the chemical flowed into his system, rendering him unconscious.

Back in the side room, the technician inserted the second syringe into the IV line. Pancuronium was a muscle relaxant that caused complete paralysis of the skeletal striated muscles, including the diaphragm and respiratory muscles, that would eventually cause death by asphyxiation if the third drug didn't do its job.

And finally, the technician picked up the third syringe and injected it into the line. The potassium chloride acted quickly, and within two minutes, the heart monitor affixed to Cristos's chest registered no heartbeat.

With little fanfare, before an audience of twenty including Jack Keeler, the medical examiner stepped into the room, read the monitor, laid his stethoscope to the deceased's chest, and declared Nowaji Cristos dead.

CHAPTER 25

JACK SAT PARKED AT the North White Plains train station, the lot nearly empty on the Friday of a summer holiday weekend.

He and Mia had commuted from this station into Grand Central until a few years ago, when the demands of their jobs turned their schedules upside down and it became more practical to drive into the city.

A black Suburban pulled to the curb beside Jack, and he recognized it at once as the car that had pulled him over on the bridge the night before, the car that had taken Mia away.

Two men emerged from the front of the vehicle, dressed casually in sport jackets and slacks. Jack caught a glimpse of the driver's shoulder holster.

The driver turned and opened the rear door. A moment passed before Nowaji Cristos, sitting in the back of the car, turned and looked directly at Jack. Jack couldn't believe his eyes as he watched the man he had convicted and seen executed less than a year before emerge from the Suburban. His black hair in a ponytail, wearing jeans and black boots, he reached back into the car, pulled out a dark blue sportcoat, and threw it on. The man took a few steps forward, approaching like a bird of prey, his black eyes focused on Jack as if ready to pounce on his next meal.

Jack slowly emerged from the Audi.

"So glad you can join our team." Cristos's deep voice was thick with contempt. "Aaron and Donal will be joining us. I believe you have already met."

The two men glared at Jack. Indeed, he knew them from the bridge. Donal, the oversized man who had pummeled Jack senseless, throwing him back into his car and sending him over the bridge, and Aaron, the skinny redhead who had struck Mia so hard and knocked her to the ground. Jack stared back at Aaron until he finally averted his eyes. No matter how the next hour unfolded, Jack swore to himself, that man would pay for what he did.

"Two *dead* men working together," Cristos said. "I told you death is not always permanent."

"How?" Jack said. "I saw you die."

Cristos smiled, taunting him. "You have a beautiful wife, Jack. You should see how she cried when she learned of your death."

"You son of a bitch," Jack said through clienched teeth. "How do I know she's alive?"

Cristos pulled out his cell phone and dialed. "Get the woman. Put her on the phone."

Cristos handed Jack the cell.

"Mia?" Jack quietly asked.

"Oh, my God." Mia's voice cracked with anguish and relief. "You're alive?"

"Mia—"

Aaron reached for the phone, snatching it from Jack's hand.

"No!" Jack yelled, trying to pull the phone back.

"Let him talk." Cristos stepped forward and stilled Aaron's hand. "It may be the last time they ever speak."

Cristos gave the phone back to Jack, indicating that he should get into the Suburban.

Jack took the phone back and climbed in as Cristos shut the door behind him.

"Are you hurt?" Jack said, doing everything to keep his emotions from spilling out.

"No, don't worry about me. You were shot. I saw you go over the bridge into the river . . . That bastard showed me the newspaper . . ."

"How many times have I told you not to believe everything you read in the paper? And remember, it said we were both dead. You and I don't go down that easy."

"The girls . . . ?"

"They're fine. I checked. Do you know where you are?"

"No idea. They drugged me. I woke up in this small room, no windows. I can hear the city noise, though."

"I will find you." Jack's voice boiled with emotion. "If it's the last thing I do, I will save you, I promise you."

"Jack," Mia said, "Those guys who jacked us last night were FBI."

"I know. How deep do you think this goes?"

"Deeper than you can imagine. Jack, do not help them," Mia pleaded.

"What choice do I have?"

"Jack . . . you have to stay alive for the girls, protect the girls . . . I'm already dead."

"You're not dead!" Jack yelled. "Don't say that. You survive, whatever happens, do you hear me? You fight!"

Mia grew quiet. "Jack, you can't let him get that box. You know he'll kill us *both* once he gets it?"

"That's why I have no intention of giving it to him. But Mia, you have to tell me what is inside."

"Jack, I can't."

"I saw Jimmy. He told me about the prayer books, about some kind of drawing—"

"Where did you see Jimmy? I don't understand—"

The car door opened. Cristos stood there, his hand out, wanting the phone. "We've got to go."

"Jack, promise me something," Mia pleaded. "Don't look inside."

"I love you, Mia."

"I love you with all my heart, Jack. Please tell the girls I love—"

And the phone was snatched away, closed, and tucked back into Cristos's pocket.

Jack felt powerless, manipulated by Cristos. "Do you have any intention of telling me what we are doing?"

"You're going to lead us down to the evidence room of the Tombs," Cristos said. "And you're going to steal the evidence case."

CHAPTER 26

THE BOY WAS EIGHT years old when his father gave him the small red leather book. It was a book provided only to those whose hearts were deemed pure, whose future would be one of devotion to their religion, their people, and the earth.

The book, used by the Cotis monks, contained pages filled with prayer, but through the simple act of wetting them, a blank page would be revealed, a secret tableau where one's thoughts and words could be written and concealed as the paper dried. Informally called the Book of Souls, it was nicknamed so because its true heart was only known by its owner.

As the son of the high priest and ruler of Cotis, Suresh was blessed not only with pure blood but also with a mental and physical aptitude that the village had not seen in decades. He was mentored by scholars and holy men, warriors, philosophers, and poets who honed his mind, body, and spirit to form a young man who would one day take the place of his father as the ruler of Cotis.

As life moved on and the student attained enlightenment, then assumed the role of the high spiritual leader of Cotis, his writing evolved. No longer would it be of just the past but now of the present and the future.

Suresh grew into a powerful young man, strong, intelligent, with a supreme focus that allowed him to absorb his teachings and to excel at every discipline, be it hand-to-hand combat, weaponry, mathematics, spirituality, or philosophy.

But with his sharp, curious mind, Suresh realized that he needed to see the world beyond the confines of his family, their wealth, and the ancient kingdom of Cotis.

Against the entire Tietien council's demands, Suresh chose to go on a pilgrimage, to see the world beyond their simple ways, beyond their forest home of temples and nature. His father begged him to stay, explaining that he had glimpsed his future and feared for him losing his spirit to the darkness of the outside world. But Suresh explained that if he was one day to rule, then he needed to do so with a global perspective, not one of isolation.

THE OPEN-AIR MARKET was abuzz with life early in the morning on a cloudless day in the small town of Rashivia, just over the Cotis border in India. Sitting at the foot of the Parshia Mountains, the town was middle to lower class, except for the northeast section, where enormous lakeside homes were built for the wealthy who spent their summers away from the chaos of Delhi, Mumbai, and Calcutta. Vendors with pushcarts piled high with produce, dried meats, breads, clothing, spices, orchids, and tools filled the crumbling makeshift sidewalks and alleyways. Small shops with open windows and doors lined the dirt roads. Crowds of people swarmed about; the singsong voices of the merchants hawking their wares filled the air. Suresh walked among the sea of people, feeding off of the energy, feeling the vibrancy of life around him. He marveled at the diversity, at the differences between this part of the world and his home just a short distance away. He reveled in his new freedom, cherishing his escape from the ritual, from the routine that he now saw had stifled his understanding of the world.

Stepping under the woven tent of a produce merchant, Suresh flipped a coin to the hunched-over old man behind the cart and grabbed an apple. Taking a bite, savoring its sweetness, he looked out across the sea of people to see a young woman racing through the streets, her long, lithe legs seeming to make her float above the un-paved dirt road. Suresh watched as her long black hair drifted behind her, bouncing in rhythm to her every stride. Her face was pure and innocent, like a fresh orchid.

But he was shaken from the moment as he realized that she was on the run. Two men, large and equally fast, were ten strides back and clos-ing. Without thought, Suresh charged from the bazaar, cutting through the aisles and past the merchants out into the open streets. People turned to watch, but their attention was distracted by the competing chaos.

The young woman led her pursuers down the road, kicking up a small dust storm with her long, quick strides. Suresh was ten paces back and closing when the woman cut down an alley bordered by two six-story decaying buildings, the two men right behind her.

Suresh rounded the corner to find that the trail to freedom was suddenly cut short by a high wall covered in razor wire.

Without a moment's hesitation, the woman leaped onto a Dumpster, launching herself up onto the rusty fire escape that climbed the side of one of the brick buildings. Her hands caught the ladder, and she swung herself in a perfect arc, like an Olympic gym-nast, forward, backward, gaining momentum.

But her long legs were her downfall. The first pursuer jumped and caught her by the ankles. She desperately clung, but his two-hundred-pound weight was too much. They both came crashing down to the filth-covered ground, the girl's head hitting the pave-ment hard. She rolled around, dazed and confused, as blood began to blossom through her ink-black hair.

The second man grabbed her roughly by the neck, seeming to ignite a new fire within her, and she rolled up her fist and hit him squarely in the eye, kicking him hard in the stomach as she turned to run. But the first man was there, stumbling to his feet, reaching into his jacket, and pulling a stun gun. She dived to the right to avoid the two metal prongs, but it was too late as they jabbed her in the neck and ended her struggle.

She fell to the ground in a heap as the two men paused, gasping for breath.

They never saw Suresh come up behind them. They never saw the snap kicks and round-house punches that came from his over-sized fists. Both were unconscious before they realized they were under attack.

Suresh crouched and examined the woman, checking her pulse, examining the wound on the back of her head that seeped blood.

He turned and flipped open the first man's jacket to find a hol-stered Glock pistol and a cell phone strapped to his belt. Suresh rifled through his pockets and pulled out a small amount of cash, keys, and his wallet. The man's name was Arthur Patel, and his address was fif-teen hundred miles south in Mumbai. His ID said he was a special envoy to the Indian government.

He took both men's guns, popped out the clips, quickly disman-tled them, and scattered the pieces. Without knowing the circum-stances, he had no intention of hurting these men any further.

THE YOUNG WOMAN sprang up from the bed as if she had just woken from the dead.

Suresh sat in the corner, his hands raised, his eyes passive. "It's OK."

The girl stared at him, her dark brown eyes darting around the room. It was small, only the bed she lay on and a single table off to the side for furnishings, with a galley kitchen in the corner oppo-site Suresh. A kerosene lamp filled the room with an orange danc-ing glow.

"You're free to go," Suresh said as he pointed at the door. "I just brought you here to get you off the streets in case anyone else was looking for you and to give you a chance to recover."

The girl looked around the room while rubbing her neck and finally noticed the bandage on her head and the ice pack on the pillow.

"Eleven stitches. I made them small. I did need to shave a very small amount of hair, but no one will notice. The ice will help with the swelling."

"Are you a doctor?" Her voice was soft and innocent.

"No," Suresh said as he shook his head, "I have had a bit of training."

"In more than just medicine," she said. "Those men had training, too."

Suresh slowly stood, picked up a tray from the lone table in the room, laid it before her, and took his seat back on the floor in the corner.

She looked down at a plate of fresh fruit and a loaf of bread. A lone white orchid lay next to the simple meal. She picked it up and took a long sip of water from a tin cup. "Is this your place?"

"For the moment." He smiled.

She again looked at the food and at the bag of ice on the bed as she ran her hand over the wound on her head. "Thank you."

Suresh nodded.

"You haven't asked me a single question." She tilted her head in curiosity.

"No," he said simply.

The moment hung in the air, a connection beginning to grow.

"My name is Nadia," she said with a hint of a smile.

NADIA DESAI HAD been on the run for almost a month. Men who had been tracking her for the last week finally made their move that morning. Tasked with bringing her home with no limits on their methods, they were to return her to Mumbai to face charges.

She was nineteen, two years Suresh's junior. She did not speak of her childhood or upbringing beyond saying that it was hard and filled with violence, although her perfect teeth and refined speech indicated that her difficult youth may have been more emotional than physical.

With no plan beyond escape, she had ventured up to the mountain region to start a new life, to find love and adventure. And she did with Suresh. He took her on jungle excursions, taught her camping and how to live off the land. He taught her how to defend herself more effectively and the importance of avoiding aggression and physical confrontation when possible.

It was a week before their first kiss, another month before they made love, and when they did, Suresh knew that he had found a partner to spend his life with.

THEIR PASSION WAS primal, their lovemaking rough yet tender. Their existence was simple, spent in the outdoors, the apartment used for expressing their undying passion, sleep, and showering. They were able to live off money earned from selling their jewelry, including Suresh's ruby ring and Nadia's gold necklace, and felt no need for the materialistic aspects of life. The world around them and their own company offered all of the entertainment they needed. Truth be told, though, Nadia indulged her one interest—photography—taking pictures of the vast jungle, of Suresh, of them dining, swimming, holding hands. She photographed them in bed, naked, within each other's embrace, photographs they shared only with each other.

IN THE THIRD week of their relationship, Suresh found the note on his door. Sitting in the café fifteen minutes later, he faced his father.

"You have not returned," his father said.

"This is my life now," Suresh said. "You are stuck in the past, you and everyone else. You claim inner vision yet are blind to the world around you."

"This life will not fulfill you." His father looked upon him with sad eyes.

"You claim to know my wants and feelings."

"No, I know your heart because you're my son."

"Then know that I have found someone—"

"Does she love you in return?"

Suresh glared at his father. "We have found a deep connection. We were meant to be together. Fate, which you so love to cite, brought us together."

"Is she committed to you, the way you are committed to her? Does she love you?"

"One hundred times a day, she says it; she has given me her mind, body, and soul."

"But has she truly given you her heart?" his father paused. "If she has, then I give you my blessing. You are then one with her and her outside world. And you are lost to us."

And without another word, his father stood and walked out.

IT WAS IN the alley, after dark, and Suresh was on his way from the produce market to meet Nadia when four thieves emerged from the shadows. They were quiet, trying to get a jump on him.

The first man stepped in front of him, blocking his way and staring at him. Suresh naively smiled, thinking the man lost, but then he heard the others approaching from behind. His teachers had trained him to sense aggression and imminent attack and to embrace the instinctual release of adrenaline and turn it to his advantage.

Suresh's senses were immediately heightened. He could hear not only their footsteps upon approach but also their flanking movements and even their breathing.

And as the man on his left rear attacked, Suresh was already in a crouch, ducking beneath the blow, spinning around, sweeping the man's feet from beneath him. The two others came at him simultaneously. Suresh dove to the left, driving his fist into the tall man's throat, the shock of the blow sending the man to the ground, grasping his neck. Suresh spun to the right, his left foot pivoting as he right-snap-kicked the second man in the nose, and he quickly followed it up with a single blow to the solar plexus and a kick to the knee, disabling the man.

Suresh turned to see their leader coming at him with a knife, driving it forward, aimed at his heart, but Suresh turned the man's momentum on him, snatching the man's knife hand and twisting it back until the knife fell to the ground. Suresh continued the motion, using the man's own weight to lever his wrist until it snapped. Twisting the man's arm until the shattered bone acted like an internal knife, he brought the man to the ground.

In less than a minute, the four street thieves lay upon the alley, disabled, wounded, but alive.

SURESH WALKED INTO his apartment to find Nadia not home. He lit the kerosene lamp by the window, its orange glow lighting the room. He turned on the stove and placed a pot of oil over the flame, then quickly seasoned the fish and laid out the produce that had all managed to survive his ordeal.

He stepped into the small bathroom, checked the wound to make sure it was minor, cleaned it, and applied a bandage. The adrenaline had quickly left his system. It had been nearly six months since he had tasted its flavor, but his defense and attack skills had returned as if he had practiced them the day before. His mind quickly let it all go, his thoughts returning to Nadia, to her smile, to her eyes that looked into his soul. He was glad she wasn't with him, relieved that she didn't bear witness to the violence he could unleash.

As he finished applying the bandage, his heart began to race, and the adrenaline returned as he sensed someone entering the apartment. Not Nadia, not the soft pad of her feet, the smell of her natural scent. It was someone else, trying to remain quiet, invisible.

Suresh turned off the light, crouched low, and peered out through the bathroom door to see an equally tall man standing at the kitchen table, rifling through the few papers that lay there. Dressed in a dark, tailored suit, the man projected an aristocratic air while his eyes scanned the room like a soldier on a mission. Suresh looked around the small bathroom. There was nothing but the box of gauze, a bar of soap, and a washcloth. He reached into his pocket and fisted a handful of coins.

Suresh took a moment, gathering his wits, and stepped from the bathroom, surprising the man. They stared at each other a moment.

"Who the hell are you?" Suresh finally demanded.

"Ah." The man turned, momentarily startled. He flashed a smile, but Suresh saw his eyes; there was no smile within them. "My name is Raj, Rajeev Sapre. You must be Suresh."

Suresh's caution escalated. Beyond Nadia, no one outside of his world knew his name.

"Making dinner for Nadia?" Rajeev asked, pointing to the pot of boiling oil, the fresh vegetables and fish.

Suresh remained silent and assessed the man before him. His tailored clothes projected a superior air, which momentarily distracted him before he recalled the words from his youth: *no one can make you feel inferior without your consent.*

"The door was open—"

"And you just figured you'd walk in?" Suresh said in an accusatory tone.

"I'm a friend of Nadia's."

"She never mentioned you."

"Nadia fashions herself a woman of mystery, but believe me, the mystery doesn't run very deep."

"I think you should leave," Suresh said.

"Did she get you with the lost-child story?"

"This is her home now. I'm not going to ask you again."

Raj looked around the small, cramped apartment, his eyes unable to hide his disgust.

"I've known Nadia for most of her life, and I can assure you, she does not consider this her home."

"Then you don't know her very well."

"She tell you she ran away, traveled fifteen hundred miles on her own? Bet she failed to mention her father's palatial estate not two miles from here in the foothills of the Parshia Mountains. How do you think she has kept that beautiful head of hair of hers so perfect? Certainly not with a bar of soap and tap water. My people have been watching her, every day when she goes for her run. She grabs a cab, goes to the estate which is vacant during this season, takes a real shower, indulges the needs she proclaims are beneath her, that are vainglorious and shallow. She usually grabs a bite to eat, watches a little television, before coming back here to play the martyr, to be a free spirit."

"This is bullshit—"

"No bullshit. She was rebelling, using you to insult her father." Raj pulled an envelope full of photographs from the inside pocket of his suit jacket and threw them down onto the table. They were intimate and revealed Suresh and Nadia in the throes of passion. "She sent them not only to him and her mother but also to the tabloids, like some American reality-TV star. She really wanted to piss her dad off, embarrass him, show him she didn't need his money or power . . . reject his wealth to be a free spirit," Raj said.

"She doesn't care about money."

"Really?" Raj smiled. "*You* don't know her very well."

Suresh tried to contain his growing anger.

"Nadia is not who you think she is, Suresh. In fact, do you even know her real name? You were her bad-boy fantasy; in you, she found danger, romance. You allowed her to explore her base needs, her sexuality. You were just a pawn, like all of us, used by a spoiled child. But like so many before, when she is done with you, she casts you away."

"Get out." Suresh raised his voice as he took a step forward. "You're not taking her away from here."

"You don't understand. We didn't track her down." Raj paused. "She called us."

Confusion ran through Suresh. There were too many thoughts to process. He knew she loved him. He saw his love reflected in her eyes, in her heart.

"On her twentieth birthday," Raj continued, "Nadia is to receive the first installment of her trust, fifty million dollars, with the proviso that she fulfills one criterion."

Suresh's head was spinning. "What are you talking about?"

"She receives her trust, provided she marries . . ." Raj paused, and a knowing smile creased his face. "Provided she marries me."

Lies. This man was lying to him. He was there to take her away, just as the men tried to snatch her back three months earlier. This man was playing his emotions to the extreme.

Raj picked up the camera from the table, turned it on, and thumbed through pictures of Suresh and Nadia. Shaking his head, he pulled out the memory stick and snapped it in two. "These last six months of her life will be erased from all memory."

"Those men in the alley." Suresh spoke slowly as the realization formed in his mind. "They worked for you."

Raj just stared.

"They weren't there to mug me, were they?"

Raj reached into his jacket and pulled out a Browning pistol. Suresh could see the worn butt of the gun. It was this man's personal weapon, one that he had had for a long time. Despite his polished appearance, Suresh knew he was up against someone familiar with violence. But no fear arose in Suresh, only concern for Nadia, and no one was going to take her.

In a snap move, Suresh tossed the coins he clutched in his hands at Raj, the cloud of metal causing the man to flinch and allowing Suresh to dive left.

But Raj's distraction was short-lived, and he quickly fired, hitting Suresh in the right arm, the echo of the gun reverberating off the small walls. But Suresh's momentum was not deterred; his left arm was already in motion, swinging upward as his hand wrapped the barrel, twisting it from the man's grasp, while his right fist caught the man upside the head.

Suresh continued moving forward, tackling Raj backward over the chair, crashing onto him. Raj rolled right, countering Suresh's move, driving his elbow into Suresh's wounded arm, stunning him.

But Suresh compartmentalized the pain, continuing his attack. And while Raj may have had military training, it was no match for Suresh's skills, which had been honed not only throughout his lifetime but by his ancestors for decades before.

With a sudden movement, Raj was wrapped in a choke hold. But this time, there would be no mercy like he had shown the pack of thieves on the street. Raj had awakened a rage in Suresh, a kind that he had never tasted before. Suresh hadn't realized that his attackers from earlier in the evening were there to kill him, but he was not making that mistake again. If he allowed Raj to live, he would surely be back with a much larger team to correct his mistake.

Suresh tightened his grip. Raj struggled beneath him, his tailored suit torn, fear in his eyes, knowing that his neck was about to be snapped.

Without warning, the boiling oil from the stove hit Suresh's skin. Like molten lava, it oozed down his side. He turned with disbelieving eyes to see Nadia standing there, pot in hand, her eyes filled with tears. He released his grip on Raj and tried to ignore the excruciating pain as the skin on his torso bubbled and rolled up. The blood of the bullet wound washed away while the fresh blood that poured from the wound congealed upon meeting the boiling liquid.

Raj kicked, scooting away from Suresh, gasping for breath.

Suresh didn't move. He did not break his stare at Nadia, standing there with a tear-streaked face.

"What are you doing?" Her voice cracked in anguish as she looked back and forth between the two men.

As she put down the pot, her questioning eyes turned sympathetic, and she took a step forward, crouched down . . .

And took Raj in her arms.

It all became clear. Raj's words were true, and Suresh was nothing but a pawn. He had opened his heart and turned his back on his previous life for love.

But before Suresh could utter a word or a question of why, Raj struggled to his feet and stood above him with hate-filled eyes. He reached to the window and picked up the kerosene lamp, removing the fuel cap.

"Here, let me cool those burns," Raj said as he poured the fuel on Suresh's chest.

And in ceremony, Raj held a match in his hand, struck it on its pack, and dropped it on the scalding oil that covered Suresh's chest. With a low whoosh, the flame leaped around Suresh's torso; the oil on his skin sizzled, charring his already burned flesh as clouds of thick smoke coiled up to the ceiling.

As he looked up, he saw Nadia's pure face, her warm eyes staring down at him. There was no sympathy, no regret or revulsion at seeing the man she had shared a bed with for six months burning to death.

SURESH AWOKE, BLINDED by the antiseptic white of the room. He found himself in a hospital bed, tubes and wires running into and around his body, the low chimes and beeps of the monitors confirming that he was alive. Outside his private room, nurses and doctors scurried in the halls, tending to the sick. A sudden confusion filled his mind as he realized that with no money and ID, he should have been dead or at least in the ward with the poor.

He burned with a hatred far stronger than the pain from his injuries. His mind filled with thoughts of vengeance.

Two men stepped into the room. The taller one moved to the corner and remained silent as the shorter, overweight man moved to his bedside.

"My name is William Riley," the man said with a southern American accent. "So glad you're finally awake. Do you know where you are?"

Suresh nodded.

"You've been in a medically induced coma for close to a week now. The burns were third-degree. Your recovery will be slow, but they will do everything to minimize the pain." Riley took a seat beside the bed. "Do you have family you would like me to contact?"

Suresh shook his head. He had left that world behind. If they were to find out how weak he had become, how he was fooled by the woman he loved, he would crumble.

"Where do you live?"

Suresh was a man without a home. "I live nowhere."

The man nodded in sympathy. "Do you know who did this to you?"

Suresh nodded.

"You're lucky to be alive. I understand Raj Sapre dispatched a street gang after you and you handled them like swatting flies."

And Suresh remembered that the attack in the alleyway was not a random mugging, that they were there to kill him. But his heart had blinded him to the obvious truth. Self loathing rose; he was angry at himself for letting them live, thinking them to be nothing more than lost souls looking to steal a few dollars.

But it was at Raj and Nadia that his rage burned brightest.

"Raj Sapre, along with his girlfriend, tried to kill you themselves. As sad as this may sound, you're lucky they set you on fire. It set off the smoke alarms, and the tenants came running to your aid."

Hearing that Nadia did not love him, did not want to be with him, that she wanted him dead, filled him with emotions he couldn't describe.

"Raj's father is the prime minister of India."

Suresh's mind turned upside down at the revelation.

"You should know he sanctioned your death. An all-points bulletin has been issued for your arrest for the attempted murder of his son. It is why you are registered under an alias, Cristos. If you're arrested, I can promise that you won't live until trial. The PM is operating for himself. He was elected through voter fraud. He has made the country's accounts his piggy bank and is willing to put this country into war with its neighbors if he can see a profit in it.

Suresh looked at the two men. While Riley did all of the talking, it was the taller man, the silent one, whose presence loomed larger. Despite his efforts to remain a nonentity in the room, it was clear that he was in charge,.

"Who are you?" Suresh said to the silent man.

The men exchanged a quick glance before Riley answered. "We are representatives sent here to assess you, to evaluate your worthiness."

Suresh felt an icy chill run through his scorched body.

"We know where you're from, we know of your unconventional training, your skills with weapons. We know how easily you wove yourself into the fabric of this community, losing yourself, living outside the system." Riley paused. "And we know the hatred that burns in your veins."

"We would like to make a proposition." The silent man finally spoke with a deep American accent.

"What kind of proposition?"

"One that will serve us both. A proposition of vengeance."

CHAPTER 27

CRISTOS SAT NEXT TO Jack in the back of the Suburban, Aaron and Donal in the front seat, a man named Josh in the rear third seat. All were silent in deference to Cristos as they drove toward the city.

"So how did you know?" Cristos asked.

"How did I know what?" Jack said.

"That I was alive. You try to act so surprised, yet you taunted me with that note."

Jack shook his head. "What are you talking about?"

"The note that was inside the case we stole from you." Cristos reached inside his pocket, pulled out the letter, and handed it to Jack. "Is that your signature?"

Jack stared at the envelope and quickly pulled out the letter. Just when he had started to think his memory was intact, this letter said otherwise.

"Who told you?" Cristos pressed him. "Or did you figure it out?"

Jack was speechless, his confusion impeding him from even hearing Cristos. Until he had received the call, he had no idea Cristos was alive. Nothing could have ever allowed him to surmise such an impossibility. He had no memory of writing it. He had no memory of placing it in the box.

Yet here he was, staring at his own handwriting, his own signature.

The envelope had Cristos's name on it. The personal stationery was Jack's, given to him by Joy for his birthday. The message was written in blue ink, with thick, heavy strokes.

> *I killed you once . . . touch my family and I will kill you again.*
> *Jack Keeler*

"NOT REALLY WORDS becoming of a district attorney." Cristos took the letter from Jack, tucked it back into the envelope, and gave it back to him. "You go ahead and keep it, contemplate it later."

Jack looked out the window of the Suburban, seeing that they were heading down the FDR, nearing their destination.

"So, Jack, before you *kill* me, you're going to help me."

Jack could hardly focus. Against all logic, it was as if he had written a letter to a ghost. His attention was pulled back as Cristos nudged him.

"You really don't have a choice, Jack," Cristos said as he held out his cell phone.

"You expect me to help you break in?" Jack finally said, trying to put aside the fragility of his mind.

"Oh, I expect you to do so much more than that. You're not only going to lead us down there, but you are going to steal the box from under the noses of the agents who are protecting that room." Cristos paused. "And Jack, you know, if you don't, your wife's death will be your fault."

Jack took the phone from Cristos, flipped it open, and quickly dialed. The phone hadn't made it through half a ring when—

"Evidence," Charlie Brooks answered.

"Charlie?" Jack asked in surprise.

"Holy shit," Charlie said, immediately recognizing his friend's voice.

"Don't say a word," Jack said quickly.

"I wouldn't know what to say. Oh, my God."

"Charlie, who's down there with you?"

"And your wife?"

"She's alive, but you can't react. No one is to know what's going on."

"You know the feds are down here looking at everything."

"I know. How many people you got down there now?"

"Three feds and an accountant. Seems I'm not the only one with nothing to do on a Friday night. Does Frank know?"

"Yeah."

"That son of a bitch, He let me go on and on. I'm going to kick his little fireplug ass—"

"Charlie." Jack cut him off. "Remember the case Mia and I dropped off the other day?"

"I have no idea what you're talking about, especially every time the feds ask about it."

"You're a good man. Smart. Don't let them tell you any different."

"Good thing you said not to log it in."

"Well, that box you have no idea about? I'm coming to get it."

CRISTOS STUDIED THE hand-drawn map that Jack had sketched out of the lower level of the Tombs, looking at the bottleneck entrance to the evidence room, the small administrative office, and the oversized warehouse-like space where tens of thousands of evidence cases, boxes, and bags lay in wait to be shepherded through the judicial system.

"I will get you the box, but you don't harm anyone, do you understand?"

"You don't really think you're in charge here, do you?" Cristos said. "We're all going downstairs except Josh here." Cristos pointed to the third man, his brown hair slicked back, his jacket a size too large. "He'll watch the guard and the lobby and keep us posted."

"Those people downstairs have nothing to do with this."

"Then their lives are in your hands. You get us the box without incident, no one dies. But if you try to warn anyone or take control, their deaths will be on your conscience."

As Jack sat there in the limo, he did everything he could to stay focused, to keep his mind off of Mia, as any fear he felt for her would only distract him from the task at hand. He had to get that case but had to stay alive in the process if he was to have any chance of saving her. He finally turned back to Cristos and asked the question that had been burning in his mind since he first heard his voice.

"How did you survive? I watched you die."

"Yes, you did," Cristos said. "But do you remember what I said? Death is not always final, not always permanent. Death is never the end."

"You're trying to tell me you came back from the dead?"

"Where I come from, life and death stand side-by-side; the divide is blurred. Our priests say they can communicate with the dead."

"Really?" Jack said, his voice filled with cynicism.

"You act as if that sounds so far-fetched. Everyone talks to those who have passed away in one way, shape, or form. How many people do you know who will talk to their deceased mother or father, hearing their voices in their ears during times of stress or anguish? Mothers hearing the cry of a child who has passed away. Or seeing people in our dreams, people who have come back to haunt or guide us. The priests from the village where I grew up have traditions thousands of years old concerning life, death, resurrection, just like any other religion."

Jack stared at him.

"They believe in magic. In not only communicating with the afterlife but also seeing the future, predicting what's to come as if they could read your fate. They say they can remember the future in much the way we remember the past."

"That's bullshit."

"Spoken like a man who can only see life in terms of black and white, right and wrong. Spoken like a scientist who can't wrap his mind around things he can't understand or . . . just like an attorney." Cristos tilted his head, as if assessing. "You look like a Catholic to me."

Jack didn't answer.

"The priest during mass, turning water into wine, Christ rising from the dead. Miracles, healings, divine intervention. Every religion has and embraces its own beliefs, the kind that some might call magical. Who are you to question their validity?"

"You're telling me the priests of your religion can see the future?"

"The head Cotis priest can look into someone's heart and see his fate and, in some cases, even help to shape it."

"If they have such a third eye, why didn't they see the horrors you would commit and try to stop you?"

"Who's to say they didn't try?" Cristos paused. "Do you believe your future is preordained? That we were always destined to meet again even though I died?"

"We shape our lives," Jack said. "Not some divine intervention."

"Really? If your mother called you in the middle of the night with a premonition of your house burning to the ground from a fault in the toaster, you'd unplug that toaster. Or if someone was to tell you that you were to die in a car accident on I-95 tomorrow and they said it with certainty, would you take a different road or perhaps avoid getting into a car?"

Jack pondered the logic of Cristos's words. He hated when people lectured him but there was a glimmer of truth to their words. "Are you telling me you weren't supposed to die that day? That some kind of magic intervened?"

Cristos let out a dry laugh. "No magic involved that time. I only needed to own two people: the technician who administered the drugs and rigged the heart monitor and the coroner."

Jack was instantly shocked. "How could you get to them from prison?"

"Once I was captured, the people who hired me were the ones who insisted on my speedy trial. They knew that if I was ever captured, I could choose to name names during the trial about who hired me and tell them about the list I had of all of the jobs I've done worldwide. And most particularly, who my employer was. They were easily swayed to my cause. We came to the conclusion that if I was convicted and executed, I'd have even more free rein to carry out future assignments."

"How could your employer manipulate our system so easily?"

"Because my employer is the system. My employer was your government."

CHAPTER 28

CRISTOS

THE SOUNDS OF THE jungle came alive at
night: birds in sweet song and raptor screech;
monkeys and small mammals on their nocturnal activities in the
enormous trees; snakes and reptiles slithering in the underbrush, taking up positions to lie in wait and snatch their unsuspecting prey as
it meandered by. The sudden howl of a macaque echoed through the
mountains, its deep growl hushing all other sounds of the night, all
bowing in fear and respect. And it was that moment of silence that
frightened most, for it felt as if the world was waiting for death.

Cristos lay under the thick green canopy of the jungle, just on
the outskirts of the Sapre estate. He had embraced his new name,
Suresh having died along with his heart four months earlier. The
fiery pain in his skin was still there, the grafts taut like an ill-fitting
garment. All of it reminded him of why he was finding pleasure in
this moment.

He had surveyed the property, performing reconnaissance for
the last month under cover of darkness. He knew every inch of the
grounds as if it were the land of his birth and the interior of the
home as if it were his own skin, able to walk it blindfolded without a

sound, without running into a single wall or piece of furniture in the ten-thousand-square-foot mansion.

It was built to resemble a Swiss chalet. The prime minister had modeled it on the lodge he frequented in Gstaad. Made of large pine timbers, it was a multistory log cabin with large picture windows affording views of the lake in front and the Parshia Mountains in back. Cristos found it pleasantly ironic that the upper reaches of the peaceful mountains the prime minister had looked upon for all of these years was not only the birthplace of his assassin but would also be the last place he gazed on in his final day.

Raj and Nadia were scheduled to be married the next day in a lavish ceremony by the lake. Three large white tents were in place, the seating for five hundred already set. The marriage was viewed as the dynastic merger of the century, the politically powerful family of Prime Minister Wahajian Sapre joining with the family of Kartic Desai, one of the wealthiest industrialists in the country. The marriage was arranged more than ten years earlier, before Nadia and Raj had met, before they had even finished grade school. Their fathers had laid out their lives for them, lives that they rebelled against in their own ways but fell in line with as they grew up.

But come tomorrow, there would be no wedding, there would be no grand merger to be covered in the *New York Times*, the London *Times*, or the *Times of India*. The headlines in the coming days would only be of death.

Cristos had formulated his plan. He would be acting on his own. His employers had already transferred five million dollars to an account in Prague, with the balance to be paid out upon completion. He requested a list of supplies and was surprised when it had all arrived ahead of schedule to the small warehouse he had rented in the slums three miles away from the estate.

A small stag party was held earlier in the evening, more akin to a Wall Street board of directors meeting than a stripper-filled, gin-mill extravaganza. Only men were on the estate at this time; the mothers, sisters, bridesmaids, and bride weren't expected until morning.

While some of the small group headed upstairs to the six guest rooms and others had left the main house to rest in the guest houses on the other side of the lake, PM Sapre, Desai, and Raj had retired to the library for an impromptu ceremony. It was a gentleman's den filled with books, leather furniture, and a fully stocked mahogany bar. The three men sat in large captain's chairs, clutching glowing Cuban cigars, as if they were gods discussing the fate of mankind.

Cristos watched it all through the high-powered scope of his sniper rifle, listening to their every word through his earpiece, which picked up the signal from bugs he had placed earlier.

Desai placed a large wooden box on the table before Raj. The two older men smiled as he lifted the lid and drew out a long golden dagger, its hilt sparkling with precious gems.

"It belonged to my great-grandfather," Desai said. "He was a prince in the times of the Maratha Empire. His father had it made for him as a symbol of purity, virility, and command. It is called the Shiant Dagger. It is said that those who possess it will attain great power over mankind. I now pass it to you."

Cristos clutched the long Galil sniper rifle, smiling as he watched the exchange. Not a word was mentioned of Nadia, the wedding, or love—just daggers, business, and politics. Cristos reached over, picked up his bottle of water, and took a long, slow swig, savoring the coolness as it poured down his throat.

Without further delay, he grasped the rifle, lined up his sight, and swept the gun back and forth between his targets. Assured of his aim and without fanfare, he exhaled and pulled the trigger. The three-inch copper bullet exploded out of the gun, traveling the two hundred yards in an instant, shattering the large picture window in the library before exploding the PM's head. Within half a second, the barrel was swung to the right, the cough of the rifle echoed along the mountain, and Desai's head was nearly torn from his body.

Cristos swung the rifle again, lining up the sight on Raj, but he had a change of heart. He adjusted his aim and fired off two quick shots. The first bullet hit Raj in the stomach, tearing out his back, while the second bullet shattered his knee, driving a hole clear through the cap and cartilage.

Cristos abandoned the rifle and broke into a full-out sprint. Covering the grassy two hundred yards in less than twenty-two seconds, he leaped through the now-empty window frame into the library. He looked at his handiwork, at what was left of the corrupt PM Sapre, at Desai, inwardly smiling that the country's richest man was felled by a two-dollar bullet.

He finally turned his eye to Raj, walking over and looking down on the dying twenty-year-old. He waited a moment for his face to register in the young man's fading mind.

"What was it you said about erasing me from existence? I just wanted to say thank you."

And as Raj's eyes began to drift, Cristos pulled out an EpiPen—an auto-injector of epinephrine—and jabbed him in the thigh with it. Raj's eye's flew open as his heart began to race.

"I want you to be fully awake." Cristos smiled. "Fully aware of the pain as you die."

Suddenly, the twin doors exploded open. Cristos spun around, a pistol instantly in hand aimed at the intruder. But he did what he swore he would never do again. He hesitated, for he was looking into the eyes of Nadia.

And despite her unforgivable betrayal, his heart still skipped at the sight of her. Cristos had declared his heart dead, replacing the pain and hollowness with rage and vengeance, but that all melted away as his eyes fell upon Nadia.

She raced to Raj, taking him in her arms, screaming in agony as she looked at the carnage around her.

"What have you done?" she cried, the same words she had said four months earlier. She glanced at what was left of her father and nearly retched. Turning her attention back to Raj, she pressed her hand on his wounded stomach, trying to stop the bleeding.

Cristos just stared at her, momentarily losing all focus.

"How could you do this after everything I did for you?" Nadia openly wept. "I stopped Raj from killing you. I kept my father and the prime minister from seeking you out. I paid for your hospital, your care. I watched over you while you were in a medically induced coma."

Cristos's head began to spin, once again not knowing what to believe. Riley was very clear that the only reason he was alive was that the fire alarm had gone off and that Raj and Nadia needed to escape before they were seen. Riley said he was paying for his treatment, that his government, in conjunction with the British, was paying.

"I'm so sorry for what I did to you." Her words flooded out on heavy breaths. "I panicked when I saw you killing Raj, I lost my mind and threw that oil. I can't imagine the pain you must have endured. I haven't slept since that night. Can't you understand? This is my world. This is where I belong."

Cristos began to panic; all logic, all reason, had left his mind as he fell under Nadia's spell once again. "Come away with me. I can—"

"Go away with you?" she screamed. "You're a monster. How could you do this? My father, the prime minister . . ."

She turned and looked at Raj. His eyes had fallen shut, his breathing coming in fits and starts as he slowly began to die.

"You've taken everything from me. Get out. Get out!"

"Raj said that—Riley said—"

"Who said what? You listen to everyone except yourself. What does your heart tell you, what does your instinct tell you?"

Cristos could see the truth in her eyes . . . and feel it in his heart. She was right. He was trained to listen to his instincts, and yet he had tucked them away, chosen to ignore them when they had been his guide for his whole life.

Cristos reached down, offering her his hand.

Nadia picked up the bejeweled dagger, pointing it at him. "Stay away from me."

"Nadia . . ."

"I have nothing. You've taken it all from me."

Cristos could see the despair in her eyes, her body shaking, on the edge of a nervous breakdown. He had come there seeking vengeance, bringing death, and succeeded in his task. But he had been manipulated by all: Nadia, Raj, Riley. He was truly just a pawn in their games. And while his heart had burned with Nadia's betrayal, looking at her now, he couldn't bring himself to harm her, for he realized that he still loved her in spite of everything.

"Please, you don't understand . . ." he said as he reached out for her.

Nadia stepped back, finally looking at her father, the prime minister, and Raj.

And without warning, without a single word, she looked Cristos in the eye and plunged the dagger into her own chest.

THE OPEN-AIR JEEP raced up the mountainside, under the canopy of night, the thick leaves allowing only shards of moonlight to penetrate. In the valley below, a sudden explosion lit up the night as the prime minister's vacation home was torn to shreds, an enormous fireball engulfing it and the remaining guests inside.

Cristos white-knuckled the steering wheel, his eyes darting between the road and Nadia, who lay motionless across the backseat, the dagger protruding from her chest.

He had nowhere else to turn. He had abandoned his culture, his people, his father, but now they were the only ones he could turn to to save the woman he loved.

Five miles up the dirt road, the hard-packed surface abruptly ended as if it had been swallowed by nature. He grabbed Nadia off of the seat, careful to avoid touching the dagger, and carried her into the jungle, still knowing the path better than anyone. The long, twisting trail meandered through the thick foliage, over rocks and streams, up a five-mile slope whose grade never diminished.

It would be at least another hour before he reached the village. He feared that he was already too late when two Cotis priests stepped out of the dark jungle, members of the Tietien council. Hovath had schooled him in martial arts and weaponry, while Prunaj had taught him of spirituality and the jungle. Each—uncharacteristic for the Cotis people—carried a sidearm on his hip. Without a word, they flanked him.

And Cristos's father stepped from the cover of the foliage.

Father and son locked eyes, a world of emotions exchanged without a word.

"You cannot come back."

"You have to save her," Cristos pleaded.

His father looked at the girl, her body limp in his son's arms. "Save her for herself or save her for you?"

"Please," Cristos begged. "Bring her back."

He laid her down on the ground, gently stroking her dark hair from her face.

"Does she wish to live?" his father asked. "Or have you taken away what she lives for?"

His father knew what he had done.

"Bring her back!" Cristos exploded in rage.

"I know what you've become," his father said softly. "My whole life, I fought it. Although I knew it to be your future, I had clung to hope. But fate sometimes is stronger than any force. The shadow hidden within you has emerged and consumed your heart and soul."

"You don't understand—"

"I do understand. I should have stopped you before all of this death. I foresaw your future but allowed my heart to fall into denial, questioning the future as some question the past."

"I love her." Cristos's voice cracked. "You have to help me."

"After what you have done—" his father said with pain filled eyes. "You will be followed; you will bring the outside world to us again. We cannot afford to protect you. We cannot allow our ways to be investigated so they may build a case to convict you. "

Prunaj and Hovath stepped forward, pulling and raising their pistols. They were trained on Cristos, and, anticipating his every move, they stayed just beyond his reach. Cristos's emotions vanished, his eyes falling on Hovath.

"We must turn you over to the authorities of the outside world," his father continued as Cristos kept staring at Hovath. "Please do not—"

And without warning, with his eyes locked with Hovath's, Cristos drove his fist into his father's gut, the immense blow knocking him sideways toward Hovath.

Cristos spun left, snatching the gun from Prunaj, continuing his motion up and into the priest's neck, crushing his larynx with the butt of the pistol. Prunaj fell to the ground, unable to breathe.

As he was taught so well, Cristos could feel Hovath's approach, could sense his finger wrapping the trigger. He feigned left and spun, firing Prunaj's gun, the bullet hitting Hovath's wrist, crippling his hand as the gun fell to the ground.

With no regard for his mangled wrist, Hovath dived at Cristos, and although he was his teacher, skilled in hand-to-hand combat, the student had surpassed him long ago. Cristos caught Hovath by the shoulder, rolling toward the ground, taking his teacher with him as his arm wrapped around the man's neck. And as they hit the jungle floor, Hovath's neck snapped from their combined weight.

With no regard for the bodies, Cristos stood and stared at his father, who was recovering.

"This is your fault," Cristos said.

His father looked at the twisted bodies of the two dead priests. He turned and looked upon Nadia, finally stepping toward his son. "Take her away from here. Never return. You are no longer my son."

Cristos slowed his breathing, focused, reaching out to feel any other attackers, but none came.

He looked back down at Nadia, shards of moonlight refracting off of the bejeweled hilt of the knife that protruded from her lifeless body. He finally realized that she would not have wanted to be saved; he had taken away everything she loved in the world. He accepted that she had used him with no regard for his heart and in so doing permanently destroyed it, killing his emotions, his feelings, his true self.

And in that moment, Cristos knew that his future was sealed.

He crouched down, wrapped his hand around the jewel-encrusted blade, and withdrew it from her chest. No blood poured from her body, its flow having long since ceased. He looked down on the face that had caught his eye one year earlier, its solemn innocence so contrary to the callous, selfish heart within. His father was wrong. Cristos had not succumbed to fate, had not followed some preordained path. His soul had been turned by Nadia, a woman of two faces, whose evil had infected his own heart.

In that moment, he vowed never to love again. Never to become a pawn of his own heart.

And in a lightning move, one too quick for his father to react to, Cristos plunged the blade into his father, lifting him upon the blade into the air, his powerful muscles flexing with effort.

He looked at his father, and his father stared back; there was no pain in his eyes, just pity, resignation at what his son had done to him.

CRISTOS SAT IN a café on the Champs-Élysées sipping tea, watching the Parisians passing by. He was dressed in a custom-made suit, his green tie set off against his white shirt. He had left Cotis and the Asian continent behind one week earlier and headed to Zurich, Switzerland, where he bought a townhouse and began to formulate a future.

"We would like to avail ourselves of your services again," Riley said. He and his silent partner sat across from Cristos, each sipping coffee.

Cristos nodded.

"How will we contact you?"

"You won't. When in need of my services, you will place a memorial posting to Nadia Desai in the obituary section of the Sunday edition of the *London Times*. I will then contact you."

"Very well," Riley said.

"I have a question for you."

"Yes," Riley said with a smile.

"Who paid for my treatment at the hospital?"

"I thought we discussed that."

"Did Nadia visit me while I was in a coma?"

The two men looked at each other. The silent man nodded.

"Yes, she did," Riley said without any display of contrition or embarrassment. "Every day."

Cristos picked up his napkin, wiped his mouth, and placed it on the table. He finally stood. He looked directly at the tall, silent man. "I will be available, but understand that if you ever lie or betray me again, you will end up like your friend here."

"I don't understand." The man spoke for the first time.

Riley looked at Cristos with a curious smile. "What do you mean?"

And as if drawing a pen from his pocket, Cristos pulled out a gun, quickly placed it against Riley's right eye, and pulled the trigger.

CHAPTER 29

L ARRY KNOLL LOOKED UP at the moni-
tor, the display showing two FBI agents leading
a group of three men into the main entrance, and buzzed them in.

In the last ten hours, his post had become the site of mayhem.
Between the various FBI, Justice Department, police, and ADA, he
wasn't fully sure what was going on, but the groups seemed to be
squared off more against each other than working in concert.

But in the last hour, a semblance of peace had been restored.
Most of the various law-enforcement officers had returned home to
their families, headed out for drinks on a Friday night, or gone back
to their offices to regroup. There was no one else in the cavernous
lobby at this hour except for detectives Myers and Reiner, whom he
had just let down to evidence to drop off some materials on a new
case.

This was Larry's third double shift in seven days. Not that he
was complaining. He needed the money. He had promised Daria
that when the baby was born, they would have no debt and a small
nest egg to allow them to give their newborn child the advantages
that neither of them was afforded. There was a comradery among

the double shifters: Charlie downstairs, Nolan Ludeke upstairs in the medical facility. They had come to be known as the musketeers, as the three of them did the work of six and did it better than those working half the time on twice the rest.

As Larry finally turned his attention to the five who walked across the large marble lobby, he did a double take as he saw the face of the man in the middle of the group. He had read the papers, had seen the news, and had actually seen him just two days earlier with his wife. Larry had been devastated at the news of their dying, which confirmed his belief that it was always the good who were struck down before their time. But maybe that wasn't in effect today.

AT 8:25, JACK walked through the main entrance to the Tombs. Aaron and Donal walked in front, with black bags on their shoulders, while Cristos and Josh were three steps behind. They had run through the plan four times, studying Jack's hastily drawn map, discussing contingencies. And while there was no further discussion of Mia or the cost of failure, the threat was abundantly clear. If Jack did not succeed in turning the case over to Cristos, Mia would die. Jack had a part to play, and he was about to play it at award-level caliber.

"Holy shit," Larry said.

Jack smiled back.

"But . . ." Larry was lost for words. "You're alive?"

"Hey, Larry," Jack said as he held his fingers up to his lips. "That's between you and me."

"And your wife, she's OK?"

"Yeah," Jack said, nodding. "Thanks for your concern."

"I didn't hear."

"No one has, and I need you to keep it that way."

Larry nodded in understanding.

"We need to go downstairs," Jack said.

Larry looked the other men over.

"Show him your badges, boys."

Aaron, Donal, and Josh flipped open their billfolds, flashing badges, quickly closing them up and stuffing them back into their pockets.

"FBI?" Larry said with raised eyebrows, turning back to Jack. "Don't tell me you've gone over to the dark side, too."

"No." Jack laughed. "I'm still a good guy."

"And who's this?" Larry pointed at Cristos. He was still on guard despite the DA standing before him.

"He's a member of the Cotis government. I've got a real hush-hush case going."

"Is that what everyone downstairs is after?"

"You might say that. Who is downstairs, by the way?"

"Charlie, he's always down there; some accountant"—Larry pointed at Aaron and Donal—"and three of their friends."

Jack glanced at the two. "I don't think these guys have any friends."

"Oh, and I just sent two detectives from Midtown South, they're just dropping off. You'll probably pass them on the way down." Larry smiled as he pushed the button releasing the security gate and waved them past. "What about you?" Larry said to Josh, who lingered behind.

"Sounds a little crowded down there. I think I'll wait up here." Josh held up his cell phone. "I'm waiting for a call, anyway."

"Suit yourself. There's a bench over there if you want it," Larry said as he pointed to the far corner of the lobby.

"Larry," Jack called out as they arrived at the elevator bank, "don't tell a soul that you saw me or that we're downstairs."

"Mr. Keeler, once a cop, always a cop. You know I have your back."

The elevator arrived, and the four stepped inside. Just as the doors were closing, Jack smiled and said, "Thanks, Larry."

• • •

FBI AGENT JOE Perry stood in the middle of the evidence room, thinking of what a misnomer its name was. The vast space was more like a warehouse or a storage facility than a room.

Perry had been assigned as the liaison with the Bureau of Courts in locating the evidence case in the possession of Mia Keeler before her death that morning.

A day earlier, an internal investigation had begun on her possible connection with evidence tampering, but he had his doubts. He had known Mia for several years, and that was something that was not in her character.

After ten hours here on top of his seventy-five-hour week, Perry was done. He was heading home for a late dinner with his wife and would crawl into bed for at least eight hours before he had to return the next morning. He was leaving behind two young agents, Bracato and Stratton, to ensure security. As both agents were younger than thirty and known for their weekend exploits and surveillance stamina, he had no fear of them being able to pull an all-nighter. Holly Rose Tremont, the analyst provided by the DA's office, was still poring over computer records and wasn't planning to leave until after nine. She had gone through the several hundred files in cases brought in since Tuesday but was forced to expand her search once someone realized that Mia might have had her evidence case stashed inside another case that was already down there.

JACK PUSHED THE button for sublevel five, and the cab began its descent. The four banks of elevators were separate and apart from the prison facility serving the sublevels up to the fifth-floor medical and psychiatric facility.

"You realize we are all being recorded," Jack said without looking up at the security camera.

Donal smiled broadly, looking straight into the lens. Both he and

Aaron reached into their pockets and pulled out small black key-fob-like devices.

"Nobody sees us unless we want them to see us. You think we'd walk into the lobby of this building allowing our pictures to appear all over the place the minute we leave?"

"So, that's how you didn't show up on video when you killed the Bonsleys?"

Cristos smiled at Jack but remained silent.

As the car passed sublevel two, Aaron reached inside his jacket and pulled his gun.

"Absolutely not!" Jack shouted at Aaron before turning to Cristos. "You want my cooperation, no guns. Let me just walk in and get the box, and we walk out." Jack felt as if he were descending into Hades with hell's minions.

Aaron shook his head, but Cristos nodded in agreement. "No guns . . . for the moment. You've got two minutes to get the case."

CHARLIE NODDED TO Perry, who stood at the exit from the evidence room, buzzing him out the security door into the lobby. Charlie didn't much like the overly stiff FBI agent who walked around his domain as if he owned it, talking to his own people with respect yet talking down to both Charlie and the female analyst from the DA's office.

As Perry left, Charlie smiled inwardly. Despite all of Perry's arrogance, all of his blowhard superiority, Charlie knew he would never find what he was looking for. As far as Charlie was concerned, he was the one who actually controlled the moment. He was well aware of what everyone was looking for, he knew its exact location, and he knew that no matter how many records people pored over, no one would be finding it anywhere in the database. And if and when they decided to go through every box, it could take them weeks before they found the unregistered evidence box that Jack and Mia had hidden away.

But Charlie also remembered how scared Jack's wife looked when asked about its contents. When he had heard of their untimely deaths this morning, Charlie knew that it was no car accident that ended their lives. Someone, somehow, gave them a little push. When he had arrived earlier in the day to see the FBI and judicial liaison waiting for him, asking if he knew where an evidence case belonging to Jack Keeler might be, he said he had no idea. It wasn't in the system. *Deny till you die*; the phrase kept echoing in his head. It was Charlie's intention to wait until things died down, grab the box himself, and turn it over to Frank Archer.

But now that Charlie knew Jack was alive, that he was on his way to get the case, a new clarity formed in his mind. Jack would set things to right. That's what he did. It's what he had always done.

Charlie turned as two cops exited the elevator and stood at the glass window.

"How's life at Midtown South?" Charlie asked the two detectives who stood on the other side of the security glass.

"Hey, Charlie," Scott Myers said. "Always fun."

"You know, the usual summertime mayhem," Sid Reiner said as he dug through his pants, searching for his ID, cursing under his breath.

Although Reiner thought his words were unheard, Charlie heard it all, their voices amplified through the speaker under the window. Everyone knew Charlie's rules. Charlie had always been a stickler for protocol, demanding to see proper ID from all cops and detectives who ventured down into this world—his world—no matter if he knew them a lifetime or a day. And if they were his relatives, he asked to see two forms of ID before he granted access. This was his domain. He was charged with protecting it, and if someone wanted to curse his ass out under his breath for enforcing security, that was just fine.

And with Perry now standing in the vestibule, impatiently waiting for the elevator, watching the exchange with judgmental eyes, Charlie was going to ensure that the FBI understood not only how seriously he took his job but also how strongly he carried it out.

Detective Myers stood at the window, holding his ID up for Charlie to see as he laughed at his partner, who grew frantic in his search. Charlie had known Myers and Reiner for a few years now. They were good detectives, but like so many before them, their passion for the job had faded, their appearance sloppy, their attitudes jaded. Charlie didn't fault them—after all, he was removed from their world, safely hidden behind a wall of glass. Myers and Reiner saw and dealt with things most people couldn't imagine and did it on a salary that forced you to live paycheck to paycheck.

As Reiner continued to fumble for his ID, the second bank of elevator doors opened, and to Charlie's surprise, Jack stood there flanked by three men. Larry hadn't called down, hadn't told him anyone else was on their way down. They had spoken not two minutes earlier confirming that Myers and Reiner had some evidence to log in, but there was no mention of Jack or three companions.

It was Perry who reacted first at seeing Jack. He stood there speechless, his mouth half open in surprise.

"Mr. Keeler?" Perry said, his normal confidence temporarily on hold.

Jack thrust out his hand in an election-style greeting.

"I'm glad to see you're alive . . ." Perry said as he shook Jack's hand.

"And you are?" Jack asked, a hint of distrust in his voice.

"Joe Perry, FBI." Perry looked at the other men, his mind beginning to spin. "I hadn't heard you were alive. And your wife?"

"Alive."

"Thank God," Perry said before reverting back to his old self. "Forgive me, but why are you down here?"

"This is my backyard, Mr. Perry, and you're asking me what I'm doing here?"

"I mean no offense, but your wife, who works for us—"

"Who is still missing," Jack snapped back.

"I'm sorry, I didn't realize." Perry paused. "But if your wife is still missing . . . why is it this is the place you come to?"

"Charlie," Jack called out, ignoring the question and hoping to keep the conversation from devolving into a situation where Aaron would feel compelled to reach into his jacket again.

"Mr. Keeler," Charlie said, "so glad you're here—"

"Excuse me," Perry interrupted. "You didn't answer my question."

Jack could see Aaron and Donal getting edgy, exchanging glances.

"I'm sorry," Jack said. His mind was flying. Before a single threat was made, Jack knew that disaster was looming. Perry wasn't going anywhere, and if Jack was to retrieve the case, something would have to give, and sadly, he knew what that was. "Perhaps we could speak in private."

Cristos looked at Jack, his eyes void of communication but his thoughts clear.

Scott Myers had watched the entire exchange from where he stood by the glass window and, like everyone else, had that same re-action at seeing Jack Keeler come back to life. But when he saw the body language of Keeler's escorts, his instincts took over, and he cautiously laid his hand upon the Glock 19 at his waist. Not a second later, a bullet caught him in the right cheek before his hand had a chance to draw his gun.

Donal, the barrel of his gun still smoking, turned it on Perry.

From behind the safety of the glass, Charlie grabbed the phone.

Aaron charged Reiner, whose hands were still in his pockets searching for his ID, grabbing him, smashing his face up against the glass as he jammed his pistol into the detective's neck, twisting his head violently to the side. Aaron looked at Charlie and said, "Drop that phone if you want this man to live."

Charlie hesitated, staring between Reiner's desperate eyes and the face of his red-haired attacker.

"Now, open the door."

Charlie and Reiner stared at each other, fear etched in the detective's face as his eyes pleaded for help. Charlie was frozen, the phone still in his hand, poised to dial.

Cristos gave a subtle nod, and Aaron pulled the trigger. The blast of the 9mm echoed in the small vestibule as the side of Reiner's head splattered the window.

Donal grabbed Perry by the back of his collar; his gun jammed into the FBI agent's neck and shoved him toward the blood-covered window. Aaron released Reiner's body and let it crumple to the floor. Donal took his place, shoving Perry against the glass.

"Care to have another go at that?" Donal said.

Charlie stared back through the blood-covered window at Jack, sharing a horrified look as they both stood there powerless.

But Aaron wasn't waiting. He reached into the black bag on his shoulder and withdrew an egg-sized ball. A small LED device protruded from the malleable substance. He rolled it around in his hand, fingered two small buttons on the LED, and jammed it up onto the bloody glass.

"You are a stubborn one," Donal said to Charlie. And without another word, Donal pulled the trigger, killing Perry.

Charlie, in shock from the sight of death close up, stared at the Silly Putty-like glob. The moment hung there as he finally realized what it was . . . and dived for cover.

The small explosion shattered the three-inch-thick window as if it was a wine glass thrown to the floor. The accompanying fireball rolled up to the ceiling and curled back down.

Without waiting for the smoke to clear, Aaron climbed through the three-by-three foot hole onto the reception desk and leaped down on top of Charlie, who rolled around on the ground with shards of bloody glass embedded in his skin. Aaron kicked him in the gut and quickly turned to the console, wiping the glass from the surface. He found and thumbed the red door button. The buzzer sounded, and Cristos, Donal, and Jack came charging in.

Donal shucked the bag off his shoulder and onto the counter as he looked around the room. He reached down to Charlie, taking his gun and handcuffs.

Cristos turned to Aaron. "There are three in there. Clear the room so Mr. Keeler can get what we came for."

Jack raced to Charlie's side, leaning over him, running his hands around his body, looking for serious injury.

"I'm so sorry," Jack whispered before being violently snatched to his feet by Cristos.

"Time to save your wife."

CHAPTER 30

BRACATO AND STRATTON SAT in the back of the evidence room at a makeshift desk, feeling like overqualified guards, as Holly whirred away at her computer, trying to locate the evidence case that might or might not be down there.

Stratton didn't mind babysitting Holly. He had always liked blondes and had been partial to the more athletic types, a description that the twenty-five-year-old Holly easily fit. He hoped at least to get her phone number by the end of their shift.

Greg Stratton was the senior of the two agents. He and Carl Bracato were in their third year as partners and had developed a substantial and successful case history in the white-collar crime division. Stratton had thought it ironic; after all of the training they went through at Quantico, all of the weapons and hand-to-hand skills they had developed, they had never even drawn their Glock 23s from their holsters. Having met on the first day of class, they were always competitive, Stratton seeming to edge out Bracato in everything from target practice to exams to navigating city streets in mock car chases.

Stratton might have been the better shot, the smarter of the two, but Bracato was the one who wasted no time in seizing the day. He had already set up dinner with Holly for next week.

"What do you say I go pick up dinner?" Bracato said to Holly and Stratton.

Holly looked up from her computer amid the stacks of paper and smiled in the affirmative.

"Sure, how about—"

The sound was muted, a dull pop, but Stratton knew at once what it was.

"Shit," Stratton said as he drew his pistol. "Holly, go to the back corner, and stay there until we come back for you."

The second muted gunshot sounded. Bracato pulled his gun and was already on the run up the aisle.

"Who the hell would try and shoot their way down here?" Bracato said. "They'll never get in."

Then the sound of the muffled explosion reverberated through the evidence room, the tinkle of shattering glass trailing off.

"Holy shit," Bracato whispered as Stratton arrived at his side. They bisected the main aisle, hiding between the twelve-foot-high rows of shelves twenty feet from the main entrance door. Sounds of commotion drifted out from the office.

Bracato looked to Stratton for direction.

"No question, they're coming in here. Stay lost among the shelves. If you take one out, quickly move your position so they don't find you."

A skinny red-haired man in a sportcoat rolled into the room, spinning into the first row of shelves. Bracato watched as he looked back, signaling a second, taller man who came in gun held high, sweeping the room. Bracato could see from the way they held their guns, the positions they took, that they were law enforcement.

Bracato stayed low, two rows back from the two men, watching, thinking. The taller man was obscured by the shelves, but Bracato could see over the evidence boxes, through the open spaces, as the man took a few steps forward. Bracato could see his eyes focused. This man was not there to capture anyone. He was there to kill.

In that single moment, Bracato made his decision. He crouched low, creeping forward, his eyes fixed on the man through the slatted shelves, watching as he approached, only ten feet away now.

Bracato wrapped his fingers around the trigger. He could hit a small target at one hundred feet, so ten feet should be nothing. But he had never shot anyone; this man would be his first. And Bracato had no intention of shooting to immobilize, to take out a leg or an arm. He was going for the kill, knowing that the man would do everything to kill him if given the chance.

He lined up his sight, shoulder high, and waited for the man to appear in the open.

And the bullet exploded through Bracato's chest, entering through the left of his back, piercing his lung, nicking his heart. Bracato collapsed face-first to the floor.

He never saw or heard the other man's approach. He was so focused on the tall man that he failed to notice the other.

Bracato was roughly flipped over onto his back. The tall man, the one who had been the bait, leaned down and took the gun from his hand.

"Where's your partner?"

Bracato stared up into the man's eyes. His face was plain, an average-Joe kind of look that would get lost in a crowd, the type of face that so easily obscured a dark heart.

Bracato knew that he was dying, a minute, maybe two, left as his lungs filled with blood, and in those two minutes, he would do everything he could from his position to save his friend and the young woman with whom he would be missing a date next Saturday.

"He left," Bracato struggled to say, stifling a cough. "He and Holly went to get our dinner."

"When?"

"A couple of minutes ago." Bracato could taste the iron flavor of blood in his mouth. "Maybe five."

The man leaned down and looked into his eyes, searching for truth. Bracato did everything his crippled body could do to convey it. It was a moment, the two men assessing each other.

Then the tall man laid his pistol on Bracato's brow. "You shouldn't have hesitated. Lucky for me, I guess, or we'd be switching positions."

And the man pulled the trigger.

JACK WATCHED AS Charlie's large body was violently hoisted up into a rolling desk chair by Cristos. Small rivulets of blood rolled down his friend's face, pooling in the collar of his white shirt. But other than the small cuts and singed hair, he seemed to be all right. Jack couldn't bear the thought of his friend dying at his expense.

Aaron stepped back into the office.

"Well?" Cristos said.

"We got one. He says the other two left to get dinner. We've swept the room, didn't find anyone, but I'm not sure."

"Then the two of you escort Keeler back there. We are running out of time."

Jack looked around at the devastation, through what was left of the window into the vestibule, and could see the three bodies lying there in intermingled pools of blood.

"You said no one was going to die. You're going to kill my wife and me as soon as you get the box, so why should I get it? Why should I help the man who is going to kill me?"

Cristos stared at Jack. "I'll make a deal with you."

"I've seen your deals."

"I made no promise about people not dying. Collateral damage, you remember what that is? You remember those teens who died in your pursuit of justice?"

Jack hated this man.

"I give you my word, I'll let Mia live," Cristos said.

"You have no word to give."

"On the contrary. If you get me what I want, she will live."

Jack said nothing, not believing the word of the man before him.

Aaron and Donal stepped over to Jack, flanking him. They looked to Cristos for guidance.

"Or how about this?" Cristos said as he drew out his gun, laying it on Charlie's thigh.

"I'll let you choose: your friend here or Mia. Could you make that choice in front of your friend?"

"Jack, don't let this guy mess with your head," Charlie said as he looked up.

"Say it, Jack, who would you choose? Could you watch the eyes of your friend here as he suffers and dies so that your wife may live? Does he even know her? Would he be willing to make the sacrifice for her?"

Jack's mind was spinning. He couldn't bear to look into Charlie's eyes. They both knew the choice Jack would make, what any person would do for the one they love.

"If you don't want to be faced with that choice, you've got one minute to go get me my case."

REMAINING IN THE shadows of row Q, Stratton watched at the far end of the evidence room as three men walked through the main door into the room. He couldn't believe his eyes when he saw Jack Keeler. Stratton did not know the man, since he and Bracato were based out of the Washington office, but he had seen his file not twelve hours earlier when he was assigned to babysit this place.

Keeler was being escorted by the two men who had killed Bracato. Stratton heard the gunshot too late, rounding the corner to see his friend lying on the ground. He had tried to take a shot but had no clear angle, and by the time he did, the two men had lost themselves in the rows of shelves, only to slip out the door.

Stratton watched as the taller man shoved Keeler forward. He was their prisoner and there was no doubt that he was leading them to the mythical box everyone had been searching for all day.

As he watched the three men walk down the aisle, he had a clear shot, and he was certain that he could take one of them out. But that one kill could lead to Keeler's death, Holly's, and his own. The second man could disappear into the oversized rows of shelves and later come back at him without warning, striking him down just like Bracato. And he had no idea how many more were outside.

But all moves be damned. He could overthink a simple decision. He held his gun in a two-handed grip, lined up the sight on Bracato's killer, and pulled the trigger.

DONAL'S HEAD EXPLODED in much the same manner as those people he had killed in the last five minutes. Sounding like a smashing melon, the rear of his head bloomed into a red mist that splattered onto Aaron's face.

Instinctually, Jack and Aaron dove for cover in opposite directions away from the carnage. Jack's eyes scanned the direction the shot had come from but saw nothing. Grateful for the help, he didn't know how much of an ally the gunman really was or how long he would live as he came up against Aaron and Cristos. Not waiting on a savior, Jack looked back at Donal's body and saw the gun he had been holding when the bullet pierced his right eye. It lay not two feet from his outstretched dead hand.

But then Aaron was there, quickly snatching it before Jack could react and disappearing back into the row across from him like a rat stealing food. Without further delay, Jack scrambled backward into row J and raced out the other end into an adjacent aisle.

• • •

STRATTON WORKED HIS way up to row C just fifteen feet from the entrance door. He knew the momentary confusion would shield his movements and that the space where the gunshot originated would soon be searched.

He focused his hearing, careful to stay within the shadows, watching and listening to both his front and his back so as to avoid the same fate as Bracato. He could hear a man speaking with a distinctive, polished accent, its origin unclear. There was no question a second man was there, no doubt a captive, as the conversation was one-sided. He couldn't make out what was being said but caught intermittent words: "death," "box," and "Keeler."

He could see through the door into the small hallway that led to the main entrance and its offshoot into the office. Shards of blood-laden glass were scattered over the cream-colored carpet, looking like rubies in the sand. He could smell burnt air, the odor of residual C4 thick in his nostrils.

Stratton moved back through the aisles, eyes darting to and fro, making sure that he was not in anyone's gun sight. He worked his way back to the far corner to check on Holly, finding her crouched in a corner, her head tucked into her knees, sitting motionless.

"Holly," Stratton whispered as he approached. But she didn't respond, frozen with fear.

Stratton turned his back to the corner, looking around as he stepped backward toward her. "Let's go. I'm going to tuck you somewhere safe, up into the shelves. You'll be fine, I promise."

But there was no response.

Stratton bent down, laying a gentle hand on her shoulder.

And she tumbled over. Blood coated the front of her white shirt. The slash across her throat had nearly bled out.

Stratton recoiled in shock, seeing the girl he had pined over for the last eight hours so brutally murdered. With the horror of death witnessed for the second time, his mind was distracted. He never saw the small charge of C4 in her lap. It never occurred to him that she

would be booby-trapped. The charge tore him and Holly apart before he had any chance of escape

CHARLIE WAS SITTING in the office chair, still struggling to
get his bearings. The ringing in his ears had died down a bit, but he
still had the sense of being underwater. The sounds of the world were
muddled and distant. He felt as if he had just been hit by a train.
His skin burned from the heat of the blast, but he was thankful that
nothing appeared broken and that somehow he was still alive.

Aaron slipped into the room, his gun at the ready. "Someone else
is in there. They took out Donal. Now Keeler's slipped away."

Cristos grabbed Charlie by the hair and pulled him out of the
chair, slamming him against the wall. "You know why we're here." It
was a statement, not a question.

Charlie smiled at Cristos. It was a knowing smile, a fuck-you smile.

Cristos slammed him against the wall again. "Where is the case
brought in here by Jack Keeler?"

"I moved it," Charlie said with a grin. "Jack doesn't even know.
Once I heard he was killed, I had a feeling something like this would
happen. And you, my friend, will never find it."

"Then I guess I have no need for Jack anymore," Cristos said as he
threw Charlie back into the chair. He shot a knowing look at Aaron.

The statement was like smelling salts, pulling Charlie to full
alertness.

"If you value not only your life but theirs, you'll tell me."

Charlie stared up at the man, ignoring the pain of the burns, the
stinging of the glass in his face. When Charlie woke up this morning, showered, dressed, and kissed his wife, Lisa, good-bye, he'd had
no idea it would be the last time he would see her. He valued his life,
something he knew the man before him did not, and he knew that
it would quickly end once he got what he came for. Charlie resigned

himself to death and in doing so would take the location of the box with him.

"Keeler's loose in there," Aaron said as he tightened the strap of the black bag on his shoulder.

"Relax. He's got nowhere to go." Cristos looked at his watch. "But we don't have much time."

Aaron looked at the computer on the side desk, its monitor cracked. "Not a chance we're going to find it in there."

Cristos stared off, his mind spinning, then, without a warning, he turned and shot Charlie in the foot, the sound of the report deafening in the small space.

Charlie grimaced as he instinctively tried to lift his now-mangled foot. But Cristos restrained his hands as he glared at him, letting the shock of the wound fade and all of the pain pour in.

"You're going to tell me where the case is—" Cristos leaned in close, eye-to-eye with Charlie, staring at the tiny pieces of glass under his skin, at the pain in his eyes. Charlie's eye lids began to flutter; he was near passing out. "Because every man has his breaking point."

Cristos pulled an EpiPen from inside his jacket, removed the needle cover, and jabbed it into Charlie's neck.

Charlie's body went rigid, his eyes flashing open as his heart began to race.

"No passing out on me now," Cristos said. "The epinephrine and adrenaline will keep your ass wide awake and your senses on fire, so you'll feel everything I'm about to do to you."

"I may be wide awake," Charlie said as he gritted his teeth, "but I'll bleed out before you find out what you need. The only person I would ever tell is the one the box belongs to, and we both know that is not you."

CRISTOS CENTERED CHARLIE'S large frame in the wheeled office chair and bound his torso to the seatback with an extension cord so Charlie wouldn't fall as he lost his strength. He pushed him out into the evidence room, guiding him from behind like a nurse, except that the gun he kept pressed against Charlie's head quickly vanquished that image.

"Aaron!" Cristos shouted as he continued pushing Charlie down the center aisle toward the middle of the room. "Keep an eye on that door."

Aaron stood at the exit door, his pistol gripped tightly in his hand, his other wrapped around the black bag strap on his shoulder, as his eyes scanned the area for movement.

"So, Mr. Keeler!" Cristos called out. "Your friend Charlie seems to have moved your little box. And he's only willing to tell you were he moved it to."

Jack stayed low, in the shadows of aisle L. He could see Charlie and Cristos as plain as day, his friend precariously perched on the chair. Blood flowed from his shattered foot, leaving a red-dotted trail behind him. Cristos stopped at the midpoint of the main center aisle beneath a harsh bright light that seemed to wash what little life remained from Charlie's shattered face.

Cristos stood over Charlie, his gun pressed down against his knee. "Mr. Keeler?"

Jack remained silent.

Kpow. The gun exploded, the large-caliber bullet shattering Charlie's knee cap, cartilage, and tendons, nearly separating the leg at the joint. Charlie grimaced in agony, but no cry escaped his lips, his pain channeled into an angry gasp.

"Mr. Keeler," Cristos said without remorse, without emotion, "I've got far more bullets than you have time. I suggest you answer me."

Jack remained silent, his soul broken as he watched his friend suffer. As despicable as it seemed to watch a friend die, he knew that it was inevitable. They had no intention of allowing Charlie or, for that matter, himself to live.

Kpow. The bullet tore into Charlie's groin. Charlie's eyes were glazing over from the pain, his staccato gasps echoing in the room.

"Your wife's survival depends on you. I suggest you speak to your friend and get me that case before it's too late." Cristos spun around and walked back down the aisle, leaving Charlie sitting there in the open.

Jack moved closer. He could see the damage to his friend, shocked at his condition: his face dotted with wounds, his lower body soaked in blood.

"I'll give you thirty seconds to talk to him," Cristos called out. "Then you've got one minute to get me the case. Or your wife will die a far more slow and horrific death than your friend."

Charlie looked around the room, his head turning to and fro, when he finally caught sight of Jack. Their eyes locked, a moment of painful understanding passing between them.

Charlie managed a pained smile and nodded as Jack emerged from the rows of shelves. He slowly walked forward, paying no attention to Cristos and Aaron, who stood in the doorway at the other end of the room. Jack put his hand on Charlie's shoulder and stared down at his shattered body. He was filled with pain, heart-rending agony at the torture of his friend. He had spent so much of his life seeing the aftermath of crimes, the horrific photographs, the witness statements, the testimony of those who had seen the evil in men's eyes, that he had forgotten the reality of the brutal origins of those pictures and stories.

"Don't look so troubled," Charlie whispered.

"I'm so sorry."

"Jack," Charlie whispered, "you have to do me a favor."

Jack leaned into his friend, taking his bloody hand in his own. "Is there something you want me to tell your wife?"

"No, she knows how I feel. No worries."

"I don't know what to say."

"Row S," Charlie struggled to speak. "Case nine-two-nine-six."

Jack looked into his dying friend's eyes. "What's in it, Charlie?"

"Just find it. You'll understand."

Jack nodded.

"And Jack," Charlie whispered, reaching out with a closed fist to place something in Jack's hand, "it's always brought me good luck. It will help you get out of here."

Jack said nothing as he looked down at the tip of a rabbit's foot protruding from his closed fist. Without a word, he slipped it into his pocket and smiled at his friend.

As he looked Charlie in the eye, he watched the light slip away; he heard the last subtle breath escape his lips as his head gently tilted forward.

Jack's head snapped up as he saw Cristos nod at Aaron and Aaron begin his approach.

Without thought, Jack broke into a full-on sprint, racing down the aisle, calling out the rows as he went. K, L, M . . . O, P . . . S. Quickly ducking in, he scanned the shelves, eyes darting back and forth. He heard Aaron's running footsteps charging his way. Moving down farther and farther, Jack finally spied it on the fifth shelf: 9296.

The box was simple, reinforced cardboard, looking as if it had been up there for years, blending with the numerous metal cases, transfiles, and accordion folders. The section was civil, not criminal. Jack didn't fully understand what Charlie did, but he realized that his friend had taken matters into his own hands when he heard that Jack and Mia were killed. He was the only other person to know about the box and its location and, Charlie being Charlie, realized that people would be coming for it, so he took it upon himself to create a contingency plan.

With Aaron's footsteps nearly upon him, Jack drew down the box and flipped open the lid. And as he peered inside, he was floored by what he saw.

AARON CHARGED DOWN the center aisle, clutching his pistol, his bag banging against his back. He had watched Jack dodge right into row S and pumped his legs as hard as he could. Cristos's orders not to kill him were clear, but that didn't mean he couldn't maim him, shoot him in the leg or the spine to cripple him. All they needed was the case's location; it didn't matter if it came out of Jack's mouth clearly or as a last gasp.

And as he turned the corner, his gun held high, double-fisting it as trained, he caught a glimpse of Jack standing there. But much to his surprise, Jack wasn't scrambling away like a trapped animal—he was facing him, his eyes focused. And when he realized what Jack was holding, it was too late.

By the time Aaron pulled the trigger, a bullet was already tearing into his own chest, straight through his heart, the force knocking him back and to the ground.

Jack was instantly upon him, grabbing his gun and tossing it away. He took his cell phone, the key-fob-like device, and finally the black bag from his shoulder before melting back into the shadows of the aisle.

Jack looked back at case 9296, the case that, besides a canvas shopping bag filled with Oreos, two bags of chips, beef jerky, and a six-pack of Budweiser, also held a loaded pistol and two clips in the event that a *situation* arose. Charlie always said this place was his home and that his home had its little touches, its little stashes for *all* kinds of emergencies.

Jack quickly ran to row Y, looked up to the seventh shelf, and found the evidence case that he and Mia had stashed away on Thursday. He quickly opened it, verifying that it hadn't been discovered and emptied. He had no idea what he was looking at, nor did he take any time to inspect it.

He unzipped Aaron's black bag, tucked the metal case inside, and threw it over his shoulder. He slipped the gun into the waistband of his pants but pulled it out as he heard Cristos's rampaging approach; his accent had all but vanished as he screamed desperately on the run, "You will never get out of here!"

Digging into his pocket, Jack felt Charlie's rabbit foot and smiled. Filled with hope, he charged out of the row, catching a glimpse of Cristos seventy-five feet away, racing toward him. Gunfire erupted, erratic and staccato, ricocheting off the floor, walls, and shelves. He pressed on, driving his legs as hard as he could.

Without looking back as he ran toward the rear of the evidence room, Jack shouted between deep breaths, "I'm going to burn everything in this case!"

Suddenly arriving at the rear fire door, Jack ground to a halt, pulled out the rabbit's foot, and stared at it—more specifically, at the three keys that dangled off the small chain. He tucked the largest key into the lock, turned it, and, with a broad smile, opened the rear emergency exit.

CRISTOS RAN THROUGH the evidence room. He needed that box at all costs. His life, his future, depended on it.

When he saw Jack race out of the shadows, he knew what had happened. Somehow Charlie had gotten the better of him. Although shot multiple times and left to die, the old man had somehow reached up from the dead and helped his friend. They had taken his gun, his cuffs, but they couldn't take his mind; Charlie had tricked them all.

Cristos had no idea where Jack was running to, but his greatest fears were realized as he saw the open emergency door, the wash of dim light pouring out of its opening. Cristos held his gun tightly, ran through the door, and charged up the stairs.

CHAPTER 31

JACK WATCHED AS CRISTOS ran through the doorway and up the stairs, waiting a few moments before he emerged from the shadows and pulled the emergency exit door closed. He knew there was no reentry and that the door exited five floors up on the opposite side of the building.

Without another thought and his plan in motion, Jack ran through the cavernous evidence room, past Charlie's dead body, and through the lobby and its carnage. He hit the elevator button and prayed for its quick arrival. He felt the rabbit's foot in his pocket and prayed that it would impart the luck that Charlie wanted to give.

Cab four on the far left arrived; he hopped in and hit the button for the lobby. He quickly stepped up on the handrail and pushed aside the small ceiling service panel. But what he saw made any hope of escape via the shaftway quickly disappear. Hundreds of pin-red security lasers bounced around the shaft, flicking on and off and on as the cab rose toward the main floor. If Jack was to break the plane of a single one, every alarm in the complex would sound.

Jack knew that the chances of getting out of the Tombs were slim. He still had to face Josh up in the lobby, but at least Larry would be there. And with the rear fire stairs exiting in the back vestibule of the building, it would be only moments before Cristos was behind him again.

With the case in his possession, Jack had the one chip that could get Mia back, the one item that Cristos wouldn't dare let get away. And as he looked at Charlie's blood on his hands and shirt, Jack decided right there that too many people had already died over this box to let it slip into Cristos's hands. This wasn't just about saving Mia anymore; it was about salvaging some meaning for those who had perished in its wake.

THE ELEVATOR DOOR opened. Jack stood there staring out at Josh and Larry, whose conversation suddenly fell silent as they saw Jack, a black bag over his shoulder, the top of a metal case protruding from the top.

"Mr. Keeler?" Larry's tone conveyed his shock at Jack's appearance, the blood on his shirt, the gun dangling from his hand.

But Jack wasn't looking back at Larry; he was staring directly at Josh, whose shock was even more evident. Josh subtly moved his hand into his jacket.

The sound of a cell phone shattered the moment, echoing off the cavernous marble space. Josh quickly pulled his phone and answered it, his eyes never leaving Jack's.

"Yeah," was all he said, listening intently, nodding his head. With Larry's focus on Jack, he never saw Josh draw his pistol.

"What's . . . going on?" Larry said, his fingers drifting toward the emergency button on his desk.

Jack gripped his pistol tighter.

Josh slowly closed his cell phone and slipped it back into his pocket. The moment hung in the air, the two men locked into each other with knowing stares.

Suddenly, Jack whipped up his gun, firing at Josh, who dove for cover returning fire, the report amplified in the large space.

"Larry!" Jack shouted. "Stay down!" Larry scrambled under his desk, quickly drawing his weapon as he reached up to the command desk and hit the single red button. The cry of the alarm shrieked through the building. All doors and gates went into emergency lockdown, the loud thud of their slamming dead bolts and bars cutting through the high-pitched alarm's scream.

Jack rapid-fired his weapon, racing for the front door, despite the fact that it was locked tight behind bulletproof glass and dead bolts. He'd have more luck trying to penetrate the solid walls.

Josh answered back, firing his gun with far more care and accuracy than Jack, the bullets slamming into the ground around him, hitting the walls, barely missing him.

And as Jack's gun clicked out empty, he dove for cover by the door. He pulled the second and last clip, ejecting the first and slamming home his last fifteen bullets.

"Larry!" Jack yelled, his heart pouring through his words, pleading for release. "You've got to let me out of here. They have Mia. They're going to kill her. I'm the only one who can save her!"

Larry stared back at the DA, one of the most respected men in the city, who stood crouched by the door, behind the large garbage receptacle, trading gunfire with the FBI agent known as Josh.

He had no idea what was going on but didn't trust the FBI agent, who had taken cover behind a marble column, with a far superior position on Jack, one that would help him triumph if the firefight lasted much longer.

Larry knew protocol. Lock it all down. No one in or out until backup arrived, until someone in command made a decision. Larry respected the chain of authority and had never defied protocol, but there was no protocol for the decision he was about to make.

It wasn't his respect for Jack, or the fact that he was a former police officer—it was simply his plight. Larry knew what he would do if someone would dare try to kill his wife, Daria.

And despite the fact that he knew he would be facing the hell of a disciplinary hearing and probable removal from the force, he hit the door release.

CHAPTER 32

JACK BURST OUT OF the front of the Tombs and sprinted up the sidewalk. Seconds later, Josh dove out the door in pursuit, his arms pumping, his pistol clutched in his hand.

And then the black Suburban came tearing around the corner, its wheels screaming in protest as the SUV dug in and raced toward Jack, the roar of its redlined engine bellowing in the concrete caverns of Lower Manhattan. Jack ran, pushing himself to the limit, but knew there was no way he could outrun the SUV. There were no alleys to duck into, no open buildings on a Friday night, no savior to pluck him from certain death.

The downtown sidewalks were empty, devoid of people for the weekend except for those cutting through to some other destination. It was just Jack and the lone black vehicle that hunted him like a wounded animal. He held tight to the strap on his shoulder, the black bag that held the case, a prize that was only leaving death in its wake.

The SUV was less than fifty yards back, bearing down on him. It would be only seconds before they ran him down, for Jack knew they had no intention of letting him live.

And as the SUV cut the distance in half, only seconds away, a Jeep mounted the curb and skidded to a stop, nearly hitting Jack. The door flew open, and Jack stared into Frank's eyes.

"Let's go!"

WITH ITS GRILLE LIGHTS flashing and siren wailing, the Jeep entered the FDR Drive, the East River whipping by.

"Do you want to tell me what the hell is going on?" Frank said as he white-knuckled the wheel. "You disappear from your house, I think the worst, and then I hear on the radio about an emergency lockdown of the Tombs."

Jack said nothing.

"Are you out of your frickin' mind? I waited and waited until I realized where you were probably headed. What were you thinking? The whole world is going to be looking for you now."

Jack said nothing as he kept looking back at the SUV, which was cutting the distance by the second.

"Do you want to tell me what's in that thing?" Frank pointed at the case protruding from the bag on Jack's lap.

"Just get us the hell away from that guy."

Frank didn't say another word as the Jeep rocketed up the FDR, swerving in and out of traffic, braking and accelerating as he barely eluded the black SUV.

As Jack looked over his shoulder and saw the approaching Suburban barreling their way, it reminded him that just twenty-four hours ago, the same black vehicle had raced up behind him on Route 22. Although last night he was unaware of what the black car would unleash on his world, this time Jack was well aware that it would deliever only death.

The Suburban's oversized eight-cylinder engine was far more powerful than that of Frank's Jeep, but power and size were not always an advantage. As Frank approached 42nd Street, with the SUV coming up on his right side, he turned hard left, taking the exit at the very last second. The SUV's weight and size made it too difficult to stop and turn in time, and it blew right past the exit.

Frank blasted down 42nd Street, his lights flashing, his siren screaming, as pedestrians and cars alike made way for his approach. The closer he got to Midtown, the more he was forced to slow, to steer around traffic hung up at stoplights.

He took a hard right on Sixth Avenue, momentarily relaxing as he headed uptown. With no sign of the SUV, he exhaled, turning to Jack, who sat clutching the case to his chest. But then he saw the Suburban, turning onto the avenue from 42nd Street, rapidly coming up behind them.

Frank stomped the accelerator to the floor, blowing through lights, crosstown traffic screeching to a halt to avoid him.

Then the SUV was there, weaving in and out of traffic, desperately trying to gain ground.

The side windows rolled down, and a disembodied arm emerged, pistol in hand, and began firing at the Jeep's tires. Frank threw the wheel hard to the right, but the SUV matched his move, still rapid-firing, as bullets danced and skittered along the road, sending the nighttime strollers scrambling for cover. People whipped out cell phones, and multiple 911 calls reported the two involved vehicles. Frank hit the brakes and then immediately accelerated, trying desperately to lose Cristos and the ever-firing weapon. And then, suddenly, the left tire exploded, shredding in seconds, the car pulling hard left on only the aluminum rim, skidding across the avenue, sparks flying from the exposed wheel.

Frank came to a sudden stop.

"Run! don't look back!" Frank shouted as he reached for his gun to give Jack cover.

And without hesitation, Jack leaped from the vehicle.

• • •

JACK RAN DOWN 48th Street toward Broadway, toward the crowds, where he could get lost, while the SUV raced onto the block behind him. Simultaneously, two cop cars tore into the street ahead of him, blocking all traffic. Four cops leaped out, charging toward Jack.

Jack turned, spinning in place, looking around. There were no open stores, no subway entrances to duck into. And then he saw it. He looked up, the shadow of a new building blotting a sliver out of the night sky, surrounded by a ten-foot chain-link fence. Jack could see no security. They were probably asleep in the construction trailer and would only emerge if the matter was life-and-death.

Jack ran across the street and climbed the ten feet of chain link, hurdling the top and landing with a bone-jarring thud. He cut through the dirt and gravel courtyard and into the unfinished high-ceilinged lobby of the new addition to the New York skyline. Work lights dangled from the ceiling, piles of custom dark wood cabinetry and shelving lined the walls, ladders and scaffold abounded. Jack looked around for a place to hide, only to see Cristos on the fence not forty yards behind him. Jack quickly chose the open stairwell. He ran into the concrete shaftway and began his ascent. Five floors, ten floors—his body screamed as his lungs fought for breath. He could hear Cristos's pounding footfalls coming up behind him but didn't dare look for fear of slowing his flight.

Jack raced up the stairs, two at a time, his legs on fire as lactic acid poured through his muscles. By floor twenty, he thought his heart would either collapse or explode out of his chest. At floor thirty, he finally looked down and saw Cristos only two floors below and coming up hard. At floor forty, Jack came upon a wide-open floor, no walls, still under construction, and raced through the construction debris, past the idle tools and wallboard to the north-side stairs, where an open second route continued the ascent.

Up the stairs Jack ran, finally coming to a bulkhead, and he rammed through a steel fire door onto a wide-open roof deck. It was littered with gang boxes, storage sheds, portable toilets, empty beer bottles, and cigarette butts. This was the haven of the construction workers, where they escaped from the toils of their day to sit above the city that they and their brethren had built over the years.

Jack realized that he had boxed himself into a corner and had nowhere else to go. It would be a standoff unless he could figure a way out or down.

He walked to the edge, staring down on the neon lights that painted Times Square in an iridescent rainbow of colors. The sidewalks were awash in hordes of insect-sized people as the sounds of the night wafted up around him. He had escaped the Tombs, eluded his pursuers through the streets of the city, only to end up there, alone, with the one person who held Mia's life in his hands only seconds behind.

"So, what are you going to do? Jump?" Cristos said as he stepped through the bulkhead. He slowly walked toward Jack, his gun aimed directly at Jack's head.

Jack looked down over the city as he clutched the case tightly.

"You go through all of that effort only to commit suicide?"

Jack didn't turn, continuing to look out over the city, at the masses who walked around enjoying their Friday night, unaware of what was happening above their heads.

"Give me the case, and I'll let Mia go. I promise."

"That means nothing." Jack finally turned around and pointed his gun at Cristos.

The two held tightly to their weapons.

"You realize, if you kill me, your wife will have no chance? I'm the only link to finding her."

"You sure about that?" Jack said.

"Quite sure. Which leaves you with not a lot of choice," Cristos said. "You jump with the box, and I promise you, Mia will be five minutes behind you in death . . . and where would that leave your girls?"

Jack looked up in shock. "You stay away from them!" he snapped.

"I don't play with the innocent lives of children," Cristos said. "But you would be. They'll grow up as orphans under the cloud of a father who went insane and didn't try to save his wife."

"What?"

"How else will it be explained that you broke into the evidence room, killed all those people, stole an evidence case?"

Jack clutched the box closer as he continued pointing the gun at Cristos. "That was your hand, not mine."

"I'm dead, remember? That's a pretty far-fetched story for a dead man. You, on the other hand, stealing an evidence case filled with nothing but trinkets."

Jack stared at the box.

"Don't tell me you didn't look inside?" Cristos laughed. "You don't even know what you hold in your hand, what you're about to give your life for?"

"What?"

"That box holds the future, the answer to questions you couldn't imagine, secrets that the world isn't ready for. It holds mysteries and miracles. It holds the truth about certain people who are beyond desperate to ensure that the truth doesn't come out. Why do you think your wife hid it away?"

The north bulkhead exploded open, and four cops rolled out onto the rooftop, guns drawn. Their eyes filled with caution as they saw the two armed men facing off on the edge of the building.

"Drop your weapons!" the lead cop screamed.

Jack and Cristos ignored them.

"The contents of that box are rightfully mine," Cristos continued.

"That's bullshit—"

"No." Cristos cut him off. "The man who was murdered, the man who possessed the objects in that box, was my father."

"The priest?" Jack said with shock. "Did you kill him?"

"That is between me and my father. How are things with your dad?"

Jack was shocked and offended at the question, at the intimacy this man invaded.

"Give me the box."

Jack looked at the four cops, their guns trained on them.

Jack stepped away from the ledge. He didn't lower his gun as he spun left toward the north bulkhead. Cristos moved in sync with him, turning as he turned, stepping as he stepped. Jack looked toward the cops. He couldn't allow the case to fall into their hands, either. The FBI was after it, Cristos was after it, and who knew how many others were under its spell trying to get hold of it.

"Will you release her?" Jack asked. "Let her go unharmed?"

Cristos stared at the box. "I give you my word, I'll let her go."

Jack looked into his eyes. He wasn't sure if he saw a moment of honesty or the shadow of a lie. But he realized that with the cops closing in, his choices were limited.

Jack laid the box down next to the open bulkhead door, his eyes filled with defeat. Cristos kept his gun trained on Jack as he reached down, collecting his prize.

Jack watched as Cristos disappeared down the stairs, clutching the case under his arm. Two of the cops raced after him, but Jack knew they would never catch him and live.

The two remaining cops approached Jack, their guns aimed high.

"Drop your weapon!" the lead cop screamed.

"Now!" the young rookie shouted.

Jack released the pistol and watched it clatter to the roof deck.

And the two cops were on him, grabbing him by the shoulders, pulling his arms behind his back, and throwing him violently to the ground. Jack's knees hit first, but with his hands behind his back and nothing to brace his continuing fall, his head hit the surface with a violent snap.

His vision filled with blackness as the sounds of the city disappeared and he was enveloped in an unconscious nightmare.

CHAPTER 33

J ACK LOOKED AROUND, LOST, confused.
He lay in a strange bed. A man stood over him,
tall and broad. A scar wiggled its way down the left side of his neck;
he had the countenance of someone who had seen battle on more
than one occasion. But despite the rough exterior, there was a sadness
in his eyes.

"Jack?" the man whispered.

"Who are you? Where am I?"

The man placed his finger to his lips. "Not too loud. Listen very
carefully to me. I've got only a moment." The man paused. "Hold on
to your mind, or you won't be able to save Mia."

JACK AWOKE WITH a start and stared around the room. The
white walls were cushioned, and there wasn't a single corner or sharp
angle in the ten-by-twenty space.

A tube ran into his left arm, the IV drip infusing him with a tired
warmth. His chest and arms were wired up, although the monitors

were nowhere in sight. A curtain was drawn across what he imagined was a large window to the outside world.

A large leather strap wrapped his chest, not enough to constrict his breath but enough to constrict his escape. Smaller, equally constraining bands wrapped his wrists.

The mental ward of the Tombs occupied the entire fifth floor of the west wing, isolated and unknown to most. Used for the insane, the mentally disturbed, sometimes the perfect place to tuck a VIP, isolating him from scrutiny while *matters* were sorted out, it was also the facility for evaluations by court-appointed psychiatrists. It was a place far worse than any cell, as not only were you locked up and tethered to your bed, but your release depended on both the judicial system and the far more subjective medical community, where the inexact science of psychiatry could condemn you for life.

As Jack lay there, he fought off panic. He had gotten so close to finding Mia, yet now, having been captured, he couldn't be farther away. There were no clocks; his watch was gone, leaving him with no concept of time.

The thought drew his eyes to his left forearm, where he was surprised to see it encased in a thick white bandage, entirely obscuring his tattoo.

"Mr. Keeler." A blond nurse, big-boned and smiling, greeted Jack. She sat quietly in the corner, where she was practically invisible. She rose from her chair and walked over, her warm smile never leaving her face. "I'm so glad to see you awake. I'm Susan Meeks."

Jack nodded as she leaned over to shine a light in his eyes, checking his pupils. "How long have I been out?"

"Not long, an hour maybe. It's just past eleven o'clock." Meeks took Jack's pulse, fluffed his pillow, and tucked his blankets in without any regard to his restraints. "We took the liberty of bandaging the injury to your left arm—"

"Injury?" Jack asked with confusion as he looked at the heavy bandage on his arm.

"—and redressed your shoulder wound."

Before Jack had a chance to respond, the door opened and man in a dark suit entered. He stood ramrod-straight, what little hair he had on his head military bristle length. He avoided eye contact with Jack as he read through a single manila folder in his hand. Dark circles rimmed his eyes, although there was no exhaustion apparent in his body language. He glanced at Nurse Meeks, who immediately left. He closed the door behind her, silently walked to the bed, and finally snapped shut the folder.

"Mr. Keeler?" The man's voice was deep and without sympathy. "What did you take from the evidence room?"

Jack was amazed at the question, at the right-to-the-point approach. "I'm sorry, I didn't get your name."

"Gene Tierney, deputy director, New York field office of the FBI," Tierney answered in a staccato cadence.

"I have permitted access and confidential files down there pursuant to ongoing investigations, which are privileged."

"I don't believe the eight dead people down there care about your privileged information."

"They were shot by others."

"Who?"

Jack glared at the man, at his brisk and brusque interrogation style. Jack did not like being on the other end of an interrogation, particularly when he believed in what he did.

"What was in the box that you stole?" Tierney pressed.

"Stole? I didn't steal anything."

"Witnesses would care to differ."

"I'm trying to save my wife."

Tierney's rapid-fire questions abruptly stopped as he pondered Jack's statement. It was a moment before he slowly asked, "What do you mean, save her?"

"A man by the name of Nowaji Cristos kidnapped her. He is going to kill her."

Tierney stared at Jack, his face a mass of confusion at Jack's statement.

To Jack's surprise, the door opened, and standing there was his doctor, Ryan McCourt, a thick medical file under his arm. With him was an elderly female in a white gown with a stethoscope.

Ryan glared at the agent. "Excuse me, no one is authorized to speak with this man until he's been examined."

Tierney stared back, but the battle of wills never manifested. The agent walked out the open door, letting it close behind him.

"Jack," Ryan said softly as he turned, having trouble meeting his friend's eyes, suddenly lost for words.

"Hi, Jack," the woman said as she brushed a few gray strands of hair from her care-worn face. "My name is Dr. Emily Sebert."

She took a seat on the bed, then paused, allowing Jack to get comfortable with her presence before laying a gentle hand on his feet. "How are you feeling?"

"Fine." Jack slowly nodded, although his emotions were anything but.

"I thought you were dead," Ryan said. "I saw what was left of your car."

Jack nodded.

"A lot of crazy accusations are being thrown around."

"Honestly," Jack said, "I couldn't give a shit."

Ryan nodded, understanding Jack's attitude. He waited a moment, allowing a comfort to grow. "Look, you're under my care for the moment, doctor-patient confidentiality. You want to fill me in on what happened?"

Jack looked at the woman sitting at his feet on the bed.

"Emily's to be trusted," Ryan said. "We work together on occasion, and she won't say a thing."

"I promise." Emily held up her three fingers in a scout's honor sign.

Jack looked between the two of them, not sure if he was being set up. He had known Ryan since grade school, since they played Little League baseball. They were close, having carried each other home after drunken parties, playing wing man for each other. They had even dated the same girl in high school, each giving her up in deference to the other.

And so Jack told him. He told Ryan everything he could remember about the night before, about waking up at home that morning. He told him about the mysterious box that Mia gave him, which he took from the evidence room before it fell into Cristos's hands. But throughout, Jack was careful to leave out certain aspects, things that he had seen, such as Adoy's translation of the tattoo, his conversation with his father, and his suspicions of the FBI, things he thought to be irrelevant or not germane to Ryan's understanding of what was going on.

"I'm terrified for Mia," Jack said. "I've got to find her before it's too late."

"Well," Ryan said, "you've got help now. No need to do it on your own."

"Can you get me out of here?" Jack said, trying not to sound desperate.

"I'm not sure yet, but you know I'm sure as hell going to try."

"Thanks," Jack said with sincerity.

"Well," Ryan said, perking up, "we need to check you out."

"What, you think I may be disease-free?" Jack tried to joke, but it fell hard.

"Let's just make sure you're OK for the moment."

As if on cue, Emily leaned toward Jack. "Do you feel any pain?"

"Where?"

"Anywhere," she said with a soft, coaxing smile.

Jack looked up at Ryan. He had never mentioned that he was shot, nor was he about to. The nurse had bandaged him up and that was just fine for the moment. He didn't want anyone poking around in his chest costing him precious time.

"She's reviewed your file. She knows the illness you're dealing with."

"I'm not tied up in this bed because I have cancer."

"No," Emily said, quickly changing the subject. "Have you been experiencing headaches over the last week?"

"No," Jack said with a shake of his head.

"Nausea . . ."

"Look, I feel fine—"

"Have you seen a change in colors? Do they appear more vibrant?"

"Just a bit," Jack said. They were more brilliant than at any time in his life.

"Do you hear any high-pitched whine, white noise? Has your hearing grown more acute?"

"A bit," Jack answered like a bored patient.

"Have you . . ." She paused, almost afraid to ask. "seen things?"

Jack turned away, thinking, remaining silent. He had avoided certain things for a reason. His silence ended her line of questioning.

A smile suddenly blossomed on Emily's face, as if she had become a different person. She reached across the white blanket and took his left arm, examining the bandage. It was thick, wrapping his arm from elbow to wrist "How did you get this?"

Jack stared at her, afraid to say that he had no idea. "I'm not really sure."

"Does it hurt?"

"No. It's a tattoo."

"Really?"

Again, Jack remained silent.

"Are you sure?" Emily spoke to him as if to a child.

"Ryan?" Jack looked to his friend. "This is bullshit."

"I know," Ryan said as he laid a hand on Emily's shoulder, a subtle indication to slow down. "We're just talking, that's all."

The two doctors paused, building up to something.

"Jack, we believe the tumor is pressing on an area of your cerebral cortex," Emily said. "It might be from the impact of the accident or just the natural progression of growth. It may be causing you to either pass out or lose bits of memory or . . ."

She looked at Ryan, passing the baton.

"It might be causing you to imagine or see things," Ryan said quietly.

Jack looked between the two doctors. "You think this is all a delusion? You think I'm running around chasing ghosts?" Jack tried to flex his restrained wrist. "You think I wrote this fucking thing on my arm?"

"Jack." Ryan tried to calm his friend.

"Don't you dare *Jack* me. Yeah, I've got cancer, but I'm not crazy."

"Jack," Emily said softly, trying to calm him.

"My body may be failing, but not yet. Don't you dare tell me I'm going crazy or dying, because I don't give a shit how long I live, as long as it's long enough to find my wife and catch the son of a bitch who has her."

"Sometimes when hit with a tragedy," Emily said as she rubbed Jack's foot, "we imagine things, fantasize about ways to save the one we lost, bring them back from the dead. With where the tumor is located combined with the stress and anxiety over Mia, this may be occurring."

"What are you saying?"

"Is it possible," Ryan asked sympathetically, "that maybe you've been imagining things? Could Mia have gone over the bridge with you in the car?"

"Absolutely not," Jack shot back.

"Our memory is a tricky thing," Emily said. "Often, we rewrite our recollections to make them more ideal than the actual occurrence, seeing ourselves as heroes, forcing our minds to paint a more ideal picture than what was witnessed. You said that your mind was blank until it was triggered by her perfume. Could your mind be blocking out her death in favor of hope?"

"No, she's alive, dammit, I feel it." Jack said through gritted teeth, although fear began to creep into his soul. "I spoke to her, for Christ's sake."

"Is it possible that this case you've been chasing after," Emily added, "all of your running around trying to find her, is just you not dealing with her death?"

The door opened, and Tierney poked his head in. "We need to talk."

"It can wait." Ryan didn't turn to acknowledge his presence

"No, it can't."

TIERNEY AND McCOURT stood in the hallway.

"I don't have time to be playing around here," Tierney said. "I've got eight dead and the world calling me for answers."

"That is my patient in there, and this takes time. If you push me, I'll postpone my findings until morning."

"You listen to me—"

"No, you listen to me," McCourt said. "Remember, you called me down here as his friend and physician to help you deal with a situation. If you want to tell me what's going on, if you want to give me a question or two, I'll get you answers. But that's your only option."

Tierney calmed himself and finally spoke. "Is he crazy?"

"Why would you ask a question like that?"

Tierney handed Ryan four files, labeled *Nowaji Cristos, James Griffin, Mia Keeler, Jack Keeler.* Ryan looked at the first, *James Griffin,* and he felt his heart collapse.

AS THE SECONDS ticked by, Jack tried to avoid looking at Emily, who sat at the edge of his bed.

Finally, the door opened and Ryan stepped back into the room. His face had gone ashen.

"Ryan," Jack demanded, "what the hell is going on?"

"Jack . . ." Ryan said. "Jimmy Griffin's body was found last night. He was tortured. Every finger, every bone in his left hand, was snapped in two, a slow, methodical torture."

Jack was lost for words.

"After they failed to get what they needed from him, they went for Mia; you were collateral damage."

"He's not dead," Jack shot back. "I saw him. I spoke to him."

"Are you sure it was him?" Ryan said gently.

"Of course I'm sure. I spoke to him for at least fifteen minutes."

"Had you ever met the man? Do you know what he looks like? Are you sure it was him and not someone setting you up?"

Jack's breathing quickened. In all honesty, he had no idea. "Ryan, what the hell is going on?"

"Relax, Jack. I'm a friend, remember that."

"Friends don't have to remind friends."

"You know what I'm saying. I'm talking to you instead of you talking to them." Ryan pointed toward the door. "I'm your doctor and your . . . well, you know."

"Can you loosen these straps?" Jack asked.

Ryan looked to Emily, who sat in silence, her hand never leaving Jack. She subtly nodded.

Ryan leaned over to unfasten the metal clasps of the strap around his chest and the Velcro leather straps around his wrists. "Tell me about this guy Cristos."

Jack took a deep breath, waving his arms around in momentary relief. "Did they tell you about him? His background? Our background?"

"Yeah, Tierney just explained it to me. It's all in this." Ryan held up a thick manila file.

"He has Mia."

"How do you know?"

"He told me. But more important, I spoke to Mia. She told me, dammit."

Ryan sat on the bed, rubbed his face, gathering himself. "And you saw him? This Cristos?"

Jack nodded. "I did a lot more than see him."

"I heard." Ryan paused. "More than a year ago, you convicted this guy of murder, sought and got the death penalty. You were the last person he spoke to. He asked for you. What did he say to you?"

"Nothing. He just spoke about life, the weather . . . and death."

"What did he say? Can you remember?"

Jack remembered . . . *death is not always final, not always perma-nent; death is never the end.* And as he thought on those words, pon-dering them in the context of his current conversation, he realized that from Ryan's perspective, they might take on a whole new mean-ing. "I don't remember."

"Last fall, you saw Cristos executed at Cronos prison. You saw him die."

"Don't talk to me like I'm a child, Ryan. He didn't die. People . . . people within our government conspired to save him."

Emily and Ryan exchanged a glance.

"Jack, more than twenty people saw him die. The coroner con-firmed his death."

"He was paid off." Jack felt as if he was arguing with a child. "Do you want to just get to the point? They have obviously fed you a bunch of lies and are playing you."

"OK." Ryan sat up, composed himself. "Jack, at seven this eve-ning, they— "

"Who's they?" Jack asked.

"The FBI guy outside—Tierney—he said you walked into the lobby of the Tombs, alone. Talked to an Officer Knoll and went downstairs. They say Charlie Brooks buzzed you in . . . and then . . ."

Jack felt his mind slipping, realizing the inference. "That's not true." Although Jack tried to avoid it, there was desperation in his voice.

"Jack—"

"I didn't kill Charlie, dammit. He was a friend. I didn't kill those cops. The only man I shot was the man who struck Mia and who was about to shoot me. There's got be video footage," Jack pleaded.

"I didn't see any video. I did see pictures of the aftermath. It looks like a war zone."

"Yeah, and Cristos was right in the middle of it, the cause of it. Pretty horrific work for a dead guy."

"Jack—"

"Did they speak to Larry Knoll, the guard at the desk? He let us through security. What about the lobby cameras? Surely they got Cristos on video."

"I asked the same thing," Ryan said. "They say the cameras were somehow interfered with, nothing but static. And Larry, the guy at the desk, is in a world of trouble for letting you out of the building."

"What about the cops who arrested me? They saw him on the roof."

Ryan shook his head with sympathy. "Just you, Jack. No one else was on that roof but you."

Jack's head throbbed. He closed his eyes, trying to find something, anything, that would convince his friend of his sanity.

Ryan took a moment, forming his words. "With such a tragedy befalling Mia, when hit with such trauma, sometimes the mind runs and hides. It plays tricks on us. With the accident, hitting your head, it probably jostled the tumor. That is why the colors were brighter, why you could hear things . . ." Ryan turned on his bedside manner. "And it made you see things. "

"And you saw the tumor," Jack said facetiously. "You saw that it moved? I don't recall any X-ray since I got here. A week ago, you said it wouldn't have an effect for several months, and yet in less than a week, I'm having full-blown hallucinations?"

"No, I haven't taken an MRI, but I know what I'm going to find. This isn't you I'm talking to. There are some things you've said . . . they don't make sense."

"Bullshit! You know me, Ryan. I didn't just go through what I went through imagining things. I saw Griffin, I went into the depths of the Tombs with Cristos—in flesh and blood, not some ghost—and his three guys. I was nearly killed trying to get that case."

"And where is that case, Jack?" Ryan's words sounded like a summation of all of the facts, bringing his point home.

Jack thought that no matter what he said, they had already tried and convicted him; they were going to rule that he was temporarily, if not permanently, insane. But with every question, Jack's self-doubt grew. He didn't remember how he got home, what happened after the accident. There were holes in his memory. And the conversation with his father kept ringing in his head. *Reality is all a matter of perspective . . .* and no one was seeing his perspective.

"The cops who arrested you said you were alone on that rooftop, that there was no case."

Jack said nothing. *Reality is all a matter of perspective . . .*

"You gave it up to a man who is dead," Ryan said.

"Jack." Emily finally spoke. "Was there ever really an evidence case, or could this all have been in your imagination?"

"Ryan, please." Jack began to beg. "You've known me forever. If I can't convince you . . . please, for Mia . . ."

"OK. "Ryan looked at Jack, his face troubled, his hand shaking. "You're right. We're jumping to conclusions, moving too fast. Let's slow down—no, better yet, let's start over. Tell me what happened when you woke up this morning. Take your time."

Jack inhaled as he smiled at his friend. "OK. I woke up, tired, groggy, struggled out of bed as I usually do. Walked downstairs. I was parched. I grabbed a Coke, looked around for the paper. It wasn't there. Grabbed it off the porch. Went back to the kitchen. Checked the garage, noticed the Tahoe was gone, assumed Mia took it since she left me the Audi—"

"Did you see the headline?"

"No, not yet."

"And the girls weren't home?"

"They're at my mom's."

"Good," Ryan said. "Remember—details."

"Right." Jack smiled "I went upstairs—oh, wait. I let the dog out when I got the paper."

"You did?"

"Yeah, actually." Jack was thinking, trying to keep order to things in his mind. "Actually, I played a bit on the kitchen floor with Fruck before I grabbed the Coke."

"With Fruck?" Ryan asked as he nodded.

"Yeah, I'd assumed Mia fed him. I let him out when I grabbed the paper." Jack refocused. "So, I went upstairs—"

"How long have you had Fruck?"

Jack smiled. "God, I don't know. Years . . ."

"Jack." Ryan spoke quietly, his heart breaking with every word. "Fruck was your dog when you were a kid. I was with you when he got hit by the garbage truck. He died in your arms in the drive-way . . . you were seventeen."

Jack's head began to throb. He looked around the room, feeling as if he needed to hold on to something.

Ryan stood up and motioned for Emily to walk with him to the corner of the room. They became lost in a conversation of whispers and soft tones. Ryan passed her each of the four files, one by one. Jack's hearing had grown more acute, but he couldn't make out their words as they nodded to each other before walking back his way.

"Jack," Ryan said in a calm, reassuring voice, "Emily is a psychiatrist, the best in her field. I respect her opinion as much as her experience."

"Jack." Emily spoke softly. "You are going to be moved to a special hospital where we can better care for your state of mind. You can undergo radiation treatment which may alleviate the tumor's impact on your brain function, but until that time, you are a danger to yourself and anyone around you."

"What?" Jack exploded. "Ryan, don't do this! Please! Mia is out there . . . you've got to get me out of here. Don't do it for me. Do it for her."

"I know. My heart is breaking for you, Jack. I can't even imagine . . ." Ryan took a slow, measured breath, trying desperately to calm himself. The last five minutes since he'd walked back into the room were leading up to this moment. He had waited too long already but still had trouble finding the way to broach it. "Forgive me for not telling you when I came back into the room, but we needed to judge your state of mind."

"Forgive you for what?"

"They found her, Jack," Ryan said almost in a whisper.

Jack closed his eyes, a sense of relief filling him, washing away his fear. He truly didn't care what they did to him, as long as she was safe. He no longer cared about dawn or whether he lived or died. Love was such a simple thing, a thing that if truly felt and experienced compelled one to give everything he had to the one he loved. He let his anger slip away. None of it mattered, as long as Mia was safe to get home to their girls, to hold and protect them forever.

But when Jack opened his eyes, he saw a tear on Ryan's cheek, Ryan, the one who was not known for emotion, the one whose wife had called heartless on more than one occasion.

"Jack, I don't know how to tell you this, but Mia's dead."

CHAPTER 34

FRANK HAD SPENT THE last hour chasing down every friend, contact, and enemy he had in the New York City Police Department to find where Jack had been taken. He had lost Jack once he exited his car with the Suburban in pursuit. They had both disappeared up 48th Street.

Frank thought of taking up the chase on foot, but Jack was long gone, and he knew he would have no chance of finding him. He quickly set to work changing his front left tire, which the men in the Suburban had shot out, finishing in pit-stop time of two minutes. He was thankful for his intense workouts and large forearms as he muscled through the process but admitted that he felt his age as he climbed back into the car with an ache in his back and a sore shoulder. He had quickly started up the car and headed up 48th Street, where Jack had disappeared. He imagined that he sought refuge within the sea of tourists who prowled Broadway on a Friday night, a far better place to hide than in some isolated hole in the wall.

He raced west toward Seventh Avenue and couldn't believe his eyes as he saw Jack carried out of on office building by three cops. Unconscious, his weight taxing the young police officers, he was stuffed into the back of a police cruiser and sped out of there. Frank took up pursuit and was quickly foiled by the slow-moving traffic out of Times Square, but the cop car managed to bob, weave, and vanish to who knows where. He flipped on his scanner, but there was no mention of the goings-on on West 48th Street. Frank knew that Jack was under VIP care, radio silence on whatever had happened, allowing the officers and the department to sort through what to do with the arrest of the city's DA.

Frank had called in favors, had called in chits, had called upon captains and rookies, but no one had heard even a rumor about Jack being arrested. There was fractional chatter about an occurrence at the Tombs, but that was being handled by the FBI, where Frank knew he wouldn't be afforded even a pleasantry. He had called out to Riker's Island but knew that they would never take Jack there, into the heart of the enemy, whose population would flay the skin from Jack's body before he was even placed in a cell. He called the central jail at the Tombs, but no one had been brought in during the last hour even anonymously. Frank headed downtown and circled back to the entrance to the Tombs, where he found the FBI poring over the lobby, dusting for prints, noting and cataloguing the bullet slugs and the scars they'd left in the marble walls and floors. Frank couldn't believe what he saw and was amazed that Jack had made it out of there alive. He had searched for Larry Knoll but was told Larry was being debriefed by the FBI at a different location. The wall of silence on the matter was impenetrable.

He had been so furious with Jack for leaving him, for slipping into the Tombs. He had no idea what prompted Jack's singular drive to get downstairs without him or any real idea of what had happened. He had only glimpsed the mythical box that Jack had spoken of, as he clung tightly to it while they raced up the FDR. And he did not get even a glimpse of its contents, let alone a mention of what was inside.

Frank was loved and respected by the NYPD, both top brass and lowly rookies, but he wasn't about to get any information from his former colleagues; no one knew a thing. He had been a cop for twenty-five years. Even though he'd retired, he still considered himself one and would until they day he died. He thought back on his career and similar situations—the arrests of movies stars, the senator from Arkansas found unconscious at the Four Seasons with his battered wife next to him, and the incident twenty years ago involving the former mayor's son, the underage girl, needles, and guns. He thought about each situation and the embarrassment it created, not just for the individual but for law enforcement, the country, and the city administration, all of whom sought legal, PR, and practical advice before informing the media and the world of a respected and loved VIP going off the rails. And the pieces fell into place . . .

Frank knew where Jack was.

JACK LAY ON the riverbank, his body broken and wet, the sound of the rushing river heavy in his ear, his body and mind enveloped by the darkness of night. Moonlight danced off the muddy shore, the wet leaves of the surrounding woods. And there was a presence beside him. The man who had emerged from the woods, cloaked in the shadows of night, knelt behind his head, just beyond the periphery of his vision.

An incredible pain coursed through Jack's body, his head pounded, his face was dotted with multiple stings, his chest throbbed on the left side, and his torso felt as if a vise was closing around it.

And a voice rose, a quiet chanting, a prayer uttered in the soft whispers of a foreign tongue. But somehow, despite the fact that he spoke no language beyond English, Jack understood the words that poured from the man's mouth.

"In between life and death, between the deepest dark of night and the first rays of dawn, in that moment where we begin to drift up from sleep to wakefulness, is where anything is possible, Jack."

The man reached over and drew Jack's naked arm to him. Under the rays of moonlight, the man withdrew a quill from his pocket, a bottle of ink from the other. He dipped the quill in the dark brown ink and began to write. His hand was that of an artist, his focus and demeanor those that of a wise man.

"You can still save her, Jack," the man whispered as he wrote, "but time is slipping away and will soon fall through your fingers, where all will be forever lost."

JACK'S EYES FLASHED open, and he desperately tried to recapture the fading thread of the dream, trying to hold on to the answers that floated up from his memory while he slept. He lay in the hospital bed, the strap around his chest reaffixed, his arms tethered back down. He was filled with such agony, such grief, such confusion.

Everything he held as reality had slipped away. Mia was everything, his better half, his lover, his best friend, and she was dead.

He reviewed the last fifteen hours in his mind, every conversation, every action he took. It had all seemed so real. Talking to Jimmy Griffin . . . he couldn't be dead. He couldn't have been an imposter. He had not set Jack up. He was her friend. He didn't lead him down some rabbit hole. He merely said that her salvation lay with the fate of the evidence case.

And Cristos, he was not some illusion, some spirit come back to haunt him. He was flesh and blood. The bullets were real, not dreamed. Jack would not go off randomly shooting his way into the Tombs. He wouldn't have killed Charlie or shot some innocents. He had seen death at his own hand in the past. It was what had brought him to law and away from guns. He wouldn't repeat those mistakes.

But above all, it was Mia's voice that rang in his ear. He had spoken to her from Cristos's car. It wasn't imagined. It was not the wishful thinking of a grieving man. He heard her desperation, her surprise at his being alive.

He had known Ryan for too many years to count; he had always been a good friend, someone he could always count on. He couldn't imagine him lying to him, making up some elaborate story. But was he, too, being manipulated? Was he drawing conclusions off facts that he couldn't possibly verify himself in such short order? Had he fallen into the trap of being fed information that could only lead to one conclusion? Jack couldn't imagine his friend toying with him. He had seen Ryan's pain when Ryan told him of his cancer diagnosis; he had seen his agony at seeing Jack tied to the bed. And above all, Ryan was not one to fake tears or grief at the loss of a friend's wife at the behest of the FBI. Ryan believed everything he told Jack . . . and Ryan believed he was crazy.

He and Emily had left the room to consult further on Jack's "condition" and "illusions," leaving him alone for the last ten minutes, which felt more like ten hours.

They never explained how Mia died, simply implying that she died in the car accident, but he had seen her kidnapped, driven away. Or had he? Everything was so murky. Had his mind played tricks on him? Had he blocked out what he had seen, suppressed the tragedy of her death? Had she been lying there next to him on the riverbank, or was she drowned in the car only to be washed downstream? Had her death been the impetus for his insanity, for some desperate act within a reality of his own making? Did a crazy man ever know he was crazy, or did he simply create his own reality?

And he thought about the parallels to Cristos. Was it coincidence that he, too, had *risen* from the afterlife? Both had been declared dead: Jack by the newspaper, Cristos by the coroner. The world, in both cases, was convinced of their passing only to have them walk the earth again. Had his current state of mind been brought about by Cristos's prophetic statement of death not being the end, the implications being that he couldn't die? Could Jack's mind have truly snapped, creating this elaborate scenario all in order to do what he had failed to do: save the woman he loved?

Jack looked at his bandaged arm. It wasn't injured as the nurse had said; the mehndi tattoo was real, his visit to Professor Adoy was real . . . the warning of death to come tomorrow at dawn was . . .

If he could somehow tear away the bandage, see the tattoo once more, it would be the anchor that could pull him back to reality, that could give his mind the footing it so desperately needed now. It could wipe away any and all doubt. For if the elaborate tattoo was there, it meant that someone had been with him after the accident and had saved him, that it wasn't all a figment of his imagination. It meant that he was being lied to, a cog in some conspiracy in much the same way as the system was manipulated to keep Cristos alive.

He pulled at his restraints, his arms straining with the effort, but it was to no avail. There had to be a way. He looked to the door, pondering escape. There were so many barriers in his way—FBI, police, building security—insurmountable obstacles, but so had been stealing the case from the basement of the Tombs.

But the biggest barrier was the fragility of his mind.

If it was a choice between an insane existence where Mia was alive or a reality where she had perished, he would simply choose the madness. And that sudden thought terrified him. Had he already made that decision subconsciously?

Hope was lost. It was lost for him, for his two girls, for Mia. And it was bone-crushing. To be faced with death by cancer was one thing. To have your body fail, as tragic as it was, was part of life. But to have your mind slip away, to have your wife ripped from existence, to leave your children alone in the world, was far more devastating, for there was nothing to cling to, nothing to give a glimmer of optimism, nothing but a forever night where the sun would never rise again.

He looked again at his arm and the thick white bandage. He just needed to see. What had once brought him confusion and panic could give him the one thing he would need. For if it was there, then, *truths* could be washed away, minds could be brought back to sanity, and Mia, despite everything he had been told, could be brought back to life.

All Jack needed was a little hope.

FRANK AND JOY rode up the elevator to the fifth floor of the Tombs. Joy had spent the last several hours poring over the old case files on Cristos while cross-referencing them with the information on Cotis from Professor Adoy and the note of appreciation Jack had received with the blue necklace from the Cotis government. Hoping for some kind of link or clue, she found none.

As they emerged from the cab, they were greeted by the security desk officer, who sat behind thick bulletproof glass similar to the setup in the evidence room. Nolan Ludeke was at the end of a double shift, a shift that brought tragic surprises that he could never have anticipated.

Frank had known him for too many years to count, since back when Nolan was on the street. He had always spoken of retiring, moving to Florida with his wife, to be closer to his kids, but as that fateful day approached, Nolan realized that work was his life, and if work stopped, how far behind would the end of his life be? So he regrouped. His years of service and his reputation gave him the inside track on a job with little to no stress that would alleviate the forever fears of his wife getting that 3:00 a.m. call of death in the line of duty.

"Frank," Nolan said in a warm greeting, buzzing him and Joy through.

"Hey," Frank said as he walked through the heavy metal door, which closed with a thud behind him. "We're here to see Jack."

Nolan looked at the two. "I don't know. He's down the hall, the feds have two posted outside his door, and they've labeled him a suicide watch."

"This still is under our jurisdiction, correct?"

"Come on, Frank, semantics."

"What can you tell me?"

"They brought him in an hour ago. He was in rough shape, out cold. Tucked him in a psych room. A nurse patched him up. A couple of doctors came in, evaluated him, and declared him nuts. A hot-shot FBI guy has been all over this thing. I heard whispers of all kinds of mayhem downstairs on sub five, but no one will confirm a thing. The rumor is it's not hard to connect Keeler to it, though that seems so wrong. I heard the guy was killed last night in a car accident along with his wife, but then he shows up here. Whole thing seems crazier than that mess years back with the mayor's son."

"We need to see him," Joy said.

Nolan looked between the two. "I've got no problem with you seeing him. He's a good man, as far as I'm concerned. Of course, getting past Tweedledum and Tweedledee may prove difficult."

"Who else from the feds is up here?"

"Tierney, deputy director of the New York office. He commandeered an office down the hall, haven't seen him in a while. I'm sure he'll come blustering through shortly."

"Let me ask, what kind of security you got on these rooms?"

Nolan's eyes filled with concern. "Please tell me you're not thinking of—"

"Nolan, relax. Just tell me." Frank had a way about him; he was trusted and used that faith to bend people to his way of thinking. "I just need to know. You know I wouldn't do anything stupid, particularly with Joy here."

"The nut rooms are for nuts—nothing in there where you can hurt yourself, no long wires, cords, phones, pretty much free of everything except a bed and a bolted-down table. The doors are keylocked from the outside. No lock access on the inside, though there is a door handle. The room Keeler is in, five-oh-four, fits the bill perfectly."

"Has he had any visitors, family, an attorney?"

"No." Nolan shook his head. "I don't think anyone really knows he's here. He is just anonymous patient nine-five-three-oh with no one permitted access.

"Well, I'm his friend, and I'm going to see him. Where's this nurse?"

Nolan picked up his phone, spoke quickly, and hung up. "She'll be right out. You're going to cause a problem, aren't you?"

"Nolan, I will not be breaking any laws, I promise you. But imagine if your best friend was stuck in a mental ward. Would you want to get to the bottom of it or just let him slip away into the system?"

"May I help you?"

Frank turned to see the blond nurse behind him

"I'm Susan Meeks."

"Sue, these two are here to see Mr. Keeler."

"He's not to have any visitors—"

"So the only people who can have contact with him are the FBI and their doctors? Do you work for the FBI or the city of New York?"

"The city."

"Who gave you the order not to let him see anyone?"

"Mr. Tierney."

"Do you work for Mr. Tierney?"

"No."

"Good, because Jack Keeler, as you know, is the DA for the city of New York. He was thought to have been killed this morning along with his wife, who is either missing or dead. He is being denied counsel, contact with his family, and all of his rights. I am his closest friend, and this here"—he pointed to Joy—"is his secretary. We are here to see him, and we will see him now unless you want to have a much larger problem that will be resolved by a judge."

Meeks looked at Nolan.

"Frank, she's good people. Lose the bluster." Nolan turned to Susan. "He's just upset. He's doing the right thing. You can let him see Mr. Keeler."

Susan nodded and led Frank and Joy to room 504 just down the hall.

"You know he's very sick?" Susan said quietly.

Frank and Joy stared at her, confused.

"What kind of sick?" Joy asked.

Joy looked at them a moment. "You said you were close friends of his?"

"What kind of sick?" Frank asked, his voice stern. "We're family. What kind of sick?"

Meeks inhaled, pausing. "He's dying. Cancer." Susan paused. "If you're his friends, you should know that, because his file says he's not dealing with it, nor has he told his wife."

Joy looked away, trying to hold back her compounding emotions. Frank remained stoic, but the shock was visible in his eyes.

They arrived at the door to Jack's room. Two FBI agents stood on opposite sides.

"Can we help you?" the first agent said.

"And you are?"

"Special Agent Matt Crews," the taller agent said.

"Have you notified Jack Keeler's family of his presence here? Have you notified anyone? Has he spoken to an attorney?"

"You need to speak to Director Tierney—"

"No, we are his family, and we are going in to see him."

"I can't permit that."

"Has he been charged with a crime?"

"No."

"Are you holding him against his will, then?"

"You need to speak to Deputy Director Tierney."

"I don't give a shit if you come in there with me, but I'm going to speak to the DA." Frank nodded to the nurse, who slipped the key into the door and opened it.

Crews stepped in her way.

"You," Frank said to Crews, "come in with me. And you," he said to the other agent, "you go get your boss. Bring him in here to speak to me. You guys have crossed the line. You have denied this man his lawful rights, and there will be hell to pay."

The short agent hustled off down the hall as Frank and Crews stepped into the room. Frank turned to Joy. "Get the car. If I'm not down in fifteen, go home, because I won't be leaving here for a long time." And he closed the door.

"HEY, JACK," FRANK said, seeing his friend bound to the bed, his eyes red and tired.

"Frank."

"They say you're nuts." Frank smiled.

"I think I am."

"Well, I'm glad you finally admitted it. Now, do you want to tell me what's going on?"

Jack looked at him. "Yeah, but first, can you do me a favor and loosen my wrists?"

"Sure, just give me a second."

Frank spun around, his gun drawn and aimed in Crews's face. "Could you please kneel down?"

"They're going to be here any second," Crews said as he complied, putting his hands on top of his head.

"Which is why we have no time to waste." Frank pulled out his first set of handcuffs and slapped a cuff on Crews's right wrist. He pulled him to the other side of the bed, laid him on the floor, threaded the cuff around the bed leg, and slapped the other cuff around his left wrist. He pulled a handful of tissue from the side table and stuffed it into the agent's mouth.

"Now, about that favor." Frank nodded as he tore back the Velcro straps from Jack's arms and released the strap around his chest. Jack sat up and quickly climbed out of the bed.

Without a word, he tore the layers of white bandages from his left forearm.

And he felt his heart fill with hope.

• • •

THE DOOR EXPLODED open, and Tierney and the shorter agent, Philippe, charged in to find Jack out of the bed and standing in the corner. Philippe drew his gun as the door slammed closed behind him, but it was too late. Frank's pistol was pressed against the back of his head.

"Either of you make a sound, he's done," Frank said, thwacking the agent in the back of the head with his pistol.

"What the hell, Frank?" Tierney yelled.

"What the hell, Gene?" Frank shot back. "You've got Keeler strapped to a bed, without counsel, family, anyone notified?"

Frank took his second set of cuffs and secured Philippe's hands behind his back, threading the cuffs through the leg of the bed, where he was awkwardly crouched.

Frank turned his gun on Tierney and motioned him to the bed. "Get your ass in bed."

Tierney glared at him. "You have no idea what you're doing."

"Oh, I have every idea what I'm doing. Now, lay the fuck down."

Tierney complied; Jack strapped him to the bed.

"You want to tell me what's really going on?" Jack asked as he leaned over Tierney.

"You're insane." Tierney struggled against his bindings.

"So I've heard."

"Where is Cristos holding my wife?"

"Your wife is dead—"

Jack drew back his fist and pile-drived Tierney in the jaw. "Don't you say that. I know she's alive."

"She died in the car accident," Tierney growled. "You know it, and I know it."

"What is the FBI so scared of? What's in that box that you so desperately need?"

Tierney said nothing.

"Can I tell you a little secret?"

"Fuck you, you're nuts."

"I wanted to be caught. I knew full well where you would bring me."

"What? That's ridiculous."

"You think so? You don't think I'm fully aware of police protocol when it comes to the arrest of high-level people, when it comes to bringing in someone like a DA on charges that no one will believe? I knew I'd be brought up here to the psych ward."

"Why would you do that? You wanted to be committed?"

"Wouldn't you like to know?" Jack said. "You're good; you had me convinced, using my friend to bear your false news. Talking about all of those dead people, trying to convince me it was all in my head."

"So you think you're not crazy?"

"I know I'm not crazy. Now, where is Cristos holding my wife?"

"Fuck you."

"You know why I think you're working with Cristos? Because once I was captured, once he got what he wanted, it would be far easier to pin it all on me, to kill my wife, dump her body where it would never be found, convince me and the world that I was crazy, no trial, just lock me up in a padded room until I succumbed to the cancer."

"That sounds like a pretty good plan," Frank said, half joking.

"But you know what? There is something in that box that Cristos was not expecting."

Tierney's eyes narrowed slightly, just enough for Jack to see.

Frank thumbed through Tierney's phone, through the names of his last twenty calls, and passed the phone to Jack. "You know this guy?"

Jack looked at the phone log, the last eight calls all to the same number, the same person. Someone Jack knew and trusted above all. "Son of a bitch."

CRISTOS SAT IN the passenger seat of the Suburban. Josh drove at a leisurely pace so as not to draw any more attention. Cristos had raced down the stairs, his prize in hand, and exited through the back of the unfinished structure. He'd cut through the alleyways and hidden in the shadows of a parking lot while police swarmed the area searching for him. He had lain motionless, the case tucked tightly against his body, blending with the shadows. He had avoided two cops who had taken up position not thirty feet away, watching the rear of the office building, keeping focus on the alleyway, never realizing their prey lay just feet away.

Cristos slowed his heart, focused his senses, and became motionless, his mind taking on a Zen quality. He had used the technique during countless situations in which he would take up a position ten hours before his mark was to arrive, patiently lying in wait until the precise moment of pulling the trigger. He would finally rise from his position, shake off the moment, and exit the area, without cramp or ache.

It was nearly an hour later when the cops were called off, and he slipped from the garage to arrive on 47th Street, where Josh lay in wait.

Josh told him the moment he got into the car: Jack Keeler was in the mental ward of the Tombs, preliminarily diagnosed as insane, with the slaughter in the evidence room blamed on him.

Cristos felt like a child with a wrapped gift in his lap. He had maintained such a singular focus on it that everything else in the world had become secondary. He had spent months tracking down his father, tracking down what he so desperately needed, secrets he was promised but in the end had to kill for.

As they turned onto Broadway, heading downtown, Cristos was actually only two blocks from where he last saw his father.

One month ago, Cristos had realized he was following him in Istanbul. He allowed it to continue through the Middle East into Africa. After a week of cat-and-mouse, he found his father in his hotel suite in Marrakech, sitting calmly on the floor, looking out the large living-room window at the Atlas Mountains in the distance.

"You survived," Cristos said, with no hint of emotion as he laid his briefcase on the coffee table and sat on the couch.

"Come home with me," his father said, continuing to look out the window.

"I'm no longer your son," Cristos reminded him.

His father sat there a moment and finally turned to look at him. "I have foreseen your death . . . and it is soon."

Cristos stared back. "You are so fond of reminding me of the inevitability of fate, of the difficulty in altering its path, and yet here you sit telling me this?"

"Our will, our love, is much stronger than fate. Surely you haven't forgotten that."

Cristos laughed. "Really? Love is what made me who I am."

"Then allow my love for you, my son, to save you."

"After all this time." Cristos shook his head in disbelief. "After all that I have done over the last twenty years . . . "

"Your death is soon, Suresh. It will come from where and when you least expect it."

"Then tell me," Cristos said. "If you are my father, if I am truly your son, then you will tell me so I can save myself."

His father remained silent.

Cristos stared at his father and for the briefest of moments remembered what it was like to be a son, to be part of the world, to be not alone. He finally stood. "I am going to get us something to eat."

He went to the small kitchen and set out a tray of bread and cheese. He reached into the cabinet and withdrew his gun, tucking it into the back of his waistband. He picked up the tray and returned to the living room

But his father was gone. He knew his son too well.

Cristos turned to see his briefcase on the coffee table, wide open, his papers in disarray. And with shock, Cristos realized what his father had done.

He had taken his red prayer book, the book he gave to him when he was a child. Cristos had written everything in this book, his entire life, every job, the people he contracted with, the fees he was paid, a record of every assassination.

And so Cristos turned the table on his father; the hunted became the hunter. Cristos tried to capture his father on the train to the port city of Casablanca, only to find that he had eluded him by slipping out of the country before Cristos was even aware.

He had to get his prayer book back for obvious reason. But even that paled in comparison with the obsession he felt growing inside himself, the desire to know his own fate. By knowing, he would change it, would stop it from ever happening, killing anyone and everyone remotely connected to his demise before it arrived.

Cristos knew that his father had recorded it in his own prayer book, a place where he wrote his most important prophecies, his greatest secrets, wondrous things that were not meant to be shared with the world or any living soul.

It became like a game, a deadly game, for Cristos would go to any lengths to extract from his father not only his fate but also his secrets, the grand mysteries and objects that he possessed and always carried on his person.

It was well after midnight, the past Monday, when Cristos tracked his father to the Waldorf Astoria Hotel on Park Avenue in New York City. The suite was large, four rooms with an elegant marble bathroom provided by the Cotis government to their respected diplomat.

Cristos opened the door to see his father sitting calmly on the couch, as if in wait.

"Come back home with me," his father said, his words filled with emotion. "Leave this world behind. It has corrupted your heart."

"I knew from the moment I killed you that you'd survive, you with all your tricks and magic. But with all that wisdom, all that power, you couldn't stop me," Cristos said.

"I'm sorry for you," his father said without reaction.

"I should have used a larger blade." Cristos walked into the room and stood over his father. "You stole my prayer book."

"You have corrupted it, using it for everything but what it was designed for."

"Oh, it contains my inner thoughts, my life, painting a pretty detailed picture."

"Of death . . ." his father said sadly.

"Where is *your* book?" Cristos said. "That's what I want to see."

"You do not want to know the future I have written in mine. Yours is very short."

"Show me the book!"

"Suresh—"

"That has not been my name for more than twenty years."

"Our identity is our heart, not what we call ourselves."

"Return my book, and give me yours, and you'll save yourself," Cristos said as he drew his gun and screwed on a silencer.

"Know that in what you are about to do, you will seal your fate. You will set in motion a series of events that will end with your own death before this week is through. If you come back with me now, you will live."

Cristos stared at his father, absorbing his words, and without further thought pulled the trigger. The bullet struck his father in the stomach, and as he collapsed on the couch, Cristos reached across and tore open his shirt, looking at his bare chest, at the wound in his stomach that began to bubble with blood.

Cristos turned to his father's bag on the floor and rummaged through it. Beyond prayer robes and some personal effects, there was nothing there.

"Where are they?" Cristos shouted in desperation.

"You will never find them," his father said as he held his stomach. "Soon to be placed in the hands of someone pure of heart—"

"I'll tear the heart from their chest."

"I'm sorry for you," his father said through labored breaths.

Cristos searched the suite, the safe, every inch of the hotel room, but found nothing.

"Does it hurt yet?" Cristos spat out in anger. "The poison in the bullet is for two purposes: to ensure that your death is painful but, more important, to make sure this time it is permanent."

"Know this, my son, it will not be long until we are together again."

Now, riding in the Suburban, Cristos looked down at the case, which he felt would soon provide all the answers. Cristos finally had what he came for; he would carry out the second part of his mission without distraction and disappear from the world like a ghost, as he had done so many times before.

Cristos finally turned his attention to the small lock on the case and smashed it with the butt of his gun.

Savoring the moment, the anticipation of victory, he took a deep breath and closed his eyes, knowing that he possessed the power to cheat his own death. He finally lifted the lid, his heart holding in expectation, the culmination of his quest; he dug his hand inside, and as he looked at the contents . . .

. . . he lost his mind in rage.

CHAPTER 35

"DO ME A FAVOR?" Frank said, pointing at Jack's former room. "Don't open that door."

Nolan looked up at Jack and Frank standing in the hallway of the mental facility. "And what are we supposed to say when people come asking?"

Susan Meeks handed Jack the rabbit's-foot key ring, a key fob, and his shoes.

"Just say you saw me but never saw us leave. Trust me when I tell you that they will be in far worse trouble for holding Jack than anyone who assisted us."

Jack looked at Nolan as he buttoned up his shirt, tossing the hospital gown onto the floor. "Someone is holding my wife. I don't have much time."

Nolan looked at Jack. "I never saw you, but if I did, I'd tell you good luck in finding her."

Nolan buzzed the door, and Frank slipped out into the small vestibule and hit the elevator call button.

The elevator door of cab one opened, but Frank didn't get in and allowed the door to close. He hit the call button again.

Cab three arrived, but Frank again let it leave without him.

It was when cab four arrived that he turned and motioned through the glass to Jack, who was buzzed through the security door and came out pushing a wheelchair stacked with blankets.

Jack raced into the open cab and without a moment's hesitation, leaped onto the wheelchair, reaching up to the roof of the cab and pushing aside the trap door. The shaftway was aglow in the red pin lasers.

The cab door closed and began its descent

Instead of continuing to climb up onto the roof of the cab, Jack simply turned to his right and snatched a canvas shopping bag, pulling it back into the cab, and quickly closed the hatch.

He quickly sat in the wheelchair and affixed a surgical mask to his face while Frank draped his shoulders and legs with a large white blanket that covered the bag in his lap.

As Jack had ridden up from the depths of the basement in cab four two hours earlier, leaping onto the handrail, opening the elevator cab ceiling to see the red security lasers in the shaftway, he had made a decision. With Cristos giving chase and the authorities not far behind, he feared he would be trapped and captured.

So he had dumped the contents of Mia's case, along with everything in his pockets—his wallet, the letter he had written to Cristos, his cash, keys, and the jewelry box, everything except his gun, Charlie's rabbit foot, and Aaron's key-fob device, which scrambled the security camera's signal—into the canvas shopping bag he had taken from Charlie's box of food and weapons and stored it atop elevator cab four.

After depositing the few contents of Aaron's bag into the evidence box for ballast, he tucked it into Aaron's black bag, jumped back into the elevator, securing the trap door, and led Cristos off on a wild-goose chase around the city, pulling him as far from his goal as possible.

All the while, Jack knew he would have to go back, and there would be only one way back in.

He was counting on being captured.

The door finally opened to the main lobby, which was abuzz with forensic personnel, mapping bullet trajectories, digging fragments out of the floors and walls, and consulting. Without hesitation, Frank wheeled Jack along the back wall to the rear hall and the rear service entranceway.

As they rounded the corner and rolled down the fifty-yard hallway, they came upon an armed New York City policeman at the rear door, with two others at the desk.

Jack could see the security monitors, ten of them showing different angles of the lobby, of the upstairs, and of the four elevator cabs. He prayed that Aaron's key fob had worked. Otherwise, he was about to have a very short conversation with law enforcement.

His heart began to race as all eyes fell on him. The surgical mask was a silly disguise, yet Frank continued to wheel him down the linoleum-tiled floor toward the exit.

The desk guard spun around to face them. "Frank," he said in his Bronx-accented voice. Sergeant Johnny Seminara stared at him a moment. "I'd ask why the camera in your elevator went on the fritz, check you from stem to stern, but seeing it's you, I'm sure it's an issue for maintenance."

Frank continued toward the rear door.

"You want to leave the wheelchair or take it with you?" Johnny asked.

"Thanks." Frank nodded.

Jack hopped out of the chair, holding tight to the blanket as it wrapped the canvas bag, and followed Frank through the rear door of the Tombs to find Joy behind the wheel of Frank's car with the engine running.

"So, I heard you're dying," Frank said as he walked with Jack toward the open car door.

"Aren't we all?"

Jack climbed into the back while Frank jumped into the passenger seat.

"I don't know, Jack. You've always been kind of a miracle man. I don't see something like cancer taking your life."

Jack looked at Frank and smiled. Some people poured out emotion and sympathy when dealing with a friend's troubles. Some put up a selfish wall, remaining silent, as if acknowledgment of the disease would somehow infect them. Others just disappeared. And then there was Frank. His gruff exterior filtered his warmth and friendship, but his simple words were all Jack needed to give him a moment of hope.

"By the way, they said I was crazy."

"It took how many doctors to come up with a conclusion I've known since I met you?"

Jack smiled. "They said it was the tumor, pressing on my brain."

"Of course," Frank said with a smile. "We all have something to blame our faults on."

"So you wanted to get arrested?" Joy asked from the driver's seat.

Jack nodded. "Kind of had to."

"That's rich." Frank laughed.

"I'm not even talking to you about all this shit," Joy said. "Cancer, stealing, psych wards. If we don't all get thrown in jail, I'm thinking of finding another job."

"Thanks, Joy." Jack smiled.

"Do you mind telling me where I'm going?"

"Yeah, to see an old friend."

CHAPTER 36

JOY DROVE UP THE West Side Highway toward Riverdale, nervously sipping her bottle of water. Frank watched the traffic silently, hoping they weren't being followed.

Jack turned his attention to the canvas bag, the one that held the contents of Mia's evidence case. It had been the desire of so many, yet it lay on his lap now. He looked at it, pondering the answers it held, the secrets that Cristos spoke of, the fear it created in Mia.

He dumped the contents into his lap. He wasn't going for the slow reveal.

He looked at the objects, so simple, yet their meaning meant the difference between life and death. He pushed aside a credit card, money, a quill pen, and a room keycard and directed his attention to the more substantial objects.

There were two nearly identical prayer books, just as Jimmy had described. Red leather covers, one hundred fifty or so pages in each, pages torn out of the back of one.

"So, what the hell was in Mia's evidence case that has everyone so interested?" Frank asked from the passenger seat as he looked back at Jack.

Jack ignored his friend as he continued examining the objects. He ran his thumb over a prayer necklace of marble-sized beads, simple polished wood with a glossy gemlike sheen. There was a bejeweled dagger looking to be of considerable value, but his focus was drawn to the passport.

He opened it and examined the picture. The man's face was strong, free of wrinkles or blemish. His eyes were caring and warm under close-cropped black hair. Jack pondered the man and his untimely death, his last earthly possessions in Jack's lap. He didn't deserve to die.

And as Jack continued to look at his face, he felt a tugging on his memory, a familiarity with the man, yet he couldn't place it. He was sure he had seen him before, but he wasn't sure if it was just his mind playing tricks or wishful thinking, attributing the vileness to Cristos while assigning a purity to this man, as if they were night and day, good and evil. Jack thought it silly to think in such terms, like some philosopher or director from a 1940s movie.

He thumbed through the passport pages, looking at the visas, and saw the man's recent worldly travels.

He finally flipped back to the first page and looked at the diplomat's name. He did a double take before the confusion set in. Marijha Toulouse was the name of the member of the UN Peace Council who had sent him the blue necklace, the blue necklace that he gave to Mia the night before.

Jack's mind was on fire as he realized that the man who was murdered early that week, whose murder Mia was investigating, whose belongings lay in his lap, was Toulouse.

But even more earth-shattering to Jack's already fragile mind was the fact that the man known as Marijha Toulouse was Nowaji Cristos's father.

• • •

"YOU AND YOUR team will continue to help him get that box,"
FBI Director Lance Warren said in a measured tone of anger.

Warren sat at his desk inside his Park Avenue apartment, dressed
in khakis and a polo shirt, the phone pressed to his ear at this late
hour. He had changed out of the suit he had worn to the bridge earlier in the day when he escorted Sam Norris. He had played the part
of the concerned friend, because despite everything, he still considered Sam his friend. It was unfortunate that Mia had become involved, but he valued his own life and freedom above anyone else's,
even the daughter of his closest friend.

"My team is growing weary," the man on the other end said.

"With the money you are all paid, you can't afford to be weary."

"Six of our own are dead already."

"A risk they all knew when they signed on."

"What is in that box?"

"A book," Warren said.

"A book?"

"A book containing everything, everything Cristos has ever done
for us, foreign and domestic, every hit, every assassination, every
plot, every coup. We don't get that book, multiple agencies are going
down. Do you understand me?"

"But he's the enemy."

"Not at this moment, and need I remind you that this enemy
works for us?"

There was silence on the other end of the phone.

"We will have no more communication until that case is safe in
our hands. Too many people are involved already. I don't want you
even to fart within a fifty-mile radius of me." Warren slammed the
phone down.

Cristos stepped out from the shadows.

"How the fuck did you lose that book?" Warren shouted.

"I never said I lost it," Cristos said calmly. "It was stolen from me."

"By a diplomat to the UN? Don't bullshit me."

"I don't *bullshit*."

"You realize the shit storm you have created by killing that man?"

"You have no idea who that man was."

"I don't know who you really are, either."

"That's best for all concerned."

"Why would you write such things down?"

"Accountability."

"What?"

"Without leverage, what's stopping you from killing me?"

"If we wanted you dead, you would have died in prison, on schedule."

"You know what I found disturbing? While I was in prison, you checked out my bank accounts, tried to access them. You betrayed me."

"That was not my department," Warren said dismissively.

"What, were you looking for a refund? You traitors made me. That doesn't mean you can unmake me."

"You'd be amazed at what we can do to you." Warren glared at Cristos as he sat forward in his chair.

"I'd be careful if I were you. You see, I'm dead. I don't exist. Remember that?"

"Vividly," Warren said with a scowl.

"And if I'm dead, then I can't possibly be accused of murder."

"What murder?"

"Yours."

And Cristos raised his gun.

CHAPTER, 37

A S THEY CONTINUED NORTH on the Saw
Mill Parkway, Jack tried to wrap his head around
the fact that the items before him belonged to Toulouse, a man he had
contact with not even a week earlier. Jack at once knew the necklace
was not some token gesture by the UN but something far different.
When Joy had researched him, it was in the context of the UN Peace
Council and its mission, with no possible connection to Cristos.

Jack knew now who killed Mia's priest, the man he knew as Toulouse. It was Cristos, his son. He had revealed to Jack on the roof of
the highrise whom the contents of the box belonged to. Jack knew
how desperate he was to possess the case and knew the man would
stop at nothing, even patricide, to gain it. All of the pieces fell together.

As Jack continued to ponder the implications of the Cotis priest's
identity, he turned his focus to the other items before him. He put
aside the prayer necklace and picked up the bejeweled dagger, or-
nate and deadly, its hilt covered in rubies and sapphires that glim-
mered under the lights of the highway. There were the two red prayer
books, which, according to Griffin, held secrets and answers to mys-

teries that many desired to gain. But Jack's eyes were drawn to something else, two drawings, incredibly lifelike.

Jack picked up the first, and his world began to spin.

"Jack, I know this isn't the time, but if we're to help you find Mia, we need to know what we don't know. What aren't you telling us? What are all those things?" Frank pointed to the object in Jack's lap. "You go running off into the Tombs with this Cristos, leaving me not only to try and figure out where you are but to save your ass . . . twice, I might add. Then the cancer bombshell gets dropped in our laps, we overlook the insane-asylum thingy—"

"Pull over," Jack said quietly.

"What?" Joy said. "No, we don't have time to—"

"Pull over!"

Joy threw the wheel hard right onto the shoulder, locking up the brakes in an angry skid stop.

Jack leaped out of the car.

Frank threw open his door in a fit of rage. "What the hell was that all about?"

"You think I know what's going on?" Jack shouted.

"More than I do!" Frank yelled back.

Jack yanked up his sleeve, pointing at his tattoo. "I think we've got this all wrong. I think we are being played. I don't know how. I don't know who's pulling the strings, but there is a bigger picture here that we are not seeing."

"What are you talking about it?"

"These items that Mia so desperately wanted hidden away . . . the murder she was investigating—the man is Cristos's father."

"You sure?"

"The necklace that Joy mentioned before, the one I gave to Mia, I didn't know it at the time, but it was sent to me by the same man, this Marijha Toulouse.

"OK, as much as that is freaking you out, at least now we've got something to sink our teeth into."

"I think we know only what people want us to know. As I said, we're being played." Jack reached back into the car and pulled out the two drawings.

"Played by whom?"

"Explain to me how this was in the case at least two days ago." Jack shoved the first drawing into Frank's face.

"What the hell?" Frank said as he backed up, annoyed by the closeness of the image. He glared at Jack before finally turning his attention back to what he now realized was a picture. His eyes slowly focused on a drawing, done in ink and charcoal pencil by an expert hand. The detail was intricate and refined, as if replicating a photograph. It was an outdoor scene, nighttime, a rushing river under a dark, cloud-ridden sky, and then he saw the body, the face pale, still, eyes open yet devoid of life. There was a bullet wound in the upper left chest. The face was dotted in small wounds, the hair and the clothes soaked.

An impossible drawing that predated its subject.

When Jack's eyes first fell on the drawing, he shrugged it off. As the DA, he had received countless threats on an almost weekly basis. Whether by phone, by letter, or in person, they were always turned over to the police and found to be nothing more than attempts at intimidation. So, when he saw the image, even though he was shocked at the detail, at the near-photographic realism of the depiction, his reaction was minimal. He understood how it must have disturbed Mia, seeing him depicted as dead, understood how it scared her. He had not once told her of the numerous threats he had received. He never wanted to worry her, much in the same way that she minimized the dangers of her own job.

But when he looked closer, his mind exploded in a wave of disorientation. For the image drawn days early and sealed away in Mia's box depicted him in the exact condition he was in early that morning, lying on the riverbank, a bullet in his chest, the cuts on his face, a spot-on match down to the smallest detail. It was as if the hand of fate had rendered him on the canvas, as if everything that transpired the night before was his destiny.

He was a pawn, or at least Alice chasing the rabbit down the hole.

He studied the picture again, its exacting detail down to the clothes he wore, the rushing river that lapped the bank. And that's when he saw the shadow. It was next to him, faint yet distinct. Whoever had drawn the picture with foresight, with an attention to exacting detail, they were sure to include the singular shadow . . . there was someone else there.

Jack didn't believe in fate; he didn't believe in God or the hereafter. He didn't believe in magic, ghosts, answered prayers, or superstitious mumbo jumbo. Yet this day had thrown it all into question. He refused to believe it, and so he cast the facts aside and focused on Mia.

"This doesn't make any sense," Frank said. "This is some trick. Cristos must have slipped it into the case to mess with your head."

"He never had the case; no one has touched the case since I put it down in the Tombs two days ago, *before* I was shot, *before* I crashed through the guardrail and awoke on the riverbank."

Frank stared at Jack, lost for words before finally realizing. "You didn't make us pull over to show us this picture. What the hell is going on?"

Jack held out the second drawing. Frank stared at it but didn't touch it, as if doing so would somehow render it real.

What troubled Jack far more than the fateful image of himself was the one in the second drawing. The picture was of a beach, the first rays of morning peeking over the horizon; gulls hung suspended in the air, scampered along the sand in search of food; gentle waves lapped the sandy shore. And on the rocks was a woman's shattered body. Jack felt his heart crumble in his chest. No doubt drawn by the same hand, it was a depiction of the future in much the way Jack's image had been rendered. But this picture drew everything Jack was doing into question, casting doubt on his chances of success, of ever saving his wife. For the picture of the dead woman was of Mia, her lifeless body awash in the first light of dawn.

• • •

"CRISTOS SAID THAT our lives are preordained, that certain people within his religion can remember the future in the same way we remember the past."

"Bullshit," Frank said from the passenger seat. They were back in the car, heading north, with Joy at the wheel.

"I agree," Jack said. "But then how do you explain the drawing of me?"

"Why do I need to explain it?"

"If there's truth to them, then Mia will die at dawn tomorrow."

"I don't believe that. The picture of you on the riverbank, what do you see?"

"I see me lying dead on the riverbank."

"But are you?"

"The newspaper said it—"

"But you're not, and neither will Mia be if we find her. So let's keep focused on that instead of all this mysterious magic bullshit. Cristos filled your head with nonsense. Quit dwelling on the words of a psychopath. It's making you sound crazy."

Jack said nothing, letting his friend's words sink in. They finally did, and he smiled.

"No offense, Jack," Frank said, "but the FBI and Cristos weren't after those drawings of you and Mia. Not to downplay them, but they are not the earth-shattering type that conspiracies are built around."

Jack nodded. "No, they were after these." He held up the two red books, handing one to Frank. "Prayer books."

"Prayer books?" Frank said as he looked through it. "Why the hell would they be after prayer books?"

Jack leaned over the car seat and opened the book. He took a bottle of water out of the cupholder and poured it on a napkin. He rubbed it on the first page, and the prayers disappeared, replaced by elegant handwriting, small and detailed

"How the hell did you know how to do that?"

Each notation was short, and there were thousands of them. Jack kept wetting the napkin, thumbing through the pages, until he came near the end, where he found a missing page, its shredded edge still bound within the book. He looked back and noticed the last date on the page before it was June 23, the week before. Whatever was missing contained pages either written about the present or blank for future entries. But as Jack turned to the next page, he saw that notations had already been made for the next week. He flipped back to the torn section.

"Whatever was written here was torn out for a reason," Jack said, not looking up from the book. "Someone didn't want anyone to see these missing pages."

Jack flipped forward, looking at dates for the next week, and as he scanned the last notation, he was suddenly shocked. There was a name he recognized, completely out of context with everything else on the page. And while the language was Cotis, there was no question of the anglicized name appearing in the text: *Mia Keeler.*

"What the hell is this?" Jack said, turning the page toward Joy.

"Oh, God," Joy said, glancing over at the book before looking back at the road.

"What the hell does it say?"

"I'll see if I can find Professor Adoy," Joy said as she looked at her watch. "But at this late hour . . ."

"Why would her name be in this book?"

"Guys," Frank said. He wet the napkin and rubbed the pages of the second book in his lap.

Joy and Jack turned their attention to the second book. Frank was flipping pages, rubbing the wet cloth on them as he went, revealing Cotis text, but the page he was currently on revealed English.

"Oh, boy," Frank mumbled.

It was all in a similar fashion, but they understood it. Small notations, dates in the corner, and they went on and on, five, ten, twenty pages.

As they continued to read, they began to realize why the FBI and the U.S. government were after this book. It contained every job that Cristos had done, every assassination, every bombing, every act committed on behalf of people and governments whose world image would be tarnished by such allegations.

As they read, they found several jobs engaged by offshore companies for which Jack knew the dots could eventually be connected back home. But on the last page, it seemed that Cristos connected those dots himself, for anyone who read the red book would find written a list of five names. Jack, Frank, and Joy knew them all; each one filled them with ever-escalating shock: a member of the Justice Department; a high-level FBI agent; two Cabinet-level positions in the current administration. And the final name—none of them would voice it, as it filled them all with confusion.

Jack understood where Cristos's help came from and why he had certain members of the U.S. government at his beck and call, for the imcriminating evidence would doom not only careers but lives for acts of treason.

He understood how Cristos's execution was a staged event of subterfuge, how he was just a pawn in prosecuting an assassin in a trial whose outcome was preordained by people pulling strings for show. Jack understood how Cristos managed to get the assistance of certain members of the FBI and the Justice Department in protecting him. If they didn't act on his precise instructions, he threatened exposure; they had danced with the devil and had become his minions.

This book, the one with more than half of its entries in English, was not being sought for national security, as leverage against other nations who had illicitly engaged Cristos; it was being sought by a select few who were operating on their own within the confines of the U.S. government—arranging hits, assassinations, and who knew what in the name of national security while standing in the face of the constitution and laws of the United States.

And those select few, those five, were listed.

Jack was on his way to the first person on that list, someone who knew where Cristos was holding Mia, someone who would tell him even if he had to resort to unthinkable means.

He personally knew FBI Director Lance Warren; he was with him Thursday night, trading handshakes and smiles. There was no doubt he had sent Cristos's men after him when they left the party. CIA Director Stuart Turner's success in dealing with foreign governments and hostile adversaries was now clear. And if Jack was to survive this ordeal, he would pay a visit to FBI Agent Gene Tierney and see to it that he was convicted and made to suffer for the rest of his days.

But it was the fifth and final name that gave him pause, that none of them mentioned, that Jack couldn't understand its presence on the list. And it caused him the most fear. For that name was Jack Keeler.

TIERNEY WALKED OUT of the Tombs humbled and humiliated. He had lain strapped to the bed for fifteen minutes, struggling with the leather bindings, before the nurse came in to free them. The two men he assigned to guard the room had left two minutes before him after being debriefed.

No one saw anything. Bullshit. Everyone saw everything. They just weren't going to cooperate.

Tierney had simply followed orders, orders he didn't agree with, but that's what agents did all the time. Once someone didn't follow orders, the entire system would crumble.

Tierney climbed into his white Mercedes. It was his one indulgence, a gift from his wife, who was the real breadwinner, toiling away her days on Madison Avenue creating ad campaigns for sneakers, soda, and erectile dysfunction medication. He started up the car and let Beethoven's Piano Sonata Number 21 wash away his ever-rising stress.

He pulled out of the garage and headed for the Brooklyn Bridge, noticing how the bright lights of the city gave it a false sense of innocence.

Although he was told not to contact Warren, the circumstances demanded it. He tried six times but still had received no answer. The lower level of the Tombs was littered with bodies, and although he made the accusation that it was Jack's doing, there was little doubt that Cristos had lost control of the situation.

Cristos wasn't looking for the evidence case for them; he couldn't care less if anyone's secret agendas were laid bare. Something else was in that box, something far worse that had made Cristos desperate, that had made him scared. And in Tierney's mind, there could be nothing worse than a scared, desperate assassin.

Tierney hit the Brooklyn Bridge. It was virtually empty, the city masses having already escaped for the long weekend. He looked to his right out at New York Harbor, at the Statue of Liberty, whose lit torch was held up in welcome.

And as he turned to look back at the roadway, the fabric of the night was shredded by an enormous fireball that rolled up high into the sky, the explosion tearing Tierney and his white Mercedes to shreds.

CHAPTER 38

FRIDAY, 1:15 A.M.

A SINGLE CAR SAT IN the driveway of the stately white colonial home in Riverdale, New York. While Peter Womack was the U.S. attorney for the Southern District of New York, earning the wages of a federal employee, both he and his wife, Katherine, came from money, the trust-fund brigade. Because of their station in life, they were encouraged to give back, to work in the service of the country that had afforded their families a life of privilege.

The porch light was on, and several windows glowed at this late hour. Jack knew that Peter was in the middle of a trial, and he never joined his family out in the Hamptons until all work was behind him. Jack had considered Peter a friend, and although they and their wives had dined out, although they had worked together, Jack admitted to himself that he never truly knew the man. They walked in different worlds, not just federal and local but background, financial circles, and privilege. Jack was a DA because of passion, Peter as a result of duty.

He was not a cynic, but when Jack saw Peter's name in Cristos's book, he was not totally shocked. As they drove to Peter's house, Jack grew angrier with every mile. It was Peter who suggested that Jack prosecute Cristos; it was Peter who limited the fed involvement, all the while knowing that Jack would do the right thing and get the conviction. And, Jack imagined, it was Peter who was involved with the false execution of Nowaji Cristos, allowing him to live another day.

Jack tried to banish the thought that Peter would have allowed Jack and Mia's current situation but would withhold judgment until they spoke. But the bottom line was that Peter was connected to Cristos, and if he didn't know where Cristos was, he knew the people who would.

Jack rang the doorbell as Frank and Joy stood back on the slate walkway.

He waited a moment. No answer. He rang it again.

After a full minute, no sound came from the home.

Without a word, Frank took off around the house, peering through the windows.

Jack and Joy remained at the front of the house as Jack gave the button one last push. But this time, he heard movement.

Someone approached the entrance hall, the lock was unlatched, and the door was pulled open. Frank stood there, his hand wrapped in his sleeve so as not to touch the knob.

"Back door was open," Frank said.

Joy and Jack stepped inside the small wainscoted foyer.

"Don't touch anything," Frank said.

Jack knew full well what that meant as Frank led them through to the study off the living room.

Peter sat behind an antique partners' desk, a Tiffany lamp's glow lighting the dark wood surface. The right side of his head was missing, the maroon curtains behind him covered in bits of flesh and bone. A pistol lay on the floor beneath his left hand.

"Look at his neck," Frank said.

Jack could see a shade of bruising around his trachea.

"Jack." Frank waited until his friend finally looked up from the body. "The list in the back of that book, the one with Peter's name on it, Director Warren's name, Tierney's . . . yours. It's not the type of list we think. It's a hit list."

THE HEAVY BOLT of the lock slipped back with a thud, and the door opened to reveal a man balancing a heavy tray precariously on his right hand. He stepped into the room; the sound of the city flowed in before he closed the door behind him. He slipped the key back into the door lock, securing it with a single turn, tucked it back into his pocket, and took hold of the silver tray with two hands.

"Brought you a little dinner," the man said with a forced smile.

Mia sat on the bed, her head hung low.

"Sorry we don't have something a bit more appealing, but this is what we're all eating." The tray had two plates covered in cold cuts, two apples, a loaf of bread, and three bottles of water.

"I'm Jacob," the brown-haired man said, trying to get a reaction from Mia, but she remained silent, her eyes distant. "Well, it's here if you want it."

When Jacob leaned down, both hands holding the tray, Mia sprang from the bed and snatched the gun from his holster.

Jacob spun around, but Mia already had the gun pointed at him.

"You're kidding me, right?" There was a mix of fear and humor in the young man's eyes.

Mia tapped the gun against his head. "Do you want to see how much I'm kidding?"

"You wouldn't shoot." Jacob's words sounded more hopeful than definitive.

"Then you don't know me very well." Mia stepped back and pulled back the bedspread to reveal long white ropes, hand-woven from torn strips of bedsheet.

"Lash your legs together," Mia said as she tossed him a four-foot length.

Jacob reluctantly sat on the floor and tied his legs, laughing as he did. "You don't have a chance of escaping."

"You'd be surprised how far a woman will go to save her family."

"You'll be surprised, then, because it won't be very far."

"On your knees," Mia snapped.

Jacob shook his head as he complied. "I'm not going to hurt you."

"Hands behind your back." Mia brought the gun close to his eye, reminding him of what she held.

As Jacob held his hands behind his back, Mia grabbed a length of woven bedsheet tied in a noose and, walking behind him while jamming the gun hard into the back of his neck, dropped it over his wrists and pulled it tight, binding his hands together. She yanked it roughly for emphasis, wrapping the excess twice more about his wrists, ensuring that he couldn't free himself.

"I can't tell you what a mistake you just made." Jacob's humorous tone was completely gone, replaced with a mix of anger and fear. He sneered. "If Cristos has his sights on your family, they don't have a chance."

Mia's temper boiled, and she drew back her arm, smashing the butt of the gun into the man's temple. He tumbled from his knees and hit the hard floor face-first, out cold. She leaned over and grabbed the elegant cloth napkins from the silver tray and stuffed them into Jacob's mouth.

She rifled through his pockets, empty except for a single key.

She slipped the key into the lock, and with a quick turn, the heavy dead bolt slipped back into the door with a click. She laid her ear on the door and listened. She wrapped her hand around the brass handle and slowly turned.

As she cautiously opened the door, what she saw shocked her. Despite the constant whine of city noise, the sounds of traffic and people, she could not have been farther away from the image the sounds of the city painted in her head.

Mia stepped into a room, and her captivity immediately took on a whole new perspective. While expecting to be met with a dingy, run-down warehouse, perhaps a decrepit apartment building, she saw before her anything but.

The room she had been held in for the last twenty-four hours was not a room but a closet, an anteroom to a large, elegantly appointed bedroom. The walls were covered with soft floral-print paper, and thick green velvet curtains framed the large windows. A canopy bed dominated the room, while its matching dresser and makeup table sat off to the side. She looked at a small stereo on the floor and felt the fool. A CD was on perpetual repeat, and the sounds of city noise, cars honking, bus doors closing, sirens racing off to nowhere poured from the speakers.

Mia's fear grew as Jacob's words began to ring in her ears, *you won't get far.*

JACK STOOD OUTSIDE Peter's house, looking at the dark clouds looming overhead, the orange lights of the city reflected off their underbellies. Flashes of summer lightning burst inside their five-mile-high confines.

There was no doubt in his mind that Frank was right. The list in the back of the book was a hit list. Reports were already coming in that FBI Director Lance Warren was dead. Being on Cristos's hit list hadn't fazed him; he was killed once already. He had never been involved in anything recorded in those books. His name was on the list for retribution, for revenge, for putting Cristos to death the year before.

Jack's cell phone rang, startling him. He saw Mia's number come up, but he knew who was calling. He placed it to his ear.

"Heard you escaped."

"Where is my wife?"

"You betrayed me while I hold the proverbial blade to your wife's throat," Cristos raged through the phone. "If I'm not holding the contents of that case, every single piece in my hands by dawn, I will kill your wife . . . not quickly. Slowly, drawn out, where you will hear her screams no matter where you are in the world. And then I will kill your children. I will do it in front of you as you watch the life slowly seep from their young eyes. Then I will render you helpless, crippled, blind, with nothing but the memories of their cries to keep you company for the rest of your days."

"You son of—"

"I imagine you're at Peter Womack's house trying to track me down. Don't bother with that list in the back of my book. They're all dead."

"Where are you?" Jack begged through gritted teeth.

"You know exactly where I am."

And Cristos hung up.

CHAPTER 39

M IA SLOWLY OPENED THE bedroom door to find a wide hallway, the ceiling at least twelve feet, the floor covered in a thick burgundy rug. She could see a cloud of dust rising up with her every footstep.

Several doors ran off in both directions, while a sweeping set of stairs lay at the far end of the hall and fell off into an enormous marble foyer. The paneled walls and coffered ceiling left no doubt about the extreme wealth of the home owner.

Mia crept down the hall, thankful for the pair of flats she wore on her feet, glad she had changed from the three-inch pumps when she got into the car the night before. She held tightly to the pistol, taking comfort in its lethal ability and the fact that she knew how to bring it to bear so well. She ejected the clip, confirming nine bullets, before slamming it back into the butt, resolving to use it only as a last resort. Her only thought was getting to her children. Jack said they were safe, but she had seen the look in Cristos's eyes. She saw the picture that he had taken of them and knew that their innocent lives meant nothing to him except as pawns of leverage in achieving his goal. And while she was terrified for them, she tucked her fear in the back of her mind, knowing that it would do nothing but cripple her and keep her from reaching them before it was too late.

She stopped at the top of the stairs and peered down into the foyer. She tuned her ears, listening for any presence, but heard nothing. On silent feet, she crept down the stairs, her pistol waving back and forth, her finger poised on the trigger, ready to shoot.

As she stepped into the foyer, she was amazed at what she beheld. The house was enormous. To her left was a ballroom-sized living room, replete with antique furniture from a bygone age. To her right was an old-fashioned library, deep cherry paneling, a fireplace you could park a car in, bookshelves covered in never-ending volumes. There were large overstuffed sofas, and high-back wing chairs faced the fireplace.

But there was a coldness to the place, a foreboding of death and abandonment, despite the furnishings, the pictures that lined the tables. She couldn't help feeling that the place was haunted. Dated pictures covered the desk and the end tables, images of a forgotten time that was only recalled by the depths of the house

She cut through the library to a set of French doors and, gently turning the handle, pulled it open. She inhaled the humid summer night air and looked around the well-lit grounds, but again, she saw no one.

She took a step outside onto a slate terrace adorned with planters filled with withered flowers. Suddenly, the planter beside her exploded, turned to gravel and dust.

The gunshot came from the house, not behind it, not from above or from the brush. It came from the porch by the front door, where two men were focused on her with guns raised.

Without thought, Mia ran for cover.

A hail of bullets erupted, tearing into the ground right behind her, shredding the stone wall to her left. As Mia kept running, she caught sight of two guards racing her way.

The cascade of gunfire continued without pause. Mia had been an FBI agent for thirteen years, and although she was well trained, her investigations had never brought her into a war zone until now.

Rounding the house, she saw a blanket of darkness before her, a shroud against the star-filled night sky. The woods were only twenty-five yards away, a momentary place to seek sanctuary, to get lost, to afford her the time to clear her head and save herself. She pushed her legs to the breaking point, the lactic acid pouring over her muscles, urging her to slow, her mind protesting, clinging to the adage, *fight or flee*. As the gunfire continued, skimming the ground around her, she thought she was about to die when she cut right and into the deep woods.

The sounds of gunfire soon diminished, echoing behind her, but she didn't slow. Branches slapped her face, stinging her skin, as she ducked and dodged through the thick nighttime forest, her footing precarious as she sprinted over the uneven forest floor, struggling not to fall as her toes caught on protruding roots and rocks. Putting as much distance between herself and death as possible, she headed deeper into the dark woods, the shadows enveloping her, and finally slowed her pace. Catching her breath, she listened for her pursuers and prayed that they were as lost as she was. She felt like an animal, hunted for sport. She knew there was no surrender, no going back. She was no longer their prisoner, and, as she knew all along, they couldn't afford for her to live.

Mia looked around the woods; shadows ran long and deep under the moonlight, its intermittent shafts slicing down through the leafy canopy reflecting off the rocks and fallen, decaying trees scattered on the ground around her. The sounds of the summer night filled the air—insects, birds, nocturnal creatures rustling in the treetops. And although she knew she was awake, she felt as if she had just been thrust into the darkest of nightmares.

And then, in the distance, like a voice calling to her, she heard the roar of a train, its howling whistle, like a beacon. It filled her with hope. It gave her a desperately needed destination where she knew she could find help.

She began to walk, gingerly, each footstep on the forest floor taken with care, trying to minimize her footfalls upon the unseen leaves and sticks.

On the horizon, five miles away, she could see the flashes of lightning, setting enormous thunderhead clouds ablaze. With each successive strike, she could see the enormity of the approaching storm, built up throughout the humid day, ready to unleash its fury on the world below. There was no doubt in Mia's mind, fate was drawing the storm toward her.

Up ahead, she saw a clearing, the last bits of moonlight dancing off a white concrete roadway. She stopped, tuning her hearing, listening, reaching out with her mind for a trap. She was so close to escape, her pounding heart racing faster as she knew that it was always when freedom was in view that the gates came crashing down.

As she stepped from the woods, she nearly collapsed, for what she thought to be a roadway was not. The sound that called to her was not a train. In hindsight, it was like the mythical sirens that called to Odysseus, tempting him with their seductive cries.

Mia realized that her efforts were to no avail. There would be no finding Jack, no way to get to her children in time. She was truly powerless, trapped . . .

For the place where she was held had no escape.

Mia stood at the edge of the forest and fought the overwhelming urge to give up. She thought herself so smart, so brilliant, in overpowering her captor, in making her escape. She had not only managed to avoid being killed in a hail of gunfire but had successfully eluded her captors.

But now she knew why they had slowed their pace, why their desperate gunfire had fallen off. They knew she'd never get away. She had nowhere to go.

Mia looked out over the sandy beach at the great expanse of water before her. Moonlight danced up the crests of the waves, swirling like lights at Christmas. A ship three miles to the north steamed through the ocean waters, its running lights like fireflies in the distance, its low bellowing horn echoed out to sea. Her wishful thinking had morphed its sound into that of a locomotive luring her here where she now stood with her feet in the sand.

And then she heard them, getting closer, closing in.

JACK WAS AT a loss. It was after 1:30 in the morning. He had less than four and a half hours to get to Mia, and yet he had no idea where she was. He was so sure he could get it out of Peter, and that was his only option.

Jack racked his brain, trying to focus, to see if there was some clue he had missed. He thought he had all of the cards. He had the books that Cristos wanted, he had the passport and the prayer necklace. He examined them, wishing that they would speak to him, give him some direction.

He looked at the two fateful pictures, of him lying dead along the river . . .

And it hit him. It was there all along. He looked closer at the drawing of Mia, at its exacting detail. The drawing of Jack on the riverbank was so precise, down to the wet errant hairs on his head.

If there was any truth to these drawings, if the drawing of Mia was done to the same standard as Jack's, then Mia's depiction was the compass that would lead him to her.

A momentary blossom of hope welled inside him as he looked at the picture. He knew the area where she lay. He knew the rocks and the trees. He knew the sandy beach like the back of his hand.

CHAPTER 40

THE WHITE HATERAS YACHT belonged to Jack's friend, Mitch Schuler. They had graduated from law school at the same time, but Mitch had never been bitten by the justice bug, heading straight into Wall Street and millions. When Jack called in a favor, Mitch never hesitated. And this time, finding out that his friend was still alive, Mitch almost leaped through the phone to hug him. He made sure that his sixty-foot yacht was fueled and stocked and was happy to play the game that Jack was still dead. He told the head of the marina that Frank Archer and a friend would be picking up his boat that night and not to expect it back until the next day.

They sped into the rain-soaked marina to find the boat already running and the harbor master standing in wait. Frank quickly greeted him, slipped him a hundred, and hopped aboard.

"Listen," Jack said to Joy as they got out of Frank's car, holding an umbrella over her. "I'm sorry I didn't tell you about the cancer."

"So, what's this mean, you come back from the dead only to have death waiting around the corner? I can't go through that again. You don't know what it did to me to hear you and Mia had died."

"I'm sorry."

"No." Joy calmed down and wrapped her arms around Jack. "I'm sorry. I can't imagine what you're going through right now. I love you, Jack, and I love Mia. And I will go on loving the both of you till the day I die." Joy wiped away a tear. "Please bring her back safe."

Jack handed Joy an umbrella as one of Mitch Schuler's town cars arrived in the parking lot next to them. She got into the backseat and, without another word, closed the door, and the town car drove away.

Jack ran through the rain, down the pier, and jumped onto the boat. He quickly released the stern line and ran to the bow.

Frank was at the wheel, familiarizing himself with the controls, when his cell phone rang. He quickly answered it as he revved the motor. "Yeah?"

"Frank, it's Matt Daly."

"What's up?" Frank said, entirely distracted with flipping knobs and levers.

"You wanted me to call you if we found anything."

Frank froze in his tracks. He hadn't thought about Matt since his last call, forgetting that he was probably still in his dive gear, dragging the river for bodies that weren't there. Everything had moved so quickly; quite honestly, it didn't really matter now if the world found out that Jack and Mia weren't in the river. But there was an urgency in Matt's tone that unnerved him; he stopped fiddling and focused all attention on the call. "You found something?"

"Yeah, we've got a body."

Frank spun around and looked at Jack, who was casting off the bow line. "Whose body?"

"We're not sure yet. It's wedged in the spillway. It may take some time to get it out. It's real tough working underwater at night."

"I'm sure it is." Frank was hardly listening as confusion began to wrap around him. "Do me a favor and call me as soon as you have an ID."

"You got it." And Daly hung up.

Jack turned toward Frank as he cast off the last line and pulled in the bumpers. "Who's on the phone?"

Frank struggled for words. "Just my wife."

CHAPTER 41

A s Mia looked out across the water, the slim chance of escape was not what scared her. What tested her mental stability was what she saw across the body of water, two miles away to the west. She understood now where the photo of her daughters at play that Cristos had left her was taken from. It was clear that he had her children under surveillance this whole time. The site she was staring at was the distant beach house where Jack was raised, the house of her in-laws, the place where her daughters now slept.

While sitting on the sandy beach behind his boyhood home, Jack would tell her tales of his youth, stories of a time before he was born, of the great island across the water, where the abject poor were buried in unmarked graves on the southern side, while for fifty years the opulent estate of Marguerite Trudeau hosted the rich and powerful at her weekly summer parties.

Mia was two miles from shore, a swim she could easily make, but it would leave her an easy target for the men who were closing in. She could hear the approach of her pursuers, and without another thought, she turned and headed back into the woods.

She headed in the direction of what she believed was south, away from the mansion, working her way through the woods for five minutes. She could hear her stalkers not far behind, the sound of their footfalls coming from two different directions. Clearly, they had split up and were closing in.

The rain began to fall in large, soaking drops. Mia was drenched in thirty seconds. The thunder was close enough to shake the ground she ran on, the deep, engulfing rumble startling her with every strike.

Before she knew it, she was in the overgrown potter's field, a world of the dead, countless souls buried beneath her feet, forgotten to the world. Brush had overtaken the footstones, and trees had sprouted long ago, their roots digging down deep into death, carrying it out of the earth, and filling the woods with an ominous cloud of foreboding.

With the storm's full force nearly upon her, the dark clouds blotted out the moonlight, plunging her into near-total darkness. She stumbled, falling hard to the ground, scrambling through the mud to regain her footing. With the sounds of the driving rain, of the constant thunder, she could no longer hear her pursuers. She spun around the potter's field as a terrible fear crept up within her, as though she was on the edge of death. She waited for the bullet to strike.

And through the sounds of the storm, she once again heard them, less than ten yards away. She froze in place, holding her gun high, her finger on the trigger. Waiting for death.

Thunder exploded, the flash of lightning briefly illuminating the darkness around her: shattered foot- and headstones, felled trees, overgrown bramble. The brief bolt left her eyes momentarily scarred with spots, inhibiting what little sight she had.

Another sound, this one just feet away. She pulled the trigger in the direction of the sound, and her gun exploded, the flash lighting her surroundings for the briefest of seconds. She saw them, two of them, rain running down their angry faces, their hair plastered to their heads. They both spun and began rapid-firing in the direction of her shot.

Mia spun left a half-second before the gunfire was returned. She raced without direction, tripping, stumbling, her legs weak with fright. She crashed into a broken headstone, her ankle twisting in pain. She hunkered down, enveloped in fear, hiding among the dead.

Mia held her gun as if it would ward off her attackers, ward off evil, blindly pointing it. She never felt so alone, so close to death.

She thought she heard movement again, but this was different. It was a rumble from beneath the ground, as if the souls of the departed had been disturbed.

And then, without warning, Mia was suddenly sucked into the ground.

CRISTOS STEPPED FROM the large speedboat onto the dock, the churned-up ocean waters sending the floating wharf rolling around, the two boats banging against their moorings as the waves washed over everything, trying to drag it all out to sea. Ignoring the growing storm, he stalked up the gangway onto shore, where he was met by Jacob.

"What the hell are you doing out here?" Cristos said.

"The woman escaped." A bruise was welling up on the side of his rain-soaked head. They continued walking up to the estate.

"Off the island?"

"No."

Walking in silence, they arrived at the front door. Cristos saw the spent bullet casings on the ground and spun around into Jacob's face.

"They shot at her?" Cristos's words were measured and angry.

Jacob said nothing.

"If she dies, you all die. Where is everybody?"

"Alex and Rizzoli are out looking for her.

"They can't find her?"

"They lost her. It was like she just vanished. They said it was as if she had disappeared into thin air."

MIA WAS IN a full-on panic, scrambling in a pool of water, her gun lost during the fall, her hands scratching the muddy walls for purchase. She could barely see, but then lightning lit up the night, filtering down into her tomb, and she saw flashes of her prison.

She was in a pit, a makeshift crypt, where countless bodies had been thrown one atop the other when space was no longer available in the graveyard, robbing them of the dignity of lying alone in their eternal rest.

About her were shattered skeletons and tattered clothing that tried in vain to hold what were once human bodies together. The heavy rains, along with her weight, had opened the sink hole like a grave where no one had been in decades, where maintenance had stopped in the '70s.

And although the illumination of lightning was intermittent, she didn't need to see to know that the four feet of water was quickly rising around her. Between her exhaustion and the freezing water, Mia knew she could only hold out for so long. If she didn't drown first, the muddy walls would soon collapse, filling in the grave, where she would never be found, where she would die terrified among the already dead.

JACK SAT IN the teak-appointed salon of the Hatteras. Frank was forward at the helm of the boat as they cut through the choppy seas. Frank had fallen silent since the call from his wife, speaking in short one-word answers. Jack knew he was either pissed, preoccupied, or scared. Jack had picked up on Frank's mannerisms from the moment they met so many years ago. He hadn't changed much since. He still had the powerful arms of a fighter, the sharp mind of a soldier, and the temper of a junkyard dog. Jack would hate to be his enemy. There was no one he would rather have at his side, living or dead, as he was about to embark on the fight of his life.

Jack had tucked all of Toulouse's effects into a knapsack. He and Frank had pored through the two books, but there were still some missing pieces to the puzzle. He understood that the feds were after the book that included the list of assassinations. He felt sure, though, that Cristos had different motives. There was something else there, something he wasn't seeing.

Jack pulled out Toulouse's passport. He read through all of the visa stamps, imagining all of the places Toulouse had traveled to in the last month. He flipped back to the front and stared at his picture. There was a slight resemblance to Cristos, but there was something else . . . He looked at the dagger, at the prayer necklace.

Jack turned his attention to his wrist, the tattoo. He could remember the man writing the words; he could see him kneeling beside him on the riverbank.

Jack closed his eyes, trying to draw up his memory. He could see the swollen river, moonlight shining down upon him . . .

"Did you give her the necklace, Jack?" the man whispered.

And Jack finally knew who the man was, who had emerged from the woods, who had written on his arm, who had saved him.

And it was impossible . . .

. . . for the man died this past week.

Toulouse paused from his writing, finally looking at Jack, staring into his eyes.

"You did not answer me, Jack. Did you give her the necklace?" Toulouse asked.

SOMETHING FELL ON Mia's shoulder. She flinched and kicked back in the ever-rising water until she heard someone calling her. She reached over to find a rope dropped down in the pit beside her. She could see nothing above but knew that if she didn't grab hold, she would surely die, and no one would ever find her.

She held tight and was hauled up. It was only ten feet, but it felt like forever; the pit collapsing behind her as her feet dug into its muddy walls.

She finally crested the rim, bloodied, bruised, and covered in mud. Standing there, holding the other end of the rope, was Cristos.

Standing beside him were Jacob and a taller middle-aged man. Jacob's face was bloodied, his right eye swollen. "If Jacob had carried out his orders, you wouldn't be here right now," Cristos said as they began walking back to the estate.

The rain had let up. Lightning still flashed, although its rumble was seconds behind the glow.

"I'm glad you survived," Cristos said. "Your husband is on his way, and how would it look if you died *before* he got here?"

CHAPTER 42

TRUDEAU ISLAND LOOMED ON the horizon, intermittently appearing and disappearing behind sheets of rain and drifting fog. The seas were rough as Frank piloted the boat through the six-foot choppy swells.

The storm burst from the dark clouds in five-minute onslaughts of horizontal rain before falling back to a fine mist. Against every regulation, they cut through the waters without running lights, invisible to anyone watching from the island and also to any other approaching vessel. Jack and Frank kept their eyes peeled for oncoming boats and ships, but it was difficult with visibility waxing and waning.

The trip out was nearing an hour when Frank passed the outer edge of the island. The tall white lighthouse on the north ridge came into view, its beam cutting through the stormy night like the sharp blade of a sword. They circled the island twice, confirming that the lights of the mansion were lit and that the estate was occupied.

After quick debate, they approached from the western side and weighed anchor fifty yards from shore.

Within the salon of the boat, Jack checked his gun, ejecting the clip, verifying his bullet count. He cleared his pockets, throwing his money, his wallet, and the envelope with the letter to Cristos—the one he still couldn't remember writing—onto the table. He opted to hold on to Charlie's rabbit foot—he chose to believe in every talisman he could at the moment—and the small jewelry box with Mia's pearl choker inside. It was like having her with him, something he could draw strength from.

Tucking his gun back into his pants, he caught a glimpse of the envelope on the table. There was nothing written on the outside.

Confused, Jack grabbed it, opened it, and withdrew the note. He looked at it, turned it over in his hand three times, and felt his head spin. It was his stationery, no doubt about it. It was the letter he had stuffed into his pocket, the one he had read in Cristos's Suburban . . . but it was blank.

FRANK AND JACK took the small skiff to the sandy beach on the western shore, far out of sight of the estate. The storm had picked up, visibility barely reaching the Hatteras one hundred fifty feet away. Jack looked over his shoulder, trying to see the distant shore two miles away where his daughters were sleeping in his parents' home. He couldn't suppress the creeping fear that Cristos was so close to them.

Working off of twenty-year-old memories, Jack led the way through the woods, finding the pathway of his youth nonexistent but his direction still accurate as they emerged at the overgrown side yard of the estate.

Staying within the shadows, they worked their way toward the docks, finding two high-speed cigarette boats in the slip. There were no guards walking around, no one in the boats.

Rounding the outer perimeter of light wash, Jack and Frank raced around the grounds to the far eastern edge, where the outbuildings, communication center, and generator were located. Frank examined the thirty-foot-square generator, a ten-ton unit capable of generating power for the house plus enough electricity to power a neighborhood. On the far side, adjacent to a separate deep-water dock, was a 25,000-gallon fuel tank, its meter indicating that it was recently topped off.

"You have no idea where she is in there, do you?"

"No." Jack shook his head.

"How the hell are we going to find her without getting killed?"

Jack looked around, at the generator, the stone mansion, the stormy ocean, until his eyes were finally distracted by the sweeping light on the north side of the island.

FRANK STOOD ON the deck of the first high-speed cigarette boat. He opened the fuel spout on the two-hundred-gallon tank and punctured the line, allowing the gas to pour along the deck, seeping into the forward cabin. He followed suit with the second boat and ran back to the communication house.

Beyond the satellite dishes and centralized communication systems, most of the thousand-square-foot house was for storage of everything from lawn-maintenance equipment to food and supplies offloaded from the nearby deep-water dock. He grabbed several gas jugs and filled them from the 25,000-gallon fuel tank, pouring and scattering them along the concrete floor.

Heading back outside, he returned to the tank and opened the lower fuel drain a quarter of a turn to allow the gas to flow out in small streams toward the main house.

Frank turned to the generator, glanced at his watch, and, laying his hand on the kill switch, watched as Jack arrived at the front door of the mansion.

• • •

JACK STOOD BEFORE the large mahogany door when the lights went out, plunging the entire estate into darkness. Jack looked at his watch; the second hand just swept past 1:30 a.m.

He pounded his fist against the door.

Five seconds later, a young dark-haired man with a bruised and battered face opened the door and pointed his pistol in Jack's face.

"Bravo," Cristos said as he stepped into the doorway. "You figured out where I was."

"Where's Mia?"

"Where are my father's possessions?"

"Where is my wife?"

"She'll be dead in thirty seconds if you don't give me what is rightfully mine."

"Then in thirty seconds, you will never see those items again," Jack said quietly.

"Do you think I'm bluffing?" Cristos stood there defiantly.

"Do you think I am?" Jack said, his eyes on fire. "I want to see my wife. Now."

Cristos stared back before finally nodding to the man on his left. "I said I wouldn't hurt her if you did what I asked. And you haven't done what I asked all day."

"Your sense of morals and honor is twisted."

"And you ran off thinking you could, what, trick me? Leave me with an empty box? Don't talk to me about honor and morals."

"You killed your father."

"I had no choice."

"No choice?"

"I chased him, sought him out, begged him to tell me."

"Tell you what?"

"My future."

"Seriously?" Jack laughed.

Cristos glared at Jack. "A naïve man laughs at what he can't understand. Those two books?"

"Yeah?"

"My father's is where the future is written. He could remember the future as easily as the past."

"Really," Jack said skeptically, although he had seen the fateful drawings of himself and Mia.

"You don't understand the power of fate."

"There is no such thing as fate. No one's future is preordained. You can't tell me some writing in a book controls destiny."

"Your mind can't grasp what it can't comprehend."

"Once someone knows their future," Jack said, "just the fact that they know it could change their actions and thereby change your so called divination."

"That may be true for some but not for my father's foresight. He was never wrong."

"Then why didn't he use it?"

"He did, foolishly, in the way he saw fit. Do you understand what one could do with that power? The control one could have?"

Jack laughed. "Are you hearing yourself?"

"My father would only write down what he chose to, and he wrote down in the last pages of his book my future. He lured me here with it, back to the United States, in hopes of either bringing me home or having me captured, having me brought to justice for all that I had done. For all of the *embarrassment* I had caused him."

"And so you killed him?"

"And got nothing for it, until now," Cristos said. "Did you look at everything in that box, all of my father's things?"

"Yeah."

"Do you understand what it held?"

"Your future," Jack said, mocking.

Cristos laughed. "Besides that."

"His books, passport, money, some papers . . . a prayer necklace—"

"It's there?"

"Yeah."

Cristos smiled in satisfaction.

"What is it, a magic necklace?" Jack taunted him.

"Sometimes the simplest of things can hold the greatest power. Like that cross around your neck," Cristos said as he pointed. "There is no greater power than faith."

Jack just stared.

"My father, our priests, have the power to heal, the power to keep one alive in ways you couldn't understand."

"And a cheap necklace is going to—"

"I can use it to stave off death," Cristos snapped at Jack. Then he quietly calmed himself. "Use it to save myself from my fate."

"You said fate can't be changed," Jack shot back.

"Right. And you said we control our own destiny."

Jacob came from the rear of the mansion, holding Mia by the elbow.

Mia stood there, her eyes red from anger and tears. Her dress was torn, wet, and muddy, her sweater buttoned up, pulled tightly around her.

"Are you all right?" Jack asked.

"Don't worry about me." Mia nodded, breathing heavily as she fought being overcome with emotion.

"Her condition is not my doing," Cristos said as he saw Jack's rising anger. She tried to escape, but I guess she thought twice about taking a swim. Now I would like proof that you have my father's things."

Jack reached into his back pocket, pulled out Toulouse's passport, and tossed it to Cristos.

Cristos flipped through the pages and smiled.

"You haven't heard my terms yet."

"There are no terms." Cristos grabbed Mia by the arm, dragging her with him. "You will take me to my father's things, now."

Jack followed them across the foyer and out the front door into the rain. They had stood on the front porch for a moment when an explosion rocked the house. A roar like thunder echoed throughout the island as an orange glow lit up the night, flooding the grounds, pouring through windows as flames licked the sky.

"That's the first," Jack said as he looked at his watch.

"What do you mean?" Cristos demanded.

"You will let Mia go and allow her to board my boat. Once she is away and she radios me that she is safe, then I will give you your things."

"Not a chance."

A second explosion ripped apart the night.

"The flames move quickly . . . the third one is right next to my knapsack. You have me. Let her go now, or—"

"Or what?"

"It'll all burn."

FRANK HAD WATCHED Jack emerge from the house—the prearranged signal for the first explosions—and lit the fuse to the communication center so that the building exploded into a maelstrom of flame. He counted down thirty seconds as he raced for the dock, firing his gun at the deck of the first boat and igniting a firestorm that tore the two vessels into enormous balls of splinter and flame. The heat set the dock ablaze. The blast threw Frank to the ground. All around him, the fire sizzled and popped as the rain fell on it, sending plumes of gray and black smoke into the night sky.

He climbed to his feet and he ran back to his position under the trees near the main fuel tank, watching as four men came rushing out of the house. They stopped at Cristos's side, looking at the nearby fires.

Suddenly, his cell phone vibrated in his pocket. He pulled it out, ready to hit ignore when he saw the number and answered.

"Frank," Matt Daly said.

"Yeah," Frank whispered.

"We got the body but . . ."

"But what?"

"It's not Jack or Mia."

Frank fell silent. "Then who is it?"

"No idea. He's got dark close-cropped hair. Maybe Asian. Looks like he was shot in the stomach, and there is some kind of black ooze running through his veins and circling his heart."

"How long has it been there?"

"Not long, less than twenty four hours."

MIA AND JACOB arrived at the western beach, finding the inflatable skiff pulled up on the sand tethered to a small claw anchor that was dug into the sand. Cristos had relented to Jack's demands but under his terms. He had pulled Jacob aside, giving him explicit instructions before escorting Mia.

Jacob pulled out his cell phone.

"What are you doing?"

"Cristos has no intention of letting you leave this island."

"What?"

"You're going to tell him that you're safely away."

"Or what?"

"I'll kill you right here." Jacob held up his gun. "Then take the boat across the water, pull your kids out of bed, and let them beg for their father, let him hear them scream."

CHAPTER 43

JACK AND CRISTOS STOOD on the front steps of the house, the orange glow of flame dancing around them.

Cristos held his cell phone in his hand, awaiting the call.

The minutes dragged as Jack awaited word of Mia's safety. And in his interminable wait, everything began to cascade through his head: waking up to the announcement of his death, the tattoo on his arm, the unraveling of the day's mysteries, racing through the Tombs, his father, Jimmy Griffin, the stranger in the psych ward who told him to hold on to his mind. Jack realized that as the day had progressed, the mystery of finding Mia, of saving her, had only produced far greater mysteries.

Ryan's diagnosis of madness echoed in Jack's head.

He vividly remembered his dog being run over in the driveway. He remembered his sad, pleading eyes, uncomprehending his broken body. Jack remembered as his last breath escaped his body . . . yet he also remembered him in his kitchen that morning, playing with him, the smell of his breath, the sound of panting, his warm eyes.

Jack's hand went to his chest, rubbing his wound. He realized that as the day went on, the pain was growing, the wound feeling new. Despite the nurse telling him she had redressed the bandages, Jack felt as if it was attacking him from the inside. He assumed it was somehow related to the tumor, to his enhanced senses.

And his senses . . . despite the darkness around him, the subtle glow of flame seemed to light the whole world for him. He could hear what seemed like every raindrop's fall; he could hear Cristos's breathing, the sound of distant thunder as it escaped out to sea.

He knew that his psyche was at the brink of failure, the tumor, the smallest of things, chipping away at his mind, the disease momentarily blessing him with a new view of the world while wiping away his sanity.

But it didn't matter. Mia would soon be safe. She would grab their girls and whisk them into her arms, far away from Cristos and all this madness.

FRANK WATCHED FROM his position by the fallen tree, hidden in the shadows of the glowing fire, his gun trained on Cristos.

One of Cristos's men had left with Mia, presumably escorting her to their boat, while the other three went back into the dark house. Frank had no idea of the possible significance of the body Daly had found, but that could be dealt with later.

There was still a nagging sensation running through him that he couldn't put his finger on. He shook it off and trained his gun on Cristos. He knew hell was about to be unleashed.

WITH THE RAIN falling around them, the distant mainland coming in and out of view, Mia sat on the edge of the inflatable skiff next to Jacob as he began dialing the phone.

She had no intention of letting him or anyone near her children.

With Jacob focused on his phone in the teeming rain, she grabbed the anchor rope and threw it over his head, pulling it tight with every bit of energy she had. Jacob's hands went for the rope, dropping the phone and his gun. Mia held tight, leaning back, keeping up her leverage, keeping the rope taut around his neck.

But Jacob outweighed her by seventy pounds. He grabbed the rope, pulling it forward, gasping for air. And suddenly, he launched himself backward, throwing back his head, smashing it into Mia's face, stunning her, knocking her back onto the sand.

Suddenly free, Jacob scrambled to his feet, searching for his gun, but as he turned, Mia spun around like an Olympic hammer thrower, holding tight to the small anchor, hitting him upside the head, knocking him into the skiff.

Mia took off running into the woods.

Jacob struggled to his feet. He found his gun, but before taking chase, he turned and shot out the inflatable skiff, plugging it with two bullets.

Mia raced through the forest, the clouds above parting; streams of moonlight poured down with the now sporadic rain. She felt a horrible sense of déjà vu, but this time, she could see . . . but so could Jacob. She saw the semiclearing up ahead and pushed toward the old graveyard.

She cut through the potter's field, staying low, watching her footing over the broken head- and footstones, leaping over fallen trees and bushes heading toward the center of the graveyard. She finally stopped, winded, catching her breath, when all of a sudden, Jacob was there, blood mixed with rain pouring down his face, his gun aimed at her heart. She looked around. There was nowhere to go; she was trapped. She thought of Jack and her children and how she had tumbled into this nightmare before throwing her hands up in surrender.

"Stupid bitch!" Jacob screamed as he ran toward her.

And he fell as the earth beneath his feet gave way, sucking him down into the crypt sinkhole that Mia had fallen into earlier.

Jacob's hands clawed the muddy ground to no avail. He looked up at Mia, his rage-filled eyes turning to fear knowing that death would soon claim him.

TWO GUNSHOTS SHATTERED Jack's hearing, despite the distance, the rain, and sounds of the night. Fire raced up his spine as he realized that Cristos was playing him and Mia. He had no intention of letting her leave the island.

Suddenly, an explosion that dwarfed the first two shredded the fabric of the night, and an enormous fireball mushroomed into the sky, turning night into day, lighting the distant ocean, casting enormous shadows. Flaming tendrils spiked high in the air from what was left of the fuel tank and the generator; shooting starlike bits tore through the sky, shrapnel rained down, crashing like tiny meteors. The blast of heat ignited trees, curling leaves, shattering the windows of the mansion. A river of fire raced toward the stone estate.

Cristos bolted in shock, diving for cover. He reached for his gun, instantly aiming it at Jack.

With nowhere to run, Jack raced into the mansion.

He cut through the foyer, its white marble painted red with the glow of flames, only to find three of Cristos's men charging his way, guns drawn.

Jack quickly cut through the parlor toward the rear of the house as gunfire erupted around him.

FRANK RACED FOR the rear of the mansion. Seeing Jack run into the house was not on their agenda, nor was hearing the two distant gunshots from where they had left the boat. Hugging the rear of the stone façade, he sought and found an open door. Stepping into the mudroom, he reached behind him and pulled out a second pistol from the small of his back. He knew there were at least three to face, plus Cristos.

GUNFIRE EXPLODED AROUND Jack. He was pinned behind the stairs, nowhere to go. He could see the muzzle flashes coming from across the hall and knew it would be only moments before he was shot or they were upon him. His mind focused. He hadn't come this far only to fail now. Somehow he would escape his position and—

The gunfire stopped . . .

And a gun came to rest against Jack's head.

"Can't kill you, but there's plenty we can do short of that." The man stood over him; he aimed his gun at his leg and began to pull the trigger.

A gunshot exploded, and the man fell dead to the floor beside Jack.

"You're supposed to run away from the house, not into it," Frank said as he crouched next to Jack, handing him a gun.

The gunfire resumed, chipping away at the stairway around them.

"I've got to get to Mia," Jack said between breaths.

"Back door. I got your back."

Frank aimed his gun and began firing as Jack raced away.

THE NIGHT WAS awash in fire as Jack headed for the woods. He had no idea where she was but prayed that Mia was being Mia, staying alive for their girls.

As he raced across the backyard, Jack saw Frank through the window, racing down a hallway, and suddenly stopped, overcome with déjà vu.

Jack was the better shot, always had been, and yet it was Frank who was facing Cristos's men. Jack knew if he was to find Mia, it was far better if they searched together instead of splitting up. He hoped it wasn't too late as he turned and ran frantically across the yard back into the house.

Entering the darkened house, the glow of flame diminishing, Jack was thankful for his heightened sight. He tuned his ears, listening, and the sound of gunfire filled them.

Jack charged down the hallway and kicked in the door of the library to find Frank pinned behind an overturned table. Two shooters had taken up positions flanking him, relentlessly shooting away. Frank stayed tucked low. Jack could see his thick arms flexed in stress as he gripped his pistol, waiting for an opportunity to fire back. Time seemed to slow to a crawl, Jack took everything in, the flame from the exploding barrels, the smoke drifting skyward in fingerlike wisps, the bullets exploding around the table, splinters shattering, flying around.

Jack drew his pistol, and with two shots, he took out each shooter, their heads snapping backward in abrupt death. Jack didn't need to confirm his kills as he raced to Frank's side.

"Took you long enough."

"Sorry," Jack said as he crouched down.

But then Frank rolled toward him, and Jack could see the crimson stain blossoming on his shirt, just above his heart, the blood pulsing out of him.

"Not again!" Jack cried out.

"Hey, you knew this was inevitable."

"No. It's not inevitable. I can change this."

"No, Jack. Shut up." Frank's speech slowed, his eyes falling to half-mast as his life ebbed. "Save Mia. That's all that matters; that is the only fate you can change."

Jack pulled him closer.

"I'm sorry I never met her."

Jack stared at him, confused at his words. "I don't understand."

"You will." And Frank's eyes slid closed as a final breath escaped his lips.

Jack's heart broke as he laid his hand across his friend's head.

His own head throbbed, events of his life merging and falling apart all at once.

"Jack," Mia whispered.

He turned to see Cristos standing in the doorway, his gun jammed into Mia's neck.

"Seems you can't save anyone today, huh?" Cristos said. "Where are my things?"

"I'm sorry, Jack," Mia whispered.

"No. This is my fault. I'm sorry."

"My things?" Cristos cut in.

"Let her go, and I'll give them to you."

"We tried that once already."

"Kill her, and it will all burn."

"I will say this only one time. No more idle threats." Cristos's voice grew calm. "If it burns, I will kill you both and pay a visit to your children. I will kill one of them in front of the other and take the second child to raise her as my own."

CHAPTER 44

JACK WALKED WITH MIA at his side; Cristos was ten feet back, his gun trained on Mia. He led them across the long front yard, past the docks, heading north, the grade growing steeper for two hundred yards until they finally arrived at the base of the lighthouse, where the wind whipped the rain into a maelstrom on the high, rocky point. The white structure stood sixty feet tall, its bright light turning in a slow arc, casting its beam out into the world.

Jack opened the door to find the floor covered in a pool of gasoline, his backpack hanging from a nail in the circular stairs. Jack grabbed the bag and reluctantly stepped outside, passing it to Cristos. Keeping his gun trained on them, Cristos knelt on the muddy ground, oblivious to the rain that fell around them.

He dug through the bag, pulling out the passport and tossing it away. He found the dagger and looked at it under the wash of the lighthouse beam, its jewels sparking so many memories, but he tossed it, too. He found his prayer book and dumped it aside, finally pulled out the second book that belonged to his father. A smile of triumph creased his face as he turned back the red leather cover. He began thumbing through it, allowing the rain to fall on the pages to reveal his father's hidden writing. He kept turning, lost in thought, as he absorbed his father's words. Finally, he came to a section near the end, and his smile was washed away.

He flipped the pages ahead, back . . .

"There are pages missing."

"I know."

"Where are the pages?

"They were already torn out."

"Bullshit!"

"How would I even know what pages to tear out?"

Cristos pondered his response.

"What is on those pages that is so important to you?"

"The names of the people," Cristos said slowly, "who kill me."

Jack looked at him as if he was crazy. "So you can kill them first?"

The rays of the lighthouse swept over them.

Cristos's mind was working. He looked around him as if some answer could be found out at sea.

He finally dug back into the bag, drawing out his father's money, some papers, the drawings of Jack and Mia, and finally, the wooden prayer necklace. He examined it, rolling it around in his hands. He finally turned to Jack. "Where is the necklace?"

Jack stared at him, confused. He pointed at the prayer necklace as if it was obvious.

"These are prayer beads." Cristos looked back in the bag, but it was empty.

"Where is my father's necklace?"

"I don't know what you're talking about."

"Blue stones on a silver chain."

Jack stared back, trying to hide his shock.

"Don't tell me that it wasn't here, that you don't know where it is."

And Jack realized . . . He avoided eye contact with Mia, fearing that he would reveal the location of the blue necklace that hung around her neck.

Cristos grabbed Mia, pulling her close, laying the gun against her temple. "Remember what I said before you had me executed? Hold tight to your family."

Jack's eye filled with rage.

"Where is that blue stone necklace?"

The moment hung in the air as Cristos dug the gun into Mia's head.

"Ten seconds, and I'm going to start with her." He scraped the gun through Mia's dark, wet hair. "Know this. Your daughters are sleeping just across the water. Why do you think I chose this place?"

Cristos wrapped his left arm around Mia's neck, holding her tight in a headlock. He turned the gun on Jack.

And as the revolving light of the lighthouse passed over them, a shard of blue light hit the jewels of the necklace in the gap above Mia's sweater. Cristos saw it, spun her around, and tore open her sweater.

And there it was, hanging from her neck against her skin, the blue stone necklace that belonged to his father, the one that was spoken of in rumor, in mystery, said to keep him alive. It was passed down through the years to the leaders of their small country and would have passed to Cristos if his heart was true, if his father so deemed.

But Cristos didn't need his father's blessing now to take possession of it, to avail himself of its power.

Cristos smiled. What he sought had been under his nose for hours.

But in all of his distraction and focus on the necklace, Cristos never saw Jack lunge for his gun.

Jack grabbed it, wrenching it away, launching it toward the cliff's edge.

Mia tore herself away from Cristos, backhanding him in the cheek with amazing strength before scurrying away for the gun. And Jack attacked with all of his strength, but the powerful man fought back, possessing the training that Jack could never match, blocking his blows, anticipating his moves. He spun a kick to the side of Jack's head, sending him sprawling backward to the ground.

But Cristos didn't continue at Jack—he dove at Mia and the gun she was picking up near the cliff's edge. He punched her hard, sending her dazed into the mud. He grabbed the gun, spinning back, bringing it to bear on Jack.

And as Jack scrambled up along the muddy ground, Cristos saw a flash of Jack's left arm and became momentarily distracted by the Cotis lettering on his tattoo.

"Where did you get that?" Cristos demanded.

Jack stared at Cristos, seeing a look on his face that he thought impossible. It was fear, a look he had seen on Mia when she had asked Jack to hide the case.

"Do you understand what that is?" Cristos said. "It's a prayer for the dead."

"I don't want to hear any of your—"

"You died, Jack, and someone saved you. Who was it? What did he look like? Was it my father? Is he alive?"

Jack covered his arm with his hand as if in shame, as Mia slowly got to her feet behind him.

"Let me see that!" Cristos screamed, thrusting the gun at Jack.

Jack slowly rolled his sleeve down, taunting Cristos.

"Let me see it, now." Cristos jabbed the gun toward Jack for emphasis.

Jack let a smile slip out, mocking Cristos. "How does it taste, the flavor of fear?"

"Why don't you tell me?" It was Cristos's turn to smile coldly. And he pointed the gun at Mia.

Without warning, he pulled the trigger. The gun exploded, its report echoing across the island. Mia stumbled backward, the bullet hitting her just above the heart. Her eyes fell on Jack, wounded, not comprehending what just happened, and she began to collapse. Jack lunged for her to catch her, but her legs gave out, and she stumbled backward over the cliff's edge.

"No!!!" Jack's scream came from his soul as he watched in pure shock as she fell away, her body tumbling end over end, crashing to the rocky shore below.

Jack turned his rage on Cristos, grabbing the barrel of the gun, wrenching it out of his hand, but Cristos snatched it back, only to toss it over the cliff.

Cristos smiled at Jack, his dark eyes filled with malice and hate. He drew back his fist and attacked Jack with a series of blows. He was the expert destroying the novice; there was no need for guns to bring death.

But despite being outmatched, Jack remained on his feet. He drove his fist into Cristos's jaw, all of his anger, all of his pent-up rage unloading into the man, shattering his jaw.

As if he had had enough, Cristos grabbed Jack, hurling him over his shoulder onto the ground, driving his elbow into Jack's stomach. Jack rolled away as Cristos grabbed the left sleeve of his shirt, tearing it away.

Like a desperate animal, Jack grabbed a handful of mud and hurled it in Cristos's face. He followed up with three hooks to Cristos's broken jaw, sending him tumbling backward. Jack leaped onto him, driving his fist into Cristos's exposed neck, his nose, every vulnerable part of his body. Despite all of Cristos power and skills, they were failing against the raging man on top of him.

But then Cristos's hand fell upon the prayer books he had tossed to the ground. He pushed them aside, finding the prayer beads, continuing to search . . . until his hand fell on his goal. With blinding speed, he stabbed Jack in the chest with the jeweled dagger, the blade plunging into the wound just below his shoulder. A fire ignited in Jack's body as Cristos dug the blade in, twisting it. Jack fell to his back as Cristos leaned over him, leering down on him.

Seeing Cristos's dark eyes, seeing the face of the man who killed his wife, Jack refused to succumb. The knife and the face above him only managed to anger him further.

Jack clawed the ground for a weapon, a rock, anything to attack Cristos with, for Jack knew that despite the hate that flowed through his veins, he was on the edge of death.

Cristos's leer curled into a smile. "How does death taste?"

Jack grabbed the hilt of the dagger and wrenched it out of his chest. He quickly turned it and plunged it into Cristos's heart.

"You tell me," Jack said through gritted teeth.

And as Jack dug the blade into Cristos's beating heart, feeling its dying pulse through the hilt, Cristos finally saw the front of Jack's tattoo, the fateful words written there. And he knew they were written by his father. They were the words from the torn section of his father's book, the prediction that Cristos had sought in vain, the clue to his future, the prophecy that he had tried so desperately to eradicate so that he could choose his own path, not the one prescribed by his father's prophecies.

But as he read them, he understood that his quest, his search, had only proven to fulfill what he tried so hard to avoid. For the phrase in the middle of the prayer of death was written to him by his father.

You shall die at dawn, on the first day of the seventh month, killed by an enraged man who has lost everything he loves.

On the eastern horizon, where the dark of night met the depths of the sea, a golden ribbon crested the waves stretching north to south, as far as the eye could see, a subtle glow that began to wipe the darkness from the night, pushing away the shadows, ushering in a new day.

And in those final moments, no longer able to breathe, his lungs on fire as his heart struggled to burst from his chest, Cristos knew that he wouldn't escape death for the second time. Jack struggled to his feet, blood pouring from the wound in his chest. He grabbed Cristos, lifted his weakened body, and tossed him over the cliff to be smashed on the rocks below.

• • •

JACK RACED DOWN the rock face, slipping, sliding, his hand seeking purchase, the sharp rocks cutting his palm. With dawn's early light still in the far-off distance, he struggled to see through the last shreds of night that danced along the rocky slope. The precarious path provided no firm footing as he tried not to slip and perish on the rocks below. He glanced at Cristos's broken body, folded over a rock near the base of the cliff, momentarily lit by the sweep of the passing lighthouse beam. A pool of blood coated the sand beneath him. And Jack slipped. He skidded downward, trying not to tumble over and split his head open. As he grabbed a weathered rock with his left hand, it gave way, the sharp edge cutting into his left forearm, turning the tattoo into a shredded mess.

Jack leaped the final eight feet to the rocky beach, where Mia lay facedown in the shallow water, bent, contorted, motionless. Jack fell to his knees at her side, quickly turning her over to see the spreading wound on her chest.

Finding no pulse, no breath, Jack laid her on the sand, tilting her head back. He began CPR, forcing air into her lungs, life into her soul. He placed his hands just above her sternum and began rhythmically pumping, forcing her blood to pump. And he could see his efforts forcing the blood to accelerate its escape from the wound.

"Please, Mia. Breathe. Breathe, dammit." Jack locked his lips over hers once again and gave her the breath of his life.

"You can't die. Let it be me, please, let it be me. Let me trade my life for yours."

He forced more air into her lungs and quickly set about pumping her chest. He tore open her shirt, laying his hands just below her bra strap, and looked at the wound. It was above her heart, mercifully missing the vital organ. Maybe, just maybe . . .

With a heaving gasp, Mia exploded with life, hacking, coughing, an eruption of water shooting from her lungs. Jack lifted her, taking her into his arms, holding her in his lap.

"Jack . . ." she whispered.

"Shhhh . . ."

Mia looked up, her eyes drifting up the rock face to the cliff so far above. "How could I have survived?"

"The water must have broken your fall."

She reached her hand up to the bullet wound, wincing at the contact. Jack pressed his hand over it, trying to stop the flow of blood.

"How did you. . . ?"

"Frank's dead."

Mia looked at him. "What do you mean?"

"He was shot."

"I know he was shot. Everyone knows he was shot. It wasn't your fault."

"I know," Jack said, his head tilted to the side, confused.

"You do? After all these years, to finally release all of that guilt . . ."

"I don't understand. What you mean?"

"Jack, Frank died fifteen years ago. Are you OK?"

And as if caught in a whirlpool, Jack's mind began to fracture and reconstitute. Frank "Apollo" Archer, shot by those two kids, dying in Jack's arms . . . Yet Jack saw Frank that very day, was with him all day until he died minutes ago up in the mansion, the same scenario . . . shot by two . . . pinned down . . . a bullet through his heart.

"Oh, my God," he whispered. "That can't be . . ."

And he thought about his father, his regrets for never speaking to him, never telling him how he felt, how he loved the man in spite of everything. He never got to tell him all of those things before he passed away six months earlier.

And the letter he couldn't remember writing to Cristos, the one he kept in his pocket, the one where his handwriting disappeared.

His dog in his kitchen this morning, killed in front of him more than twenty years ago when he was seventeen, run over before his eyes in the driveway. If only he was there a moment sooner to save him . . .

Things from so long ago, lost to time, things that could never re-appear.

All dead . . . But Frank was seen by others, had interacted with everyone. He was no ghost, no figment of Jack's imagination. Frank helped him save Mia, helped hunt down Cristos. Jack glanced over toward Cristos's broken body, and his mind snapped, for Cristos was not there. There was no blood, no sign of him ever falling on the rocks.

And he thought on Ryan's words, on Emily's suggestion that it was all in his mind. The tumor. Was it causing the delusions, causing him to see the dead, to imagine those he lost around him? But Jack couldn't be losing his mind. Mia was there before him. And then he thought, if they were dead, did that mean that he . . .

"Jack, don't you fall apart on me," Mia begged, seeing the pained look in his eyes.

"Mia, Ryan said I would become delusional, see things. The tumor must be pressing—"

"What tumor?" Mia said in shock.

"I tried to tell you, early in the week. I'm sorry, I didn't know what to say . . ."

"What, Jack?"

"I'm sick."

Mia looked at him, confused. "Jack, you're not sick. You're as healthy as could be; you just had a full physical a month ago."

It was Jack's turn to be confused.

"Jack," Mia whispered, her eyes filling with tears as if revealing the death of a friend, her heart breaking with her every word. "It's me. Don't you remember?"

"What? No, the file, in my desk . . ."

"That's my file, Jack. It's me. I'm the one who is sick. I'm dying!" she cried. "Maybe six months . . ."

Jack stared at her, his mind a jumble. And he held her tight, his mind becoming unhinged with grief. "No, please . . ."

"Oh, Jack, please don't lose it. You have to survive for the girls. You have to be strong."

"No. Mia, you have to survive. I saved you."

"Oh, Jack. I will fight, but you remember what Ryan said the chances are?"

Jack's heart was breaking anew. Everything he had struggled for, everything he had gone through to save her . . .

Mia looked up into his eyes with her warm, caring heart. "You saved me today . . . and you'll go on saving me, day after day, until you can save me no more."

Jack held her close. He had fought so hard to change fate, but it was all for nothing.

His senses were suddenly filled with the smell of Mia, the odor of her perfume, as if it filled the air around him. Her smell from the powder room that had sparked his memory, that he smelled on her pillow at night, that was forever part of her.

Jack looked at his wrist. He saw the large cut he had sustained coming down the cliff face. And as he looked at it in the light wash from the lighthouse, he became aware of a stunning reality. The tattoo that had so frightened him, that had scared Cristos, was gone. No evidence was there of the Cotis artwork. Not a drop of ink, not a word, just his arm bleeding profusely.

And the light from the lighthouse softened, becoming moonlight . . .

JACK'S EYES FLASHED open. He found himself lying on the riverbank, the raging Byram River just feet away. Moonlight danced off the wet leaves and rocks, the thundering river painting the soundscape. There were pieces of the car washed up on the shore by his feet, packages and bags from the rear of the Tahoe. The air was filled with Mia's perfume, her signature smell, as if it inhabited the world around him.

And as he turned his head, he saw Mia lying facedown in a shallow eddy of water. He scrambled to her, turned her over, draping his body over hers.

Ignoring his pain, he ran his hands around her face. "Mia? Please, Mia . . ."

He laid his mouth over hers, breathing for her. He pumped her chest as he had done moments ago on the beach. Praying with every compression, "Please, God, please don't let her die. Take me, take me instead."

He glanced over to see the crumpled wreckage of the Tahoe, both airbags deployed.

He turned his eyes back on her and found her staring up at him.

"Jack," Mia whispered. Moonlight reflected off the stones in the blue necklace that he had clasped around her neck just fifteen minutes earlier, its explosion of color filling his eyes.

"Jack, are you all right?"

Jack looked into her eyes. She was alive; somehow he knew she would live.

Jack's memory was clear, unhindered. And he saw the last moments.

The SUV hit the bridge pavement . . . the rear wheels lost their traction . . . the Tahoe went into a sudden fishtail, he held tight to the wheel as it skirted left to right and back again. He pulled hard to bring the vehicle under control. Mia's left hand shot up and gripped the passenger strap above the door. Their collective breath caught in their throats as the car spun headfirst toward the guardrail . . . crashing through, diving toward the raging river. They knifed into the rushing current, water exploded upward, and despite the airbag deployment, Jack's head smashed into the steering wheel, and all faded to black . . .

Jack looked at the car door washed up on the riverbank beside them, at the objects that littered the muddy ground around him, the raging river having washed it all up onshore. There were soccer balls and tennis rackets; the girls' blue and brown bears, their hair matted, covered in mud; there was the half-open birthday present for Joy, the expensive black purse he got for her birthday next week; Mia's shopping bag from the department store, the rose-red lipstick sitting in sharp contrast to the muddy ground; three bottles of Mia's favorite perfume shattered, shards of glass twinkling in the moonlight as the fragrance permeated everything around them.

And all of the pain flooded in, as if a pause button had just been released on his nervous system. His head was throbbing, the cuts on his face feeling as if they had been doused with acid, his chest on fire with a pain he never knew could be so severe.

Jack finally looked at his chest. A shard of metal protruded from the left side, running clear through. His left arm was mangled and bloody. There was no sign of a tattoo, no sign that anyone had written on him . . . no sign of being shot.

The contusion on his head was severe; he didn't need an X-ray to tell him that his skull was cracked, to tell him that his wounds were fatal.

As the pain grew, overwhelming him with agony, he began to falter, his eyes struggling to remain open, his breathing heavy, focused as if he could fight off the inevitable. Despite his strength of will, he finally collapsed onto his back.

It wasn't until 4:30 a.m. that the broken guard rail was noticed by a passing vehicle.

It was just after 5:30, the glow of dawn on the horizon, when Mia and Jack were rushed to the hospital.

CHAPTER 45

RYAN McCOURT RACED FROM his home to find his friends in the emergency room. He looked at Mia's X-rays, the CAT scans and MRIs side-by-side, two versions, the ones from ten days ago when he had told them of her diagnosis and the ones moments old. He compared them, up close, side-by-side. Dumbstruck, he quickly pulled them down. No one would believe it, for there could be no explanation.

HOPE KEELER'S SIX-YEAR-OLD eyes drifted open; she could hear the sound of the crashing waves on the sandy beach as she lay in the oversized bed at her grandmother's house. And as the first light of morning washed through the slatted window shades, she saw her father standing there in the early-morning light.

"Hey, baby," Jack whispered, the sound of his voice painting a broad smile on Hope's face.

And with the sound of his voice, Sara stirred and rolled over. "Hi, Daddy."

"Daddy's going away for a bit." Jack smiled.

"Where?" Hope asked.

"Not far, but always remember I'm with you," he said as he reached out and touched their hearts.

"Where's Mommy?"

"Mommy's fine. She's sleeping. You do me a favor and tell her I love her."

Hope and Sara nodded in unison.

"Give me your hands," Jack said as he took their small hands in his. Unfurling their fingers, he gently kissed their palms.

"A kissing hand, Daddy?" Hope giggled.

"A kissing hand, baby. When you miss me or need me, you just place that against your cheek, and you'll feel me right beside you."

Hope placed her palm against her cheek and smiled. "It's warm."

Sara mimicked her sister.

Jack smiled. "It always will be."

JACK SAT ON the edge of Mia's hospital bed and ran his fingers through her hair.

Her eyes slowly drifted open. "Hi."

"Hi back," Jack said.

"You're alive."

Jack smiled.

"Ryan said . . ." Mia choked back her tears. "How's it possible? What did you do?"

Jack touched the blue stone necklace around her neck. The words from Marijha Toulouse's note echoed in his head, peace and love, healing and long life . . .

Jack stared at her a moment, memorizing her face. He leaned in and kissed her tenderly on the lips, all of his emotions pouring forth. He kissed her cheek, ran his hand through her hair.

"You know I can't stay," Jack whispered as the early rays of sunlight washed over his warm face.

"No, please, don't leave me . . ." Mia could barely breathe through her quiet sobs.

"Mia," Jack said softly as he took her face in his hands. "It's OK."

"Don't you do it," Mia pleaded with tear-filled eyes. "Don't you leave me, Jack. I can't survive without— Please."

"Mia," Jack said, his abbreviated smile creasing his cheeks, "you're going to live. You're going to be fine for a very long time. You need to love our girls, teach them the lessons that I would have. Teach them of me and my heart. But most of all, tell them of how I loved you so they may understand and find that most precious of things someday." Jack looked into her eyes. Lowering his voice, he whispered, "Give me your hand."

She laid her hand in his, her palm open, facing up, and he kissed it with love, gently, forever, as if he was pouring his soul into her. And as forever came to an end, he grasped her fingers, curling them around the warmth he left within her palm. He enclosed her hand in his, holding tightly, and smiled.

Mia watched, crushed with grief, as he began slowly to slip away. Their eyes locked, his warm smile fading . . . and he was gone.

EPILOGUE

"REALITY IS ALL A matter of perspective,"
Jack's father said as they stood on the beach in
front of their house, staring out at Trudeau Island. Jack was all of ten,
holding his father's hand.

Jack nodded.

A warm breeze flowed off the ocean as the sun crept up from the
horizon, morning's first light painting the sky.

"Are you ready to go?" Jack's father said.

"No," Jack said. He was an adult now, walking beside his father.
"Why did you come back?"

"You know. Somebody's got to watch out for you and because . . ." David looked at Jack and smiled. "because you're my son."

THE FUNERAL WAS on Wednesday. Mia sat in the front right
pew, her girls at her side. Frank's widow, Lisa, was there, Jack's mother,
Mia's parents, and Joy Todd.

Ryan McCourt gave the eulogy, speaking of faith, hope, love,
and, as he looked at Mia, miracles.

Jack was buried in the Banksville Cemetery near his father. Only immediate family and friends were there as his casket was lowered into the earth under the warm rays of the summer sun.

Jack's final act, his gift of love, had somehow saved Mia. She didn't know how, whether it was a miracle, magic, or faith, but somehow Jack had saved her. Mia reached up, wrapped her hands around the blue necklace, and smiled.

AS THE CROWD began to disperse, leaving Mia and the girls to say their final good-byes, Joy walked over to Mia's father. She took a moment, drying her eyes, allowing her presence to call his attention.

"Mr. Norris? My name is Joy Todd. I was Jack's assistant. I'm sorry for your loss."

Norris nodded.

"This is from Jack." Joy handed an envelope to Norris. He stared at it, confused, as Joy walked away without another word.

SAM NORRIS WALKED into his study. It was after 10:00 p.m. Mia and his two granddaughters were asleep upstairs. They would all be staying with him and his wife for the foreseeable future.

He reached into the breast pocket of his sportcoat and withdrew the envelope, tearing it open. He read the note once through and turned his attention to the large mahogany box that Jack had made and that Mia had filled with cheap fishing gear, giving it to him for his birthday—the night of their fateful accident.

He picked up the eighteen-inch-square box, turning it around. It was of excellent construction, pure, nearly invisible seams. He regretted not complimenting Jack on the impressive work. There was always such regret for things left unsaid when someone passed away.

Norris lifted the lid of the box and looked inside; he pulled out the lures and line and stared at the brass plaque that Jack had affixed: *Forever Young—7/1/38 to Eternity.* He let out a half-smile and closed it. He laid his hands on the left rear leg and the front right leg as the note had described. Each leg was only a half-inch tall, raising the case barely off the table.

He pushed them at the same time and heard a subtle click. He then reread the letter. And this time, did the same thing with the other two legs. A second click sounded from the inside. He lifted the lid as the written instructions stated, and the front of the case slid forth, allowing a large drawer to pop out like magic. Norris reached in and withdrew a large glassine bag marked *Evidence.*

There was a second note inside. He withdrew it and began to read.

Dear Sam,

If you are reading this, then something has happened. We never know the path of fate. Reality is all a matter of perspective. And sometimes the unexplainable occurs. We cannot see the road that our lives will take, but the contents of this box may beg to differ.

These items along with a gift of a blue necklace were sent to me by a Cotis priest.

He and I had an appointment, but for now obvious reasons, he never arrived. It seems he has died, a matter that is currently under investigation.

He had implored, speaking to me about his son, Nowaji Cristos, who was executed for the murders near the UN nearly eighteen months ago. As his son was executed as a result of my conviction, I felt I owed the man at least five minutes of my time. Over the phone, he spoke of knowing the future, of things to come, of warnings I should heed, a statement I immediately dismissed and surmised would be the topic of our future conversation.

The day after his death, I received these items . . .

Norris thumbed through the two red leather books. The pages in the first were all in a language he couldn't comprehend, while the second was half foreign, half English, with dates and times in a diary fashion. And on the final page were five names.

He closed them both.

Norris picked up the single detailed drawing; it was of Jack dead on the riverbank, a drawing from five days ago . . . predating the accident and his death.

> *I am unsure who killed the priest, but there is a nagging*
> *fear I have.*
> *I ask that you look into this matter, using your utmost*
> *discretion, keep these items safe, and watch over Mia, as I know*
> *you will. I have and will love her forever and always.*
>
> > *Your son-in-law,*
> > *Jack*

Norris looked at the writing on the top of the drawing. The lettering was cursive and rich, in an odd but beautiful language. His eyes fell on the text below it. It, too, was hand written, in cursive lettering, written in English.

Your future can be glimpsed in the magical hours at . . .
Half-past dawn.

Acknowledgments

L IFE IS FAR MORE enjoyable when you work with people you like and respect. I would personally like to thank the following:

Gene and Wanda Sgarlata, the owners of Womrath Bookstore in Bronxville, N.Y., for their continued support; without their friendship, you wouldn't be reading these words.

Sarah Branham for making sense of it all and for performing a herculean task in record time. Peter Borland for your encouragement, insight, and that amazing ability to understand what I'm trying to say. I'm truly blessed to have you not only as my overseer but as my friend. Judith Curr, the most forward-thinking professional in the publishing world, and Louise Burke, for her unwavering support and belief. I could not be in better hands. Nick Simonds for keeping it all together; Dave Brown for getting people to sit up and take notice; and especially Joel Gotler, my Obi Wan guide in the West Coast cinematic world.

And heads and shoulders above all, Cynthia Manson. First and foremost for your continued friendship; it is something I truly treasure. Thank you for your innovative thinking, your continued faith in the face of adversity, and your unlimited tenacity. Your inspiration, guidance, and business acumen are exceeded by no one.

Thank you to my family:

To my children, you are the best part of my life. Richard, you are my mind, your brilliance and creativity know no bounds. Marguerite, you are my heart, constantly reminding me of what is important in life; your style, grace under pressure, and sense of humor are examples to all. Isabelle, you are my soul; your laughter and inquisitive mind keep my eyes open to the magic of this world we live in.

Dad, for always being my dad and the voice of wisdom that forever rings in my ear. Mom, you were always my champion on terra firma, and you no doubt still are. How else can I explain my good fortune since your passing?

Most important, thank you, Virginia, for your love even when I don't deserve it.

I marvel at how you are even more beautiful than the day I spied you in gym class.

You fill my heart with hope and possibilities, opening my eyes to the joys of living that can become so obscured by the trials, tribulations, and everyday distractions of life's journey.

Thank you for making me laugh in the darkest of hours. Thank you for raising such amazing children; they are truly a reflection of you. Thank you for dancing; I marvel at your modesty, talent, and beauty as you lose yourself in the magic, achieve the impossible, and entertain the world around you. Thank you for making our life exceed my dreams.

Finally, thanks to you, the reader, for taking the time to read my stories, for reaching out through your notes, letters, and e-mails. Your kind words inspire and fill me with the responsibility never to let you down.

Richard